The Valiant

Captains

The Valiant Captains

BY

Sheldon A. Jacobson

Published by:

Educare Press Inc.

PO Box 31511
Seattle WA 98103

(206) 781-2665

Library of Congress Cataloging in Publication Data: 90-80517

ISBN: 0-944638-01-5

To Eric, Ira, and Ruth.

"Daddy, tell us a story!"

Foreword

I was at sea in a ship of the United States Navy when the German capital ships Scharnhorst, Gneisenau and Prinz Eugen made their famous passage through the English Channel from Brest in occupied France to German waters.

Dismay spread through the west. How had this been possible in the teeth of the redoubtable British Navy?

In all the comments that I read, I found no mention of the fact that, as I happened to know, it had been done before. In 1599, a Genoese in the service of Philip II of Spain had taken a squadron of galleys from Lisbon to the Spanish Netherlands. I subsequently looked for analogous feats, to write them up on the theme that history does indeed repeat itself.

Here is the book.

Sheldon A. Jacobson

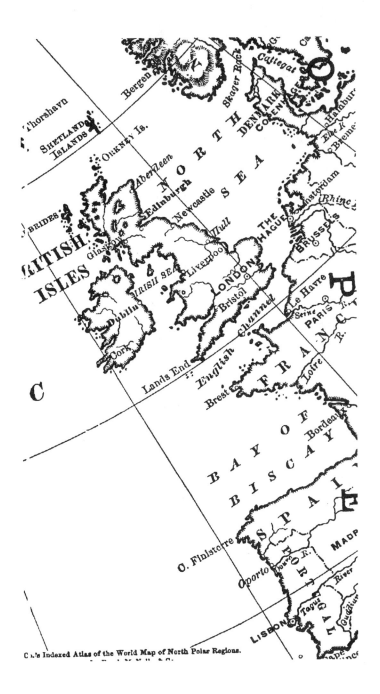

Contents

The thing that has been is the thing that will be.

Thucydides

The First Wager

*A*s far as the eye could see, great angry waves rolled from the southwest. They raised their grey bulk; they advanced, joined, parted, formed smaller waves upon themselves, and wavelets upon these. They massed now and then to build up into superwaves of daunting size and power. The troughs yawned deep and wide; the crests blew off in white foam. Near, the snarl of the seas could be heard even above the howl of the monstrous wind that whipped them into being. Above, the atmosphere was torn into scudding mists that hid the sky.

It seemed impossible for any life to exist on that ocean under the battering of the storm. It was hard to imagine even the creatures of the deep not being beaten and torn to an ugly death beneath the savage power of the sea.

But life is stubborn and strong. A galley of Brittany rode the wrack bravely. Mast lowered, and towing a crude sea anchor, she rose gracefully to each oncoming swell, till at its crest she pitched her bow downward and slid dizzily into the trough. There, concealed by the watery windrows that surrounded her, she settled to repeat the maneuver. As she neared harbor, her people, despite backbreaking fatigue, bailed with endurance born of desperation.

One other craft, invisible to that crew, lived in the wild sea. In her Manannan Mac Lir stood erect, and needing neither oar or sail, directed her to the Irish beach by his divine will.

The goddess Boann greeted him as he stepped ashore. "Was it whim, or to carry word of your dread power, that you spared that last ship?" she asked.

"A little of each; but in addition her men had fought so bravely, forcing the Channel, that I was moved to reward them."

She nodded approvingly. "A pattern has been set. Once done, the feat will be repeated."

"If you mean that future warriors will drive their ships through these waters against far stronger defenders, I say that you err." He looked at her with a superior smile. "Your domain is merely the River Boyne. What do you know of the toils and conflict of the ocean?"

"I propose a wager. Let us sponsor another such attempt. If the invaders cannot carry it off, I will build you a horse of pure gold, and endow it with the power to draw your chariot over land and sea."

"Done!" he exclaimed. "And if you win, I will do the like for you, and you will be drawn by your shining steed over the waters and waysides of Boyne."

"And done. In time we shall see."

So they planted the seed of a new venture. And if the seed was long in ripening, what were years, or centuries, or even millennia, more than a moment in time to gods?

Thus they demonstrated that even a god may be mistaken.

Prologue

THE SWIMMING BULL

In the wind's teeth and the spray's stinging
Westward and outward forth we go,
Knowing not whither nor why, but singing
An old, old oar-song as we row.
A long pull,
And a long, long pull to Mydath.

The Galley-Rowers — Masefield

Caoilte the bard was a seventh son of a seventh son; and his
mother was a woman of the shee. So when Gormliath, king of
Munster, one day said. "'Tis weary I am of the battles of my house;
sing me kings beyond the pleasant land of Munster, beyond the grey
waters that wash the beaches of Eire," the fay-born singer made reply:

"Eastward the wind blows, and it blows across the sea where
Manannan Mac Lir drives his chariot, drives it on the tossing waves
that he esteems as a fair flowered mead; eastward it blows, across the
high dark mountains of the Cymri, dark with the spells of the warlocks
of the well sworded Cymri; eastward it blows, across the barren
downs where the Britons do be riding in their chariots, and they all
yellow with the war-won gold on arm and car and noble horses. There
by the smoky northern sea rises the caher of Kilhwch och Bedwyr. In
the hall of Kilhwch sits the princess Granu.

"Spear-proud is her walk, her waist like the poplar tree; her
red-gold head blazes like the sun in his rising; down her back fall the
locks like the creeping tongues of the inswelling tide, and on either
side a strand lies gently, gently against the lovely young breasts of her;
her lips are like the blood of a swan bleeding from an arrow, till its
blood drips fading in the waters of Shannon. Well fitted those lips to
kiss the lips of a king, or anon to command a host of heroes! Her eyes
are limpid as the waters of the lakes of Connemara, save when anger
flashes from under imperious brows. But her hands are for the
caressing, and the wind in his longing drives the folds of her gown
deep between the sweet promise of her thighs."

Then Gormliath raised his goblet and cried, "Now happy the
hero-king who weds such a maid; and be her bridal pledged in this

good mead!" But the bard raised a staying hand. "Not so, oh king! For Kilhwch her stepfather has betrothed her to a craven. On Midsummer Day will be her bridal, and she weeps to think that Nann ap Gwilym will take her to wife."

Gormliath looked with a grin upon his spear-hurling heroes. "Will he so? I think there will be some unbidden at that bridal!"

Caoilte cried out in alarm. "Do not think it, oh king! For I see heart's blood drip on your bosom! Though I hear not the Davna-na-Mairv for your death."

"Do you indeed? I think you see wrong; in any case, Caoilte mac Diarmuid, my father's son was not born to die tamely in bed." And the hall rang with the pledges of his warriors.

Thrice a hundred bulls the king bade slaughter, for the tanning of their hides. The wood rang with the axes as they felled oak tree and yew. Next, the axemen shaped the gunwales, sixty feet long, thick and strong for the stiffening of the keelless hulls, that they might neither sag nor hog when the seas raised them by ends or middles. Then they bound the springy ribs in place, and the beams across from side to side. Lastly, they sewed hides together as they sewed them to the framework of the great curraghs. And they payed the seams with pitch.

In a grey June dawn they put out from Lairge. On a brave southwest wind they reached across the Irish sea for Britain. All day they drove, the sun and sea favoring them with sparkling weather; the men sat high on the windward gunwales as the cowhide sails strove to force the lee rails down to the level of the reaching waves. Misty Eire sank from their sight, and ocean was all their ken.

A bit of the horizon seemed more solid, rose grayly from the sea, and was the Cambrian land. The afternoon wore on, and eve was approaching ere they neared that shore. Then the watchers of the Cymri espied that fleet afar; and the Druids kindled fires, and burned cauldrons of things known only to themselves; and a darkness as of a too early night swept like a cloud out to sea, and the curraghs were benighted. On an island off the coast they beached and ate and slept.

Through another glorious day the Irish reached across the broad bay of the Severn. Then the watchers of Devon espied that fleet afar; and the Druids kindled fires, and slaughtered birds and passed them through the smoke; and a heavy rain hid the seascape, so that the voyagers were fain to make for an island, and they beached and ate and slept.

There was hard rowing to the southwest the next day, and slowly they closed with the coast of Cornwall. Then the watchers of the Cornishmen espied the fleet afar; and they beat upon their drums, and the wind blew hard from the northeast, so that the frail curraghs, never daring to make sail, were borne helplessly for many leagues, bailing for their lives as they drove, till at dawn they found themselves at the Scilly Isles; and they beached and ate and slept.

Now they drew their vessels well above the tide line. Carefully they payed the seams with tallow, for want of pitch, to make them tight again against the searching fingers of the sea. And when they had slept again, they put out once more, and entrusted themselves to the good southwest wind.

For six days through the narrow sea they ran, sleeping on the beaches only where marsh or cliff made those ashore unaware or indifferent to their presence. Twice they provisioned their ships, paying scrupulously for what they took; for they would soon be returning this way, and had little desire for a countryside aflame for revenge behind them. Then, with the shores of Gaul looming to the south, they greased their ships' seams for the last time on the outward voyage. Now they did not land; they wanted no word to precede them. So ships were taken in turn aboard other ships for treating their seams at sea. Lastly, they turned into the estuary of a great river.

Deep was the drinking in the hall of Kilhwch. On the morrow his stepdaughter would be wedded to Nann, whose father Gwilym was high king of the down country. Much did Kilhwch hope to prosper therefrom in lands and gold. The hall rang as Nann and Kilhwch pledged each other in the mead; and deeply did their captains quaff from the never-emptying flagons.

When at last the hall of Kilhwch was silent and dark, men came stealthily from the river. Of a sudden there were smoke and flame, then screams and the clash of fighting. Nann awoke to see the specter of Gormliath with naked sword at his door; he screamed once before the invader sliced off his head. Kilhwch died in his drunken sleep.

Then a serving woman, Gormliath's sword at her back, brought him to Granu. Long he looked upon her.

"I was minded to steal you, lady, as one steals a jewel from a weakling who cannot hold it.

"But now it is with me as once when I rose from a long battle wound; my life has come again to me, and what is past is pale and like a mist that lies over Glen Imaal and then is gone.

"Lady, my soul's within you. I am asking you to reign by my side as queen in fertile Munster, where the breezes do be ruffling the hair on sleek cows and the fattest of sheep. Do you not be refusing me, mourneen; if you do so, easy may you rest in this your land, but my grief will be big over the sea. Oh 'twill be a rare sorrow on me without us to be wedded!

"Yellow gold have I in plenty, pulse of my heart, but any craven may have that. The steel of my sword it is that is my treasure, and it will be for the guarding of you and the winning you honor. Ah woman of my pity, do not be saying me no! Lovely mouth of the honey of the Vale Avoca, may I be pressing you with mine?"

The Princess Granu did not frown or smile. With level brow she looked upon the bearded champion.

"An hour ago I had no hope but to be the wife of a fool and a coward. Now a hero king comes to me as a wooer.

"Proud I will be to be your queen!"

Oh, it was a grand sacking of the hall of Kilwch, and many the goodly shields that opposed the swords of Gormliath in vain. They gathered great store of gold and of well wrought silver, of arrows and spearheads and of swords with gem-encrusted hilts. Then the men of Gormliath took to their ships and turned down the river to the sea; and at the side of Gormliath sat Granu in his curragh.

But for four precious days they lay stormbound at Sandwich, while the runners of Gwilym mustered his men and his ships.

Then, in a rare calm, they set out and pulled strongly for the west. They left Dover astern, and Hythe; and there off Dungeness the men of Rye lay in their numbers.

Caoilte laughed aloud. "My king," he said, "long will the harpstrings twang to the songs of this day's slaughter! Oh, 'tis a grand gathering of the Britons I see before me! Where the sword of Gormliath swings, will the fish drink red and the gulls grow fat on the fallen!"

Hot was the battle on the oily swells. Ship after ship lay alongside the king's great curragh, and ship after ship he cleared with flashing blade. But the Irish in other vessels were faring ill; the stouter wooden ships of the foe clove hull after hull with nought but bull's hide to oppose the British bows. The king's helmsman, however, had averted the first thrusts, and thereafter the enemy hulls lashed alongside barred such attacks on him. Nor had all the other Irish succumbed; many the Britons who fell bloody and helpless across a rowing bench or overside.

And indeed after a half hour or more, Gormliath and two more of his ship captains drifted among a fleet of the dying and dead.

Then, ahead, the sea was black with Gwilym's vengeful ships.

Gormliath smiled grimly at his helmsman Conchobar. "The Morrigan will rejoice this day! She will see the grand feast for fish, hawk and shark!"

But Conchobar did not laugh. "Aye, the war goddess will rejoice indeed. And is it your queen who will be the daintiest tidbit for the feast?"

The king looked upon the smiling Granu. "Caoilte," he called, "do you charm us a fog, that the hundred ships of Gwilym may seek us in vain!"

"My harp strings are slack with the damp of the sea," he said, "and my throat is thick with its rheum."

"Then pluck the lashings on this shield of Kilwch," Gormliath replied, and he produced a flask and one of the tiny drinking bowls used for the scarce morat, the precious liquor of mulberries, "and wet your throat with this that is better even than the uisgebeatha, the water of life; for you will sing here this day, or I think you will sing in Hel this night.

Then Caoilte sang. He sang the lay of the line of the Princess Granu, the line of chariot-fighting kings and of proud, chaste queens; he sang of her birth and of the death of her valiant sire, overwhelmed in battle; of her mother, wedded perforce to cunning Kilhwch. Then he sang of Granu's growing and the promise of her girlhood; of her wisdom and her pride and her generous giving of gifts. Then he sang of her beauty, and sun and sea listened in delight. Lastly he sang of her dark hour, when it seemed she must needs be lost to the shameful Nann; of her rescue, and now of her imminent death in the cold dark sea. And the sun veiled his face for grief, and deep fog walked upon the water.

And so the Irish ships passed unseen by the fleet of Gwilym.

Gormliath turned to his bride in triumph. "We have passed through the narrow waters in despite of all the power of the High King's ships!"

"And despite him I am yours, head and hand and heart!"

In Gwilym's ship was a warlock of the Cymri. He drew his bow and shot blindly into the fog. The arrow pierced Granu's bosom.

And as his ships bore Gormliath homeward in his anguish, the blood from the heart that had just become his dripped down upon his breast.

The Second Wager

*H*ard pressed between the giants of Jotunheim and the black-robed messengers of Christ advancing from the south, the Norse gods were making their last stand. But even so they spared time and attention, now and again, for their customary ways. Mighty Thor addressed Njord of Noatun.

"Do you remember how the Irish king Gormliath passed through the Channel despite the massed power of the Britons?"

"I remember. It was bravely done."

"Bravely indeed. I think that such a feat will never be repeated."

"What has happened once will happen again."

"Does the Vanir race dare to dispute with a god of Asgard?"

"The sea is my domain," Njord replied proudly. "It is I who ordain what haps upon its bosom."

"And war is mine. I decide the fates of men engaged in the iron game. If you can contrive to send ships through that same Channel against impossible odds, I will give you my hammer Mjollnir, that returns to my hand after each cast."

"And if not," interjected Freyr, who had joined them, "Thor may have my ship Skidbladet, that always commands a favoring wind."

So they contrived a new venture. But they had more immediate concerns, so that it was long indeed evolving.

THE DAY OF THE DRAGONS

This is the tale of Earl Godwin and of the Revolution that he wrought in the year 1052.

History has dealt harshly with the Earl - perhaps justly. To add rebellion to the agonies of a land struggling for its life against foreign enemies seems an ill deed; one wonders whether anything can excuse it. The ostensible reason - to obtain justice for a city which was being wronged - will not quite wash against the background of the grim and faithless dealings that were so common in that time and place. A selfish desire to keep for oneself the revenues of what was not after all the first or second town of the realm could not have been the motive either; the earl was wealthy and powerful enough to take such loss in his stride, rather than hazard total ruin. An attempt at self aggrandizement? He was already the first subject in the land, and his power waxed yearly.

Let us, with the insight enjoyed by the novelist but denied the historian, inquire into the problem. To do so, we must start with the life and deeds of Wulfnoth, his father.

WULFNOTH

I

Dire deeds are come
Bringing hard battle and bitter strife.

The Battle of Finnsburg.

A land of woe and bitter grief was England.

From south to north stretched the brooding weald; and in its shadow ranged bear and wolf and sought their prey. In the clearings the grudging soil fought plow and harrow. Dangerous seas rolled round the isle; and from the eye of the fisherman fogs would veil reef and bar, and the reaching hills of home. But a stout yeomanry toiled mightily with sickle and with sail, and the axemen little by little widened their fields.

The fearfulest foe was man.

Hard pressed on the restless continent, the Romans had abandoned Britain. From Scotland, from Ireland, from Germany, the wilder men swept in to pillage, ravish and kill. Came the Saxon, and conquered the land; but there was still no peace. Mercia and Wessex, Northumberland and Kent, the kings were each at the other's throat for glory and for land.

And then, says the unknown scribe of the Anglo-Saxon Chronicle: "In this year 787 there came for the first time three ships of Northmen and then the reeve rode to them . . . . for he did not know what they were; and they slew him. Those were the first ships of Danish men which came to the land of the English."

II

Thought shall be the harder, heart the keener,
mood shall be the more, as our might lessens.
Here our prince lies low, they have hewn him to death:
Grief and sorrow forever on the man that leaves this
warplay! I am old of years, but hence I will not go; I
think to lay me down by the side of my lord, by the side
of the man I cherished.

Lay of the Battle of Maldon

In high exuberance Wulfnoth rode through the March sunshine. Again and again he retold himself the words of his beloved king.

"You are young," Edward had said. "When were you born?"

"In the year 958, my lord. In three days I shall be twenty."

"Only twenty. Still, you are, I am told, steady beyond your years. Certainly you should have learned enough of seamanship from your father, God rest him! And your family has been outstandingly loyal. Ceorl Wulfnoth, I appoint you to the command of my dragon-ship 'Daedfruma.' Take her, my boat-ceorl, and make her in truth a Doer of Deeds!"

Then they had parted, and the king had ridden on with his score of men-at-arms on the Swanage road. King Edward, too, was happy, this beautiful afternoon; he was on his way for a visit with his thirteen-year old half-brother Aethelred and Aethelred's mother Aelfthryth. In their Castle Corfe, Isle Purbeck, Edward would rest for a day from his nagging ministers.

Perhaps, thought Wulfnoth daringly, fortune might favor him; on some day of desperate battle Daedfruma might succor her hard-pressed king after all others were fled or slain. To youth all things are possible.

But Wulfnoth would be content with less. Far, far less. The ceorl had been schooled by his father in the ancient Teutonic code. There was nothing greater than glory. A chief's glory came through victory; his henchman's through service to his chief. And with a young man's idealism, Wulfnoth dreamed almost eagerly of falling in some battle-swirling ship at the side of his king.

Twilight found him at the shore. There as expected was the beached ship by a huddle of huts and sheds with the clutter of a much used repair shop and a landing.

There were lights in the parchment windows of a longish structure. The door opened to his knock and he entered. Some score and a half of men sat at a refectory table that ran down the middle. One of their number, a prepossessing chap slightly older than the visitor, rose in greeting. "I am Bernhelm, boatswain of the king's ship Daedfruma. Will you join us at mess?"

Wulfnoth thanked him. "I am Wulfnoth, commanding officer, and here is the king's warrant. I shall be glad to eat, but first I want to take a short look at my ship!"

Daedfruma was some seventy-five feet long - the boatswain nodded at his estimate - and less than one-fourth as wide. The hull was five feet deep, and open. She was built with sixteen planks on a side, and each side showed, coincidentally, a like number of oar-holes. A dragon's head rose on a long stem, and the sternpost was almost as high. Not much more could be seen by the fading light.

There were thirty-four stout fighting men in the crew, they told the captain - almost all trained rowers and seamen. A likely looking lot - all but a youngster who seemed sullen.

"He has a young wife alone in a hut in the marsh," the boatswain informed him. "She is about to give birth to the first child, and the thane has forbidden any leave until the ship has been inspected by him."

"The thane runs the squadron," growled Wulfnoth, "but I run my ship. What's your name?" to the youngster.

"Waltheof, captain!"

"Then get you gone, Waltheof, and look to your wife. Who is attending her?"

"Only a stupid girl from a cottage nearby."

"Have you money?"

"None, captain."

"Then take this and get her a midwife. Never mind thanks - - show yourself a good servant to the king when you return."

Without even waiting for dawn, the lad was gone.

The skipper accepted what remained in the pot. (He found, suddenly, that he was hungry.) Then they entered the huts - there was a little one for the captain - to sleep.

It was not much later that the pounding of hooves brought Wulfnoth out of his cabin. A man flung himself off his horse and asked excitedly for the captain.

"The king is dead!"

"What?" And then, "How?"

"Murdered!"

They stared at him in horror.

"We rode in to the castle courtyard. The prince's men came forward to greet the king with honor and affection. So it seemed. They grasped his hands - firmly, because he tried on a sudden to pull away. There was the flash of steel, and he fell. And then the courtyard was filled with armed men, and there was fighting. I was at the rear of the train, so I wheeled my horse around and fled for my life. You were the last vassal to see the king alive, so I thought at once of you. And here I am."

Wulfnoth looked at him in grief and rage.

"Your king was killed before your eyes, and you survive him?"

"What was I to do? We were much outnumbered."

"This!" exclaimed the other. He snatched up a maul that was lying by, and brained the hapless messenger. "Thus should be the fate of the man who deserts his lord!" And he dragged the body to the edge of the water and flung it in.

Then Wulfnoth was minded to take horse and die at Castle Corfe for the honor of his beloved young king. But the boatswain grasped him by the arm.

"Captain, with whom would you fight? Aethelred is a thirteen-year-old boy! He could not have planned this thing! And, in any case, you will not get near him!"

"With the thanes at the castle. True, I cannot kill them all. But if I can dispatch only one before I fall, my lord will not have died wholly unavenged." Tears of grief and rage were in his eyes.

The other nodded. "Well spoken. But not well thought. Do you think that they were the principals in this plot?"

"Aethelred is, as you said, only a boy. He could not

have...Oh, I see what you mean. It is that cursed Aelfthryth who must bleed."

"And do you think that she will be unguarded?"

"I can die trying to reach her with my sword. And woe to the first who tries to stop me!"

"Yes. You can do that. And so the murderess lives in triumph, and sees her son crowned King of England!"

There was a pause before Bernhelm went on, "It is good to die with one's lord. But it is even better to avenge him. This is my counsel, Wulfnoth. Flee this area - the devotion of your father to our murdered king is too well known. Let us put to sea, early though the season be, and flee to a loyal vassal of our poor lord. There is Alderman Aelfere. With him you will be safe, and you can bide your time for revenge." He sniffed the air. "The wind is fair for the Bill of Portland and Daedfruma is ready for sea. Let us embark, so that we will be safe from Aelfthryth's troopers, and anchor in the harbor; and with the first light let us get under way to the west."

"Be it so," the young man agreed at length, bitterly.

"Then I am your man," the boatswain said, "and I will seek your vengeance with you till you or I have swallowed steel."

There can be no more fateful act than the unmooring of a ship. One is safely bound to the firm and immutable land, to the patent and the certain; the weighing of an anchor or the mere casting off of a mooring line and you are the Ocean's, the creature of its vastness, its darkness, and its unmatched passions. Let no man unmoor himself lightly, for there may well be no going back. Even if fortune smile, and he make the same mooring again, it will be different, by subtleties of hand and gear, from that which was before. But more significantly, the man who moors again is not the same man who left that mooring a minute or a lifetime ago. The Ocean has worked on him; and although it may have marked him long before, its face is forever changing. Have you known happiness, pride, and effortless delight in your ship? Be sure that a dimension has altered within your soul. Have you known terror, anguish, fatigue and thirst? Be sure that you bear their stamp, pressed deeply and ineradicably into your very marrow. No landsman can come to the vaguest apprehension of these matters; nor can any seaman approach you too nigh, because your farings have been different in the infinite variety of Ocean, and the metal upon which it rang its hammer is not the same in you as in him.

Little thought of all this had Wulfnoth as he cut him loose from country and law, to commit his poor bark to the winds of chance.

No mariner anticipates quite all that may hap, or he would bind him closer to the world of benefits and values he has known. And well that it is so; or naught would ever change in man or man's world; and men would be moored fast within the harbors, the valleys, the ideas in which each found himself at the dawn of time.

As predicted, there was a fine easterly, and the ship drove rapidly under her square sail around the dark cliffs of Dulston Head. Then beyond the blue waters rose the chalky heights and green downs of Dorset; but Wulfnoth, his heart burning within him, had no eye for its beauty.

He did have an eye, however, for the clean run of his ship, with only a little bow wave and a quick obedience to the slightest motion of the steering sweep. She rose sweetly to the following sea, and would obviously be as dry in a seaway as one could reasonably expect.

When the gigantic figure of a man on horseback appeared white on the downs, they closed with the coast, and beached in the mouth of the Wey River. They built their cooking fires and found shelter in the barns of local geneatas.

But not the captain. Wulfnoth's impatience drove him, just before evening, to the purchase of a horse and the start of the long ride north.

Aelfere was already an aging man, but still vigorous - tall, handsome, decisive. Beside him sat his lady - - likewise, obviously alert and awake. He listened to Wulfnoth's tale.

"Only yesterday a rider brought us the news," he said. "Deep is the sorrow of all who loved the king - all of my thanes, as well as myself."

"Will you fight the usurper?" asked Wulfnoth.

The alderman shook his head. "Were there another claimant to the throne, such a man as could lead us in battle, and with a good title, I would follow him. As it is, the standard of revolt would be the signal for the drenching of the country in the blood of a civil war between I know not how many contenders. I'll have no part of it.

"I can take you and your crew into my service. But mark you, I will not be drawn into revolt. And if I hear of any such plans on your part - or any one's else - there will no longer be a place for him in Somerset or Dorset. Is it understood?"

Wulfnoth gave grudging consent. "Whatever I may do or plan," he said, "I shall keep my own counsel."

"So be it. For the time being I would not have anyone here to connect me with the affairs of Corfe Castle. Is your ship in all readiness to put to sea again?"

"She is. And so am I."

"Your father was one of the few Englishmen to voyage abroad. Have you ever sailed with him to Germany?"

"I have been to the Warnow."

"You must go further, to Jomsborg on the Odermouth. Harold Gormsson, King of Denmark, has established a settlement there for Viking fighters from all over the north. His cousin raided here and we took him; his death is worth less to me than the good will of the Danish king. You will carry him. And then, if Harold Bluetooth permits it, it would be well for you to remain there until the following spring." "Or longer," the lady of the manor put in. " Cool your hot blood in the cold Baltic, and if word of your doings comes to the English court, perhaps it will be forgotten. And your ship."

Wulfnoth spent the evening and the night at his patron's manor. He had no eye for the attendants upon Aelfere, and he certainly had no eye for an eight-year-old girl who gazed at him with big round eyes of wonder.

III

O'er the sea-monsters' home
They drove their foaming deep-flanked ships.
Oft on the wave the stout wood stood
The blows of the billows. The ocean roared.

Elene—Cynewulf

So Wulfnoth became Alderman Aelfere's man. And so he returned south to the Wey, provisioned his ship, and on a warm March evening, with a moderate southwest wind heeling Doer of Deeds slightly to port, he stood eastward along the coast, camping for a night on the way, then out across the straits for the continent.

March was early for such a traverse, but Wulfnoth dared not delay. His men had been given their choice; only a half dozen had declined the voyage. He was favored by an unseasonably benign whole-sail southwest wind. They took departure at dusk, so as to arrive at the Dutch coast during daylight; and after a run of some eighteen hours were piloted by a fisherman into the Scheldt. And here they lay while gale followed gale for ten days.

Northeastward then they crawled along that nightmarish

coast. Sometimes they ran before a favoring westerly; sometimes they lay beached while squall after squall blew itself out; sometimes they pulled at the oars against a chill easterly, partly to make easting and partly to keep a semblance of warmth in their bodies; once they made excellent way under oars in an unbelievable calm and with a good two-knot current in their favor; once a late snowfall caught them, and again and again the fog. The murderous sandbanks often kept them far enough off the coast to confuse their reckoning, but not far enough to avert the danger of stranding. Occasionally, too slowly shelving beaches prohibited drawing the ship up out of the water for a decent night's rest. Once (this was by Bernhelm's sage counsel) they lay at anchor just to leeward of an unseen bank that turned the seas over it to a welter of boiling fury amid a grey, howling, formless waste. During the scanty hours of rest that Wulfnoth allowed himself, Bernhelm the boatswain, almost equally tireless, acted in his stead.

They rounded the Skagen, threaded their way through the isles of the Danes, and rode the bluff rollers of the Baltic to the mouth of the Oder at last. Human enemies had troubled them not at all; the few towns they had touched at had been friendly either for the sake of the English king (they knew nothing as yet of what had happened) or of the Dane who was their passenger.

At the Oder, they removed the dragon's head from the bow, as Viking law required, before entering haven. The sail came down, and the oarsmen pulled upriver. They beached Daedfruma among the ships of Harold's fleet. Wulfnoth and his passenger took the path up the hill.

By a heavy gate they passed through a circular rampart of wood and earth and entered the Danish camp. In each quarter were four buildings - barracks, shops, storehouses, and a mess hall. In the center was the great hall of the king.

The travelers passed by the sentry. Half the space in the wooden walled structure was occupied by a long table and chairs; the other half was cleared, with the king's chair of state and his couch behind it.

Harold Gormsson received his kinsman with delight. The mead flowed well that evening, and Wulfnoth had to tell of his passage in all detail.

"This was a somewhat early voyage," the grateful king told him. "We don't usually undertake it till a little later, and now you know why. And you have also seen why we prefer to sail right across the North Sea rather than along the Flemish and Frisian coasts; although if, like you, I had reason to depart in haste, I suppose that I should have done the same." And there was gold for the arm of Wulfnoth, and a gift for him to carry home to Aelfere.

"I like the looks of your ship, and of her crew. And I like the way you sailed her. In two months we fare on the summer raiding - no use to go till the crops are in and the stock spring-fattened for our taking. Some sail to Scotland, some to France." Tactfully, he made no mention of the Saxon lands. "Come with us! Glory and wealth are yours for the taking!"

Skathi the skald raised his mead cup on high. "When men of the sword-bearing Danefolk make music, 'tis the woeful wailing of empty-armed widows, the howl of the wolf pack that scents in its hunger blood of men in the blaze of the bower."

A grin lit the scarred face beside him. "There's better music than that! How'd you like a screaming, struggling lass under you, eh?" and a guffaw swept the room.

Wulfnoth thanked King Harold. "But I've no quarrel with Frenchmen or Scots," he objected, and then, in an inspired flash of cleverness, "nor would Aelfere my lord appreciate my involving him in a quarrel not of his seeking." He had once seen the sickening aftermath of a Viking raid, and wanted no part of it.

The king eyed him thoughtfully. "What will you be doing, then?"

"I don't know."

"Is the ship Aelfere's or yours?"

"Mine."

"Sell her to me. Or, better, trade her to me for a merchantman. I have a fine Swedish round ship swinging at anchor below here. Take her and I'll let you have a cargo of metalware that we captured in a Frisian. At the eastern end of the Baltic you can make yourself a rich man trading for furs. I must have that dragon ship of yours!" And so they agreed.

IV

Much he endured
On wintry seas, with woe in his heart.
Dragging his oar through drenching-cold brine,
Homeless and houseless and hunted by Wyrd.

                                        The Wanderer.

*F*enja was a knorr, about as long - seventy-five feet - as the dragonship, but with a beam a third of her length and with slightly higher sides. She was straight-ended, with a vertical cutwater fore and aft. They loaded with copper and iron pots, basins, knives and the like hardware; linen cloth; mead; flour; and a few other items.

Wulfnoth had little interest in trade, but everyone has use for money, and in any case he dared not return so soon to England. Some of his crew expressed disappointment at his rejection of the king's proposal that they go raiding; the captain released them with a suitable reward and his best wishes. With the boatswain and seven seamen a merchantman was well manned. They set up the mast with deadeyes and lanyards at the base of either shroud, took up on the backstay with a windlass, hoisted the sail on its yard, weighed anchor and were under way.

Fenja showed a fair turn of speed with the westerly pushing her along. The square sail of homespun bellied out more than the captain would have liked, even though reinforced by a grid of diagonal strips of thicker material. Trial showed, as he expected, that she would lie no closer to the wind than eight points. On the return voyage, toward Jutland, therefore, he would simply have to wait for an easterly slant. A heavy cargo ship could be rowed into or out of harbor - if no strong river or tidal current opposed her - but a long passage under oars would be out of the question.

So northward he stood to the inner Baltic. By good fortune there had been a Finn at Jomsborg waiting for transportation home, and his pilotage took much unease from the shoulders of the youthful skipper. It was bitterly cold, even in April, as he passed the Aland Islands. But there would be no use, he knew, in looking into the Gulf of Finland; the local goods would already be gone or contracted for. A tramp merchant like himself would have to go further afield for his cargoes - and for his markets. So on they ran with the good beam wind through the fine days of spring, and huddled nights, two men in a sleeping bag, trying to keep a little body warmth under the tented sail.

Harold had not misled them. At journey's end there was such store of furs, and such beautiful ones, as Wulfnoth had never seen. His Finn stayed long enough to interpret between Lapp and the Germanic lingua franca of the northern seas. The odd-looking, strange-eyed little men with their curious colorful costumes were eager enough for the metalware of the south.

When the wind blew from the east, they took advantage of it to set the homeward course. Not to waste it, they ran by night in mid-sea, and glad they were of the fur garments in that biting air. Three times they were stopped by cruising long ships; but Harold's script saw them safely through. For two weeks they lay wind-bound at

Nynashamn on the Swedish coast, until another slant released them. But once in the tidal currents of the belts, they needed merely to keep off reef and shore with sail or oars, and they transited the straits and stood triumphantly out to sea. Wulfnoth and Bernhelm breathed deeply in relief.

Now fortune smiled. On a fine easterly, under sunny skies, they ran across the North Sea in four days and nights. The best market for Wulfnoth's goods would, of course, be London; but he dared not show his face in Aethelred's capital, and in any case others would likely have preempted the facilities. The latter would be true in Edwinesburgh on the Firth of Forth as well. But the cold of northern and western Lothian assured a demand for what he had to offer; so he overruled Bernhelm's urging and set his course for the Moray Firth.

And here he almost came to grief. Boats packed with armed men put off from the shores of the harbor, and his ship was too slow to flee, his crew too small for defense. But a hail from another boat following upon these dispersed them; and Wulfnoth gave thanks for the chieftain who realized that in the long run trade was more rewarding than plunder. So here he sold a small part of his cargo, for woolen cloth and silver. Then he coasted (at a safe distance from the beach) to more civilized Aberdeen, where he found a merchant who could take on more of it at a good price. Then he ventured to Tynemouth in Northumberland - English, but hardly more than in name; and here he disposed of the rest.

In all this time - amid the critical study of the knorr's characteristics and performance under various conditions of wind and wave, equally critical study of the individual members of his crew, storm, wet, cold, entertainment by a king, seeing, studying and learning new seas and shores, trading, deciding where to go and how, not for an hour did bitterness against Aelfthryth cease to smoulder within him. All of this was to gain time and opportunity to avenge his king. No more - not for a moment anything more.

Wulfnoth's real problem was simply this - to determine the nature and means of his revenge. As to the bloody queen, it was a simple matter. When his chance came, he would kill her. But the matter of the boy king Aethelred was more difficult. He had probably not been involved in the plotting. (But perhaps he had!) He had benefited by the crime nevertheless. And, most heinous of all, he was of the accursed blood, and that blood must all be shed.

But even given the opportunity, to kill a child was a mean sort of vengeance. What he must do, then, was bide his time until the boy should become a man. And if he must wait for the son, he must wait as long for the mother; for if he should be so lucky as to have a chance to smite one, certainly there would be no second opportunity. It must be both at a blow.

So Wulfnoth bided his time. With a cargo of salt fish and hides he stood boldly across the North Sea; it was a four day passage in the fine weather of late summer. He fetched the Skaw as expected, transited the Kattegat and ran up the Baltic to Jomsborg.

Harold Bluetooth was, as Wulfnoth had anticipated, only too glad to buy supplies and provisions for his growing army. And quite willing for Wulfnoth to winter there with his ship and crew.

Wulfnoth waited in the Danish fort, then, while the equinoctial gales raged over the sea at their front door; and while thereafter the snows fell and frost ruled the landscape. And as he waited he brooded over his revenge, making and discarding one fantastic plan after another to make the hated blood flow in atonement for its treason. Occasionally he wondered for what conquest Harold was assembling so great an army. But in the meantime he drank and caroused with them; there was a plenty of mead and of slave girls in the king's hall, and the king was kingly in his largesse. There were good harpers, too, and skalds sang in right good verses of the bravery of Harold and his line. In fine weather there were hunting parties in which the Englishman joined - with ill success, for the game had long since been decimated - but the sport was good nevertheless. Above all there was practice with bow, sword, axe and spear; and in these too Wulfnoth took conscientious part. Boatswain Bernhelm saw to it that the crew too had its share of training.

A man must live, however, and the boatswain would inform his captain, whenever possible, of the advent of the occasional traders. These came down the river from the vast, unknown hinterland. Wulfnoth managed to buy - this took some arranging, for even if he could have outbid the king he dared not give offense - silk cloth, wine, and some attractively decorated pottery, and a lovely Wend to be his leman. And he bought most of a shipload of plunder offered by his hosts.

Some of those he met he could have liked, had his mood been friendly; as it was, he kept himself at a distance. Once or twice he narrowly escaped having a quarrel forced on him; the combination of weapons and strong drink is not conducive to a placid existence. He was an outsider, however, and had sense enough to control his temper. His life was not his to throw away.

But the spring came; and then there were the endless caulking and painting and oiling and carpentering and sailmaking and metal polishing and the thousand and one chores incidental to making a ship ready to sail. It was done at last.

He embarked his crew and they put to sea.

Hedeby was sited at the head of the Schlei, on the eastern side of Sillende, the base of the Jutland peninsula. The beginning of its decay could be read in the empty warehouses seen here and there, and the poor state of repair of some of its houses. It was still an important trade center nevertheless; more important to the nation, perhaps, was the fact that its semicircular fifty-foot city wall constituted the Baltic anchor of the Danevirke, a protective earthwork that stretched ten miles westward to the marshes of the North Sea.

The skipper laid his craft neatly alongside a pier between a Frisian cog and a great merchantman of Skuldelev. Ashore, he threaded his way between and among sailors, washerwomen, armed horsemen, ladies gaudily attired, urchins, dogs and a pig or two. He dodged a dray, stepped under a lintel-piece bearing the carcass of a goat in sign that the householder had sacrificed it to one of the gods, and entered an open market shed.

In a few days he had done his chaffering and laden his ship with additional bronze work, arrow and spear points, sword blades, and well wrought marine hardware. He also invested in a few slaves, male and female, mostly young adults, but a woman among them begged so hard that he bought her little son as well, grumbling to himself in the knowledge that he would have to throw in the child for nothing when he resold the mother.

Now northward he stood, with a Norseman happily available as pilot. The pottery, silk, and wine had gone in the trading; there would be little use for such luxuries where he was bound.

Strange indeed to the Englishman was the inland passage behind the reefs and islands of the western Norwegian coast; but stranger still were those nights in which the daylight never quite disappeared, and the sun itself set as if reluctantly, sliding sideways down the horizon for a scant hour or two of rest before resuming its duties.

Arrived at Lade, he found the eager acceptance of his manufactured goods on which he had counted. In their stead he bought the thickest, most beautiful furs he had ever seen - of marten, bear, otter; sleek reindeer hides with the hair tanned on; the precious ivory of walrus and whale, and almost as precious, long line plaited of seal- and whale-hide.

Now back he coasted along western Norway, and then east for England once more. And with no little emotion he changed the cliffs and fiords of Scandinavia for the soft green fields of the Humber. And gladly did the merchants of York and Hull purchase his treasures of the north for the good white silver. He received it with the satisfaction of a job performed, but without joy. And when he had sent a seaman with a gift and a letter to Aelfere, the answer was such that he put to sea and spent yet another winter among the Danes.

This time, when cruising weather came, he loaded with goods from the north and headed southward toward the land of the Franks. He rounded Normandy and Brittany, rowed into the Loire and came to a mooring at Nantes.

The peoples of the north - Saxons, Flemings, Danes, Norse, Germans, Swedes - understood one another with some difficulty. But here in the south it was another matter, and Wulfnoth had to hire a translator to do business. But the trading was bareiy under way when some yells were heard from the summit of a watch tower, and then there was screaming and running, and men-at-arms appeared, and people were rushing behind the city walls, and they slammed the great gates. Wulfnoth could have accompanied them, he supposed, but to do so might well mean to share their fate, whatever it might be; and he preferred to carry his destiny in his own two hands. So he boarded his ship, and in a few minutes a Viking fleet swept into view.

Fortunately, the writ attesting to Harold's friendship still held good. So they merely relieved him of his cargo, and left him ship and crew - and life. So back he sailed to Jomsborg.

Harold received him in a friendly enough fashion, but only laughed at the report of his misfortune. Wulfnoth had expected nothing more. But the king offered to lend him a cargo.

"Do you still have Daedfruma," the captain asked him, "or is she sunk or lost?"

"She is still in my fleet."

"Then take back the ship I have, if you will, and let me take Daedfruma and go home."

"Take her," said the king, and put two gold bracelets on Wulfnoth's arm.

It was not too expensive to buy slave rowers - his armed crew could control them. Three years after he had left, Wulfnoth sailed Daedfruma back to the Wey. Leaving boatswain Bernhelm in charge of ship and crew, the captain took his way to the manor.

V

The famous prince
sat unhappy and suffered dire grief,
the aetheling good for the thanes who had gone,
when once they had traced the track of the enemy.

Beowulf.

Aelfere gave the returning captain a great welcome. Wulfnoth greeted him and his lady; he was hardly aware of a ten-year-old girl who was lost in rapturous wonder at his every word.

"The land fares ill," Aelfere told the seaman. "Last year men saw many times in the welkin a great red, in the likeness of fire - or of blood; it waxed till midnight, but was gone by day. They say that it is heaven's sign of displeasure with the murder of the old king and the accession of the new. This year the Northmen raided again. They swept like a storm from the sea. They burned farms, killed or stole the cattle, murdered the old, seized the young for the slave markets of the continent. They stormed and plundered cities."

"And what of the king and council? Did they remain idle?"

"Not so," grimly. "He consecrated a new bishop."

"But," he went on in different vein, "I have removed the remains of King Edward from his shallow, hastily made grave, and reinterred them at Shaftsbury with honor. There was a great assemblage of those who took ill at the anointing of the new king with blood. But nothing else has been done." His lady took the alderman's hand between her's. He glanced at her tenderly.

Aelfere was less than fair. The council had tried to counter the raid from the sea, but to little avail. Men looked askance at the call to war issued in the name of a king whose legitimacy hung under a cloud. And the peasant militias were short-sightedly reluctant to fight for any farms or hamlets but their own. So each earl or alderman defended his own lands with what little aid he could get; and it was seldom enough.

So the Danes came down on Dorset, and the people of Portland learned about the sacking of a city.

Tragedy came to the manor. Its dame, old but seemingly hale, died suddenly. Aelfere bade his wife a heartbroken farewell.

"You were the delight of my youth and the dear companion of my later years. Beautiful I found you when first I unveiled your dear body in the bridal bed, and beautiful I found you when the passage of years had frosted your hair. You were my stay in time of distress and despair, and the sharer of joy in time of success. Warm you were and loving in the chamber, and wise in the hall of council. When you pleased me I loved you; when you angered me I loved you still. Oh that I might have died in your stead, or else that I might have been the sharer in this your dark journey!

"Oh, my love, my love! God be tender with you, and may I soon rejoin you in bliss! Or if there be indeed no marriage hereafter, then what would I of Glory? Without your love Paradise will be but a wretched guerdon.

"You were indeed the darling of my heart. May I not linger long in this cold and lonely world. For I too am dead, but this rebel flesh refuses to succumb."

Aelfere was very old, and the day came when Wulfnoth walked sadly at his funeral. His son Aelfric succeeded him. Even more than his sire, he resented Aethelred as a murderer and usurper, and Wulfnoth found in him a man of like mind and purpose.

Aelfric began to inquire cautiously of this thane and of that, how he liked being ruled by this nithing king, this fratricide and stealer of crowns; and of what might be concerted to his confusion. And he sent Wulfnoth abroad with letters of purport that here were rich rewards to be won, and assistance in the winning of them, for any princeling bold enough to risk a landing.

Wulfnoth did his lord good service. There were quarrels in which he bore himself manfully. And the longships, now two, now three, assailed Aelfric's own coast. Out then came Daedfruma and her two sisters; they closed and grappled the Norsemen. Wulfnoth, axe flashing, would leap over the gunwales at the head of his men; he would parry a few swordcuts and bring his weapon crashing through shield and helm. Bernhelm's shield was ever at his master's side. Briefly the captain could vent the bitterness of his soul - briefly, because within minutes the melee was ended with the surrender of the few raiders still on their feet. And to the question, "What shall we do with the captives?" his answer was, on each occasion, "Sell them!"

He made some further trading voyages in Aelfric's interest - to Flanders, to Friesland, once even as far as Lisbon.

It was seven years after Wulfnoth's flight to Aelfere that the alderman said to his half-sister one day:

"Child, it is time you were married. Our father always gave as much thought to you as to his children by his wife."

"He was good to me, my lord."

"It is time you were married. I cannot, as you know, marry

you as well as my other sisters. Perhaps that is in a way an advantage - since we cannot look to the sons of earls, the number from whom we can choose is so much the greater."

"I do not aspire to an earl, my lord."

"Possibly a thane could be persuaded."

"I do not need or hope to marry so high, my lord."

He looked at her searchingly. "No, you do not. It is in my mind that a certain ceorl has been long in your heart."

"Ever since first I saw him, Aelfric, I have thought of no other man."

"This Wulfnoth is no man of gentleness, my child. He is embarked upon a course that may destroy him - that may even lead him to the gallows. You will find little ease or comfort by his side."

She looked imploringly at her brother. He sighed.

"Well, the man has elements of greatness. He is brave and capable, at least. Are you sure, child, that that is your wish?"

And so, a day later, the alderman summoned the captain to his closet.

"By the law of the Saxons, Wulfnoth, having made three voyages abroad in command of a ship, you are entitled to be raised to the grade of thane."

The other nodded.

"The Danes mount ever greater attacks upon our land. The future of each of us is uncertain - I see no end, late or soon, to battle. I think we should delay your elevation no longer.

"I have an estate in Sussex, I give it to you. You know Ethelfleda, my sister by my father's leman Elfrida. Does she please you?"

"She pleases me well, my lord."

"Then take her to wife. And serve me as before."

"My deep thanks, my lord. I shall serve you as well as God gives me to do. Together, we shall carry out the great mission."

"Let that lie still within your own bosom."

So Wulfnoth became thane of Sussex. He found himself master of a modest manorhouse in a vale of the Downs. Above, the slopes, part oaken and part pasture land for sheep, led to the heights; below, a ghyll opened into a tiny harbor in the white cliffs, sufficient to furnish mooring or beaching facilities for his longship.

The cluster of houses held men enough to tend sheep and till the corn land. A small mill ground its yield. A grey church held the men and their families on a Sunday, or when the father celebrated a wedding mass.

It was a pleasant abode, and the grain and wool were, if not abundant, sufficient for the thane and his people; and a man could live here in peace and contentment. If he had not a flame in his bosom.

"I congratulate you, my lord, on your elevation," Bernhelm said to him. "Even more than before, you will now be Aelfric's faithful retainer. But I urge you, keep some of your own counsel, and even your own power, to yourself."

The newly created thane looked his astonishment. "I hope you are not suggesting that the alderman is not to be trusted!"

"I am not, my lord. He will deal with you loyally enough. But I do not trust his judgment. There is a streak of rashness in him that will bring him to destruction. Look to it that you do not share in his fall."

Bernhelm too had taken a wife - the daughter of a ceorl in Aelfric's service. Wulfnoth gave them a cottage. To this and to his wife the boatswain was to return at the end of the sailing season each autumn.

Many of the crew made less permanent arrangements. There was a floating population of blowsy women in a cluster of huts near where the ships were laid up for winter.

Aelfric had been only just in time with the gift. Inevitably, someone talked of his machinations. A horse, foaming bloodily, his flanks heaving, appeared before Aelfric's manor, and the rider flung himself out of the saddle and through the door. Then the alderman was calling for a horse, and within minutes he was spurring for his life.

But it was not the king's men-at-arms who banged with their sword-hilts, too late, at the alderman's door that evening. Goda, thane of Devonshire, had seen his opportunity; and he had joined with a Norse raider to enlarge his lands while proclaiming Aelfric a traitor to the king. The charge was plausible enough for Aethelred to look the other way.

Wulfnoth was on his lands in Sussex at the time. Too late to aid his benefactor, he tried to pick up the pieces of Aelfric's conspiracy. But presently one came with greetings from Aelfric in Wales, bidding him lie low till further word; and messages in the same tenor continued.

Then, three years later, there was another incursion in the west, and Goda fell at the hands of the raiders he had once favored. It was a great slaughter; when he heard of it, Wulfnoth hurried to the area with his ceorls and seized aldermanship for his absent lord.

Aelfric returned, and again King Aethelred ignored the matter.

On occasions when the king and his mother were together, Wulfnoth made attempts to approach them; but the coolness of the people toward their king of darkened accession assured that he was well guarded. Not even a thane could produce convincing reason for access to royalty.

In the twenty-first year of the reign, Wulfnoth learned that the king was taking Aelfgifu, an alderman's daughter, to wife.

It was a happy day in the same year as Aelfric's return when Wulfnoth's son Godwin was born. The thane raised the infant proudly in his arms. It was large, well formed, vigorous, and had a lusty cry. Here was his succession! If he should fail in his mission of vengeance, here was a manchild to take it up! And he dedicated the boy to the extirpation of the line of hated Queen Aelfthryth. He did not forget to kiss his wife and put much gold about her neck.

But it was an ill time into which the boy had been born. The Viking cloud was darkening. Fugitives, one after another, found their way to Wulfnoth's manor. He listened to their stories, and took horse toward the West.

Aelfric made him welcome.

"The hit-and-run raids, apparently, are developing into something more," said the host.

The thane nodded. "They come now as whole armies, in fleets of nigh a hundred sail. The men I have brought are from the ruined countryside. Ask them what they have seen."

A ceorl of Hampshire spoke. The raiders had taken gold and silver, all small articles of value, all costly raiment. What they had not taken, they had destroyed. They had spat in the faces of bishop and priest.

A monk nodded. "I was a guest in the house of thane Wilbert. I was walking with the young children of my host, when I saw the Danes approach the manor. I hid with the little ones; I heard later how the thane looked on in misery as a dozen grinning ruffians in succession ravished his wife and elder daughters. I saw the pirates drive forlorn gangs of pretty girls and able-bodied young men to the ships and slavery."

A slave with raw wounds where ears and nose had been, spoke in a curious thin voice. "They tortured the wealthy to make them disclose the hiding places of possible treasure; when they had it, they tortured them some more in hope that there might be some silver that was still concealed. They tormented us poor for sport."

The monk added, "The Vikings spread out into the countryside, and the air became foul, first with the smoke of burning homes, later with the stench of putrefying flesh."

Aelfric and Wulfnoth sat late in talk.

"It is too late for the king to organize a defense this year," said the former. "In the spring he must make a great effort to oppose the Danes. I shall again see what I can do to persuade some of his people to abandon his cause."

Wulfnoth shook his head. "You tried that before. Let me, though there is no reason to anticipate any better success now - especially since all may feel that now more than ever they must unite for safety under the king."

"We should be able to make some sort of capital out of his distress."

The thane nodded. "Seek a reconciliation. Pretend to be eager to serve. If you succeed, you can then work more effectively within his forces."

"I think you are right."

"And I shall be at your side to assist as opportunity offers."

"No. Remain aloof. If you are not compromised, and I fail, you will be available to me for possible succor; or if not, you can resume the great design alone!"

Bernhelm had not been present at the conference; but he had ears and eyes, and was uneasily silent that winter.

As Aelfric expected, the king began to organize a fleet for a struggle against the invaders in the coming year. His councillors, turning every way in their desperation, accepted Aelfric's proffer of his services, and made him one of the four commanding generals of the royal forces. They hoped to trap the Danes at sea.

The clash took place in the spring. There was a great rout of the king's ships.

"Have you heard about Aelfric?" one of his fellow thanes asked Wulfnoth thereafter. "He betrayed the battle plans and disposition of forces to the enemy."

"Incredible! Are you sure?"

"Quite sure, unfortunately. Perhaps we would have lost in any case, but the traitor made certain of it!"

"What has been done to him?"

"The rascal took ship and fled, but was captured by the Northmen - no doubt by design."

The slave who was serving the mead spilled a drop upon Wulfnoth's cloak; the thane gave him a savage buffet.

The visitor regarded him sympathetically. "We are all in a rage. If only the traitor were here under our hands!"

But King Aethelred had his vengeance. In the following year one led to Wulfnoth's door a youth with blood still oozing from empty eye sockets. This was Aelfric's son Aelfgar, made to pay in this horrible fashion for his father's crime.

With grim satisfaction Wulfnoth wrote Aelfric in his Irish refuge: "King Anlaf, with young Olaf Tryggvason, led ninety-three dragonships into East Anglia. They sacked Staines and Sandwich; Alderman Brinoth fell in a gallant but futile defense of Maldon; then Anlaf laid Bamborough too in ruins, took his ships up the Humber, and ravaged Lindsey and Northumberland."

King Aethelred faced his council in despair. "If this army continues to march plundering through my kingdom, I shall have nor throne nor land nor people. No arms prevail against them. What are we to do?"

It was Archbishop Siric who spoke the fateful word. "My king, there is but one thing left to try. Let us call these Vikings to a parley and try to buy them off."

The king received young Olaf Tryggvason in pomp. For ten thousand pounds Olaf swore to depart and trouble England no more. And as he promised, so he performed; and indeed a higher destiny kept him in his own lands thereafter.

The next year Wulfnoth wrote to his lord, "Anlaf has come again, and sat down before London with purpose to burn it; but the men of London showed him harder handplay than he was wont to encounter. So he ravaged widely and horribly; Essex, Kent, Sussex, Hampshire, all became a waste. Then they paid him sixteen thousand pounds in silver on his oath to go away and return no more." And he too kept his word.

But the yeomanry groaned under the ruinous weight of the Danegeld; ceorls lost their holdings and became geneatas, and many of the latter became little better than serfs. Instead of King Aethelred, "King of Noble Counsel," men began to call him "Unraed," the "Uncounselled," which time and error were to make into "Ethelred the Unready."

Never did the disaffected forget murdered Edward. More and more they spoke of him as a saint; and so he became. They withheld their support from Aethelred; his campaigns were failures on account of it; men said that his failures were a judgment upon him.

Domestically the king fared no better. Gentle Aelfgifu bore

him sons and daughters and then died. As the grief-stricken husband
followed her to the grave, he felt that he was abandoned of God and
men.

The Norsemen now felt strong enough to establish winter
quarters at some defensible site, and remained in despite of king and
nobles, and in the spring resumed their scarcely suspended
depredations. The dragonships operated from islands begirt with
shallow water; even when the English could bring larger fleets to
challenge them, the more heavily built English ships could not pursue
and engage without running aground.

VI

What is woman, that you forsake her,
And the hearth fire, and the home acre,
To go to the old grey widow-maker?
                    Harp Song of the Dane Women: Kipling.

Wulfnoth's son Godwin had a happy childhood. His father's estates were lucky enough to escape the attentions of the invaders. His loving, gentle mother sang him the immemorial songs of babyhood, then told stories suitable for a little boy. His grim father came and went, played with him occasionally, felt the growing muscles and smiled. For playmates there were the children of the ceorls and geneatas about the manor; they early began to use wooden swords and spears in mimic warfare.

He was in his sixth year when a monk of the abbey nearby came at the thane's behest for the boy's education. Reading, writing, and the study of poetry came easily to the little pupil, and elementary arithmetic only a little less so. A smattering of history and of geography followed, and the rudiments of Latin.

Godwin took all this without too much suffering. It cannot be said that he enjoyed it; a boy is a half domesticated animal who would much more willingly be roaming the woods than sitting caged in a classroom. Nevertheless he endured it, as boys usually do, partly because he realized dimly that these were tools essential to the business of coping with the world, and partly because he realized that his parents would allow him no option in any case.

Much more to his liking was the instruction in arms and equitation by one of the house-ceorls. An eight-year-old, he was given a set of weapons scaled down to his strength. He learned to catch blows and missiles on his shield, to wield sword and axe, to fling a spear at a target, to string and shoot a bow, and what qualities to look for or avoid in choice of weapons. He was instructed in the care and diet of a horse, and in the ordinary and extreme limits of endurance of the animal. And of course there was from time to time the ecstasy of a hunt.

And there was husbandry, at least as much as he needed to know to be a prudent lord over his cottagers, neither slack nor overly exacting. He had to join, at least occasionally, in the plowing, the sowing, the cultivating, the reaping; to milk a cow, shear a sheep, slaughter and butcher a swine. There were even sessions in the kitchen; a wise thane should have some idea of how many loaves to expect out of a bushel of grain, how and how long the beer is brewed.

Evenings there would be a song by his mother, a stirring reminiscence of some long-past battle in which his mentor had fought, a tale of olden days by the reverend father.

Sundays he went to Mass with his mother and the household. He sat in the long, high nave that characterized the Saxon church, and gazed at the sculptures, paintings, and hangings that adorned it. And afterwards there would be stories of a far-off land to the south and east and of strange doings long ago that he accepted without thought or question.

Aelfere's daughter lived in a philosophic acceptance of what, in that age and land, had become woman's lot. She had long given up any hope of drawing tenderness out of her thane's granite breast. He never abused her; he insisted that all, including himself, give her the deference due her rank. If he was enwrapped in concerns that he never shared with her, and if he occasionally took an hour's pleasure with a purchased woman or a captive, she had never expected otherwise.

Except in winter, she almost never saw her husband. With the onset of spring he was off to see about the refitting of his ship, the assembling of his crew, and other business of which she knew nothing. With the onset of autumn the thane would bestow his ship for the season, and set about disposing of his trade goods, if indeed they were trade goods, and come home.

Almost indifferently he had sired the handsome and well-built Godwin, and for the most part he treated the son as he treated the mother. By reason of the attendants to whom Wulfnoth had entrusted the boy's education, the paternal neglect did not greatly matter.

Childhood must end; and cruelly for some. Ethelfleda had learned not to expect attention from her strange and preoccupied lord. He did not observe how, while his son was still but a lad, the mother gradually lost flesh and strength. It was only when she developed a swelling under the jaw that her husband became aware of something amiss. He discovered that she was running a low fever.

The leech took porlock leaves, lily roots and helenium shoots, chopped very fine and pounded for a fomentation. It did not help. He bled her from the right arm. She became rapidly more debilitated. The swelling grew larger; he incised it and released thick whitish pus. For a few days thereafter she seemed improved; then there was a relapse. They bore her to the shrine of St. Swithin at

Winchester, but a week thereafter she died.

The twelve-year-old orphan wept continually for a week. Wulfnoth duly observed the rites of burial, and then considered what to do about the boy.

"Son," he said at length, "as young as you are, you know how uncertain are chances in England. No place is secure from raiders; our weakling king cannot defend his kingdom. When you are a man, there may be no estate left for you; and if there is, it is doubtful how long you will be able to enjoy it.

"A thane must know the arts of war; but there is no reasonable assurance, as things are, that he can expect favorable conditions for defense. Even if you were willing to take a command in the royal army, there is so much folly and defection among the king's officers that you would, more likely than not, fall victim to what should have been a friendly force.

"I am a man of the sea, and the sea may be your salvation. There is danger on it, but danger of a kind that, with luck, a man can cope with. As long as you have ships, and know how to sail them, and how to lead your men, you can protect yourself and, if necessary, recoup your losses. Your true estate should be the sea. No one can envy you it; no one can seize it.

"A first-rate seaman knows his ship. He knows how she will perform and why, he knows her limitations as well as he knows his own, he knows how and when to repair her, and he knows how to judge a builder and a ship he is going to entrust with his life.

"And so, Godwin, I am going to place you, for a few years, where you can learn all these things. Then, you will come to me."

Wulfnoth took his son to the shipwright Heca, one he had known for many years, with respect for the man and for his work. Heca had migrated to Cornwall; and in a tiny cove between low ridges sloping into the sea he had bought a site on the waterfront from the local fishermen and set up a shipyard. Behind it, scattered among the beeches and elms, were the cottages of the fishermen and of his workmen. There was little here to lure raiders, and it was not too far out of the way for merchants and others to come for ships of every sort. Here the thane judged that his son would be safe - or as safe as might be in those troubled times - and would profit by Heca's instruction.

Godwin found enough and more than enough to fascinate a boy despite his grief. As they rode down the slope toward Heca's yard they passed a team of horses drawing an oaken log, and a double team hitched to an axle with high wheels on which there was a larger one. Then the shipyard came into view.

Heca proved to be a kindly, grizzled, muscular, middle-aged man who gave the lad a hearty welcome. As the three went through the establishment Godwin saw a long roof under which a man was splitting logs into planks with axe, maul and wedge; another, with axe and adze, was smoothing and thinning them to size, leaving projecting butts which looked to be some 15 inches, center to center. Another artisan was trimming and shaping these, then drilling them; answering the boy's question, his father explained that these were for binding the planks to the ribs.

They passed through a blacksmith shop, where the forge was in use for the manufacture of ships' hardware, the sail loft (where at the time no one was doing anything with the bundles of homespun canvas), and the small boat shed, where a pair of tenders lay.

But the most exciting sight, to Godwin, was a longship on the ways, whose skeleton artisans were beginning to plank. A noble-seeming dragon she was - 80 feet long, Heca told them, 18 feet in beam and seven in depth. The boy looked at her with shining eyes and saw himself at her steering sweep.

Heca was an exacting master, he found in the days that followed.

Godwin had dressed a section of gunwale. Egelric looked at it, and said, "Roll up your sleeve." The boy did so. "Now pull your arm along it." As he complied, the old man pressed upon him; when Godwin winced and looked at the blood oozing from his skin, his mentor said, "Now how would you like to slide along that with your full weight on the arm, when she pitches in a gale?"

The lad had forged a rivet. Elnoth examined it, then asked, "Do you think I can use this rivet in the ship?" "Yes." was the proud reply. "Well, let us make a wager. If it stands up, you get my portion of mead for a month; if not, I get yours. Agreed?" "Agreed." The smith took hammer and chisel, and demolished it at the first blow. "You did not temper it properly," he said with a grin.

When the lad had acquired some skill, Heca directed him to make a floor, a connecting piece above the keel for opposite ribs. There was no piece of oak around of suitable size and shape; rather than cut down a larger one, Godwin took a piece of hemlock that he found and laboriously worked it, as he thought, to perfection. He took it to Heca, who threw it in the fire.

"It could not stand up under the load," he said. "You should have used oak."

"But I saw you use hemlock for a wagon," the boy protested,

"and you said that it is just as hard as oak."

The ship builder nodded. "For a wagon, it is. But let it get thoroughly soaked, and it becomes soft and worthless."

Nevertheless, Godwin enjoyed learning the crafts of a shipwright. And on feast days there were the grand dinners and the games, and sports with boys of the shipyard and the village. Sometimes a fisher lad, when they had leave, would take him out in a skiff and he learned more about the arts of the sea.

He saw his father about twice a year, at the end and just before the beginning of the sailing season. Often there was a bitter tirade against the king. Wulfnoth had no fear lest a careless word on the part of the boy should betray him; then, as many times before and since, the disorder was such that children carried secrets which could if betrayed lead to the gallows.

VII

Loud to the harp   the lay resounded
And many a noble   who knew aright
Said he had never   heard better song.

Widsith— The Minstrel.

Men began to fear Wulfnoth. He had become all too ready to use fist or sword in anger; and anger came readily. Only with his son and his crews did he keep a strict curb upon his temper.

At last the Great Chance came.

Alderman Paley was one of those who secretly hated the ruling house. The Danes made a landing in the south; and Paley felt that the time had come to declare himself. He sent to the Danish army and engaged to meet with it in Devon with all his ships; and to Wulfnoth, now in the lower Thames, he wrote that the evil queen mother was at Bath with but few men-at-arms to defend her. If Wulfnoth, with his crew and what men he could collect, would march swiftly a hundred and fifty miles across country toward Swindon, the regicide would be caught between the jaws of a nutcracker and brought to book.

So, while a great battle was fought at Alton in Hampshire in which the king's forces were again beaten, Wulfnoth and his men took horse and dashed westward. As Paley joined the invaders and menaced the queen from the south, Wulfnoth blocked her escape northward and, full of anticipated triumph and revenge, began to close in.

Too late. With the town of Bath already in view, Wulfnoth intercepted the royal messengers who carried the news of the old vixen's peaceful death of old age.

In rage and despair the thane killed his captives. He retraced his steps and took ship for Norway and safety.

Gunnlauge Serpenttooth, the Icelandic skald, had been sojourning among the Vikings. His harp had won him gold and honor. He had however a serious defect; there were times when he allowed his tongue to run too freely. And now he had offended Jarl Eirick with what the Jarl held to be an intolerable insult.

Barely in time, the poet fled to the port just as Wulfnoth was reading advices that the English court had not connected him with Paley's treason, and that he might safely return to England. As he was about to embark he was accosted by Gunnlauge with an urgent request for passage.

It is a pity that he could not have known how fateful for Aethelred and England would be his consent!

There were, of course, temporary successes for the English arms. After one of these, in the twenty-third year of the reign, Gunnlauge Serpenttooth the skald came to the English court. Aethelred feasted him as his fame required. According to custom, the skald, having eaten and drunk, was expected to show his skill; and the graceful thing to do was naturally to sing the praises of his host.

He was really a very good skald indeed. And he brought out some lines with which he himself instantly fell in love. The Saxon tongue had not moved so far from the Norse dialects but that Aethelred had been able to learn them well.

The king, naturally, was delighted, starved as he was for recognition and praise from any source other than his own courtiers. The generosity of his gifts outdid the former rewards of his celebrant, and Gunnlauge left with the happiest of impressions.

But then the Northmen came again, and roamed at will over the agonized country.

Harried and beset, King Aethelred turned in desperation to seek support from overseas. Across the Channel was the powerful duchy of Normandy. Duke Richard had a sister, Emma, and Aethelred was a widower. He sent Bishop Elfric and Alderman Leofsy to woo for him. They returned without a definite commitment.

Shortly thereafter, Gunnlauge the skald visited the court of Normandy. At a banquet he heard mention of Aethelred. The French

speaking ducal house still understood Norse. Remembering his felici-
tous lines, Gunnlauge rose, took his harp, and extolled the English
king.

An artist knows occasions on which the wellsprings of
invention dry up, and conversely others on which inspiration soars.
Gunnlauge found himself that day in really good vein. So, in love
with his own artistry, he was quite carried away, and celebrated
Aethelred's courage and resourcefulness in war, and wisdom in council, in truly moving verse.

Emma, tall, stately, handsome in a hawk-nosed, imperious
fashion, had been raised on sagas of the prowess of her race. Only a
hundred years had passed since her great forebear Rollo had come
storming out of the mists to wrest the duchy of Normandy from the
feebler Frankish kings. She listened enthralled to the poet; when he
had finished she cried, "Richard! Grant Aethelred's suit! Give me to
him for his queen!"

So Emma went to England.

VIII

Queen Sigrid the Haughty sat proud and aloft
In her chamber, that looked over meadow and croft.
Heart's dearest,
Why dost thou sorrow so?

The Saga of King Olaf—Longfellow.

But it was a strange sort of kingdom, she discovered, whose
crown she had assumed. Her lord seemed powerless in the face of the
invaders from across the North Sea. The ravagers came and went
almost at will. Under their wasting and the well-nigh equally ruinous
Danegeld the people were sinking into despair.

Aethelred first learned the depth of her disgust when he
broached the possibility of a Norman fleet to help him fight off the
pirates.

"God's death!" she burst out. "Am I to tell my brother that I
wedded a King who is too feeble to hold his throne? A king? Hardly
even a man!" She was in this unjust; Aethelred had always acted with
what vigor his circumstances permitted. "Not a hundred years have
gone by since my forefather, Hrolf Gangr, wrested his dukedom of
Normandy from the grasp of France; the dukes of Normandy have

held it to this day, and woe to him who brings war into their lands! What manner of king are you, who cannot hold fast what your father left?"

Aethelred gritted his teeth and rushed from the chamber. Weakling, was he? He would show this insolent female something! The Danelaw, to the northeast, was a recurrent source of support and refuge for the armies of the Danes. It would be so no longer.

He summoned his earls.

Within a week his soldiers drove across the border. Through the Danelaw they swept, killing and killing. When they had finished, no Dane capable of bearing arms remained alive, and with them lay the corpses of more than a few women.

Among these was the sister of a king!

Perhaps, even if his sister had been spared, King Sweyn of Denmark and Norway would have sailed to avenge the slaughtered Danefolk. Perhaps, even had there been no massacre at all, Sweyn, whose dead father Harold Bluetooth had forged the deadly instrument that was his army, would have unleashed it against the nearby kingdom of Aethelred. At any rate, once spring had made the highway of the sea passable again, he hurled his troops against the hapless English.

Incredibly, Aelfric had been restored to favor; even more incredibly, he was given high command in the king's army. Then, when the two forces should have engaged, Aelfric pretended sickness. There was a retreat, and the Danes advanced, plundered and burned.

But then, before the traitor alderman had a chance to evade the royal patrols and join the Danes, they had taken ship and were for the time being gone.

Aelfric fled to Wulfnoth. "This time I am finally finished in England," he said. "And apparently Sweyn does not want me either. You must carry me to safety."

"Where would you go?"

"The north countries are closed to me, I fear. Nor would I trust myself to Scotland or Ireland. And in France the king has his queen's people.

"Take me to Iceland!"

It was not too difficult to hide Aelfric while the thane provisioned his ship and made it otherwise ready for the voyage. Then, Aelfric and his crew on board, the thane prepared to sail. He sent for young Godwin, now a strong fifteen-year-old. It was high time and more, he felt, to begin the boy's apprenticeship to the sea; and what better opportunity?

IX

O'er the sea from the north there sails a ship
With the people of Hel, at the helm stands Loki;
After the wolf do wild men follow.

Voluspo—The Poetic Edda

Although he had crossed the North Sea, Wulfnoth knew
nothing of the art of measuring a ship's progress north or south; he
had always navigated by the rough art of dead reckoning which in
skilled hands is so remarkably dependable - but not for long voyages
through a stormy ocean.

This time, an experienced kentmand embarked with him.
The navigator brought a soldbradt, a board divided into half-wheels,
and corresponding tables of these half solar diameters for every day of
the year, with which to determine, by observations of the sun at noon,
latitudes as they changed from day to day. For direction he had tables
of the angular distance of the rising and the setting sun from the north
star, measured in the same half-wheels, likewise for each day of the
year.

Young Godwin almost regretted having been taken when the
unaccustomed chop of the Channel asserted its power over his
protesting stomach. Almost - not quite. There was a strain of tough-
ness in his constitution, already manifest at his tender age, and he
fought grimly with his weakness. And soon he began again to enjoy,
first the air, then the beauty, last even the motion of his first cruise.
His silent, somewhat awesome sire was more relaxed and communica-
tive than usual.

The lad had questions. "Father, the wind is against the
rowers, and only half of them are pulling, and even they don't seem to
be working too hard; yet, judging by the shore, we seem to be making
good progress. How is that?"

"The wind, as you say, is against us; but we have a strong
favoring tidal current, and the oarsmen have only to keep her from
blowing astern. The current does the rest."

And, "Father, the biggest man, instead of rowing, is merely
steering. Why is that?"

"Would you like to steer?" with a twisted smile.

"Oh, yes!"

He found the answer to his question.

Again, off the Lizard, as the huge Atlantic rollers

began their sport with the hull, "Father," in alarm, "I have just been looking along the gunwale, and the seas twist her half a handsbreadth out of true! What is wrong?"

"Nothing, son; besides trenails and rivets, we use, as you know, many lashings in our construction; and you notice that the upper half of the planks on each side are not even made fast to the ribs, but merely to one another. That gives our ships a lot of elasticity and makes them more sea-kindly. I sailed home from Friesland once in a curious lateen-rigged ship of Genova. She was hard-fastened throughout, and it was pound, pound, pound against the head seas all the time. I imagine they pound themselves to pieces in relatively few years."

"Why does the sail have all those diagonal strips of cloth, father, that divide it into a pattern of lozenges?"

"In earlier times, son, our people used leather sails. When cloth became available, they found that it was so much lighter and more flexible and altogether more manageable that it was adopted. But it stretches badly; and these reinforcements help it keep its shape."

The thane did not tire of his son's questions, endless though they were. Again, in the new intimacy, he told the boy about the assassination of King Edward, and about the Great Purpose.

"The upright man holds by his lord. His lord's honor and power are his whole concern. If the lord prosper, he honors his henchmen in word and by gift of gold. When you see a man with much gold upon him, then know (unless he be merely a trader) that he values it not for its own worth, but as token of his dear lord's regard.

"In battle, his lord fights for victory, but the henchman fights for his chief. And if the latter fall, his followers are in honor bound to die about his body, wreaking what vengeance they can for his death. Or if they survive, it must be only to avenge him thereafter.

"And so I live in hope to wreak vengeance for my king upon the body of the man who stole the kingship from him. If I die, it will be your duty to take up my task."

The boy felt a new dignity and importance. He had a mission!

It took three days of sailing and rowing (they camped ashore at night) to reach Penzance Bay. The next day was cloudy, with the frequent westerly wind of Britain. The youngster found it demanding of a thick woolen jacket as they pulled to and around Lands End. But then, as they turned downwind for the run northeastward along northern Cornwall, it seemed suddenly to become warm!

"It's always warm when you are running with the wind," his

father explained. "But when you are going into it, it whistles past you like the icy breath of the Rime Giants!"

Evening found them at Milford, close under Harland Point. In the morning the wind was northerly. "Just as well," Wulfnoth remarked. "Tomorrow we will rest and overhaul the gear. We'll not get ashore again before the Outer Hebrides, five hundred miles to the north. The coasts will be unfriendly all the way."

The southwest wind blew them merrily up the Irish Sea. Godwin gazed happily at the sparkling blue waters, the heights of Wales (he had never seen a high hill), and the Mountains of Mourne in northern Ireland.

It was not all loafing. Wulfnoth kept him moderately busy at minor tasks - whipping ropes' ends, making splices, polishing, polishing, polishing and oiling arms and other metalwork that tarnished almost as fast as they could clean it. But the boy wolfed down his dried bread, peas and smoked fish, and slept dreamlessly under the tent amidships.

Mostly they ran all night, keeping well in the middle of the wide waterway. When the moon was down they tried to lie in the lee of a headland or island. Nevertheless, they almost came to grief on the Maidens, a group of rocks well off the northeast Irish coast. But they never ventured ashore. The Welsh, the Norse rulers of Westmoringsland and Dublin, the Scots, and for that matter the Irish kerns themselves, all were enemies.

Only when, nine days from Lands End, they reached the remoter Hebrides, did Wulfnoth and Thurkill the kentmand judge it safe to lie ashore. This was a great comfort, although it was only less cold on the beach than at sea.

Now northward they stood again, through a wide, lonely ocean. The mounting seas were grey and unfriendly, and here the boy experienced a wonder - the nights were amazingly short, and the days correspondingly long! And well that they were so; otherwise the cold of a long night would have been bitter indeed; and the lookout was glad of the shortened hours of blindness.

The third dawn disclosed to them, not far off on the port bow, a group of rugged, treeless hills. A clinging fog hid the lowlands from their view.

"The Faeroes," The kentmand proclaimed.

"Who lives there?" asked Godwin.

"Only a few Norse. Sheep find browse, I have heard, and the fishing is good."

The kentmand looked at Wulfnoth.

"There is nothing for us there," the thane decided. "If it were nightfall, we might risk a visit there for comfort. But the weather is fair, and we had better make the best of it."

So they kept on, only altering course a little toward the west.

The wind grew steadily stronger; not in storm, but as though here it were in perpetual bad temper, and would yield no friendly gesture toward men. And indeed, it turned adverse, and for three days they lay to a warp, while the breeze whistled overhead and they huddled in all of their garments for warmth.

Men first wondered whether the kentmand would ever find the island in this enormous watery desert, then they doubted, then they were sure that he could not, and despaired of their lives.

It blew again from the south, and they resumed their northing.

One noon there was a sudden shout that directed all eyes forward - and there, faint on the horizon, floating on a bank of mist, were the noble, glacier-capped peaks!

As they approached, they saw that the southern part of the land was low. They coasted it and finally entered a commodious harbor and found the town.

It did not take long to bestow Aelfric in the house of Jarl Thurkyll.

In the last of summer, the ship took departure for the Faeroes. Only a day on the return journey, Wulfnoth ran into a southwesterly gale. Again, as many a time before, they ran helplessly before it, bailing for their lives. To the violence of the immense seas, the lash of icy spray, the terrifying howl of angry nature, was added the numbing effect of the unremitting wind. Fasten their garments as they would, it searched out every gap and worn spot relentlessly; they were miserably cold by day and agonizingly so by night. Through low, scudding clouds they glimpsed an opaque gray sky. There was never the mercy of a warm snack or drink to bring the illusion of a moment's comfort to their beaten bodies.

Day after day the vicious wind blew. They learned to give thanks even for the bitter mercy of giant seas sweeping interminably upon them; for there were spells of confused wave formation that were worse.

Wulfnoth spoke ruefully to the kentmand about the northing they were making so reluctantly, and that would all have to be made up by painful working to the south.

"Be glad that the gale is in this quarter," said the older man.

"Were this a norther, the cold would be unbearable; we might well be too numb to work the ship, even to feed ourselves. Furthermore, I am not sure that all of our run has been to the north. You noticed spells of irregular shape and motion of the waves. They indicated sudden shifts in wind direction, such as occur in these seas. Without sun, moon or star to observe, we could not judge direction."

"Does that mean that you do not know even approximately where we are?"

The other could only spread his hands helplessly.

Now even Wulfnoth could not have kept heart and life in his men but for the resolute backing of the ever loyal Bernhelm.

On the high seas there are two things that oppress; infinity and menace.

There have been many accounts of "endless voyages," and a famous voyager speaks of fear that is always present as an obbligato to the enjoyment, the freedom, the merriment on a small boat passage. Your seaman speaks of the sea with a casualness that hides from others, but never from himself, his awareness of these two brooding specters that haunt his every hour. Why else does he go to sea, but to measure his manhood against their horror?

Menace and infinity. Peril at sea has a thousand guises. It comes as storm that may pitchpole the frail craft end over end, or cause her to broach to and swamp, wrench her timber from timber in despite of the cunningest of fastenings. It comes as reef, uncharted or simply unrecognized, that may tear the bottom out of her, or as softer but equally treacherous sand that may swallow her whole and drown her people in foam. It comes as foe, human or animal, pirate or grasping arm of the horrible kraken. It comes as rust or rot, that weakens the frail shell which is all that stands between man and the devouring depths. It comes in guise unguessable, sweeping clean a vessel of her people, leaving her afloat and unharmed for the bewilderment of her finders.

Infinity and menace. What lies beyond that fleeting horizon, but ever more of the same emptiness? One sees the distant land writ clearly on the chart, or in the mind's eye of experience. But is it really still there? Can one be sure of surviving the fatigue, the hunger, the cold, actually to attain to that mythical shore? The endless suns wheel through the empty heavens, and they far outlast the few allotted days of man.

Menace and infinity. Are they not, in truth, one and the same? What are the timelessness and shorelessness of ocean but

menace of the gaping gates of doom? What is the menace of that
yawning deep of ocean but the portal by which man passes from the
finite and homely world into the terrible infinite?

When after eleven days the weather turned fair at last, there
was a council to determine their course. To the east was either the
wide North Sea and Norway, no friend to English ships; or, if they had
drifted far south, Scotland. To the south was open ocean, but warmer;
unless again the ship had driven eastward, which would threaten with
the terribly dangerous rocks and sweeping tides of the north of
Scotland or the isles.

The sands of the most trackless of deserts have almost always
the boon of guidance by the great beacons of the sky. The shade of
the Amazon jungle, if it has no other clearings, is broken in places by
streams which offer an opportunity for observation of the celestial
bodies, or in favorable places a tree can be climbed for the purpose.
Even in its rainy season, the tropical ocean has frequent periods of
clear skies by day and by night. One cannot be long in doubt, in any
of these or other areas, of the cardinal points of the compass.

But in the wild northern seas, for weeks on end the firmament is hidden in a sombre shroud. Forward, abeam or astern, above
or below, one sees only a characterless, trackless immensity of gray.
There is nothing to tell that here lies, ultimately, safety; and there,
death. To the anguish of the flesh is added the despair of the soul.
How, in his doubts and fears, is bedeviled man to find the way of
salvation?

"My lord," Bernhelm offered, "in the east there is certainly
danger. But the men are no longer in condition to fight this southerly
wind. They must have rest. Let us hope for shelter among some
unfrequented skerries even if we are far north of England." So in the
end, the captain and his navigator gave their starboard quarter to the
wind, and steered for what they hoped might be home.

After a long run, they raised a high, broken coast which the
kentmand guessed to be northern Norway. By now their stocks of
food and water needed renewal, so they closed with the land to seek a
likely haven. At this unfavorable moment, the wind picked up, and
shifted to blow directly on shore. It was a very rocky coast, with
many indentations.

The sail lowered, the mast stowed, they took to the oars till a
narrow channel disclosed itself; on the thane's order the steersman
directed the bow to the entrance. Rowing in a seaway is difficult.
Disaster struck.

Entering a narrow passage in a high sea is always a chancy business. A sudden huge wave grasped the vessel and swung her broadside to the beach. She struck heavily upon the rocks at the entrance. In vain they strove to shove off; the waves pounded her heavily against the fanged edges of the harbor mouth, she filled and lay rolling and grinding in the seas.

Wulfnoth, even though handicapped by assisting his son, was one of the first to gain the shore. And there he stood, sword out and sweeping, to bar the way to safety to those who came empty-handed after.

"Back!" he cried. "Get your weapons! Without them we'll die!" Seconded by the faithful boatswain, he drove them back into the perilous mass of seething timbers to feel for what swords, axes or spears they might salvage.

Three of the crew were lost. The rest, half drowned and more than half frozen, huddled shivering on the beach.

Slowly, with great difficulty, they got a fire going. A tiny brook flowed into the sea nearby; at least they could drink. By great good luck the yard, with the sail wrapped around it, detached itself from the wreckage and drifted ashore. They contrived a shelter and slept.

Exploration the next day confirmed the impression that they were on an island a few miles long and very much narrower. At the head of a little bay stood a lone hut with outbuildings; here a small family lived and ran some half wild sheep and cattle.

"We shall winter here," Wulfnoth decided. "The stock will be just sufficient to sustain us till the sailing season next year. During the winter we'll build a new ship."

The householder did not protest at the raised spear. This was the way of the world. They might have told him, before he died, that his people had done as badly and worse in England, Scotland, Ireland and the isles; but there was no point in doing so. He knew it. The woman they kept alive for their cooking, cleaning, and recreation. When she grasped the feet of the nearest man, imploring, they sheathed the knives again and let the children live. They were honest sailors, and none of your riff-raff.

The first thing to do, now that survival was assured - always assuming that a greater force didn't come upon them from sea or land - was to salvage the remains of the ship and gear. Her back, they found, had been broken and there was hardly a usable timber in her. Some parts had of course broken away and drifted off; the rest they managed to drag ashore. While it dried, and before the snows began, they built their facilities and cut timber.

A section of beach, above the reach of winter storms even at high water, was carefully levelled. Upon it they laid a huge pine log for the keel. It was squared with adzes - one they had and another they appropriated from the house - and scarfed at either end to receive stem and stern posts. Then, still working with pine - they would have preferred oak, but there was not a good grade of it on the island, and in any case, lacking the resources of a carpenter's shop, they could not easily have worked the harder wood - they split logs and split them again to produce a long plank from each half.

By now the wreckage of the ship was sufficiently dried that it would be consumed in a brisk blaze. They burned it, therefore, for its iron; while the smith set up a forge to remake nails and rivets.

Next, using so far as possible, naturally curved pieces of wood, they fashioned ribs and knees (for these particularly they would have liked the abundant natural crooks of oak trees). A garboard plank was fastened along the keel on either side. To this they made fast the ribs, and sewed the planks to the ribs up to the heavier strake at the water line with spruce roots. Above, the planks were riveted through the ribs to knees at the level of the decks, and beams were laid and riveted on the tops of these.

Spars and oars were not hard to shape - some in fact had been recovered from the wreck. The "old woman" block they nailed on the keel slightly forward of amidships to take the thrust of the mast.

Meanwhile, details cut firewood against the bitter northern cold, and caught and butchered the half wild cattle and sheep. Fishing parties took cod, mackerel and herring. They would have relished some grain, but the small supply available did not go far among the relatively large number of men who consumed it. Both meat and fish were smoked and dried for their further voyaging.

The dark of the subarctic winter was of course a great hindrance in their work. In midwinter, there was no bright daylight for more than an hour or two. They were of course impatient to be gone before a Norse fighting unit should stumble upon them; but danger or no danger, a midwinter voyage across the North Sea was not to be attempted. By the same token, Norse military operations were not undertaken in the cold months; but there was always the danger of chance discovery, and in the sheltered sounds a naval expedition could even be mounted against them. But they were not detected.

The spring came, and they could advance the work rapidly. By the time that darkness was reduced to a small part of the night, the ship was finished - at least, in so far as needful. They assembled their supplies and prepared to depart. After a brief discussion between Wulfnoth and Bernhelm it was decided that the captives would be more trouble than their worth in the slave market could justify; they were therefore set free to struggle for life as best they might.

On a fine late spring day Wulfnoth declared the ship ready. Launching, lading and embarkation completed, they stood out from shore, the woman and her three children staring expressionlessly after. Their livestock gone and their breadwinner dead, they would probably starve.

The English stood down the coast of Norway, far enough off not to offer a tempting prize for some chieftain to launch a flotilla to take them, yet not so far but that in the event of storm they might run in and hope to find a hidden shelter. Keeping the land in view, furthermore, helped them to keep some idea of their southing. They gave Trondheim a wide berth; when Bergen was near, they hauled the wind and stood out across the North Sea.

The wind held fair as they reached to the westward. In the morning of the third day there were low islands ahead and to the south, with higher land visible beyond.

"The Orkneys," said the kentmand. "We'd better keep clear of them. The Norse rovers are established here."

So they altered course to the south. The wind dropped, and in one of the infrequent calms they took to the oars and coasted along the island chain.

But it was not the islanders who came grimly with death in hand toward the voyagers. A westerly had sprung up at noon, and they were reaching along close to the southern end of the archipelago when Godwin's keen eyes picked out a ship to leeward, and then another, and then a fleet of a dozen sail strung along the horizon to the eastward from north to south.

"Raiders," said the captain, the boatswain and the kentmand together.

"We are cut off in three directions," Wulfnoth stated flatly. "We must take to the oars again and make the best of our way to windward. Let us hope that before they can catch up a change of weather may conceal us from them."

The kentmand nodded. No use to seek sanctuary ashore among the countrymen of their assailants.

So westward they pulled for their lives. They made good progress, as they could see by their passage along the Ronaldsay coast. It seemed as though some giant hand must be pulling them through the strait. Obviously, there was a strong tidal current.

Their pursuers did not yet feel it, so they gained despite the more numerous oarsmen in the rovers' ships. The enemy were a good two miles astern when they too caught the favoring stream. And then the kentmand, peering ahead in the bow, gave the dreaded cry, "White water!" Ahead, extending southward toward the distant Scottish shore, was a line of breakers.

At the captain's order, the steersman threw the sweep haft to port and headed north in the desperate hope of losing the foe among the passages and islands. But it made little difference in their progress. The current bore them crabwise onto the zone of destruction.

Almost - not quite. At the near northern edge of the strait, close under the shore of the island of Hoy, the waves were still passable, though rough. Through this gap Wulfnoth directed his ship. They struggled desperately in a sea of rapidly mounting fury. Then they were through, and the passage closed astern of them in a welter of foam.

There are places at the edges of the world's oceans where complexities of shore contour and bottom have a terrible effect, imperfectly understood, on the tidal streams. At one moment the surface of the water is, if not tranquil, such as to present no threat - not even a problem - to the pilot. Then comes the turn of the tide, and within a quarter of an hour no boat can live.

One of the worst is this western entrance to the Pentland Firth off the island of Mey in the Orkneys, infamous among seamen. At the westward flow of the tide, especially if the wind oppose it, it raises seething eddies and confused waves known among sailors as the Merry Men of Mey.

The English, exhausted, rested on their oars and gazed astern. They could do no more.

Had their pursuers been men of the islands, they would not for their lives have ventured near the area at this stage of the tide. But they were Norse, without local knowledge; and assumed that wherever their prospective victims went, they too could go. But by now the northern gap in the surf was closed. As they approached, and saw what lay ahead, they reversed course, and tried frantically to flee the white death ahead. But in vain. In the grip of an eight-knot current, they were swept into the frightful maw.

Never had they seen such a sea. The firth was become a cauldron! It boiled. Swirls spun them helplessly about; steep seas assailed them from both sides at once; some flung the laboring bow in air to let others pour in at the stern, and then reversed; a sudden subsurface current heeled a ship at the very moment that a sea swept in upon it.

The pirate fleet ceased to exist. Only the last two ships managed to make the shore. Not one swimmer survived to join them.

X

Must their ever-ravening eagle's beak and talon annihilate us?
Tear the noble heart of Britain, leave it gorily quivering?
Bark an answer, Britain's raven!

Boadicea—Tennyson

Wulfnoth had used every stratagem he could think of to approach the king, but to no purpose. Summers on the high seas, winters at his manor, he grew ever more obsessed with his long thwarted revenge. Late in the summer of the third year of his widow-hood he encountered the archbishop Siric - they were both overnight guests of a thane while on their separate travels.

"I have heard some very good things about you, Wulfnoth," said Siric. "Aelfere, whom God have in his keeping, told me long ago that you were one of the finest seamen in the kingdom for courage and craft.

"Have you ever given thought to serving the king? There can be glory and profit in the king's fleet. You have a son. Perhaps you can leave him wider lands than you hold now!"

Here was the thane's opportunity. But he made a show of reluctance. "I had not thought of it," he answered. "I like my freedom of action; I would lose it in the royal ships."

"No man is free, Wulfnoth - your freedom is an illusion. In the king's service you would have a master, true; but as it is, you have a hundred. Would you trade? You are at the mercy of the whim of the market. Would you enter a certain port? Perhaps for this reason or that it is closed to you, and you must sail whither you would not. Is a merchant impatient? You must humor him if you have to sell him your goods. Would you go pirating? Every man of your crew must be conciliated."

So the thane let himself be persuaded.

He brought Godwin with him to the king's dragonship, and

kept him thereafter at his side.

The horrors of the Viking raids were again enacted, and on a larger scale than ever. Year after year they swung their hammer blows upon the despairing Saxons. In vain did Aethelred send army after army into the field. Each was outmaneuvered, outfought or betrayed. In vain did Ulfkell Snillingr give the Danes, as they confessed, harder handplay than ever they had encountered. In vain did the king raise the crushing tribute to unheard of heights. And the worst famine in the memory of man afflicted the land.

The king met one day with his council.

"My lord king," said Bishop Aelfeah, "let us give the half of the realm to Anlaf the Dane, that he come here and defend us against his countrymen."

Ulfkytel, who had never flinched from Danish steel, sprang to his feet. "For shame, my lord! Are we to give these pirates our fair land? Mark you well - they will not stop till all of it is theirs! The great Alfred learned that to resist the foe, he must not await their pleasure, but sally forth and destroy them on the sea! Let the king use all the strength that is left him to build a mighty fleet that will over-whelm these pirates and drown them in the sea they think of as their own!"

And so the word went forth through the land. Every man who possessed over three hundred hides of land was to provide a ship for the defense of the kingdom; those less wealthy were to contribute for the ships' stores; and every man who possessed as much as eight hides was to equip himself with helmet and breastplate and be ready to man one of the king's ships. Throughout Aethelred's realm there was ringing of axes and adzes, weaving and sewing of sailcloth; and a great fleet took form on the beaches.

In hope and pride Aethelred numbered them before his queen. "Here is what will save the kingdom for ourselves and our children!"

She sneered. "A fleet is no better than the commander who wields it. And as for our children -" she left the sentence unfinished.

He strode off. The curl in her lip did not change as she looked at her sons Alfred and Edward, and saw his features in their childish faces.

That love was a stranger to the royal apartments had not prevented the births of the princes and of the princess Goda. Emma had become Queen with the firm intention, despite the king's nomina-tion of his son Aethelstan as heir, of using any means whatever to bring about the succession of her own offspring, rather than the seed of her predecessor in the king's bed. But so strong grew her scorn for her incompetent husband that she found the feeling extending even toward their sons. Oddly enough, she did not regard her growing step-children with the like aversion; they did not embody her unfortunate union with Aethelred, and she could look upon them with no stronger feeling than indifference. So her little princes were abandoned to the care of nursemaids and governesses, and they sought forlornly for the motherly love that was forever denied them.

The shipwrights wrought well, and the levies came in. A goodly fleet was arrayed at Sandwich.

Wulfnoth, now commander of a squadron of ten ships, approached a shipmaster.

"Cedric, what think you of the king's prospects?"

The other, never known as one of the most dashing of Aethelred's captains, shook his head gloomily. "Fate has never favored us in battle."

"And should we then be sacrificed to the king's rashness? Do we owe loyalty to a lord who throws away the lives of warriors?"

"What do you propose?"

"Sweyn is a king who understands far better how to use his ships and troops and how to win, and without the loss of so many valiant fighters."

"Are you suggesting that we desert our king?"

"I am for Sweyn. What say you?"

Had the other uttered a word of demurral, that would have been his last. But he was persuaded.

Wulfnoth met with a second. "Ulfric, are we to shed our blood for a king who came to his throne by murder? Your sire was a strong prop of Edward's throne. What would he say to your serving a regicide and a fratricide?"

To another whom he knew to be covetous of treasure, he whispered, "Sweyn has gold beyond what this impoverished monarch can ever bestow; and he is generous as Aethelred has never thought to be."

And again, "How many years have you served this ungrateful lord, Arnulf? Is is not far beyond the time when he should have made you thane?"

To Ulf, "When your brother was condemned and hanged, did you not appeal to the king to annul the false verdict, and in vain?"

Boatswain Bernhelm had followed Wulfnoth faithfully through all his chances. The thane could not keep his plans a secret from him. The boatswain challenged him.

"My lord, I have followed you faithfully for these thirty years. I have seen you change from a true, open-hearted man to a darker and darker vessel of hate. You have become more like a Viking ravager than a countryman of this dear land. I will not betray you, my lord, but here we part. I follow you no more."

Like the stroke of an adder, Wulfnoth's sword was at his throat.

"Kill if you must, my lord. Perhaps this has to be."

The thane might have struck in the same motion and made an end of him. But once he hesitated, the matter was decided in the other's favor. For the last time in Wulfnoth's grim life, human decency possessed him. Bernhelm, bound and gagged, was delivered into the hands of some outlaws - they were not hard to find in those troublous times.

"Deliver him, alive and unharmed, with this note to the steward at my manor house in Sussex," his master ordered. "He will pay you well. You will be imprisoned for two months," to the boatswain, "and then released. Farewell."

Brihtric was one of the captains whom Wulfnoth had not approached. Brihtric's brother Edric had been created alderman by the king; and while there was known to be bad blood between the two, the younger being notoriously hostile to and jealous of Edric, Wulfnoth preferred to take no chances on a sudden reconciliation.

But Elheard, one of the plotters, had been overzealous enough to do some recruiting on his own.

It was not a recrudescence of brotherly feeling that led Brihtric to betrayal. It was on the contrary an intensification of his feeling of envy, and the chance, as he saw it, of exceeding his hated elder in service to, and consequent preferment by, the king.

And so, when in answer to Wulfnoth's summons the conspirators foregathered, Brihtric was not seen among them. And on Elheard's anxious inquiry, someone told of having seen the missing captain taking the path to the royal headquarters.

"Then we are betrayed!" cried the arch-plotter in a rage.

"We must scatter, and return to our ships! We must abandon our plan!" exclaimed another.

"On the contrary," Wulfnoth rejoined, even in the ruin of his plans making a lightning recovery of coolness and wits. "Now we cannot return to the king even if we wish to. He will have a full list of our names, and within the hour his men-at-arms will be arresting us for hanging or worse. We must board our ships with as many of our crews as we can round up within minutes, and be off. The greater part of the fleet is about to sail northward around the Isle of Thanet; we will set out for the west!"

And so they did.

In his despair Wulfnoth lost all semblance of restraint and scruple. All the coast of England became the target of his hate. Once committed to war against king and country, it was no great step for him to open piracy - especially in view of the fact that the Danes, their only potential allies, were similarly engaged. He went raging along the coast. Villages, farms, manor houses went up in smoke; and in the ruins were the slain and women who, with children and breadwinners dead, would willingly have been included in that number.

Then, learning of treasure missed in the sacking of a great house at Ramsgate, Wulfnoth's pirates turned back in that direction.

Brihtric meanwhile was basking in the royal favor. He was not content however to leave the matter thus; when his luck was running, he was the man to ride it. And so, when the reports and despairing appeals from the south indicated the traitors' near approach, he sought and received the command of a fleet of eighty ships to capture or destroy the villains. With a superiority of four to one over the enemy, as the king remarked to those who questioned his new favorite's competence, he could not lose.

Ramsgate was separated from the sea by a broad bank of shoals. Beginning a couple of miles to the westward, a few deeper channels cut through the sands. The outermost entrance, about a mile offshore, led into a fairly wide passage which was the one always used, and was marked along its seaward side by pieces of brush stuck at its edge by fishermen. Less than a quarter mile inshore a second entrance extended for two miles, only to lose itself in a number of impossibly narrow and shallow branches. It was at this village that Wulfnoth took temporary haven for a council to decide on further activities.

Here, then, his lookouts announced the approach of a strong fleet from the direction of the North Foreland. His captains clamored for a decision to flee at once, lest they be trapped. But the commander demurred.

"Let them come," he said. "A fog is making up, and tomorrow will bring a rising wind. With the devil's help, we will teach this wretched kingling a lesson he will never forget."

And indeed, as the fleet approached the channel entrance, a thick fog shrouded the markers. Unwilling to challenge the navigational hazards and the doubtful chances of battling blindfold, Brihtric beached his ships to await a change in the weather.

Wulfnoth went into action. In a few skiffs his men, communicating in low-pitched voices, pulled loose the brush markers and set them in the corresponding positions along the false passage.

In the morning, a rising southwest wind blew away the fog. As Wulfnoth had expected, a gale was brewing. But Brihtric was unwilling to wait and risk the escape of his prey. He had high respect for Wulfnoth's seamanship; and gale or no gale, he feared to be cheated of his glory. He overruled the protests of his captains, launched his longships, gained his offing with some difficulty, and entered the supposed channel to the haven. Once on the way in with the wind blowing straight from the stern they should be safe.

When his ship, leading the van, went aground in what was apparently mid-channel, he had at first no suspicion that he had been tricked. He supposed that there had been a slight shift in the contours of the bottom, such as can happen in sandy areas after every storm. With difficulty, compounded by the fact that the second ship in line was pressing upon him, he backed off; but his soundings now showed shoal water on all sides except directly astern. And in the rising wind it would have been hard to row in the reverse direction, even had ship after ship not been crowding upon him in the narrow passage. Maneuverability was quickly lost. With the flooding tide and the stiffening gale seas began to sweep over the outer banks, higher and higher. Ships were first stranded along the lee side of the false channel, then filled, then swept; men and gear were washed out; ships were capsized, carried over the inner shoals, to be beached as useless hulks. The few of their people who reached shore (men cannot swim in foam) were slaughtered mercilessly by the revolted crews. Most, however, perished in the surf, Brihtric, by good fortune, among them.

Wulfnoth's crews gathered firewood and burned the stranded ships.

In the royal fleet morale plummeted like an anchor thrown overboard without its cable. The king returned in despair to London, with the aldermen and the nobility; the ships followed. So all the labor came to naught.

"So this," said the raging queen, "is the result of your labors! You made your brag - you had assembled the greatest fleet ever seen in England! You were going to be a second Alfred, beating back the invaders by land and sea!"

"Enough! I was betrayed!"

"Betrayed! Of course you were betrayed! You are always betrayed! Who of your people give either love or confidence to such a weakling!"

"Enough, I say! It is time for you to write your brother and ask his aid. Perhaps Norman ships and men can still retrieve our fortunes and put an end to the intolerable harassment! Tell Duke Robert that if he wants his sister to retain her kingdom, he must come to her help."

"And let him know, from my own pen, that he married me to such a nithing king? Never!"

"Have you no thought, woman, for your children?"

"Had you no thought for them when you sent that fool Brihtric to lead your ships?"

Aethelred stamped out in a fury. Emma murmured to the closed door, "If you were a king indeed, even a man, you would have flung me into a dungeon for speaking to you thus!"

Part 2

GODWIN

XI

Friends to this ground.
And liegemen to the Dane.

Hamlet, Prince of Denmark.

Ever harder fell Sweyn's hammer blows upon the disintegrating kingdom. In vain was the bravery of Ulfkell Snillingr; in vain the accession to the English standard by Thorkell the Tall. The English armies melted away by battle and desertion. Queen Emma and her children took sanctuary at the court of Normandy, and the king followed. In the year 1013 Sweyn assumed the crown of England.

Not long did the new king enjoy his triumph. Late the following winter he died; and the game began again. Aethelred was briefly restored to the throne. Battered and despairing of success, he pinned his hopes on his firstborn Aethelstan; but Aethelstan died, and the broken father followed the son.

Wulfnoth, his belly filled with blood and plunder, had led his ships to Sweyn's standard. Any foe of Aethelred had been his friend. And, doughty seaman that he was, and knowing all coasts of England as he did, he had risen high in the counsels of the Danish king.

His joy over the downfall and death of Aethelred were tempered by the fact that it had not been his hand that had brought an end to the life of his enemy. All the bitterer, therefore, was his hatred when Edmund, Aethelred's son and Emma's stepson, raised an army and made a bid for his father's throne. The thane raged against the prince and against his countrymen for the support that many of them gave the claimant.

The fleet declared for Sweyn's son Cnut. Wulfnoth approached him.

"England will fall to you if only you seize the royal title and power. Never let a son of that accursed Aethelred hold the throne!

Carry steel and torch from Cornwall to Lothian!"

Cnut looked at him curiously. "I will have my father's throne," he said. "But shall I rule over a kingdom of corpses and ashes? I do not hate the English, Wulfnoth, as you appear to do. I am a Dane; but I am not in love with ravaging overmuch. This is a new age. In the Danish isles and in the hills of the north there are many challengers for power."

"You can meet them."

"I can meet them, yes. But I have seen too many kingdoms broken by contest between the sons of a king after he has died. I must have many lands to divide among my sons - if the fates grant me sons. At any rate, here in England I shall be an English, not a Viking, king. I shall rule as well as may be. Therefore did I take an English bride, not a girl from the viks. Aelfgifu of Northumberland gives me a foothold in the north."

"And do we take the field against this pretender, Edmund?"

"At once. And I look for the same good service from you that you gave my father."

But Edmund proved no such weakling as his enemies had hoped. Again and again he engaged them to such good purpose that men called him "Edmund Ironside" in admiration. It was in a hard fought field that Wulfnoth, his son Godwin fighting beside him in the full strength of his young manhood, met the arrow that fate had prepared for him. The raging inner fire burned out at last.

Godwin buried his father with the proper rites. But he was not prostrated by grief. There had been too little tenderness in the older man for affection to make a vigorous growth; and he could remember a sad, neglected, unloved mother.

"I regret his death," said Cnut when he learned the news. "He was a fine seaman, and a stout fighter in my father's cause and mine. But his character was flawed. I sensed too much hate and too little of any other human feeling. He was the sort of man of whom, when they come to power, the most monstrous tyrants are made." And then, to himself, "It is well that he is gone. He would have been too wild and unruly for the England I wish to rule, and too valuable for me to dismiss or destroy."

Now the stalwart twenty-year-old Godwin took his father's title as Thane of Sussex, and his place in the fleets and councils of the king. He paid good blows by sea and by land. But what was more important to his lord, he was wise in council, as his father had not been. He it was who, as the war swayed with even fortunes hither and yon, advised Cnut to make peace on the basis of a division of lands.

"Have no fear," he said. "Rather than face a doubtful issue, with defeat or an utterly ruined kingdom as a result, settle for part of the realm. The land cannot longer exist as a divided kingdom. One way or another, it will all be yours." And indeed, when Edmund died in the year after his accession, Cnut became king of England.

He did as he had purposed. The harrying of the Saxons came to an end. Cnut raised the Danegeld for the last time to pay off his troops and send them back to Denmark. "And now," remarked the king to Godwin, "I can make of my kingdom what I will."

"Not yet. There is one thing more you must do to secure your throne."

"What is that?"

"In Normandy there are still two princes of the blood of Aethelred. You must either have them assassinated—"

"That will be no light matter. I do not fear Richard of Normandy, but I want no quarrel with him."

"Or marry the dead king's widow, Queen Emma, their mother. That will legitimize your throne even in the eyes of the partisans of the house of Aethelred. And Richard will have no reason for resentment."

"But Aelfgifu is already my wife."

"She will not serve your purpose."

"If I divorce her, I have strife and hatred in the north. Besides, she has in no way deserved that I put her aside."

"You need not put her aside. When you wedded her, did you promise that she would be your queen?"

"No."

"Then keep her as a wife, and take Emma as your queen."

"And have two wives?"

"Did not the great Charlemagne have a half dozen?"

"It is an idea. What, think you, will Emma say to a wife senior to herself?"

"From what we hear, Emma will care nought for that, so she be your queen, and her son inherit the throne."

"I will never agree to that. I did not become king of England for Alfred or Edward to inherit. It is my own seed that will sit on my throne when I am gone."

"Did I say anything about the sons of Aethelred? Emma is still young enough to bear your children."

Emma had scant scruples about agreeing to Cnut's proposal. For years she had regarded the children of her despised husband with some of the same contempt in which she held the father. Let it be admitted that as the object of Norman charity she led a life without a future; and let it be adduced in her defense that even though she swore away the boys' rights to the throne of their ancestors, there was scant prospect that either would ever sit upon it; and that as a reigning queen she would be better able to make some lesser provision for them. Let it even be considered that to become Queen of England, Denmark, Norway, Ireland, Man, the Scottish Isles and part of Sweden, and overlord of Scotland, the abandonment of two unloved children might have been a small price to pay. At any rate, the young princes - the elder was now twelve—and their sister saw their mother, cold mother though she had been, forsake them to cross the narrow seas.

So Cnut swore that his and Emma's issue should reign in England and in Denmark; and he and Emma were wed. Presently, the unmotherly mother bore Harthacnut, heir presumptive to the throne, and then his sister Gunnhilde.

The king's henchmen were not forgotten. Before all the council the king declared, "Godwin Wulfnothson, I create you Earl of Sussex, with sake and soke, toll and team, and infangeneath," and the son of a rebel found himself a nobleman possessed of all revenues of his earldom. "And Godwin, it is time you were married. What say you to the Lady Gytha, sister of my brother-in-law Ulf of Denmark?"

So Godwin wedded Gytha, and she bore him Sweyn, and Harold, and Tostig, and Leofwine, and Gyrth. And Edgitha.

These were good years. After his stormy boyhood, Godwin was well content to spend both his martial ardor and his cunning in the service of Cnut. So he lived at peace with his king and watched his children grow in a security of both position and emotion that he himself had never known. While the boys were still quite young, each served for a term in the king's ships. Ever and anon their father admonished them, "Breadth of lands, horses and men-at-arms are good. But I tell you as my sire told me - the fortune of our house rests in the ships. Know the sea, and love it."

Not that there was peace for the land. Englishmen were drawn into and died in Cnut's wars in Denmark and Norway.

So wars went on, as in the days of Aethelred. But there was a difference. Fair England was ravaged no longer, and the people had peace at least in their homes. A man reaped where he had sown, and none were dragged off to slavery and death in a far-off land.

Now and again, word of Edward and Alfred, the unwanted sons of Aethelred and Emma came to Cnut. They were an embarrassment to their successive hosts. Their education as knights began in the court of their uncle in Normandy; it continued as they dragged themselves to one petty potentate after another. Rouen, Nantes, Brittany, Flanders - throughout northwestern Europe the homeless pair wandered without sponsor or prospects.

XII

*Ygdrasil, the tree of boon, the tree of bane,
Shakes out invisibly many branches.*

Leifsaga—Chapin

𝔉or nineteen years Godwin served Cnut in England; then, with shocking suddenness, Cnut died. The turbulent days began again. To Emma came Godwin, the bishops, and the nobles of the south. The queen spoke first.

"We must prevent, by any means, the elevation to the throne of my weakling stepson Harold Harefoot," she said. "I admit, of course, that I should probably favor my son and Cnut's, Harthacnut, in any case, as against Cnut's son by Aelfgifu. But even were the elder ten times my son I should oppose him. He has not the making of a king. He is not the man to hold the throne and kingdom against all challenge! If he reigns, he will be the tool of Mercia and Northumberland."

"He is not even a well man," put in Archbishop Ethelnoth. "I fear that his rule would not be long; and then again we would have strife."

Godwin nodded. "And where then will the council cast its eye? Perhaps on Alfred or Edward. There is still some misplaced loyalty to the line of Aethelred in the land." He looked askance at Emma, but she seconded the thought vigorously.

"That must never be! Aethelred was no true king; and our sons, I fear, share the weakness of their father."

"I am with you, " Godwin assured her, and to himself he added, "but for my own reasons. I carry on my father's feud against the house of the murderess!"

They held out as long as they could, with all manner of pretexts and prevarications. But in the end the north prevailed. Leofric of Mercia and his party installed Harold Harefoot not indeed as king, but as a regent in the joint interests of his half brother and himself. To Emma they allowed Wessex, with Godwin and her son's henchmen to keep her state.

And so, for the time at least, things might have rested in this cockpit of politics, but for Alfred the forgotten. One day a royal messenger came to Godwin with order that he ride to the regent with all speed.

Harold Harefoot's face was dark. "What do you know of this business?" he demanded of the earl.

"What business, my lord?"

The other studied his face for a minute. Then, "Aethelred's son Alfred has landed in England!"

"My lord!"

"Are you sure you knew nothing of this?"

"Nothing at all, my lord! This is the first I hear of it!"

"If you are plotting against me, I'll find out, and have your head!"

"My lord, I am sworn to hatred of the house of Queen Aelfthryth as my father was before me. He was a loyal liegeman of the martyr King Edward, and gave his life to attempts to avenge him. Surely you know, or your scribes know, that he was Aelfric's man, who strove many times against King Aethelred! And that he himself brought Aethelred's last great naval expedition against your father to failure!"

"It may well be so. What of Emma? Does she know? Did she instigate this landing?"

"I do not know, my lord. Does he come in force?"

"With a small troop of French knights. He claims, I am told, that he merely wishes to visit his mother. This is a poor time to renew family ties. When the crown wavers from head to head, royal visitors are unwelcome. Perhaps he is simple enough actually to intend only the visit, as he says. But I must assume that more than filial affection brings him. I take his appearance here very ill. Earl Godwin, see to it that he learns his lesson!"

Two days later the earl's men-at-arms apprehended the hapless prince.

Godwin ever afterwards disclaimed the guilt for what happened next. He protested that almost immediately the prince was taken from his custody. Perhaps he spoke the truth. What followed was that Alfred was blinded. Probably the cursed instrument was thrust too deep; within a few days the rash young man was no more.

The earl was somewhat subdued at the council called by the

regent. "My lords, I like not the events of the past weeks. We must consider what we may do to avoid the overturning of the realm by some mad adventure. A regency is ever in a parlous state. Earl Leofric, what say you?"

"My lord, there are two things to be done. First, it were well to consider whether we might not end your regency by a formal disposition of the crown. Second, it were well to consider who might have entertained designs against the present rule, and take steps to ensure that it may not happen again."

"My lord of Northumberland?"

"I am of the like opinion, my lord. I propose that the council declare that you, eldest son of Cnut, be crowned as rightful King of England!"

"My lords spiritual?"

The archbishop of Canterbury spoke. "We have had some prior discussion among ourselves, my lord. We are of the opinion that to ensure the peace of the realm, it were well to crown your highness without delay."

"Earl Godwin?"

The earl of Sussex had opposed the nomination of Harold Harefoot once; it would not be wise to push his luck too far. "I agree, my lord."

The archbishop rose to his feet. "Long live King Harold!"

"I thank you, my lords, and I accept the crown. God grant that I may wear it worthily. We will discuss the promulgation of this your decision, as well as the date of coronation and all other pertinent matters, hereafter. But now there remains Earl Leofric's second matter to deal with. Has there been treason?"

There was a long silence. Then from Northumberland, "My lord, Queen Emma will always be a possible source of dissension, if not worse. Perhaps she summoned the luckless Prince Alfred to come hither with a design against the peace and safety of the realm; perhaps not. In any case, she has another son who might some day try to claim the throne. She is a danger to your country and your crown."

The primate spoke again. "And her supporters?"

All eyes turned to Godwin. But Harold smiled thinly. "A month ago we might have distrusted the earl of Sussex," he said. "But after the events of the past weeks, he is in our camp, and would be even if he wished otherwise. But as to the lady Emma, she was our father's queen but not our mother. We pronounce upon her the doom of banishment."

"It is winter," Godwin protested.

"She will find a ship; what happens thereafter, is the will of God. My lord of Sussex, do you go to her and assist her to leave the country. It will be better for her to have a friend to do the necessary offices. No, my lord, in commanding you thus, we do not mean to express doubt concerning your loyalty."

So Godwin found her a stout ship and a daring captain at Dover. For a week he watched the weather carefully, while each day, under the eyes of the king's lieutenant, Emma waded out till she was neck-deep in the frigid waters of Dover Strait. Then the break came. She boarded the ship along with its crew and they crossed to Calais, pulling for their lives in an unseasonal calm. Emma found refuge at Bruges.

Archbishop Aethelnoth had seen only too clearly into Harold's prospects of longevity. In four years the king died.

Indeed, this was an ill time for the kings of Britain. In the north, Macbeth murdered King Duncan of Scotland. In the east, Norway had just broken away from the English-Danish crown; so that Cnut's only surviving son and his regent in Denmark, Harthacnut, found it prudent to join his mother Emma at Bruges. Then Godwin joined with the earls of Northumbria and Mercia; and the united council offered Harthacnut the crown. He came accordingly to England, and his mother Emma with him. Dane and Saxon alike received him gladly.

But bitterly they rued it, for he proved to be a tyrant. Again the hapless Saxons suffered extortion and outrage at the hands of a Dane.

He was, however, very sensible of the claims of blood. He reestablished Emma's court at Winchester, and showered wealth upon her. But he looked hard upon Godwin on account of his half-brother Alfred, blinded and slain after his arrest by the earl. In vain Godwin protested innocence. So, says the chronicler, "Godwin gave Harthacnut a ship beaked with gold, having eighty soldiers on board, who had two bracelets on either arm, each weighing sixteen ounces of gold; on their heads were gilt helmets; on their left shoulder they carried a Danish axe, with an iron spear in their right hand."

The king's anger was not proof against so princely a gift, and Godwin was restored to favor.

But it was not well with the king. He had fits of dizziness, and episodes of severe headache; sometimes nausea and vomiting would occur. The leeches bled and physicked him, and assured him that the indisposition would pass. But Harthacnut was not deceived. He had no son; so for the succession he bethought him of his half-brother Edward, living in exile, and brought him home to England; he gave him a seat of honor at his court.

For two years Harthacnut trained his half-brother in the arts of kingship. Then, at the marriage feast of the daughter of an earl, as the king stood with wine glass in hand, he fell to the ground in a convulsion, lived for two days without power of speech, and died.

Only Emma mourned him.

Thereupon, even before the burial, the people acclaimed Edward, son of King Aethelred and Queen Emma, King of England. The abandoned and penniless wanderer became ruler of the land of his fathers.

It was still, to some extent, a strange land to the exile of twenty-five wandering years. By now, Edward was more practised in French than in English! And to lessen his feeling of strangeness, he brought over from the continent a growing number of Norman-French. The result was predictable. The Saxons and the Danes at court sank their differences in a common dislike and resentment of the foreigners. And the French, feeling their isolation, reacted with stronger reliance upon the king, and a consequent arrogance toward the men of England. This was not lessened by Edward's bestowal of the hand of his sister on Count Eustace of Boulogne.

Young Edward had eaten the bread of bitterness too long and too recently to be magnanimous. He rode unheralded to Winchester, Godwin in his train; and there in a rancorous confrontation he stripped the cold-hearted mother of the considerable treasure that Harthacnut had granted her. He even took from her whatever she had of personal effects in gold, silver, or other precious things; Bishop Stigand her counselor lost his bishopric and his lands.

Godwin continued to prosper. His sons had grown into stalwart manhood. All were brave and hardy; but the second, Harold, was the best liked among all who knew them. He was always courteous, never too busy to give a word of congratulations on a day of good fortune, or of counsel - wise counsel - on a day of ill. He was never overbearing, never fawning.

Under the driving of Wulfnoth's obsessive hatred, Earl Godwin had spent his growing years in bitter enmity to Aelfthryth, King Aethelred's mother, and all her house. This seemed to have been resolved with the Danish conquest; and Godwin had slid quite easily into service under Sweyn and his sons. But now that Edward of the hated line reigned, the old antagonism stirred once more.

For long it did no more than that. Edward sought to consolidate his position by friendship with the most influential men of the realm. Since the time of King Sweyn, thanes had become fewer, and more earls were being created. So there was an earldom each for Godwin's sons Sweyn and Harold.

In one of those chances which, though surprising, are not rare, there had sprung from the bitter stem of the house of Wulfnoth a rose of beauty, grace, kindliness, and even learning. To bind himself more closely to the three powerful earldoms, King Edward wedded this daughter of Godwin, Edgitha, and raised Godwin's nephew Beorn Estrithson also to earldom. For the present, then, Godwin was content to wait and see what time and fate were preparing for him and for the king.

The earl was now the first subject in the land. It was hardly to be expected, therefore, that he should bear himself humbly in the face of the sneers and slurs of the Norman-French coterie in the court. He gave as good as he got, and better. What he did not know was that his utterances were being subtly altered and so relayed to the king.

The king was addressing his council. "My lords, we must look to the defence of the realm. Let us hear your thoughts."

The Norman Bishop William spoke. "Let each earl, to begin with, raise a company of three hundred knights; and let every man who possesses fifteen hides of land be prepared to come at the king's call with sword, axe and bow."

Leofric frowned. "Knighthood is the way of the Franks, and I do not decry it. But the men of Britain have ever been more accustomed to the shield wall. We fight on foot."

Godwin gave his opinion. "Even if ultimately we defeat an invader in the field, by the time we have mustered, organized and found him, much English land will have been ravaged. The king, your father, attempted many times to stand up to the Danes; he always failed. Not," he put in hastily, "by his own fault; he was many times betrayed. And a seaborne enemy has the great advantage of superior mobility; he can choose the time and field of battle.

"There was only one king who prevailed against the invader. That of course was the great Alfred. He knew that the Danes must be met on the sea. This is an island kingdom; its power will always lie in its ships."

Norman Earl Ralph sneered openly. "Naturally, the Earl Godwin opts for a fleet; he has never, so far as I know, faced a foe on horseback with only his good spear and shield between himself and death. Were I in his place, I too, I confess, would seek to shun the hazard of battle."

Godwin, livid, was on his feet. "Damn you for a villain! Let us see, outside, how you love the shock of the fight!"

"My lords!" imperiously, from the king. "Dare you affront us in this fashion? For this time you are pardoned; the next so to offend will suffer. Earl Ralph, ask the earl's pardon for the slur. Earl Godwin, ask his pardon for the 'villain.' There will be no combat."

Sullenly they obeyed.

The earl of Mercia interposed. "My lord king, I like well what Earl Godwin has said. Has he a suggestion as to how we are to raise such large fleets as we will need? The royal treasury, we all know, will not bear it."

At that moment Godwin had the great idea of his life - the idea that was to serve his country well for centuries.

"Let the king ordain and establish that certain seaport towns shall have the duty and responsibility of furnishing ships which, on command, shall assemble as the royal navy; in return for which, they shall have such privileges and exemptions as your highness shall be graciously pleased to grant."

"Excellent!" said the king. "I like that well! What say you, my lords?"

There was a general murmur of agreement. But Odda attempted a rear guard action. "Are the servants of the king to go sailing around the seas instead of fighting the wars here in the land?"

"Enough of this," Edward rejoined. "Earl Godwin, which towns do you suggest for this duty and honor?"

"Dover and Sandwich, of course," and, thinking rapidly, "Hythe and Hastings and, oh yes, Romney, my liege."

"Then be it so. They shall be known henceforth as the Cinq Ports. And, Earl Godwin, we do hereby appoint you Lord Warden of the Cinq Ports. You shall advise us of how many ships each is to furnish; with how many men, how found, how victualed, together with all other things needful."

XIII

Should not the dove so white
Follow the sea-mew's flight?
Why did they leave that night
Her nest unguarded?

Longfellow—The Skeleton in Armor

The wild blood of Wulfnoth was not tamed. The fierceness of his life burned again in his seed.

Sweyn Godwinson it was who first troubled the peace between his father and the king. Sweyn was sent to southern Wales with an army, to confirm the wild men of the mountains in their loyalty to the English throne. His way thither led through Leominster. There he stopped at an abbey for refreshment.

The abess, Eadgifu, was the daughter of a thane. She was one of those women whose beauty does not lessen; the years seem not to touch them, until, perhaps not till the sixties, age seizes suddenly upon them. Eadgifu was three decades from the sixties. An unblemished milky skin was all the more striking by reason of the black veil that framed it, and even in its shapeless covering her body could be seen to move with a grace that enchanted.

Every night, as Sweyn lay in his tent or hut, his mind's eye beheld the lovely abbess. A hundred times his imagination tore away the somber garments, and a passionate woman emerged to share his raptures. He looked with indifference at the Welsh women captured and enjoyed by the men of his command; he was obsessed by the lovely nun.

The old paganism was not quite dead. So young Sweyn dared think and dream - and act - in a fashion that would come to be incredible thereafter.

When the young general returned victorious with hostages in his train, he ordered that Eadgifu be haled to his manor.

Eadgifu had renounced the world unwillingly. The thane, her father, saved almost miraculously from the tusks of a boar brought to bay, had returned home to find that a daughter had been born to him. He and his wife were an unusually devout couple, and had vowed the girl to God. As she matured, and her beauty developed, she wept bitterly whenever the convent was mentioned, and they forbore to compel her. One day, after a troubled discussion of the matter, her eldest brother had drowned. This they took as evidence of divine displeasure. So the girl, with despair in her heart, had sworn herself to asceticism.

She had taken her vows seriously. Now for the first time she found herself given over to the passion of a man. She resisted conscientiously, first with religious exhortations and pleadings, then with such physical strength as she possessed. It was futile.

She was not horrified. Certainly, she would not have chosen to be ravished. But she was not thereby, like a woman of the outer world, deprived of the right of free choice in the bestowal of her body. Neither had she the same sense of outrage as a voluntary bride of Christ. She had done her duty as far as fate had permitted; now she surrendered first to curiosity, then to an awakening passion.

Sweyn could be skillful and winning when he chose; and he chose now, partly as a connoisseur of the woman's unusual endowments, partly in response to an ardor that rose to match his own. In the event, there was an idyllic passage such as neither of them had experienced or expected.

When the inevitable demand came from the furious bishop, the earl sought to carry it off with a high hand. But when the king's messenger arrived, Sweyn, to his surprise, found himself demanding her hand in marriage. The answer, of course, was no. In vain he offered half his lands for a writ of indulgence. It might not be.

Not all of Godwin's influence could gloss over the flagrance of his son's offense. Eadgifu was dragged weeping back to her convent; Sweyn was stripped of lands and title, and with a small fleet he fled to Denmark.

Rash and ungovernable, young Sweyn was no more able in Denmark than in England to control his passions. Within two years he was forced to leave this refuge, and with eight ships he arrived back and landed at Sandwich, where his brother Harold and Beorn his cousin lay with the king's fleet. He asked them to be his sponsors in an attempt to make peace with King Edward, and meantime to give him lands for the sustenance of his men. They however, knew him too well to credit his pretenses of reform, and refused to help him; and the king, when he heard Sweyn's suit, would have none of him.

The exile of course blamed Harold and Beorn for his ill success. Harold he dared not touch. The vengeful Sweyn approached Beorn again, pretending repentance and humility, to such good purpose that Beorn agreed to help his cousin. They took horses to ride to Sandwich; but at Bosham, where Sweyn had his fleet, his men overpowered Beorn, bound him and slew him.

Now Sweyn was formally proclaimed an outlaw. Two of his

ships were attacked by the king's men and their crews slain; four deserted him; with the remaining pair he fled to Bruges.

Rascal or no, Sweyn was still the son of the greatest lord in the land; a year later, his sentence of outlawry was reversed. But now Edward looked upon the arrogant seed of Wulfnoth with a jaundiced eye.

To trouble him further, the Norse raids, held in abeyance during the reign of the dynasty of Denmark, began again, and the Irish made a descent on Wales.

Small wonder that Edward, like his father before him, began to look to Normandy. But unlike his father, he was more a Norman than an Englishman. More lands and offices were going to Normans. Norman castles were rising in the land.

XIV

More than a thousand Franks of France
And Ganelon came, of woeful chance;
By him was the deed of treason done.
So was the fatal consult begun.

Song of Roland

William, now Duke of Normandy, came with a retinue to visit King Edward. There was no public pronouncement on the object of the visit or on their conversations. Rumor, therefore, was naturally rife. Edward had been unable to beget a successor; in Normandy the story ran that he had promised the crown of Britain to William upon his demise.

This, of course, he could not lawfully do. Even an English king's own son could not succeed to the throne without the approval of the council; all the less could a foreign prince. But there were those who believed the story. Of course, Edward could, for what it was worth, have recommended the man of his choice to take his place; he could furthermore, have set in train machinations to set William upon the throne, even if it should mean thwarting the will of the council and the people. Resentment grew.

Edward's brother-in-law, Count Eustace, came on a visit from Boulogne. After a short stay, he took leave of the court to return to his own land.

A week later came a missive to Godwin from the king. The earl summoned Abbot Siric and Thane Ethelgar of Dover to his manor.

He assumed a stern mien and faced his liegemen. "You see here the King's seal," said he. "He writes that Eustace of Normandy, who had been here on the King's business, came to Dover to take ship for home. One of his retinue, offering to rent a bed for the night, was assaulted without cause. When his companions tried to defend him, a body of armed men, who had been ready in advance, fell upon them in overwhelming force, through sheer malice and hatred of his nation. They murdered all but a few who, with Eustace their lord, were hard put to it to flee with their lives back to London. What say you to this wickedness?"

"My lord," said the abbot, "I swear to you, by the holy body of St. Dunstan, which I have venerated but now, we are maligned. Eustace and his men came to Dover fully attired in armor, with arms at the ready, spoiling for trouble. One of his men strode into a house without so much as a by-your-leave, and demanded that the master vacate his bed for him. There was no offer of compensation - not that it mattered. When the owner of the house declined to oblige him, the Norman drew and would have put him to the sword; but that the other, though wounded, being marvelous skilled smote him to death. Thereupon, the rest of the Normans came charging in and slaughtered the unhappy man like a beast on his own hearth, before the eyes of his wife and children. They then laid about them at random and slew some score of our people before it was possible to counter with a sufficient force. In the melee that ensued a like number of the marauders were slain, and many wounded. The survivors fled, and carried lies to the king - as we feared they would."

"I have orders here to ravage the city of Dover."

They grasped his hands in importunity. "Do not so, lord! Do not shed innocent blood!"

"Are you saying that the Lord Eustace lies? The brother-in-law of your king?"

"We do not call him a liar, but—" the abbot began, but the thane interrupted.

"Yes! He lies in his teeth, damned French-gabbling Norman that he is! Were he twice the king's brother-in-law, I should still call him a rogue!"

The abbot spoke again. "Lord, do not lay waste your fine city of Dover! We implore your mercy!" And the thane, "We implore your justice!"

Earl Godwin nodded. "I had guessed that the matter happened as you say. But I have the king's writ. He is very wroth. It is a heavy matter to disobey the direct order of a king."

"And if you obey it," spoke the thane, "where next will you be required to strip yourself of wealth and of men? And where after that? And where will it end?"

Godwin nodded again. "I have thought of that too. King Edward is less friendly to me than of wont." Nevertheless, he raised a volunteer troop in his south country of Wessex, and he wrote his son Harold to raise men in his earldom in East Anglia, and to Sweyn in the Welsh Marches. And from Langtree in Gloucestershire, he sent to the king at Gloucester to say that Eustace and sundry other Normans who had been lording it high-handedly in the king's realm must be handed over in chains to justice.

The king's writ went to Northumbria and the Marches, bidding Earls Loefric and Siward to march to his support. But the men of the north had small stomach to fight for the alien French against their countrymen. The earls proposed an armistice and a friendly meeting.

King Edward raged. "Does this Godwin think himself greater than the king? How dares he condone the injury to my guest and kinsman, Eustace? And still more, how weary I am of him! I will attaint him of high treason to the crown!"

"His sire sought to betray the king your father in the Danish wars," said the Normans. "His house has ever been an enemy of yours."

"Then now is the time when I shall crush this upstart. Did not I create his cursed brood earls? And shall I not take back that which all too generously I gave? Let us march on this rebel and destroy him!"

"Let the king destroy him indeed," was the counsel of Leofric. "But let us delay until all our troops are assembled. My men-at-arms come daily. So do the forces of Earl Ralph. Let the King reply with soft words. Meanwhile, to delay, let the King affect to be grieved at the prospect of letting so much English blood, and be persuaded, reluctantly, to a composition. Let us propose that we exchange hostages, and meet at London with Godwin and his sons for a conference. Then we will be ready to try conclusions on the field of battle."

Earl Ralph spoke, " Better than that, my lord. Let me send subtle tongued messengers to Godwin's thanes and try what they can effect."

To Thane Ethelnoth of Wight came one in the dress of a bishop, craving lodgment for the night. And they sat long at drink that eve.

Eadulf, thane of Dartmouth, fell in with a merchant, who showed him some excellent weapons. And much besides.

A Cornish captain was rejoiced to encounter in an inn of Bath a Pictish horse trader; he was weary of the alien Saxon accents, and glad of an evening of talk with one whose native tongue was so like his own.

Thereafter, the thanes and the Cornishman spent some few days in reflection, and then took their ways home. And as desertions occurred, those who remained became uneasy, both over the lessened battle force and the very fact of others' disenchantment with the cause. And as the King's power grew, Godwin's army began to melt away; slowly at first, but the trickle became a stream, and the stream a torrent.

Again, and more imperiously, came a summons to Godwin and his sons. But friends at court warned the earl that Edward was resolved on his ruin, so the earl demanded hostages for his safety.

The exultant king now proclaimed Godwin, together with wife and sons, outlaws, with the customery five days allowed to reach sea and safety. His vengefulness extended to his queen. Was she not guilty of being the daughter and granddaughter of rebels? The heart of Edward was too atrophied by years of maternal denial to be capable of love - or even of its fairly satisfactory substitute, tenderness. Without even the grace of an interview the hapless woman who had shared his throne and his bed was hurried off by an armed guard, without jewels, silver or wardrobe, shorn of lands and titles, and immured in the convent of Wherewell under the cold eye of the abbess.

Godwin and his wife, the former earl and countess of Wessex, and their sons Sweyn, Tostig and Gyrth, were luckily on their estates near the Channel. They took what treasure was portable - and it was much - and embarked for Flanders. Baldwin of Bruges gave them sanctuary.

Earl Harold and his brother Leofwine, however, were cut off in the west. King Edward sent a force under Bishop Aldred to seize or slay them, without the lawful five days of grace. But the brothers rode hard with a troop; in the mouth of the Avon near Brigstow Sweyn had readied a ship for just such an eventuality.

They found the ship, and a half dozen more that they seized. The pilots looked at the lowering skies and shook their heads. But behind them Bishop Aldred with his squadrons pressed hard; and behind him was the army of England. So they embarked.

The west of England is quite different from the eastern Channel. Relatively mild winds and seas characterize the latter area. But the west has the weather of the open ocean; and in winter the north Atlantic is the roughest ocean of the temperate zone. The fleet put to sea nevertheless, having no other choice.

A cold rain soon fell. The breeze became harder, and harder, and on the darkening sea the ships began to labor. Harold signalled to make a bay just visible on the Somerset coast. By the time he led the way in, it was blowing half a gale.

Two of his vessels did not make it. The southwesterly blow in the narrow waters of the upper Brigstow Channel was opposing a strong ebb tide with the growth of a nasty steep sea. One ship foundered; the other was driven helplessly to pile up in the surf.

Harold and those with him spent an anxious night at anchor in a sheltered cove. At dawn the weather had moderated. They got under way and a few days later they were seeking and receiving hospitality in Ireland.

So the house of Godwin sojourned, that winter of 1051-52, in Flanders and in Ireland. And in England King Edward built the strength of the French, whom alone he trusted. On the farms, in the churches, in the ships, Saxon and Dane looked gloomy.

Queen mother Emma died that winter. The old she-wolf sensed her end, and sent for her son the King. He came, hardly knowing why he bothered.

"So, my son, you deign to visit your mother for the last time."

"I obeyed your summons, madame. I hope, however, that you are mistaken."

"You neither hope it nor fear it. Let us not at this late date pretend to one another."

"Indeed, madame, you have given me little to make me feel too warm toward my mother who was seldom there to mother me."

"Your mother who betrayed you, do you mean?"

The king shrugged. "Since you have said it, madame, yes."

"You are your father's son, Edward. He was a weakling, and I had no better hope of his children."

"Yet now, madame, I seem in a fair way to prove you wrong. Earl Godwin was my enemy; more, this subject was more powerful than the king! Who would ever have believed, a year ago, that he would be attainted a traitor, fled, and broken, while the king he - and you too, madame - despised, would be triumphant?"

"You are your father's son, Edward. He was a fool, and so are you. Earl Godwin is fled, yes, but he is not broken. A wise king does not drive away his crafty and powerful henchmen. If he cannot win their loyalty, he destroys them. And only the dead are destroyed. You have made three unkingly errors. First, you made Godwin too great. Secondly, you quarreled with him. Thirdly, having quarreled with him, you let him escape alive. Look to yourself, my son; this Godwin has not finished with you. He comes of a line that never forgets and never despairs."

"Even if it be as you say, madame, my friends the Normans have everything to lose by letting him prevail against me."

"You are even more of a fool if you think that the Normans are your friends. The Normans are no one's friends. I am Norman, and should know. Friendship, like love, is foreign to the great houses of Normandy." She grimaced. "Do you think that Duke William will wait for the throne of England until you die a natural death?" She coughed. "My advice to you is ... to recall Godwin and reign as king; but let him wield the power."

Edward smiled grimly. "Never! And my advice to you, madame, is that you commend your soul to God." He crossed himself and left.

She looked at his retreating back. "It is no use. Why do I care?" She sighed.

One other died that winter. For various misdeeds, the Church laid upon wild Sweyn the penance of a pilgrimage to the Holy Land, and even his father endorsed it. So little though he liked it, Sweyn set forth. On that journey, to the relief even of his family, he perished.

XV

Sea-runes good at need,
Learnt for ship's saving,
For the good health of the swimming horse;
On the stern cut them,
Cut them on the rudder-blade
And set flame to shaven oar:
How so big be the sea-hills,
How so blue beneath,
Hale from the main thou comest home.

Volsungasaga

It was spring. King Edward was in council with his earls and bishops. Earl Odda spoke.

"There came to me this day a Flemish trader, my lord king," he said, "and told me that there is activity among Godwin's ships at Bruges. And for what would he ready them but for mischief along the coasts of England?"

"That hell's spawn again!" exclaimed Edward. "Will I never be quit of his insolence? What think you my lords?"

"I think, my lord king, that he can be planning nought else," from Archbishop Robert. "Let us forestall him."

The king turned to Earl Ralph. "What is the state of the fleet?"

"The shipwrights have been hard at the repairing of the damage of the last season, my lord king. The new ships will be ready within a fortnight. In a week there will be a royal power afloat such as a Godwin could not meet; in three weeks the royal fleet could, if need be, face an attack by another king."

Odda spoke again. "Let the king's ships gather at Sandwich. Then, if the rebel dare move toward London, we can close him in as he sails up the Thames and annihilate him. If he plans to raid to the westward, the Fleet can follow and cut him off from a retreat. When it brings him to action, it can crush him for good and all."

"What say you, my lords?"

There was a general agreement.

"Then be it so, and you, my lord bishop, offer our prayers that we may be free of this rascal forever."

Godwin had been making his ships ready for sea, as the

king's informant had told. But he purposed much more than a raid. The seed of Aelfthryth had spurned him, and it was bitter war between them!

With the fleet of three ships the earl stood down the river and made for Isere. There he met a fisherman which had run across from England. Her skipper sought him out.

"I have been sent to you, my lord earl, by the men of Dover. They have not forgotten how you saved them. The king has been told that you are sailing for England. His fleet is massed at Sandwich."

"My thanks to you, boatceorl. And my thanks to your townsmen of Dover. With God's help, we will yet lift the Norman scourge from their backs." He handed over a purse. "Tis nothing. Those who are loyal to me can always look for my favor."

Despite the need for haste, Godwin lay at Isere for a few days, until the southwesterly wind shifted to the east. He then put out shortly before daybreak on what promised to be a fine day at the end of May.

His judgment of the weather was not wrong. With eased sheets and braces the squadron ran along the low Flemish coast. Spirits were high as they shared their dried herring, peas and bread. All day they sailed, with never an oar in the water save the big steering sweeps.

It is hard to judge of one's progress along a characterless coast. Where hill and bay and city follow one another, one sees them slide astern, and knows that the coast is gliding with them. But where one sees only a succession of sand dunes, each just like the last, it is only the reassuring chuckle of the forefoot and the bubble of the wake that mark the way of the ship.

By the same token, it is difficult to locate oneself under such circumstances. So Godwin and his pilots argued and speculated, as the afternoon, wore on, about their whereabouts. True, there had been a tiny fishing village that might - or might not - have been Dunkirk. But at dusk a larger one appeared, and was Calais.

Now there was a decision to make. The English king would certainly have his spies about, and Godwin could assume that his arrival and departure would swiftly be reported in a despatch from Calais to the court of Britain. On the other hand, if he gave the city no matter how wide a berth, the Straits of Dover floated many traders and fishermen, any of whom might see and report him.

True, he could slow down by reducing canvas, and pass the straits in the dark. But then he would reach England with exhausted oarsmen after a night run; and he could assume that Edward would quickly be aware of his appearance in the kingdom.

He decided to put in to Calais, rest and refresh his men, and cross to England in the daytime. He would almost certainly have the respite thereafter of another night; and his men would then be fresh and equal to whatever might be before them. He made the harbor. This was still Flanders, and he received the friendly welcome on which he had counted.

The good easterly still blew on the next day. He set out on the crossing. He had picked a period when the tides so ran that even if he lost his wind when halfway, a favorable current would carry him home.

Which is just what happened. The wind dropped, then began to blow from the west. His crews sat to the oars, and at dusk they made the Naess.

Godwin went ashore and sought out one he knew. But they had not been long in converse when a servant came with a hurried word for his master.

"You have been recognized," the latter said to Godwin. "The tavern keeper is a hound who licks the boots of the Normans; he has just taken horse and rides hard toward the east."

From Dungeness to Sandwich is some thirty miles in a straight line, half again as much by road.

"Then they will be down on me by tomorrow eve, weather favoring," the earl replied. "There will be no time to send for our friends; I must be gone by daybreak." He gave some instructions about beacon fires, and departed.

In the morning the little flotilla set out accordingly. There was a light northerly air; they used it as they could, rowed as the tide served, and stood westward. At Pefensey, a day's sail away, Godwin beached again.

In the meantime, the king's troops marched on the Naess from Canterbury, and the royal fleet set sail to the westward from Sandwich. But as it neared the Naess, a gale arose from the west; and Earl Ralph and Earl Odda, its commanders, were glad to take shelter at Romney. There was one Northumbrian squadron of a dozen ships, however, which had made somewhat better time, and was able to put in at Rye, further to the west, some thirty miles from Pefensey and Godwin.

While all of these lay stormbound at their three places of refuge, Earl Godwin went about his business. Burne Manor was four miles away; messengers rode north, west and east to gather a council.

"Come back to us, my lord earl!" Thane Wigheart implored

him. "We have had enough and more of these French usurpers!"

"Mother Church is thrall to alien men whose very Latin is spoken in accents so barbarous that the flock feel they have lost their shepherd," put in Haeston. "Yes, I am an abbot now - I have lost my see; but of that -" he shrugged.

The stout Thane Waeforth was the most forthright of all. "Go back to Bruges, my lord," he said, "and return in force with what power you can muster. We will restore you and unseat these foreign upstarts."

"Nobly said," was Godwin's answer. "But I once raised my standard against the king's oppression, and I was deserted by my followers."

"Not by the ships," exclaimed boatceorl Aethelmaer. "You were betrayed, my lord, by cattle drovers and husbandmen worrying lest the king's troopers ravage their fields. But we in the merchant and fishing fleets, and the landsmen too along this south coast, remember well how you stood up to king and court in defense of your city of Dover. Return, my lord, and with a fleet as backing for your army, we will overthrow the troops of this French-loving king."

"You convince me," the earl replied. "Perhaps because I want to be convinced. I shall leave then, for Bruges, and return again. Do you my work among the men of the coast."

The king's ships had sailed to the Naess in vain. Finding their prey departed, they returned discouraged to Sandwich. But the Northumbrians made sail for Pefensey, to catch the rash earl unawares. The men of Fairlight saw the squadron while it was yet far off, and lit a smoky fire on Fairlight Hill; and when they saw it, the men of Senlac did the same; and a seaman burst in to Godwin to tell him that there was smoke over Bexford.

"Take me with you, my lord!" the boatceorl begged.

"Come aboard, then, and let us get under way."

They rowed in a calm till a light easterly sprang up, and pushed them along for the rest of the day and night. Hour after hour they coasted by the low Sussex shores that Godwin knew so well; and by the next noon they skirted the Looe off Chichester and entered the Solent, that flows between the Isle of Wight and the Hampshire main. Here the accelerated tidal current carried them rapidly westward, and at dusk they made camp. At Weymouth, just under the Bill of Portland, that long, narrow neck that makes out for five miles into the channel, they cooked, ate and slept.

They had not been unobserved. At dawn a friend of Godwin's came running into camp to report the approach of the king's reeve with a body of men-at-arms from Portland. The earl hastily reembarked his men; they stood out and to the east, when there came a swift sailor from the Isle of Wight with the news that the islanders had seen him pass the Solent, and had sent word of his passage to the pursuers. And sure enough, as Godwin turned again, here came the dozen ships from the direction of St. Albans Head.

It was beginning to blow from the west, and they took to the oars in its teeth. Godwin gazed wrathfully at his pursuers, northern ships, by their lines and rig. Boatceorl Aethelmaer spoke.

"Better steer further south, my lord! This is the last of the east running tidal current. This westerly is going to freshen; it will be evil off the Bill of Portland when the flow is against it."

A sudden memory sprang into the mind of the earl. "Do you remember the Merry Men of Mey, my helmsman?"

"Well, my lord."

"Would you slap the face of this French king?" Godwin asked.

"Aye, my lord."

"It may be that these northerners do not know about the tidal overfall at the Bill. The tides are taking on; tomorrow the moon will be full. When that fleet reaches the Bill, the water will be at its worst."

The helmsman showed his teeth in a grin. "I take your meaning, my lord."

"Then let us pull like the very devil, that we may pass the point close aboard; we can rest on our oars just beyond it."

The Northumbrian thane who commanded the King's squadron watched his quarry row close under the southernmost point of the Bill of Portland and disappear around it. He gave order to follow.

A king's officer eyed the sea dubiously. "I have heard bad reports of that point, my lord."

"Reefs?"

"I think not, my lord, but boisterous water."

"Look at it! I see no disturbance. Godwin passed it easily; nor did his ships labor as he did so."

"True; but the wind is rising."

"Let it rise. In an hour we will be past the point that worries you. Anywhere Godwin's ships can go, mine can too." And he and his squadron followed in Godwin's wake. He rejoiced in the speed by which his galleys had out-distanced the rest. Fame and the gifts of a grateful king were riding in yonder fleeing ships.

But all of a sudden, as the ebb tide set strongly against the rising wind, a fearful broken sea made up about him. The thane cursed as his ship struggled for her life against a sea which had suddenly become a monstrous thrusting, pulling, hurling thing without period or orientation, and which rose under bow or stern - often under both together - too fast for buoyancy to push the end of the ship up and out of danger. Seas swept from two directions at once, and poured into his hull. The oars were snatched from the hands of the rowers, sometimes to be hurled into the ship at the heads of his crew and himself. He suddenly realized that he was in peril of drowning.

Others of the squadron were in like case. The last few had hesitated on perceiving what had happened to the leaders, and were turning to run back to safety.

This was a wicked, wicked sea. But it was not the Merry Men of Mey. Most of the Northumbrian ships survived. But the battered, weary men in the hulls awash with sea water were in no condition to continue the chase.

Godwin's pilot studied the sky.

"My lord, the wind will veer, and there will be a northeasterly gale by evening."

"And have you stomach for this gale, my boatceorl?"

"The men of Hythe have never feared the taste of salt water. Let us put to sea, my lord, and let the king's ships catch fish for their trouble!"

That night in the bailing wells of Godwin's ships men toiled for their lives. The little craft pitched wildly to their sea anchors in the wicked waves of the Channel. The seamen prayed aloud. None worked harder with bucket or gear than Godwin; none was readier with a word of cheer.

In the dawn the blow moderated. The earl's ship lay alone. They got sail on her and steered for Dover Straits. Calais received them again, and half a day later one of the other two craft limped in. Of the third they never heard again.

During the wild night the royal ships were drawn up on the beaches. When their crews sought further, they had their labor for their pains. They waited until they had a westerly air, then returned to Sandwich.

The king was beside himself. Godwin had been in his grasp, and fools and traitors had let him slip away! In a rage he relieved the earls and their lieutenants of their commands, and ordered the fleet to London. In high dudgeon Ralph, Odda and their associate fleet commanders delayed at Sandwich, debating the royal commands and voicing their anger both at Godwin and the king. Ship after ship detached herself and made for her home port. Finally, the earls with some fifty sail returned to the Thames.

Godwin was in a frenzy of activity at Bruges. With the enormous treasure that he had brought with him on his flight, he bought and fitted out ships and hired crews. A swift cruiser went to Ireland with a letter for Harold and Leofwin.

Upon receipt of the news of the break-up of Edward's naval force, Godwin set sail with some forty ships and made the Isle of Wight without misadventure. This he chose as one of the two coastal areas that had made an unfriendly gesture. He now proceeded to strike a double blow in stripping the farms and great houses of food and wealth; he thereby, recruited his supplies and demonstrated the danger of hostility.

Harold Godwinson was in his thirty-second year, great of strength and stature, contemptuous of luxury, inured, despite the family wealth, to hardship and toil in the world of ships. He and his brother had enlisted a force from Dublin and the other Danish cities of eastern Ireland, and fitted out a squadron of eleven sail. They crossed to Porlock in the now unfriendly earldom of Somerset.

The local levies stood valiantly in defense. But in a stiff action the raiders slew the Somerset thanes and overwhelmed and slew or scattered the spearmen. Then pitilessly, Harold swept through the coastal area, killing, burning and pillaging. He re-embarked, and like a fire swept along the hapless north Cornish coast; he rounded the Lizard and carried the rapine to the south. Then he sailed eastward to reunion with his father in the mouth of the Plym.

Godwin greeted his son in joy and pride. He had passed through the narrow seas in despite of all the power of the king's ships!

"You see, Harold, I gave you good counsel when I told you that the sea bore the fortunes of our house. Study her, trust her, never neglect her, and she will serve you well."

Harold never forgot the admonition but once.

Now Godwin, reinforced, turned east again. The cruise became almost a Royal Progress. Ships and men flocked to them enthusiastically. They landed on luckless Wight once more to pick up any items they might have missed in the first place, then continued on. The further east they went, the more enthusiastic their reception; in Romney, Hythe, Folkestone the boatceorls rallied to Godwin almost to a man - with their ships. In Dover, church bells were rung on their arrival and a holiday was proclaimed. Sandwich, Northmouth defected to the earl. And then with still swelling power he turned up the Thames toward London.

King Edward called his earls to council. His words were calm, but he looked at them with desperate eyes.

"My lords, the traitor Godwin comes on with a great power of ships and men. We must decide by what strategy we are to destroy him."

Archbishop Robert was the first to speak. "We should have brought him to battle when first he landed, my king. But your city of London made stout defense in the past; I doubt not but what we can hold it until the levies are again come from the north and the west. Then we will bring him to battle and, with God's aid, we will break his power for all time."

"That pleases me well," was Edward's reply. "What say you, my lords?"

There was a minute of silence. Then Earl Siward spoke up.

"My lord, it is late for such councils. Godwin is much stronger now than last year. With the fleet for offense or retreat, he can fight, fly or even do nought at will. It is he who will decide on the time and place of an action. And the issue of such an action is in doubt."

"Then what do you advise, Earl Siward?"

"My lord, it seems to me that the king should consider terms of composition."

"Never! Sooner will I myself fall in battle at the head of my loyal troops!"

"Spoken like a king!" cried Bishop Ulf.

"Spoken like a fool," said Odda under his breath; the king would survive Godwin's triumph, but for the Normans and their toadies such as Ulf, it would mean complete ruin. Naturally, they counselled resistance. But aloud he said, "My lord, I do believe that we can crush Godwin's forces."

"That word rings well in my ear," exclaimed Edward joyfully.

"But bethink you, my king, in what plight such battle would leave your kingdom. I say nothing about our earldoms and their reduced state, in farm and field. But what of the king's realm? It would be impoverished; the best of its manhood would have fallen; England could offer scant resistance to any power that came from overseas. It is only a generation since the horror of the Viking raids; we should be naked to their swords once more. Nay, even the Welsh and the Scots would take from us what they willed. And that might well be the kingdom itself. My king, I urge that you be reconciled with Godwin."

"Never! Never, never, never! I am a king, and he is now less than a subject! Were I to submit thus tamely to this outlaw, I could never wear a crown again! Leave me, my pusillanimous earls, before I show that my wrath is still to be feared!"

Days passed with the king's army and the earl's fleet in confrontation. Edward wrangled with his nobles. There were sessions in which he fell into rages, after which he would seek his chapel and call down the vengeance of God on Godwin and on his counsellors who spoke of surrender. His followers began to lose heart. There were desertions.

In the camp of Godwin, on the other hand, confidence, high in the beginning, grew steadily. His men, thanes and commoners alike, clamored for battle; at times the earl had much ado to restrain them from raids on the hostile ships. But, like the noblemen of the king's party, he was not eager to waste the strength of the land, feeling, as he did, that victory would come his way without it.

And so it did. The day came when, after a sitting of the royal council, Earl Ralph sent for Bishop Stigand, and in the presence of Edward sitting grey-faced and silent, bade him repair to Godwin and arrange for a meeting, with hostages to assure good faith on either side.

And while Godwin and Stigand were making their arrangements, out from the city on the other side rode the Normans, Archbishop Robert at their head, with Ulf and such other Englishmen as had hopelessly compromised their cause with the foreigners; they cut down wantonly any defenseless men whom they encountered, and dashed toward the sea and safety.

Then a great gemot was held at London, attended by all the nobility of the realm; the king heard Godwin and declared him guiltless of the offenses that had been charged to him. So Godwin and his house were restored to lands and favor and honor, and poor forsaken Eadgytha was recalled from the convent and made queen once more.

Says the Chronicler:
"And they outlawed all the Frenchmen who had promoted injustices and passed unjust judgments and given bad counsel in this country, with the exception, as they decided, of as many as the king should wish to have with him, who were loyal to him and to all the people."

This was the great achievement of Godwin's

life, and for it he is remembered. When the earl reflected upon it afterwards, he felt that his entire previous existence had been but a preparation for this exploit. His indoctrination in ships by his formidable father; his introduction to stress of weather on the voyage to and from Iceland, that gave him the skills and confidence for his passage back to Flanders through storm and peril; the passing unscathed by the Merry Men of Mey, that taught him what to expect off the savage Bill; the incessant training in piloting both by day and by night; all of these carried the earl through and across the narrow waters in despite of the Royal Navy. The triumphant procession up the Thames and the humbling of the king were almost an anticlimax.

And here in the pride and gratification of restored wealth and honors we might leave him. But let us follow further the history of the talented but turbulent house of Wulfnoth.

It was the end of summer; but Godwin lived not to see another. On the second day of Easter, as he sat at meat with the king, he sank suddenly from his seat, speechless and powerless; on the Thursday he died. Harold succeeded to his land and titles.

PART III

HAROLD

XVI

*Many a man
Weighted with sorrow and presage of woe
Wished that the end of his kingdom were come.
That evil ended. So also may this!*

Deor's Lament

Edward was a broken man. He abandoned direction of affairs to his counsellors. He turned his attention to religion - to such a degree, that men later called him Edward the Confessor.

Among the earls there were three whose wealth and power made them, under the crown, the rulers of the country - Siward of Northumbria, Leofric of Mercia, and Harold.

Now fate opened her hand to Harold Godwinson. The earl grew in stature. To some men, fortune grants the means to fame. Many let the chance pass by unused. Of those who grasp it, most are unworthy of the gift. They abuse it, and character shrivels in the flame of the temptations of mastery and money. But there are a few who grow to meet the challenge of opportunity.

Harold's first stroke of good fortune came from the north. Malcolm, son of the murdered King Duncan of Scotland, crossed the Scottish border, to avenge his father by slaying Macbeth and to claim the throne. With him went the army of his grandfather, Earl Siward of Northumbria. Siward gained a great victory in the battle of Burnam; but his heroic grandson fell in the carnage.

The bereaved earl returned to his castle. For a year he grieved, and then died. His younger son was but a lad, and the troubled earldom required a stronger hand than his. The succession fell to Harold's brother Tostig, and the house of Godwin, with two of the three greatest earldoms, was preeminent in the kingdom.

Harold answered the king's summons.

"Can we never have peace in this wretched land? Just as the Vikings raided at will, withdrawing at need to the sea and safety, so the Welsh raid, and when resistance is strong, they retreat to their mountain fastness!

"Aye, again; and while you were in the south, in your own manor at Hereford!"

"Indeed, my lord!"

"Indeed. And worse - your bishop Leofgar took sword against them. After much marching and countermarching, fighting and fleeing, the end is that the bishop and many good men lie slain, to no avail!

"I need hardly urge you, Earl Harold, to proceed to the west and pacify the border! Be off at once."

"Aye, my lord!"

The earl marched to the border. There was no large scale action; the Welsh knew that they would lose. But one of the skirmishes brought Harold to an isolated manor. He had but few troops behind him at the moment; the manor was stubbornly defended; it was Harold himself who, battle-axe swinging, battered down the door, dashed in, and engaged the men-at-arms within. He did heavy execution; almost before his men joined him inside, the resistance was crushed.

It turned out to be the residence of a prominent henchman of the Welsh king. In one of the rooms, locked from the outside, was a strikingly beautiful young woman.

"Who is this?" he asked.

An old serving woman answered. "We call her Edith Swan-neck," and it was easy to see why.

"Who are you, girl?"

"I am the daughter of Thane Guthfrith. Rhys - this is his house - murdered my father on a raid last year, and I was captured. I have lived in misery with him since then."

"I will return you to your family and lands."

"I have no more family. And the lands were so ravaged by Gruffydd and his ruffians that there is nothing left."

Harold looked long upon the girl. "I think I could love you well," he said at length. "Will you cast your lot with me?"

She looked him full in the eye. "If you will love me, my lord, I am content."

In this wise Edith Swan-neck became the leman of Earl Harold. And with her person she gave him her heart.

After some fighting Gruffydd submitted. He swore to keep peace on the border, and acknowledge the over-lordship of King Edward of England. But not long did he keep that oath.

King Edward sent for Earl Harold.

"My lord?" asked Harold.

The king turned a troubled face upon him. "The Welsh again. King Gruffydd ravages at will; when I send troops against him, it only adds to the number of his slain. Yes, you had some success on that border; but as you know, he has broken the peace again and again. Is it possible to crush him once and for all?"

"It is possible, my lord; but not as the king has been doing. When Gruffydd is beaten, or when he thinks he might be, he retreats to a mountain fastness. When they harry him from one valley, he leaves it for another. If pressed too hard and too far, he takes ship to another part of his realm, and falls without warning upon the king's men from an unexpected quarter."

"So?"

"My lord, my father bade me ever to take to the sea. There, he used to say, is the salvation of our house; and perhaps the safety of England itself.

"Let me, therefore, embark a force from the west coast. I can overawe and pacify the Welsh of the coastal towns. Meanwhile, let my brother Tostig lead his footmen - not cavalry, who have met with disaster in that terrain - and press Gruffydd from the east. Between us, we will crush this bandit king as one cracks a nut!"

"Your counsel likes me well. Let it be done. What ships and what troops will you need?"

In May, Earl Harold embarked a large force and set sail from Brigstow. Northward along the Welsh coast he led his ships. They landed at every town or village. Ruin stared the hapless Welsh fishermen in the face as the earl seized or destroyed every vessel down to the very skiffs.

At Caernarvon he found what he sought. The royal fleet of Gruffydd lay an unprotected prey, and fell helpless into his hands.

Meanwhile, Tostig's army was closing from the east. Gruffydd's overmatched raiders were driven into the rugged heart of the country, where the heavy infantry of the English king could not follow.

Now Harold revealed the second part of his plan. He rearmed and equipped his men as a light, highly mobile but numerous striking force. They struck inward from the sea; and wherever they came, the Welsh farmers stared appalled at the burning of barns, stores and houses and the slaughter of sheep, swine and cattle. Nothing stood between them and starvation.

Gruffydd still eluded the English, but his realm was being ruined.

It was too much. As destruction spread ever more widely through the land, the hapless Welsh turned to the only thing that could save them. They assassinated the king who had brought upon them so much misery.

And so, Earl Harold presented his monarch with the head of Gruffydd and the ornate bow of his galley.

Edith came in great excitement to Earl Harold.

"My lord! I have just learned that my brother Osred is not dead! He was taken alive, and sold for ransom to a Dane, who sold him in turn in Flanders!"

"I am delighted, I rejoice for you!" And, satisfied that the news was authentic, the earl added, "In a fortnight I shall be free; I have wanted to visit there for reasons of my own. I had better see to your business myself. I'll ransom him, and bring him home!"

But for one reason or another, the fortnight became two, and the month did likewise. When Harold was finally free to go, the king demurred.

"This is not the season," said the king frowning. "I fear that you will come to grief on this voyage."

"Do you forbid me to go?" asked the earl.

"No. Go if you must. But I think it foolhardy."

At home, Edith hung weeping upon his neck. "Do not go,

my lord! Much as I would have you ransom the last male of my house, this may now be an ill voyage, and I fear lest it bring us great grief!" The earl kissed her tenderly, but smiled and was off to his ship.

And indeed a sudden storm arose. It swept him helpless to the south, and wrecked him upon the coast of Ponthieu. Harold made the shore alive, to be seized by the men of Count Guy; but Duke William in Normandy heard of it and saw his chance. He demanded his prisoner of the count. Count Guy dared not refuse.

For months Harold was the guest of the duke. He was treated with honor. They feasted, hunted and hawked together. When the duke campaigned briefly against one of his neighbors, Harold rode with him into combat. Yet whenever he spoke of going home, the Norman put him off with smiles and protestations of friendship.

In England, poor Edith wrung her hands and blamed herself most bitterly for having sent her lover to what fate she knew not.

Finally, when Harold became insistent, Duke William said, "Let us delay until tomorrow. Then, I promise, we shall resolve the matter," and he laid his arm across the earl's shoulders in brotherly fashion.

On the next day the duke led Harold into a chamber where behind a chest laid with a cloth were two nobles and two bishops of the realm.

William addressed the earl. "Your King Edward is, and will almost certainly remain, childless. He has no heirs of his house. Therefore, as nephew and only living heir of Queen Emma. I claim the succession to the throne. Your king has promised it to me.

"By casting you on the shore of France, God gave me this opportunity to further my claim, and it would be impious were I to reject His gift." The duke laid his hand upon the chest. "Put your hand on mine, and swear that upon Edward's death you will accept me as your rightful king; that you will give your sister as wife to a Norman nobleman; and, to cement our alliance, that you will take my daughter to wife. You will then be, as you are now, the highest man in the realm of England, under the king."

Harold thought fast. If he refused, it might well cost him his life, certainly his liberty; the duke would not dare let him further enjoy even such quasi-freedom as he had now. On the other hand, an oath which was not freely given was of doubtful validity; more important, the crown of England was not his to bestow. It would be up to the Witan, the great council. So Harold covered the duke's hand with his own and said, "I swear."

Then William removed the cloth, opened the chest to Harold's gaze, and said, "You have sworn over these holy relics - a sandal of St. Peter, a piece of the cloak of St. Augustine, a fingernail of St. Dunstan, and a lock of hair of St. David!"

Harold affected to be greatly impressed. He was not. He still considered the oath completely invalid. But the seeds of war, sown long since, received their first watering in this wise.

Then William sent his prisoner home to England.

Edith's hapless brother Osred had perished in his prison.

Harold's brother Tostig might have lived in power and honor in his earldom of Northumbria. But the wild heritage of Wulfnoth appeared again, and he oppressed his people beyond endurance. They rose against him, and offered his honors to the Mercian Earl, Edwin's brother Morcar. Tostig called on the royal troops to suppress the rebellion; Edwin marched in support of his brother.

It was Harold who mediated. Custom was for each automatically to uphold the rights of his house. But the Harold whose father had valiantly stood for his people of Dover listened to the woes of the Northumbrians. A wonder occurred. The claims of family yielded to the claims of the people! Morcar became earl, and Tostig went into exile with bitterness in his heart.

On the fifth day of January in the year 1066, King Edward yielded up the life in which he had found so little joy. In all that realm there was but one man whom the council judged worthy of the throne.

Harold faced his love with sadness in heart. "I am a king now," he said, "and you know what I must do."

Edith looked at him bravely. "I have always known that this day must come. You have a duty to marry to the profit of your realm. But I love you, and you love me, and nothing can change that."

So the newly crowned king married Ealdgyth, sister of the earls of Mercia and Northumberland. Now all of the greatest men in England were allied to him by the claims of blood.

XVII

The West-Saxons fierce
pressed on the loathed bands;
hewed down the fugitives,
and scattered the rear,
with strong mill-sharpened blades.

Anglo-Saxon Chronicle

N ow faster and faster flowed the river of time.

Duke William of Normandy asserted his claim to the throne. Harold rejected it.

Ships one after another - merchantmen, fishermen, and longships - came with the message, "Guard well, oh king! In Normandy Duke William is mustering a mighty host, with which to snatch the crown of England from your head!"

"He needs must come in ships," said Harold. "The strength of the house of Wulfnoth is the sea. We will see what this Norman can do against my dragons!" and he joined his fleet at Sandwich when the fine days of spring opened the watery road to the invader.

But the summer passed, and William the Norman did not come. Harold's fleet dispersed, and he turned his back on the sea and returned to his capital.

A messenger came spurring to Westminster and cried, "Oh king! Tostig your brother is landed on Wight! He comes with a large fleet, and is ravaging the isle!" The king sent command to his captains. But on the following day came a rider from Southamptom with a like message; then from Cisseceaster came a cry for help, then Brighthelmston, then Friston, Pefensey, Sandwich sent calls for aid.

"My lords," Harold addressed his council, "where think you we should meet this renegade brother of mine?"

Earl Waltheof made answer. "Obviously, he is proceeding along the coast. He will soon enter the estuary of the Thames."

"These are nuisance raids," was the Archbishop Aldred's opinion. "A small, light, mobile force is all that is needful."

The king frowned. "Tostig was taught in a good school. He will not continue in a line whereon he can be intercepted."

And indeed, after a raid up the Humber, Tostig disappeared. He was next reported in Scotland with a dozen longships.

He was not there long. Word came from the north that the

King of Norway had landed in Northumbria, bent on conquest, and Tostig had joined him. As Harold gathered his troops, Earls Edwin and Morcar loyally opposed the invader - only to have their forces crushed in battle. The countryside lay naked to the foe!

This was the time that Harold forgot his sire's advice to cherish the sea.

"I cannot remain here," he said, "while Norway ravages my kingdom!"

"And what of William?" Archbishop Aldred asked him.

"The season is advanced. Perhaps he will not come. In any case I must deal with one assailant at a time. Now I need an army, not a fleet."

The Saxon ruler led a two hundred mile forced march against the invaders.

In a last access of family feeling, Harold offered his traitorous brother Tostig a third of the kingdom to return to his allegiance. "And what for my ally?" Tostig is said to have asked.

Harold's fierce reply has passed into legend. "Seven feet of English ground; or, as he is said to be a tall man, we will allow him two feet more!"

In a surprise assault Harold's tired English levies smashed the invaders at Stamford Bridge, killed Tostig and his too ambitious royal ally and sent the submissive Norse fleet back to its own shores.

The English king was given no time to enjoy his victory. Across the now unprotected water Duke William had sailed his army. Word came from the south that the Norman had landed on the 29th of September with 2000 knights, 3000 archers, footmen and sailors, to make good his claim to Harold's lands and throne. He was spreading death and ruin through the fair Sussex hills!

Harold made another forced march, and mustered what fighting men he could near the channel coast. They begged the Saxon king to rest his weary troops and wait for fresh forces to gather. But the Harold who had once ravaged Cornwall and Devon and Wight said only, "My people are calling to their king."

King Harold took his stand against the Normans on the hill of Senlac, close by the village of Hastings.

After the battle, only Edith Swan-neck could pick out the mangled body of her lover amid the mass of the slain.

The Third Wager

The winged and haloed souls of Noah and Jonah had watched as Godwin evaded the royal fleet in the Channel.

"It was dirty weather," Noah remarked. "But you must remember that when I went to sea, there were no protecting shores, and the seas made up in a fetch from clean around the world."

Jonah shot him a supercillious glance. "Truly to understand what is happening in a storm, you must experience it not only on the surface, but below it as well."

"One who went over the side can hardly speak with the same authority as another whose seamanship enabled him to ride out the storm," sneered Noah. "In any case I am sure that it will never be repeated."

"On the contrary – what has happened once can happen again. As mortals say, history repeats itself."

Ezekiel flew by, but turned and alighted. "In my opinion," he started to say. But they turned on him with identical words.

"Who are you, a frequenter only of the river Kebar, or at most, perhaps of the Tigris and the Euphrates, to discuss ships' business with two blue water sailors!"

He fled from the rout.

Jonah looked up. Here come Michael and Gabriel. Let us ask them to try for permission to arrange a similar episode? Then we will see what happens. If you are right, I'll stand your watches for the next century as petty officer of the celestial detail on maritime affairs."

"I accept the offer. And if you are right, I'll take on your duties as watch stander of the starboard watch in addition to my own."

The two archangels appealed to, consented. "But," Gabriel warned, "I have some things to do first. There is no hurry. Here in eternity we can be extravagant with time."

"Not too extravagant," Michael interjected. "We never know when He will command that last trumpet blast of yours, and then there will be no more sea."

Even so, it was, by human standards, many a lifetime before they got around to it.

A PRIDE OF LIONS

Genoa is the ocean's town. In the innermost gulf she is enthroned, where the hills of Liguria meet the sea. The lads of Genoa walk with the windsong in their ears and the salt spray in their faces. The boyish eyes mark the comings and goings of tall ships of commerce and of war.

With the ships come wealth and pride. The city's late and brief renaissance left her studded with rich palazzi and made the Via Balbi the most beautiful avenue in Italy. Elsewhere the nobility scorned the bourgeoisie, and the bourgeois hated the nobles; but in Genoa, pride of achievement drew them together in fellowship and even in marriage.

In a tapestried room of a great house in Genoa, a secretary scratched busily with his pen. A tall woman, imperious of face and voice, strode up and down.

"Black shame is upon us! The thirteenth century is drawing to a close, and the arrogant followers of Mohammed still desecrate the Holy Land! After two hundred years of fighting, we have lost Jerusalem, and cannot regain it. Cowards and fools have tainted all our efforts.

"Since the men act like women, it is for the women to play the man! I have raised a regiment of the Dames of Genoa, all armed and armored. We will not fail! We only await your blessing, Holy Father....."

From this iron woman were bred the warriors whose names stand out like points of glittering steel in the roll of the Spinolas of Genoa.

1. The Twig Is Bent.

May my name be strong as flint, as thou art,
resisting the rust of the ages, and
above the loud traffic of the world
may it resound clearly.

Salamanca

from the Spanish of Miguel de Unamuno

In the year 1571 the Turk made his supreme attempt to make the Mediterranean an Ottoman lake. The peoples of southern Europe mustered their ships, and Don John of Austria led them in a great battle at Lepanto. Their galleys smashed the Moslem fleet, and freed Europe from the peril of enslavement. There were ships of Genoa in that armada, and there were Spinolas in those ships and in the allied ships of the Knights of Malta.

In that fateful year the Palazzo Spinola heard a baby's first cry.

Filippo Spinola and Polissena Grimaldi named their second son Federico. As would be expected in a great and rich house, the infant throve, and grew into sturdy boyhood. But while he was still a child, death took his father from him.

Polissena was no helpless, weeping widow. However much she mourned her husband, she acted firmly and wisely concerning her sons, Ambrogio and Federico. Her marriage had represented the union of two great banking houses. There was no material lack.

Ambrogio, the elder boy, was of course to follow the family career in finance; the younger son was destined for the church, as in so many of the noble families of Europe.

Despite their orphanhood, the boys had a happy childhood. Federico always remembered his mother as a stately lady, well built, with a proud, fair face, always garbed in an ample gown of some rich, black stuff, one corner of whose high square collar stood stiffly behind her head.

Their tutor taught the boys Latin and a little of the New Testament Greek, music, poetry, geography, history, and of course mathematics. A friar strove early to build up in them a devotion to Holy Church. Even before they entered into their teens, a household guard, a veteran of Lepanto, began their training (for every gentleman, even one destined for the church, must understand the use of arms) in the martial arts. Federico never tired of his trainer's reminiscences of war; and he pumped every male visitor for stories of military exploits and military prowess.

For this perhaps his family was partly if unwillingly responsible. His mother felt it her duty to acquaint the lad with their past. He learned at her feet of Viscount Oberto of the tenth century, founder of the line; of his sons, Belo, the first to style himself Spinola, after the mountain of that name. But it was from an uncle that he heard the exciting tales of Zacharie Spinola and his great pride; pride that drove him, in his single galley, to attack the two ships of the outrageously insulting Vincentello, and, despite the odds, to capture both of them after a desperate battle. He learned of Paolo-Battista Spinola, who, in the service of Edward the Sixth of England, fought through a whole day to a victory that saved that monarch's throne and probably his life.

Federico learned from him of that Agostino Spinola, ever the first to take arms and the last to lay them down, whether in his own quarrel or in the service of his country, and of his sons, Antonio and Hector, as brave, as redoubtable, as high-minded and righteous as their father.

From another uncle he had the account of Quirico Spinola, scourge of the conquering Turks by sea and by land. A cousin told him about Alessandro Spinola, who, almost a boy, had the command of the African army of Emperor Charles V; and was first into the breach at La Goulette, and for it received the mural crown at the emperor's own hand.

Small wonder that as the youth rode along the Via Balbi, or wandered along the wharfs redolent with the city's commerce, he dreamed more of gleaming armor than of black robes, and more of swordcuts than of masses. This was not in any case too surprising; among the great houses of northern Italy faith though prevalent was tepid. And even a banker might aspire to high command; although any title would go to the elder brother, in those cities there was none of the strict social stratification that was known elsewhere. The wealthy commoners moved in the same circles as the nobility.

Rank respects rank nevertheless. So the great families of Genoa, since the immortal Doria had brought the city into the Spanish orbit, were oriented accordingly, and gave full allegiance to the Spanish king.

Childhood passed into youth. In Federico's sixteenth year his mother's ambition sent him to prepare for his career in the church. Seville was the Spanish city in which the Genovese enjoyed a status of privilege; many in fact had there married into Spanish families. The city was flourishing. It had reached a population of 150,000, river port though it was, for much shipping came and went at its wharves.

Federico applied himself diligently to his studies. But the good mother would have been somewhat surprised had she had detailed and timely information on those studies. Instead of theology and homiletics, the ardent youngster devoted himself to mathematics and engineering, with particular reference to their application to warfare; and he read voraciously all that he could find concerning the art of war, ancient or modern. His maturing frame was shaped by tournaments and impromptu jousts. Equitation, swordplay, and, when the local garrison made it possible, the service of the great guns complemented his formal studies. In the intervals between all this, there were drinking (not too much), dancing, flirting, poetry, and song.

So a few years passed, profitably and agreeably enough. But the eighteen-year-old began to chafe at the bit. The great Armada had made its tragic voyage against England; had he had his way, the impatient Federico would have cast his lot with the troops embarked for that horrible fiasco.

Niccolo Crespi, charged with a mission to Lisbon on behalf of the Most Serene Government, stopped in Seville and greeted Federico. After the customary salutations, he came to the point.

"I have been requested by your mother, Messer Federico, to visit you and send her word of your progress."

The younger man smiled. "I trust that your report will rejoice her."

"Well, not altogether. In fact, perhaps not at all. Donna Polissena believes that you are preparing for the priesthood. Yet when I inquired for you at the Faculty of Theology, I was told that you were almost unknown. Only by dint of numerous efforts have I found you at all."

"I regret your inconvenience, Messer Niccolo. But, as I am sure you have found out by now, I am preparing for a career in the field. However, there is no need to distress my good mother with such matters."

"But what am I to write to her?"

"Say that you found me well, as you see, and cheerful. Say further that I am diligently pursuing my studies, which is also true. And say that as a loving son, I send her my warmest embrace."

"Federico, our families have long been friends. I cannot so deceive her."

"Look you, Messer Niccolo," and steel appeared in the eyes and in the voice of the younger man. "If you value that friendship, as, be assured, I do, you will write as I say. I have made up my mind, and am not to be otherwise persuaded. Remember that my brother Ambrogio is about to reach his majority, and that he will be then, as, practically, he is now, the head of the house. My brother and I are very close. He will take no more kindly than I anything done to embarrass me."

11. First Blooding

There nowhere lies
A foreign land
Or distant strand
That does not feel,
Whate'er its flag,
My crushing might,
Admit my right,
And to me yield.
My only treasure a pirate ship!
Pirate's Song.
From the Spanish of Jose de Espronceda

The son of a great family was not wholly his own man. Noblesse oblige played a great role in his life; the ambition of a man, like the heart of a maid, lay often at the mercy of a family council, or worse, of a family autocrat. Nevertheless, the first act of rebellion on the part of young Federico broke out on a visit home during the summer of the year.

The corsairs of the Barbary States - Morocco, Algeria, Tripoli, and Tunis - had been playing havoc with European shipping. Their long, lean galleys would sweep down upon the luckless merchantmen. Swift in wind or calm, with sail or oar, they would overhaul the helpless prey, grapple, and board. Resistance against their massed crews was hopeless. Ships and goods went to swell the pirates' coffers. If passengers (rarely, of course, mariners) could arrange for a sizeable ransom, well and good. If not, the strongest of the men were used for the bitter service of the oar, which was a living death. The other men became slaves ashore. Young women and little girls were sold to the harems and brothels of the Levant; pretty boys accompanied them. Older captives, less saleable, were simply killed.

Be it said in extenuation, if not in excuse, that the Moslems who fell into Christian hands fared no better.

It was while Federico was homeward bound for a visit that a far ranging Algerian rover made a landing at Sesti Levante, some thirty miles east and south of Genoa herself. There was complete surprise, and she encountered no defense. There was time enough, before fugitives could reach the greater city and summon help, to loot the considerable treasure of the cathedral, all privately owned silver and jewels, and the recently gathered harvest of winter grain; to seize practically all of the youth of the village; to commandeer a coaster at anchor before the beach; to load the plunder and sail off to God knew where - certainly the bereft parents, cursing alike the pirates and their own misery, did not.

This was in Genoa's own state of Liguria! Young Spinola arrived to find the city in a fury. His mother, brother, and sisters exclaimed in helpless anger.

Not everyone had the same sense of futility. Federico encountered an old companion.

"Gian Strozzoli!"

"Federico Spinola!"

"How is it with you, Gianni?"

"Well enough. I have been on the estate, and came to town but yesterday. And you?"

"I too am just come, from the university at Seville."

"Of course. You come in good time, Federico! You have heard - nobody talks of anything else - about the recent outrage at Sesti Levante. Well, this time it's too much and too near. Tomasso Fieschi, a kinsman of mine by marriage, is fitting out a squadron to take to sea and teach those villains a lesson."

"He'll never find them!"

"Of course not - not the same ones, but what difference does that make? The idea is to let the heathen know that they'd better steer clear of Liguria in their unsavory calling! At any rate, the big news is this - I'm going along with the troops embarked in one of the ships!"

"How I envy you!"

"Come along! If I present you, I'm sure Signor Fieschi will take you too as a gentleman volunteer!"

"I'll do it! Now!"

"Bravo! Let's go!"

Ser Tomasso was a grave, bronzed man in his late fifties, who had fought as a young man at Lepanto. He received young Spinola courteously, with a complimentary remark upon the youth's descent and his own certainty that the blood had not run out. He consented to make a place in his fleet for the aspirant.

So Federico signed the roster as cadet in La Loba galley. Of course there was indignation at home, followed by tears, followed by appeals to the family. But Federico stood his ground, pointing out that if he withdrew now, it would seem like cowardice; and that he had earned this adventure by his obedient submission to studying at Seville (he did not of course go into details as to these studies). Finally his mother ceased her opposition and started to assemble his necessaries, as she saw them. If he had not interfered, she would have outfitted him for a circumnavigation of the globe.

One item be bought for himself, because his mother would never have thought of it. This was a copy of Waggoner's "Mariner's Mirror"; and the young man studied it faithfully.

The Knights of Malta uniquely concerned themselves with cleanliness. As possible, they sank their galleys in shallow water to cleanse them of their human ordure.

But Federico needed no guide to the area of the wharves where the galleys were berthed. Hundreds of rowers were chained by one foot to the rowing benches; there they worked, ate, slept, and carried out the more repulsive if essential functions of the body. Despite frequent hosings, the stench extended a long way. "Others get used to it," Federico told himself, "and I shall too."

La Loba, he found, was the oldest and least of the squadron of five galleys. But who regards his first ship with critical eyes?"

"She's beautiful!"

Federico gazed at her in rapture. Scarlet trimmed with gold, with allegorical murals on her deck house, "She-wolf's" still trim lines spoke of swiftness and terror. There were two masts with lateen yards.

The master-at-arms of the watch met him at the wharfside end of the gangway. "Come aboard, young sir! Are you sailing in La Loba?"

"Yes, I've signed on for the voyage. I'm Federico Spinola. She-wolf looks like a crack ship!"

"She's seen her best days, sir, but never doubt that she'll give a good account of herself. I'm Pablo Gonzalez, Master-at-arms' mate. Welcome aboard!"

"How big is she?"

"A hundred thirty-five feet long overall, sir, a beam of seventeen feet at the waterline, and she draws six. The telaro here makes her twenty-two feet across." Federico looked at the timber rectangle that furnished an outboard fulcrum for the oars. On it, on either side, was a walkway where, in action, soldiers stood above the oars ready to attack or to repel. A raised catwalk ran down the middle of the ship. Between this and the gunwhales were twenty-five rowing benches on each side, three men on each. As usually in port, they were shaded by an awning.

Forward of it stood a tiny tabernacle through which, slightly off center, rose the stumpy foremast with its yard and lateen sail. The offset proved to be due to an immovable piece of artillery set amidships to fire dead ahead. There was a smaller one to either side. The tall mainmast stood further aft.

The petty officer on watch followed the youngster's eyes. "The quarter cannon is a ten-pounder, sir, a half palm in calibre. The other two are falcons — two-pounders, and you see two-and-a-half-pounders, falconets, at the stern. And along each gunwale you note four esmerils, that throw a pound of metal each."

Forward of the guns was a small triangular foredeck, ending in a strong bowsprit. Again Spinola's informant followed his gaze.

"The forestay to the masthead is fixed at the tip of the bowsprit. We hope that in combat the spar may break the enemy's telaro and cripple him. Aft of the rowers' benches you see the poopdeck, where the captain and some of his officers have their posts; then you see the cabin house, and astern of all the helm. As you see, the fifteenth bench on the starboard side has been replaced by a boat housing, and the same one to port by the cooking hearth."

Gonzalez led him aboard and presented him to Luis Valdez, the thick-set, grizzled patron.

"Happy to have you aboard, Signor Spinola," the executive officer greeted him. "The captain, Messer Guido Morosini, is not aboard right now. Strozzoli is below, and I'll have him show you around. I understand that you chose to enroll as cadet rather than as gentleman volunteer."

"I thought, Signor, that I should learn more seamanship in this role."

"There's no doubt about that. Most young gentlemen however would have preferred the other status."

Federico made deprecatory sounds. As he looked about the crowded deck, Valdez sent a sailor below to summon Gianni.

"Valdez is something of a martinet," his friend told Spinola. "You should have joined as gentleman volunteer, and you would have had less to do with him."

"I'll make it my business to get along. Meanwhile, I won't

look for trouble."

Federico met Ottavio Imperatrice, the navigator, a tall, slender, lively fellow whose tongue betrayed his Neapolitan background, Franco Amico, who combined the functions, as was usual, of sailing master and rowmaster, Lieutenant Pietro Forli, third officer (second officer Ricci was absent on some errand), ship's chaplain Fra Bartelommeo, and the barber-surgeon, Carlo d'Amante.

The ship's company was divided into three parts, over all of which the captain exercised command. Under him the executive officer controlled the Men of the Sea — sailors, their officers, gunners, and such specialty personnel as chaplain, barber-surgeon, etc., and the Men of the Oar. A sergeant-major was embarked with the infantry detachment, the Men of Combat, who served as marines; he was responsible directly to the captain.

As ill luck would have it, there was a serious shortage when the ammunition was delivered; and the commodore elected to sail with four well supplied ships rather than delay or divide what he had among five. La Loba, the least able of the squadron, was of course the one to remain. It would be several days before she could be supplied. She was detached from the command, and ordered to operate on her own when ready for sea.

Federico and Gianni watched the fortunate four pull out of harbor. They knew in their despairing hearts that those ships would sweep the seas clean of pirate shipping while La Loba was still harbor-bound. In the bright lexicon of youth there is no such word as tomorrow.

So they waited and drilled, and tried to accustom themselves to the impossible crowding, the strict timing of every activity, and the pervasive stench. (At least they could still, most of the time, eat ashore.) Until at last the ammunition appeared, and they stowed it aboard and made ready for sea.

On a bright day in early July, with flags and pennons aflutter, La Loba stood out of harbor under oars and headed south along the coast. Federico joined a knot of sailors in setting sail, and the galley slipped along under a fine southwesterly. There was enough of a swell so that the two young men began to feel queasy; the more so, by reason of that inescapable smell. Gianni was able to lie down and obtain some relief, but Federico, as cadet, had to stay on watch and accept a hundred petty tasks in connection with final stowage and disposition of running gear.

A few days sufficed to give them their sea legs.

Federico had been to sea, briefly, on the way to Spain. But

he found that the experience was entirely different now that he was a member of the ship's company. It was not only a matter of the duties assigned him; he identified with the vessel in a fashion which was impossible for a passenger.

He was kept busy. When they sailed with a favoring wind, there were endless sail trimming, taking in on shrouds and halyards, learning the mysteries of the tiller. In adverse wind or calm, when the rowers plied their oars, there were cleaning, marlinespike seamanship, and interminable (and, as he thought, useless) overhauling of lines, hardware, and canvas.

Early evening brought the crew their only taste of leisure. The coarse fare came from the raised quadrilateral hearth, lined by sheet iron and half filled with sand. After the snack there was time for gaming, chatting, washing soiled clothes, and yarn spinning. At set of sun the Salve Regina rang sweetly over the sea. Then came the dark, and sleep.

It was during the night watches that, tired though he was, the youth experienced the fullest flavor of the new life. The galley drove through a darkened sea, her dimly lit deck representing, even more than by day, a tightly constricted living area. There were infrequent commands; otherwise, the gurgle of the water alongside and the creaking of hull and rigging were all the sound that came to his ears - unless a higher wave uttered its susurrus under the forefoot.

On those days when the cadet was dismissed after the evening meal, he was glad enough to seek sleep while he could. In fine weather he would try for a space on deck; when it rained he went below to the santabarbara, the fourth from the bow of eight spaces, in which the impossibly crowded crew had their berth. The gently reared scion of the rich Spinolas found, to his surprise, that he was able to sleep crowded closely among snoring sailors and soldiers reeking of garlic, not to mention a knot of men playing cards noisily under the lamp.

After six days of aimless cruising they put in to La Spezia (a galley, with her very limited cargo capacity and her enormous crew, could not go for much more than a week without renewing supplies of food, water, and fuel). They learned that they had missed the rest of the squadron by two days. A day of active labor served for replenishment, and they put to sea again.

This time fortune favored them. Early in the afternoon of the third day they were running before an easterly when they spied a sail to the south. They altered course to intercept her, and soon by her rig they identified a Moorish raider.

Or was it good fortune? As she closed, it became evident that the stranger was somewhat bigger and more powerful than La Loba.

To the amazement and consternation of Federico and the other cadets, the captain elected to flee. They looked at one another in horror when he directed the helmsman to steer again toward the west, and then looked down in deep shame for him, the ship, and themselves. The Moor changed course to pursue. Larger and faster as she was, she might well hope to make a capture.

But as time wore on, Federico became aware of the fact that among the older and more experienced members of the crew, at least, there was neither frustrated pugnacity nor apprehension. He ventured a question to the grizzled gunner standing by the largest piece of artillery, next to his own action station.

"Of course the captain's going to fight!" was the reply. "Look at him! Does he look scared?" And indeed the commander presented a picture of quiet confidence, even though the enemy was slowly closing the interval. Her sails, like La Loba's, were billowing full, and the bone in her teeth was large.

"In a few hours," the gunner continued, "the sun will be low - low enough to dazzle the eyes of the Moorish gunners and archers. Not only that, but this wind is going to change and blow from the west, if I am any judge, and I'm sure the skipper is counting on that too. So the smoke of the enemy guns will blow right away astern, leaving us a clear view of her; whereas that from our own will just about keep pace with our speed, and partly conceal us when we reverse course and row toward them. Ser Guido is an old hand at this game."

"You said 'archer'. Don't the Moors use the arquebus?"

"They do, of course; but there is usually a greater number of bows. The English too still like their longbow, and use a few of them. I understand there are those among them who would return altogether to the older weapon."

"Why? The firearm is more accurate, and has a longer range, and hits harder."

"Yes. But it must be admitted that it takes long to load. The bow has a much greater rate of fire."

The gunner proved to be a good prophet. As the sun approached the horizon, the easterly died and was quickly replaced by a lively western air. Under Ser Guido's orders, the sails came down and the rowers turned to and pulled at moderate speed toward the Moor. The soldiers took position at bow, at stern, and along the gunwales above the beating oars.

The enemy opened fire, but without effect; the shots fell short or went wide. "Hold your fire!" called Ser Guido, then, "Full speed ahead!"

The oarsmen bent to the more rapid stroke. The galley leaped ahead at 5 1/2 knots. They could maintain this for only a half hour; but minutes would suffice.

By now the gunner, sighting along his piece, was too preoccupied for conversation. Federico turned with a question to an older sailor.

"Her guns are a little heavier. She can outrange us," was the reply; and after a minute or two, "We're coming into range now, but I don't think the captain is ready to open fire."

"Why in the world not?"

"Fire is not very accurate at this distance, unless you get a lucky shot. The hull can train the guns fairly well, but in a seaway pointing is usually high or low. The skipper will wait for close range. Its effect is more deadly, and at this speed there will be no time for a second shot from the great guns before we close."

Young Spinola was by no means devoid of fear, and this would be intensified when the guns began to speak. But he was eager to perform as he should, and most curious; these feelings mitigated the former.

The gap between the ships closed rapidly.

The head of a soldier suddenly disappeared, and the body of a man behind him became a horrible bloody jelly. But La Loba was now within a hundred and a quarter fathoms of her opponent - short range. "Open fire!" came the command, and the guns roared. The knot of figures about the great gun of the Moors disintegrated. "Well done, gunner!" called the captain.

Four Genovese fell to the shafts of Moorish archers, now buzzing thickly. But Moors were seen to fall as the arquebusiers opened fire.

"All seamen and soldiers except the bow detail, lay aft on the double!"

The extra weight aft brought La Loba's bow partly out of the water. Seconds later the two ships came together with a crash; the bow of the Genovese rode up and over the Moor just beside the latter's bowsprit - the optimum point of contact.

"Boarders away!" rang the command. The bow party, higher than the pirate deck, had been able to hold while their people rushed forward in support; then the Genovese spilled onto the enemy ship.

It was desperately hot work. Federico's bowels churned, but his limbs did their duty. In helmet and breastplate, sword in his right hand, shield in his left, he attempted, with a column of sailors and a pair of armed rowers (the more reliable often fought in hope of pardon or mitigation of sentence), to force his way aft along the starboard gangway. On the port side a column of soldiers with pikes, swords, halberds, and daggers was similarly engaged; and along the midships catwalk a mixed group engaged the main body of the Moors. From the elevated points of La Loba arquebusiers kept up a hot and effectual fire. The Moslem marksmen were of course doing the same.

Close to Federico, Imperatrice, the navigator, struck down a pirate, but as he did so a scimitar swept for his throat. Federico had just time to bring his shield up under the blow while spitting a man who was striking at him. Imperatrice spared a swift glance to identify his rescuer.

Once a rally drove them back almost to their own deck. But several Christian slaves, shackled though they were, seized weapons from the fallen and attacked the Moorish crew in the rear. At the same time, Ser Guido, fighting like three men, led a counterattack that swept the pirates back once more.

The hearth and the small boat, positioned like those of La Loba, formed a slight barrier behind which the corsairs held a line across their deck. A Christian slave swung his oar with the muscles of two years' toil on the benches; it swept the defenders off the elevation of the hearth. The attackers surged on, engulfed the group resisting valiantly from the ship's boat, and mastered the rest of the deck. The ship was theirs.

It had come dearly. One out of three were casualties - mostly dead or severely wounded. A few would survive only as cripples. The sailing master was dead, and so was third mate Forli. Federico grieved to learn that Gianni Strozzoli had been pushed overboard in the melee and in his heavy harness had sunk like a sounding lead in the sea.

The barber-surgeon and his mates worked late that night. Some of the wounded perished while waiting their turn. Perhaps they were the fortunate ones.

But La Loba rescued half a hundred European slaves from the oars, took three score Moors for ransom or slavery, and, most lucratively, brought a fine ship back to Genoa as their prize.

Federico's reward was the demonstration to himself that despite his fear he had acquitted himself well. But, he wondered, what was the nature of fear, and of courage?

"Everyone fears," Lieutenant Ricci told him. "That is, almost everyone. There are some rare individuals who seem, so far as I can tell, to be devoid of fear. But most of us know it only too well.

"How do we conquer it? The answer is not an easy one. Of course, there is our self-respect; when others are standing up to the danger, apparently without fear, we cannot do less. So each fools his fellows and himself."

"The philosopher Socrates," Spinola remarked, "said that the brave man is he who knows what things to be afraid of."

"Meaning shame, I suppose, and disgrace. Yes, that was well said. Others are driven by ambition to master their fears in hope of promotion or other reward. Most of us have, I suppose, a mental picture of ourselves that we must try to measure up to."

"We are told that to fall in battle against the unbelievers is to assure ourselves of a glorious resurrection, and eternity in heaven. We ought, therefore, to be as contemptuous of death in reality as in our posturings."

Ricci laughed. "And yet we want very much to live, even with the likelihood of later sin wiping out our gains. But I have known men whom I suspected of complete lack of belief, with no hope of an afterlife, and they too could be brave."

"I have wondered about the Homeric heroes, who expected only a dim, joyless existence in a dark hereafter; yet many of them went eagerly to war."

"Didn't they hope for the Elysian fields?"

"That doctrine came much later."

"I see. There is also the matter of a distinction between embracing the prospect of danger, as we did when we sailed, and how one reacts to its immediate presence. In the army, a defeated man or body of men has usually the possibility of running away. At sea that is impossible. One may be allowed to surrender, but that means death or slavery."

Her crew and her stores replenished, the galley issued again from Genoa. This time she had not long to seek the enemy. Early on the second afternoon the lookout sang out for a sail to windward, and then another, and then a third and a fourth. By this time the strangers were known by their rig to be Moorish.

Spanish naval doctrine, which Genoa, being in the Spanish orbit, had adopted, prescribed that two ships should not shrink from engaging three; three ships, four; four ships, five; and five ships, seven. One to four, however, was impossible odds, and no shipmaster was to accept such unequal combat. Ser Guido, therefore, turned tail and fled downwind in earnest, the foe in pursuit. The more modern galleys from the Barbary coast made better speed. Well before dusk they were able to open fire.

La Loba found herself in peril. Even if the bow armament of her pursuers had not outranged the two falconets on her quarters - and in fact they did not by much - it cast a heavier weight of metal. For a time the people on the Genovese poop watched the splashes as the hostile shot fell short; then the missiles began to plunge into the sea abeam, closer and closer.

The bow guns of galleys, as has been indicated, were fixed along the long axes of the hulls. They could not be trained around in azimuth, although wedges could be introduced to vary the range. Aiming, therefore, was in the main done by maneuvering the vessel herself, and not all gunners were adept at the art.

A shot crashed through La Loba's buttocks. It did little damage below, except to some stores, and the carpenter began emergency repairs to the hull at once. But another projectile hit home; it plowed through the group standing on the poop, and the galley lost her patron, her pilot, and a pair of seamen.

Luck did not immediately favor the African gunner again; but it was only a question of time before the Genovese craft would have to turn and face desperate odds, be battered into helplessness, or yield. But in the last hour, the lookout hailed the deck once more with the report of sails dead ahead; and as they closed, a pair of Spanish galleons hove into view.

To a galleon immobilized by calm, by stranding, or by being locked in combat with another ship, galleys are dangerous antagonists. They can attack the almost undefended bow or stern, and at close range destroy the ship's framework with repeated salvos from their light armament. Or they can board and overwhelm the defenders by sheer weight of manpower. But in enough wind for steerageway the ship's heavier weapons can be brought to bear, and batter the galleys to pieces (lightly constructed for speed as rowed vessels must be) while they are still at a distance. And there was a good sailing breeze now blowing. When the Moors perceived the change in their enemy's strength, they fled, to be lost in the ensuing darkness.

"We seem able to manage the Moors," Spinola remarked to Lieutenant Ricci at supper.

The other nodded. "Given an equal chance, we can stand up to them. But when we finish them, as, by God's grace, I hope we soon shall, we have a more dangerous enemy in the north."

"Do you mean the Dutch?"

"I mean the English! They are aiming at - and perhaps winning - the mastery of the sea."

La Loba was sailing before a moderate wind. Her fore and main sails were drawing well; her oars were shipped but lashed immovably above the water.

"Why do we fix the oars thus, signor?" Federico asked Lieutenant Ricci. "They don't add to our speed when the men are not rowing."

"As a matter of fact, they do, very slightly; they catch a little wind, as well as some seas, when as now we are running free. And they serve as a collective outrigger, making for additional stability if the helmsman gets careless and lets her quarter swing around, or if a sudden knock-down puff comes from abeam."

"Is that a danger?"

"Not a great one, under ordinary conditions. But these craft have very little reserve flotation. In the event of a capsize with open hatches (which, to be sure, seldom occurs), a relatively small amount of sea water pouring in would overwhelm her."

"When do we take this precaution?"

"On a reach, with the wind more or less on the beam, the oars would impede her progress with their drag. And if there is a high sea running, it can work the oars so mightily that a broken telaro may result."

"So when we need this protection most, we cannot use it?"

"That's right."

"A paradox!"

"There are many such. For instance, there are many harbors whose entrances are impracticable in bad weather; when you need them most, you can't get in."

It had been a beautiful blue and gold morning. But Federico noticed the captain casting thoughtful eyes at the heavens; and when a few clouds appeared in the south, he gave command to prepare for dirty weather.

They were, as it happened, farther out at sea than usual. Storm was a threat to all shipping, but the lightly built galleys were most vulnerable. The wind soon hauled from east-southeast to south, and began to blow harder, while a grayness overspread the sky. The rowers unshipped their oars and lashed them lengthwise on the benches. The motion became more violent. Seas came close to the deck.

"Are we going to shorten sail?" Federico asked a sailor.

"I don't know. That depends on whether the captain decides to run for port. If he does, we'll shorten sail, as you say, and make a dash for it. But I think we're too far out, and in any case he won't risk being driven onto a lee shore. I think he'll ride it out at sea. In that case, he'll simply furl all sail, and probably lower the masts as well."

Which is what he did. With her top-hamper down, the galley rode better in the mounting seaway. He put her head to, paid out timbers on a bridle from the bow to serve as sea anchor, raised the steering sweep, and let her ride.

The sea became more boisterous as afternoon waned. The sun sank sullenly in an orange haze, and darkness came early. It was a wild night. On almost each wave the bow started to sag off, until the rode brought it up with a jerk. The ship pitched and rolled, to the misery of more than a few, including Federico. But he was less badly off than some, and pride drove him to stand his watches, despite occasional hurried trips to the ship's side. Now and again a wave sent a shallow river across the deck, but good caulking prevented more than a little leakage through it. Some water found its way through the seams of the hull, but pumps easily controlled it.

But morning brought the sight of endless combers, which looked even higher than they were, swarming upon the galley from the horizon. They raised the vessel in turn by both ends and by her middle, threatening to break the slender hull in two. But she stood it; and by noon the gale had begun to abate. During the night they got a rag of sail on her, and the following day found her bound for port under a whole sail breeze.

This, as much as his first battle, was Federico's testing, and his officers were pleased with his conduct.

Not long after the autumnal equinox, the fiercer and more frequent gales of winter laid up all galleys for the season. Federico went back to Seville for the last time, with the invitation of Ser Guido to rejoin him for the next summer's cruise.

There followed another winter of study; of what military practice the environs of Seville afforded; of wining and wenching, both in moderation; of completion of growth to goodly stature. The boy had become a fairly tall, well built, handsome young man, with an air of strength and of quiet confidence about him. Men began to follow his lead.

111. A Sip of the Wine.

I only sail to set the country free,
And rescue lives in direst jeopardy.

From Galera real, Juan de Mallara.

With the approach of sailing weather Federico returned to Genoa and a family council to determine his future. Or so his family believed; he had already determined it. His elder brother, Ambrogio, was now the recognized head of the household, as he was head of the Spinola family bank. Their mother spoke first.

"Federico, you have had three years of study at the university, although from what I have been able to learn, you are not much nearer to the service of the church. It is time for you to put aside childish things, and dedicate yourself unreservedly to the service of God."

"Mother, I quite agree that the time has come for me to take up a man's role in the world, and this I am eager to do. And I shall always serve God, I hope. But there are many ways of serving Him, and by no means are all of these in the Church. Who serves his king, serves God.

"And, mother, I feel called to serve the king. My taste has always run to the arts of war; and last summer, I think I may say - at least, my officers said - that I showed the ability to bear the sword with honor to myself and profit to the king. All of my desire is toward this end. Mother, one does not try to make a racing steed into a plough horse. I have neither the temperament nor the desire to be a priest - or a bishop, or even a cardinal."

"You are too young, my son, to make such a decision. And you know too little of the world. Do you think that all a soldier does is fight? Believe me, son, he may do almost none of that. Statecraft and politics, for which I think you would have little taste, may make up much of a soldier's career."

"I know that you are right, mother; but they may make up still more of the duties of a churchman, especially of one who has attained the rank which I know you hope for, for me. And if I wait until I know the world, I shall spend my whole life in preparation for things that will never be done. I might as well tell you that my mind is made up, and that nothing can change it."

"It was your father's purpose that you wear the cloth."

"Unhappily for all of us, my father died before he could know what manner of son he had sired."

Ambrogio intervened. "Men of the cloth have directed armies, Federico."

"True. But I do not care to be another Pope Julius."

Donna Spinola tried again. "Are you not a believer in tradition, Federico? For generations, we have given a younger son to the Church."

"Traditions must sometimes give way to altered circumstances, mother. And it is not my fault that the Lord took my father at an early age. Had He not, there might have been a yet younger son for the priesthood."

Ambrogio spoke again. "Mother, I think that we must yield on this. As long as my brother would embark on a course that bids fair to bring honor to the family name, I think we must give him our blessing."

Uncle Ascanio opened his mouth for the first time. "Sister, be persuaded. I can see that this is to be. But, nephew, I do not think you should flout us entirely. Let me counsel you. There is no future in the galleys. They are coming to be, more and more, a mere adjunct - and a decreasingly important adjunct - to the fleets of galleons. And they, in their turn, are merely adjunct to the army. So have a military career if you must, but be ruled by me - go to Flanders. There, in the service of the great Alessandro Farnese, is the foremost school of warfare of our time. The family's interest can procure you an appointment."

Ambrogio nodded. "That is good advice, Federico."

"I recognize that it is, although I have some reservations regarding the role of the navy, and even of the galleys. I shall do as you say, uncle. But first give me one more season to nail down my understanding of ships. Even if the navy be, as you say, less important than the land forces, no serious student of warfare can afford to ignore it." And so it was decided.

Federico rejoined his squadron, but this time as gentleman volunteer in the Capitana under Guido Tomassini as commodore. Don Felipe Gutierrez, most senior of the captains, sailed in the rear as second in command.

With the Capitana in her usual position in the van, the galleys left the confines of the harbor, and at once, by order, formed line abeam with the Capitana in the center. They were massed with sail or oar room, but not much more.

A white banner was waved forward and aft in the Capitana, following which, a few minutes later, an arquebus was discharged. At once the galleys changed formation to line astern. La Loba, as the weakest, was near the center in all conditions, that she might be more readily aided by her sisters.

"There are many signals, Signor Spinola," said the sailing master, "and you must learn them all. Signals may be made with oars or sails; with gestures, brandishing of weapons, display of flags or pennants of different colors hoisted or handled in various ways. There will be sounds of trumpet, of drum, or of other instruments, or of the guns. At night, lanterns or firebrands may be exhibited."

For days and weeks the commodore kept them at practice, assuming, maintaining, and in various ways changing formation, under oars and sail, in all conditions of weather, by day and by night. The cadets and junior officers were instructed in the advantages and disadvantages of each fashion of closing with the enemy.

"When do we finish practising and do what we came for?" Federico asked Lieutenant Celebrezze one day.

"As to the first part of your question, the answer is, never! No commander ever feels that his ship, squadron, or fleet has perfected its routines and needs no further practice. Even if all goes without a hitch, there is always the time to be lessened. As to the second part, whenever we sight a foe, we're ready to engage."

It was mainly in waters distant from her coast that Liguria suffered from the depredations of the pirates. Genoa particularly, and her smaller cities to a lesser extent, lived by a far-flung commerce. In any waters the roving craft of the Barbary states might seize upon helpless merchantmen.

The Turkish disaster at Lepanto, almost a score of years before, should have made the Mediterranean safe for European shipping. It had not done so for two reasons. The hostilities and jealousies of the Christian powers had caused the alliance to break up within the year after their great victory; whereas the Turk on the other hand had demonstrated a remarkable will and ability to replace his losses and threaten Europe again, albeit not as critically as before. So Tomassini did not long ply the waters of the Gulf of Liguria, but sailed southward for the richer pickings of the Strait of Sicily.

He snapped up a Tunisian raider in the first week, but thereafter had to put into one of the Sicilian ports several times for supplies. Then he chased a Tunisian that was too swift for capture.

It may have been she who was responsible for an Algerian squadron that appeared on the second morning following. The Genovese were sailing in line abeam with a moderate wind when the enemy appeared over the horizon ahead. They were six ships to Tomassini's five, and they were rowing in a double file. The Genovese at once went to action stations.

"An ideal target for a demilune formation," Celebrezze remarked. "The commodore will get the galleys under oars, with a faster beat at both wings, so we'll hit them like the horned head of a bull."

"I don't think so," Lieutenant d'Agostino replied. "I think on the contrary that he'll order an arc formation, with the center ahead; the Moors will probably form line abeam and then we'll be all set for a break-through."

But the minutes wore on, and the galleys were still under sail. The two fleets were two thousand, then fifteen hundred, then one thousand fathoms apart.

There was the smoke of a Moorish gun, followed by its report; and the Moorish formation changed to line abeam.

"The commodore is signaling for the oar," called one of the cadets, and a moment later, "Close the intervals!" Galleys under oar needed less sea room between them than galleys under sail. Then, "Full speed!"

"Open fire!" was the next command, and the Genovese guns spoke.

"Look at that!" exclaimed d'Agostino in admiration. "He picked the moment when all of our ships were converging, so our fire was concentrated on the middle of the Moorish line!" And indeed the central two Moorish ships had suffered casualties, as could be seen even at that distance, and one of their guns had been dismounted.

But the enemy were firing too. Hits could be seen on some of the Christian vessels, and men were down. San Giovanni and another Genovese managed to get in a second shot before the fleets came together.

The intervals between the Africans were rather large. Tomassini signalled for a pass-through, and then for the hoisting of a single sail on each mainmast.

"Bow gunners! Hold your fire!" called Tomassini. "Others, fire at will!"

The Genovese slipped neatly through the Moorish line, then, needing no further order, wheeled sharply to attack. The Moors of course swung around to face them, but by reason of their commodore's tactic, the Christians, sheeting home their mainsails, had the wind assist by blowing their sterns around; they completed the maneuver faster than the foe could meet it.

"Fire!" commanded the Genovese captains, and at a range of only a few yards poured a devastating mass of shot into the crowded African decks. The result was frightful.

Before the Moorish troops could reform, the European boarders were upon them. They flooded irresistibly over the African decks in yelling, slashing, thrusting waves; and death was in their weapons.

Not all of them. Two of the Genovese ships had not raised their storm sails - the art of signalling was in its infancy - and their opponents had been as fast on the turn as they. On one of these, it was the Moors who did the boarding; the other found herself engaged with two enemies at once, and her people were desperately trying to maintain a defense. It would have been in vain; but three of their squadron, having won their engagements, came to her aid and that of the fifth vessel; and the day was theirs.

The victory had come dear.

Dead and wounded Moors were consigned to the sea, the survivors of the Moorish crews enslaved. Christian galley slaves were freed; the others changed one master for another. It made little difference to them.

The remainder of the season was less eventful. Twice they arrived on the scene in time to drive a pirate from his prey. Once they raided a Moorish coastal village. It netted them little of use, but they destroyed the livelihoods of some scores of impoverished peasants.

In late September, Lieutenant d'Agostino lost his grip while descending from the masthead, where he had been inspecting some gear. He was taken ashore with a not too badly broken back - that is to say, he had control over his legs. The injury would probably heal, although not soon. The captain temporarily appointed Federico to be third officer.

It was the last cruise of the season. To celebrate at once the approaching end of a successful summer's operations and the day of his patron saint, the commodore had set aside the makings of a cream pudding for the officers' mess. This was now broached.

It turned out to be tainted. Within hours, almost all of the officer complement of the flagship were groaning with severe cramps, and running back and forth from their berths to the heads, where the movement of their bowels was often still more agonizing. Federico had happened to be carrying a message to another ship, and so had missed the meal and was alone unaffected.

In line astern, the squadron entered a sound. Scarcely had it done so, when one, then another, then a line of Moorish ships appeared, transiting the pass in the reverse direction. The Genovese column was cutting the projection of their course, so that the two fleets were on opposite and slightly converging courses.

The ailing commodore hoisted a "Follow me!" signal. Federico was assigned to the bow station. The other officers physically fit for duty clustered at the stern. And then it happened.

A green and overzealous powder monkey brought up from the hold more ammunition for the stern-chasers than was required. Somehow, the gunner's smoldering punk touched it. There was a flash and a roar, and bodies fell. "The commodore's down!" somebody shouted.

"Who's in command?" asked Federico.

There was a moment's hesitation. Then, "You are, sir!"

Even for the quick-witted Genovese it took a moment to digest this stunning information. Then he made a rapid survey of the deck; most of the crew were on their feet, and the hull was not seriously damaged. And then he realized three things.

The enemy had continued to row forward in line astern. The steering sweep of Federico's galley had somehow become wedged with its blade slightly to starboard, so that the ship was describing an arc in the water, first slightly away from, then as slightly toward, the enemy line. And decision would have to be a matter of seconds.

Federico of course knew that the command of the squadron now devolved upon the senior captain, Gutierrez, who was at the rear of the line. But before Gutierrez could be notified, establish his authority, make a plan, and act, precious time would be lost.

Federico looked around. "Signal quartermaster!"

"Yes, sir!"

"Signal, 'All ships turn to starboard!'" And then, "Engage the enemy!"

Almost immediately thereafter, in what he recognized as lunule formation, his squadron was racing toward the Moors, two out-thrust horns on its flanks, the center slightly astern. Not for nothing had the youthful lieutenant spent so many days in the library at Seville. He knew the formation as the "Implexa" of ancient galley warfare, and as that with which Leon VI, Emperor of Byzantium, had won a notable victory. This was a very effective form of attack given two premises: That the most lateral and advanced vessels, those of the horns, be the strongest, and that there be a reserve in the rear.

Unfortunately, the latter of these conditions did not exist.

If the maneuver were successful, it would be a glorious victory. If not - but he must not think of that.

The Moors, meantime, had likewise executed a right turn, and the two squadrons, about equal in strength, were closing rapidly. Federico dared give no further orders to the other ships; but the captains knew their duty. At point blank range as many of the ships as could bring their guns to bear poured their fire into the central galleys of the Moors. The bow of one disintegrated, and the final shots of the secondary batteries made her decks a bloody ruin. By the time the squadrons closed, she was out of the fight. The Genovese too had suffered, but all vessels were still fit for combat.

At the flanks too there had been heavy exchanges of artillery fire. The Capitana, damaged by the explosion, and without her officers, could not exert her proper strength. The Moors directed a heavy fire onto her decks, and then the boarders poured into her. Federico and his men were forced back, desperately as they resisted. At the hearth they made a stand, until the young lieutenant went down under a blow to the head. Without an officer on his feet, the crew surrendered.

In the rest of the squadron it was a different story. The Genovese center held. At the right flank, one galley managed to row around the African line, and attack one after another of the enemies from the lightly defended rear. Scarcely had the fallen Federico awakened to misery and shame when his fellows came storming aboard to retake the ship.

He returned to a hero's welcome.

Don Felipe Maria Magdalena de Medina Gutierrez was beside himself with fury. A Genovese upstart, a mere acting lieutenant, had usurped the authority that had rightfully been his, had stolen the chance for glory, and, worst of all, had achieved a brilliant success! And even so, had had, in the event, to be rescued (together with his ship) by him, Don Felipe!

There was a court of inquiry. Don Felipe saw to that.

"Were you not aware, Senor Spinola, that when the commodore was disabled, the officer next in seniority became squadron commander?"

"I knew that, illustrissimo."

"Then how dared you, a mere acting lieutenant, arrogate to yourself the privilege and responsibility of command?"

"There was no time, illustrissimo, for an orderly succession. If I had tried to proceed in such fashion, there would have been no effective command, and no coordination whatsoever, at the moment of contact."

"Did you consider yourself a trained and qualified tactician?"

"By no means, illustrissimo. But I have been taught that any commander is better than none."

Gutierrez had some influence, but the Spinolas were important, too. Federico was cleared. Gutierrez brooded on his wrongs.

There are people on whom Fortune forever turns her back.

Throughout his career, Gutierrez had missed his chance. He had never been around when great things were being done. He had been a member of the ill-fated Armada of 1588, but no one won glory in that venture, and Gutierrez was lucky to have survived. He had been an officer in a galley of Portocarrero's squadron at Cadiz, where his ship had taken part in the inept attempt at defense against Raleigh. Otherwise, through no fault of his own, he had hung about the fringes of great achievements without ever having had a chance to win distinction.

For this he blamed not merely ill luck, but machinations on the part of authorities in Madrid. Right or wrong, he was convinced of this; and his temper, never very amiable, had grown worse with the desperation of approaching old age.

But Federico had tasted the sweet, heady draft of command, and the even sweeter one, of success.

In the Palazzo Spinola there was no more talk of the Church.

When the ship was laid up for the winter, Tomassini offered to make Federico's lieutenancy permanent. The young man thanked him, but demurred. "I'm off to Flanders and the duke, excellency!" he explained.

Commodore Tomassini tried to change his mind. "You will do well there. In fact, you will do well anywhere. But in the army you will have thousands of well born, able, diligent men as rivals for honor and promotion. In the galleys, there will be relatively little competition, and none, I think, that would threaten your success. You have a talent for the seafaring life. Remember what Caesar said - "Better to be first in a village of Gaul than second in Rome."

"I think your point well made, excellency. But I wish to learn something about war on land. It will make me, I think, a better naval officer when I come back to the ships."

IV. School of the Soldier

Are these, perchance, the famous ones, the strong,
The warlike men who troubled far the world,
And, furious, shook the powerful realms of earth?
Ode on the death of Don Sebastian. From the
Spanish of Fernando de Herrera

In the heat and pressure of great affairs, character can undergo strange metamorphoses.

Somber, fanatical, cruel, treacherous, unforgiving, and relentless as a wolf on the trail - such was Philip II of Spain. It might readily be assumed that he had been born as some monstrous malformation, some malign sport of nature on the human spirit.

Such was not the case. Philip had been a generous and open-hearted youth. When his father, the Emperor Charles V, had punished German mercenaries fighting for the French by hacking off their feet, young Philip had pleaded, vainly, for mercy. When his bride, Mary of England, had doomed her heretics to agonizing death, he had sought to soften her heart.

But time and power had darkened in the young man's soul all that was light, and poisoned the wellsprings of generosity. Unsuccessful in his bid for the imperial crown that had been his father's, he was remorseless in enforcing his kingly claims. Disloyalty to the king he equated with disobedience to God, whose earthly representative, for temporal power, he considered himself.

However pure be the inception of a religion on high, it is transmitted, interpreted, and promulgated by mortal men. Priests of all degrees, ministers, rabbis, mullahs, Brahmins, even prophets are but men, good and evil, wise and foolish. The things of the spirit pass through the minds, worse, the mouths, worst, the hands of these men; and like sunlight shining through clouded and unclean filters, they are darkened in the passage. To this the Catholic Church is no exception. Its darkest aberration was the Inquisition—the "Congregation of the Holy Office, by the Mercy of God, Cardinals of the Holy Roman Church, Inquisitors-General throughout the Christian Commonwealth against Heretical Pravity." They found the pravity. And nowhere burned their torch hotter than in brooding Spain.

Absolutism of the royal power and fanatical devotion to the Church became the twin touchstones of Phillip's existence. The expansion of his kingdom in Europe and the stamping out of heresy wherever it dared show its face were the lifelong obsessions of the king. For them he was willing to ruin his people.

Let it be said in justice that Catholics had been burned in Protestant England and elsewhere. It was Elizabeth's boast that although their priests were banned, Catholics enjoyed freedom of conscience in her realm. This was literally true; but they paid for it with a ruinous tax.

And Jews were practically everywhere recurrently fair game for lovers of torture and death.

For thirteen years the Spanish Netherlands had been in revolt. The edicts fostering the Inquisition had proved intolerable even to the Catholics.

That war has been represented as one between Spain and the Catholic south Netherlands on the one side, and the Protestant north on the other. Actually there were initially no more Protestants north than south, and in neither region did they constitute a majority. It was the king's bigotry and despotism that led to the estrangement of Netherland subjects of both faiths and of both speeches, Flemish and French. The cruelties of the infamous Duke of Alva had fanned the flames of resentment to an inextinguishable fury. And so when Alva had gone and the king had entrusted the high command to Alexander Farnese, the redoubtable Duke of Parma, it had been a greatly shrunken Netherlands which Parma had received. Only the French-speaking Walloon provinces of the south and Flemish Drente in the northeast had still held for the king.

Of course there were practical reasons as well as dynastic for Philip's fight for the Low Countries. These were the fertility of the soil, the industry of the inhabitants, the richness of their fisheries, their widely borne commerce, their militarily and commercially strategic position at the mouth of the Rhine, and, of immediate value, the incomparable gun founders of the Walloon provinces.

Parma had added Low Country bays to his laurels of Lepanto. He had captured Maastricht after an obstinate resistance, and surprised and taken Gortryk. By military or diplomatic action Oudenarde, Eindhoven, Dunkirk, Greve, Neusz, Gelder, Sluys, Gertruydenberg, and Yper had fallen to his sword. Brussels and Antwerp had been his greatest gifts to his royal master.

Now only the provinces about the Zuyder Zee and the adjacent islands of Zealand still defied the authority of the king. Little land enough; but here rivers, lakes, and arms of the sea split the terrain. And the Beggars of the Sea controlled the tideswept estuaries with their ships. They succored the Dutch at need while denying supplies to the Spanish-held towns. In the free Netherlands there were prosperity and pride. And if it must be conceded that, although against the wishes and exhortations of their leaders, the now largely Protestant north too had become intolerant of schismatic worship in public, religious conscience was still free, and the stake and the faggot were not in use.

In the south where the cities had submitted to the king, a sullen peace existed. But where the troops of Spain had stormed a town, not a virgin or a guilder had remained. There is almost nothing worse than war - except an intolerable peace, which leads to a bigger and bloodier war when the explosion comes.

It was in such a war that young Spinola presented himself at the quarters of Parma's adjutant. His letters won him a warm welcome, and assignment to a cavalry regiment. On the next day there was an audience with the great man himself, who, after some complimentary words concerning the galley exploits, gave Spinola a piece of advice.

"You are in a Spanish army now, Messer Spinola, and are like to serve his majesty for a long time. Prejudice exists here as everywhere, and it is well to eliminate unimportant possibilities of friction. If I were you, I should spell my name henceforth in the Spanish fashion." So Parma's newest lieutenant became Federigo, and will be so named in the balance of this history.

Spinola had come too late to study with the great general. The Parma who had aroused the admiration of Europe was no longer what he had been. He was worn out in the service of an ungrateful master. His health was broken. Worse, he who had devoted himself wholeheartedly to his king was no longer trusted; maddening accusations of treason - not, to be sure, acknowledged by the treacherous Philip - dimmed his hard won glory. Not least, the overweening king drew him and his forces from the main theater of war to dissipate them in the side-show of campaigns in France.

So Breda was lost to the royal forces, and Zutphen, Deventer, Groningen, Delfzyl, and other strategic places.

Nevertheless, the young Spinola learned about war. He learned, as all soldiers learn, that war is principally boredom, with mud, wet, and cold in the winter, dirt, heat and vermin in the summer, and at all seasons disease and death. There were marches and countermarches, sieges and the raising of sieges, and wait, wait, wait.

He learned of the politics of war, as well. Elizabeth of England and Henry of France were involved in the struggle, too - now openly, now less so. Once he marched with a vainly protesting Parma to France, and there beheld the masterly tactics whereby Parma outmaneuvered Protestant Henry's stronger army without a battle, and saved Paris for the Church. Once (only once, alas!) there was the opportunity for the young man to distinguish himself in a skirmish.

Perhaps Federigo learned less from friendly Parma than from a Dutch enemy. Maurice of Nassau, son of the martyred Willem the Silent, was a new kind of soldier. Just out of his schooling, the youngster evoked patronizing smiles from the men who had spent years in camp and field. The young man was above all a student of mathematics. For the dogmas and doctrines of the past, he substituted an engineer's analysis of problems of transport and siege. Where Parma's last foe, Henry of France and Navarre, had exhibited a reckless courage based on sheer love of adventure, Maurice was equally daring but only when, for instance, it came to a reconnaissance which he felt demanded his very own eyes. Equally with his sire he was devoted to his country's cause, but he faced military problems with a cold, objective mind that brooked no sentimental confusion.

One of the first things he did (and which Federigo was subsequently to imitate on a small scale) was to reform the organization of the army. Units and weapons were standardized as never before. He drafted new pay regulations so that officers could no longer pocket any of their men's pay, or present imaginary rolls on which to collect. What he did, in short, was to create the modern army.

And he used it - used it well. Breda was taken by a daring trick. Steenbergen too, and a number of strong points on the Maas, fell to the young Stadtholder. Parma came raging back from France, but Zutfen, Deventer, and Delfzyl fell to the Dutch. And after the onset of cold weather, which normally put an end to warfare, Maurice seized Hulst and Nymwegen.

Luck had kept Spinola far from each action; that is to say, each defeat. His chance came after two frustrating years in the field.

The fortress of Rhodsenburg lay strategically close to the important city of Nymwegen. Maurice with his army was in the north across two wide and deep rivers. Parma decided to strike. He crossed the Waal, which protected the fortress to the south, and prepared for an easy conquest.

But the garrison of Rhodsenburg, though small, was no such easy conquest as the duke had imagined. After pouring into the enemy an intense artillery fire, Parma sent his troops to storm the wall. To his consternation, they were repulsed with great loss.

Maurice meanwhile had wasted no time. Immediately on receiving word of the prince's appearance before the stronghold, he abandoned further conquests and marched rapidly to the relief of Rhodsenburg. Within a week he confronted Parma.

Maurice sent a small picked force of cavalry to reconnoiter. Parma sent against them his own lancers under Nicelli, whose adjutant was Spinola, and a large force of other Italian and Spanish cavalry. The Netherland States' troops fled before the much larger force, and the royal cavalry pursued.

Suddenly Spinola became aware that they were following the enemy into a narrowing area between two groves, and he reined in his horse, shouting to Nicelli, beside him, "A trap! A trap!"

Nicelli gave him an irritated look and beckoned him on. But at that moment the fleeing horsemen were seen to draw rein, and attack in turn. Even as Spinola perceived this, a devastating small arms fire on the left emptied many saddles, and from the right a larger cavalry troop made for the royal soldiery. In a few minutes the two forces were hotly engaged, with Maurice's pikemen hurrying in to bring support. Nicelli himself was surrounded, disarmed and taken.

It was Federigo who rallied the bewildered cavalry, led them in a breakthrough and brought the terrified troopers back to their lines. They had left at the ambush sixty killed and one hundred fifty prisoners. Parma attributed the salvaging of the force to the quick-wittedness of Federigo Spinola.

He raised the siege of Knodsenburg forthwith.

"Spinola," he said shortly thereafter, "you have demonstrated understanding of the field, courage, and the ability to think fast and clearly. I am prepared to offer you a regiment, of foot or horse as you desire."

Federigo fumbled for words. Then, "I deeply thank your highness. But I have been thinking that I can better serve the king at sea. Give me a post on one of his majesty's ships and let me aid in harassing Dutch and English shipping instead."

"Be it so."

So Spinola found himself a lieutenant in Asuncion, a galliot - that is to say, a ship resembling a galleon, but smaller. And serve he did against the English and the Dutch; harassing their commerce, and taking defenseless merchantmen, to the profit of his royal master and the dismay of their owners. But the memorable incident in this service came otherwise.

The dregs of humanity from all nations had drifted together

at Dunkirk. Here they had organized themselves into ship's crews, stolen ships, and set up as pirates.

And as such, they outdid the freebooters of Tunis and Algiers. They respected no flag. In small swift vessels they searched out and pounced upon the hardworking mariners of the northern seas, carried their prey by force of numbers and sheer ferocity, and took their plunder. But that was not all. They nailed the hapless seamen to their own decks or chained them in the rigging and let them drift wheresoever death might find them. Or, if they wanted to keep a ship for themselves, they simply threw the wretched crew overboard.

Spinola, now promoted to Patron, second in command in the vessel, was cruising off Brest when they espied a large Spanish merchantman being set upon by two pirates. As he closed, they moved in to attack. Had either of the Dunkirkers been alone, she would not have dared such combat. Together, however, they felt they could overwhelm their assailant, and not only save their prize, but capture a handy fighting ship for their further ventures.

The ensuing movements of the three ships were like a ballet. The pirates tried to keep between their assailant and their prey, in order that the former would hold her fire for fear of hitting the Spaniard. In this they were partially successful, and got in more shots at Asuncion than she at them. She sustained damage, and casualties.

Then, one on each side, they closed and grappled.

The clash of weapons is daunting enough; so is the war cry of a foe. But to these was added the crash of guns firing into packed masses of human beings. Many men were sick with fear. But almost all were able to put a good face upon it, and to conceal the weakness from friend and foe. The boarders poured in - men reckless of death or wounds, trained in a hundred combats.

Federigo happened to be at the bow when the rush came. In a moment he and those with him were slashing, thrusting, parrying for their lives. After a few minutes he became aware that the pirates were retreating, then that they had gained considerable but not enough success aft, and were carrying back the captain of Asuncion to one of their vessels.

Without even thinking he shouted, "Follow me, men!" and was first over the rail and onto the enemy deck. By dint of desperate fighting the party fought its way to the captain, then continued until the pirate vessel was in their hands. The other cut loose and departed.

Spinola was the hero of the day. While the captain slowly recovered ashore from his wounds Federigo became commanding officer.

Only reluctantly would Philip give up his dream of controlling both France and Spain, to the end of sweeping heresy out of Europe. He blamed Parma for the defeats in the Low Countries that he himself had brought about by his French adventures. But Parma, prematurely aged by a life of hardship in his monarch's service, died in time to avert the disgrace of dismissal.

Fuentes became commander of the Spanish in Flanders. He retook Cambrai, Hulst, and Calais. But Maurice cleared the northeast of the royal forces.

In the twenty-seventh year of his life, Federigo was a guest one spring day at a wealthy home in Antwerp. He was in the garden with his host and hostess when a strange dog found his way in and set the lady's cat scampering up a tree. It could not be induced to descend. The guest volunteered to bring it down.

At the highest point of his climb he glanced over the wall. In the garden next door a cherry tree had been shedding its petals; the trunk was standing as though in a drift of pink snow. In this, her back against the tree, a comely young lady was seated and reading a book. She wore a white dress. The combination of pink and white amid the surrounding green, with touches such as her scarlet girdle and golden hair, presented a picture that was utterly charming.

"Who is the young lady?" Federigo asked his hosts.

"Alisette de Vlaine. She comes of a very distinguished family, and a wealthy one."

"Would you arrange an introduction?"

"The governor is holding a reception on Saturday. Her family will certainly attend. That will give us the opportunity."

The young man was captivated. On every available occasion he spent his time with the de Vlaines. They welcomed his suit; his too was an ancient and distinguished family, and as a banking firm it put him beyond suspicion of mere fortune hunting - not that that was held so reprehensible in that day and milieu. He fell deeper and deeper in love.

And he had reason to believe that the lady reciprocated his feeling. Certainly she gave every sign of pleasure when he appeared and seemed stimulated to brightness and a happy appearance. They exchanged the usual histories and confidences of lovers (somewhat handicapped, of course, by the circumstance that a well-brought-up girl of good family never saw a young man alone). He dreamed delicious dreams of a blissful future with Alisette as loving bride, and ultimately happy mother of a new generation of Spinolas.

V. The Shadowed Road to the Sea

Grace and beauty had the maid.
Could anything more lovely be?
Sailor, you who live on ships,
Did you ever see
Any ship or sail or star
As beautiful as she?

Song. From the Spanish of Gil Vicente.

The Demoiselle Alisette de Vlaine was the daughter and granddaughter of men who were prudent and wise. While she could relish sweet nothings as well as her less gifted sisters, she had an appetite for stronger fare.

"Tell me," she asked, "when really do you believe that the conquest of the lowlands will be completed?

"The way it is being carried on, never!" Federigo replied.

Her raised eyebrows invited him to explain. And he found himself thinking aloud, just as though he were conversing with a brother-in-arms.

"On an equal basis, no troops can stand against the Spanish infantry. But it cannot fight on an equal basis. The Netherlanders make brilliant use of their chief resource - the sea. We can block the roads, but they supply by ship. When they need more men, they meet the need on the water. Our armies must wait and wait for wagon trains of supplies, but the enemy transport is quick and easy. Food is not spoiled or pilfered; powder does not deteriorate in storm. The troops they bring are unwearied and ready to fight."

"Why do we not do the same?"

"They have well fortified bases and ports of supply. We have none - at least, none here. The ports of Flanders once held much of the shipping of Europe. But they have silted up, and are no longer usable - some will not even float a fisherman at low tide."

"Is there no way of making them available to ships once more? Cannot they be dredged?"

"It would not be practicable, madonna. But," brightening suddenly, "there is a possibility. I have sailed in the galleys of Genoa. These are ships of shallow draft - they must be, for they must be light, that the rowers may drive them. That much dredging we could do. Of course, their capacity is far below that of the sailing merchantman. But we could multiply their number; they are cheaper to build than the great ships."

He warmed to his subject. "And they have another advantage. Your great ship may be wind bound in harbor for days and weeks. Even if the wind is favorable, if the harbor mouth itself necessitates a windward leg, the ship may be unable to negotiate the channel. But the galley can be rowed right into the teeth of the wind. Once free of the land, she can sail to leeward or be rowed to windward at will."

"Can she fight well?"

"In calms she can lie off and pound her opponent to pieces. Or, a squadron of galleys, avoiding the lanes of fire of the big guns, can approach and overwhelm a ship with manpower. When the ship has steerageway, however, the galley has no chance against her broadside."

The demoiselle gazed at him thoughtfully. She saw a man to admire, handsome, with the brown hair of Liguria setting off a smiling face. Perhaps he was the man!

On his part, Federigo attributed to her the intelligence she had led him to exhibit. As we all do. But he was not far wrong.

Federigo spent many hours thinking about galleys and the Netherland war. He made computations as to loads, expenses, dredging and wharf construction.

He also spent hours thinking about Alisette.

One day he requested an audience with the then governor, Archduke Cardinal Alberto. The Archduke heard him with interest.

"I think you are right," he said when the younger man had expounded his views. "But I am not the one to make such a decision. I will send you to the king."

That evening Count de Vlaine received Federigo in a lofty, ornate room.

"I have, of course, been aware of your interest in my daughter," he replied to the young man's suit. "I have heard good opinions of you from the army; and, of course, I realize the greatness of your house." There was talk of a dowry and other financial and practical details, and then Federigo was permitted to speak to Alisette alone.

It would be nice to be able to report on the beautiful and poetic language in which he couched his proposal - a formality, of course, since marriage was considered too important a matter to be left to the determination of young people when there were families to do the arranging. (His, of course, was far away). But candor compels the confession that the fluent, well educated, debonair scion of one of the great families of Europe hemmed and stammered like any schoolboy having to recite on an imperfectly understood topic. She heard him out with patience, however, and sent him home in the delighted, superworldly mood of an accepted wooer.

The Cardinal's letter, the Spinola name and the reports of Federigo's services procured him an audience with Philip II. But in this year of 1596 Philip was preparing another armada against England, and Federigo was kept cooling his heels while the one hundred twenty-eight ships and seventeen thousand soldiers were prepared and set sail for Ireland. But almost immediately a tempest smote the fleet; forty ships with five thousand troops went to the bottom of the sea. The rest returned to Spain to refit and to renew the attempt in the spring. Meanwhile, the hate-obsessed monarch ordered his governor in the Low Countries to collect an army at Calais, and send it to invade England in such small craft as might be available. Whom the gods destroy they first make mad.

Under the circumstances, the king had no ear for a young Genovese captain's hare-brained ideas. So back to Flanders went Federigo, disappointed.

The city of Amiens was one of the most important in northern France. More, it was only three days journey from Paris, and between it and the capital were only open fields, no natural barriers being anywhere about. If Spanish forces could capture it, Paris, which meant the French monarchy, would be in danger.

Hernan Telle de Lanza, Spanish governor of the city of Dourlens, was a little, dried-up, yellowish man but one of energy and boldness. He conceived a plan for the taking of Amiens. One morning, when most of its burghers were in church (they relied on themselves to garrison the city), a party of some dozen and a half of de Lanza's soldiers, disguised as peasants, appeared at the gate. One of their bags of nuts became untied; there was some scuffling between the peasants and the soldiers on guard, during which a wagon-load of lumber came along the road. The portcullis was raised for its entrance, but in the confusion dropped on the wagon and so remained partly open. There was a whistle; the supposed peasants drew weapons, and were reinforced by troops hiding under the lumber. They killed all of the guard.

De Lanza appeared at the head of fifteen hundred men who

had been nearby, dashed into the city, and quickly subdued it.

There were the usual pleasures of a Spanish conquest - almost all the treasure and the pick of the women were enjoyed by the comparatively few of the occupying party, and the city was Philip's.

Of course, high honor followed for de Lanza. And so, when he asked for the hand of the lovely Alisette de Vlaine, pressure was brought on her father that he found injudicious to resist - even had he the desire to do so.

So Federigo, disappointed at Madrid, returned to find the bitterness of a closer, more personal disappointment. In vain he raged at the Sieur de Vlaine; in vain, when after strenuous efforts and much maneuvering, he gained an audience with his love, did he pour out his heart. Alisette, the delicate, the beautiful, the spiritual, also had an eye to the main chance. And although she shed a tear or two for the dashing young Genovese, she had no intention of doing anything foolish.

The rejected suitor brooded over his two misfortunes; and they became as one in his mind. Phillip would not authorize his project. Phillip was old and sick; he could wait for another Phillip. He had lost his affianced bride to the man who had given the king a city? He, Federigo Spinola, would shame the de Vlaines and his supplanter by giving his king a kingdom!

And so, as the monarch's evil life drew to a close, Federigo sent a spy to England, to survey the south coast and its defenses. And he studied anew the coast of Spanish Flanders.

In 1598 Philip II breathed his last. And as soon as he could obtain permission, Federigo was off to Madrid with his proposition for Philip III. To what extent was the Enterprise of England the result of Spinola's professional ambition? To what extent the result of his disappointment in love?

He did not unfold all of his plans on this occasion. He knew that if he introduced too ambitious a scheme to his royal master, there would be endless consultations and conferences with this one and that, and the project would be damned, if only out of inertia or jealousy. So he broached only his plan for harassing the Dutch by sea.

"If your majesty, then, will give me command of a squadron of galleys, I will undertake to man and equip them at my own expense, and we will show the rebels that two can play at their game. We will raise havoc with the French and English commerce, and haughty Holland will tremble at your name."

"The ports of the Spanish Netherlands are too badly silted up to float any vessels, even galleys," said the Minister of Marine.

"The approaches to Sluys are still navigable, your Majesty," Federigo replied. "And Spinola funds will dredge a mooring basin at Dunkirk."

"What experience have you had at sea?" the king wanted to know.

"I have served in the Genovese galleys against the Moorish pirates, sire! And in your majesty's ships off Flanders."

"I have investigated, your majesty," the minister put in. "During a battle the commodore and his officers were put out of action. Senor Spinola took command of the squadron and won a notable victory. He also performed brilliantly in the north."

"Then let us give him six galleys, and let him show us what he can do. In the meantime, senor, you have authority to make your preparations. The navy will furnish the crews and soldiers; you will pay them."

During all Federigo's planning, appeal and interview, not for an hour had the faithless Alisette been out of his thoughts.

There followed a year of intense activity. There were supplies and equipment of all kinds to assemble, scarce though they were after many years of war. He had to study anew all information concerning the coasts of Spain, Portugal, France, the Low Countries, and England - and even Ireland and western Germany; there was no telling where stress of weather might drive him. He had to read endless records of weather along his proposed route; all possible harbors of refuge had to be carefully studied not only from the point of view of practicability but also of politics, fortifications, supplies, and so forth. And of course political orientation was subject to change without notice. There was equipment to be contracted for, and he could not take quality for granted. Personnel had to be checked; a commander ordered to make available so many men of such and such ranks would always seek to rid himself of the slothful, the incompetent and the unruly.

In March there was a flying trip to Flanders. Spinola engaged contractors for the dredging at Dunkirk. Two hundred Italian shipwrights were set to building two more galleys, and two great ships as well - he was not quite putting all of his eggs in one basket.

Don Felipe Maria Magdalena de Medina Gutierrez had dwelt with pathological intensity on that episode of long ago. He had gradually convinced himself that Spinola had deliberately deprived him of his great chance, and, further, that the Naval Board of Inquiry had likewise been resolved to frustrate his ambition. He had reached middle age. Distinction had not come his way. If he was to achieve anything of note, it must be soon - very soon.

It came to his ears that a squadron of galleys was being readied for service. This would be his great opportunity! He sought eagerly for details - to learn that that upstart Spinola, who had cheated him once of glory that was rightfully his, was to have command!

Never, if he could do anything about it! His family connections secured him an audience with the Minister of Marine. He stated what he considered to be his claim.

"I have served for thirty years in the galleys under all conditions, in all places - more years than this Spinola has served months in them. I am a hidalgo of Spain; he is a foreigner. My family has served the crown, in peace and in war, ashore and afloat, for centuries! I can effect more with a squadron of galleys than some boy whose cheeks, a dozen years ago, had never known a razor!"

"This may all be true, senor. But are you aware that Senor Spinola is meeting all expenses from his own pocket? The royal exchequer is in sad state; we are fortunate to be the recipients of his generosity."

"What generosity? Does not a subject owe all that he has to his king?"

"He does, of course. But as you are aware, senor, there are all too many who ignore this obligation."

"With the gold of the Indies at the king's disposal, must he beg of a Genovese? Only three years ago, the Guadalquivir received the greatest treasure shipment ever!"

"It is gone, senor."

"And is a hand made filthy by moneylending to be raised over one that has grasped the sword for a lifetime?"

The minister sighed. "To this we are reduced. It pains me inexpressibly, Don Felipe, that I cannot grant your request."

It might seem strange that a squadron of expensive ships, to say nothing of their personnel, would be entrusted to a commander with no more than Spinola's experience. But in the Spanish navy of that day, as in some other navies of other days, family connections and sometimes mere wealth counted for far more than solid qualifications.

To be sure, a captain was backed up by at least some subordinates at whose background one could not cavil. Bernardo de Moreo was Patron, second in command of the flagship. He had spent his third, and a half of his fourth decade in the galleys. A petty hidalgo from the arid plains of east central Spain, with little of land or money, his home acres were almost as spartan and easeless as his tiny shipboard stateroom. Ricardo Mendoza of Barcelona, that breeding place of sailors and separatists, as sailing master commanded seamen and rowers in a Catalan accent. Hardy, wiry, and slightly undersized, he displayed such incontestable mastery of seamanship that even the gentlemen respected him. The navigator, Lorenzo Denia, was like Mendoza a man of some forty-odd; he too had served the oared vessels since boyhood. He had a large collection of charts and portolans; in the latter was an enormous number of descriptions of landmarks and harbor directions, as well as the compass bearings of all practicable sailings from port to port.

Lieutenant Francisco Ybarra served as mate, and the next in command. Lieutenant Felipe de Feria, a very small shoot from a very big tree, was second mate. Lieutenant of Infantry Juan de Idiaquez commanded the marine detachments of all ships. The physician, Maestre Bernal Carvalho, cared as best he could for the health of squadron personnel; in each galley a barber surgeon was supposedly under his oversight. Fra Sancho Olesa, a Dominican, and Fra Estevan de Guzman, a Franciscan, completed the roster of officers aboard.

Federigo did his best to know his officers. What with the thousand things to be done while getting ready for sea, he had little time. He was able to form a personal, and to a lesser degree, a professional estimate of the officers of his own ship, and of the captains of the others.

A gentleman of Lisbon, Vasco da Costa, captained Santa Elena, Lorenzo de Cerralbo commanded in La Luna, Raimundo Fuentes in Lealtad, Cristoval Odo in El Apostol, and Carlos Mendoza in San Miguel.

These galleys were larger than those Spinola had known in the Mediterranean. They had four rowers to the oar, and high, beautiful poops.

With Gutierrez, Federigo and the squadron of galleys had become an obsession. It is not rare for people at his time of life to suffer an emotional imbalance; sometimes this goes on to madness. Don Felipe had convinced himself that Spain had turned against him. He decided to be revenged.

A number of places of gossip had grown up in Madrid. One of the most frequented of these "mentideros" - lie places - was the steps of the church of San Felipe el Real, at the head of the Calle Mayor. Here Gutierrez, nosing for scraps, encountered a man whom he recognized as a petty clerk at the Ministry of the Marine. On a sudden inspiration he greeted him.

"A good day to you, Don Agostino! May I buy you a drink in the tavern yonder?"

The other was delighted, alike by the gesture of gracious condescension and by the title to which he had no claim. "I should be honored, Excellencia! I trust I see your grace in health?"

"Never better, thank you ..... Landlord! Some of your best Canary!"

The bottle was quickly brought. They chatted. Then Gutierrez remarked offhandedly, "I saw Senor Spinola yesterday. Let us hope that he is successful in his mission."

"Oh, so you know about it, Excellency? It was supposed to be secret. Yes, when he reaches Holland, he should do good service against the Dutch and the English."

So that was the way the wind blew! "Let us also hope that the English get no inkling of what is afoot!"

"Let us, by all means! If they could intercept him, their ships would make quick work of his galleys in those windy waters!"

"How true! Some more wine, Senor?"

"I thank your Excellency, but I am due back at the Ministry."

The Minister of the Marine, somewhat embarrassed at having had to decline Gutierrez' request, felt himself compelled to accede to the latter's application for the command of a galleon. Don Felipe thus became captain of the Santo Tomas. Within months he managed to replace the most loyal and honest members of the ship's officer staff with others more amenable to his control and without annoying scruples. Having coaxed some vagueness into his orders, he prepared to put to sea and to set a course for the English Channel.

Half mad with his sense of wrong long continued and with his jealous hatred of Spinola, Gutierrez plotted nothing less than treason. He had heard of the confusion reigning in London; he planned to contact a British ship and send a message to the effect that Spinola's squadron alone was sailing against them, and that it would necessarily sail close to Brest. There it could be confronted and annihilated.

Gutierrez was angry enough, and brave enough, to challenge Spinola's galleys with his ship alone, and under favorable conditions he might have won. But his crew, hard-bitten and disaffected as it was, might well have mutinied at the order to fire on the Spanish flag - not, indeed, out of idealism, but out of a loving regard for their necks.

In judging and condemning him for his treachery, it should be borne in mind that in the Europe of that day nationalism had not reached its subsequent development. Enough of the spirit of the feudal system survived that loyalty was not so much to a nation as to one's lord. Great men sometimes took service under enemies to their countries, and if their kings could not or would not punish the defections, their honor was not held as tainted.

Spinola stole an afternoon from his duties to visit the theatre. The drama pleased him; and especially was he taken with the appearance and fresh, clear voice of one of the actresses, a Senora Leonora Mondego. The "musketeers," however, the self-styled critics who, although devoid of education, knowledge, or taste, infested the Spanish theatre, decided to dislike the performance. A chorus of boos and whistles was about to drive the performers from the stage, and Spinola left in disgust. As, just in time, he sallied from the door, he saw a group of armed men entering and barring the portals, with the proclamation, "In the name of the Holy Office!"

Something or someone had aroused the notice of the Inquisition. He lingered for a moment, and saw a young woman with a large hood exit through an inconspicuous side door, close to where he stood. As her hood blew back he recognized the Mondego woman.

A sentry ran up from the main entrance. "Didn't you just come out?" he asked her.

The actress was in a tight spot. If she raised her head, her stage make-up would betray her. On an impulse, Spinola took her arm in his. "As you see, fellow, the senora is passing by with me." They walked off.

She gave him a look of mingled gratitude and terror. "Thank you, thank you, senor! Thank you a thousand times!"

"Your servant, senora! I will escort you wherever you wish to go."

She gave him the name of a nearby inn. But there too they found a sentry at the door.

"For the love of God, senor, let us walk on, before he sees my face!" And a moment later she explained. "They have just arrested my father, and are looking for me! My family is a Moorish one, very long in Spain. That is enough for the Holy Office to suspect us of apostasy. They just missed us in Saragossa, and have traced us here!" She hesitated. "I must find another inn!"

"It will be useless, senora. The officers will search them all. If you will trust me, I offer the hospitality of my quarters. You will

come to no harm there, and you can consider what is next to be done."
He introduced himself.

She regarded him earnestly. "All that I have is at the inn, or
in my father's possession. I must take you at your word."

His word, she found, was good. For several days she
remained under his protection. Very discreetly, he set in action an
investigation into her father's fate. Apparently there had been an old
conviction, and the man was doomed.

After she had finished weeping, she thanked him for the
hundredth time, and proposed to depart.

"Where will you go? How will you live?"

"That is not your responsibility, senor. I can no longer
impose upon your charity, or let you bear the danger of my presence."

"I am not concerned about the danger, senora. But you
cannot return to the theatre, and there is little else that you can do. I
have become fond of you, senora. If you could love a sea captain who
will be away from you most of the time, my heart and my home are
yours."

She became his mistress.

It might be thought that he was taking shameful advantage of
her distress. But he was a wealthy aristocrat, she a penniless
commoner of a hated race; and what man would wed the daughter of a
condemned heretic, who herself was wanted by the dread Inquisition?
In family-conscious Europe of that time, not even her father would
have expected Spinola to give her his name.

VI. Line Astern!

One would say
That the earth is the way
Of the flesh,
That the sea is the way
Of the soul...
      A voyage on the ocean,
How it resembles the voyage to death,
Voyage to life eternal!

From the Spanish of Juan Ramon Jimenez.

On the third night preceding the scheduled sailing, Spinola gave a banquet for the officers and their ladies. The latter studied the host who would be so decisive in their husbands' careers. They saw a wiry young man of medium height with the auburn hair that the Goths in the north and the Normans in the south had so liberally engrafted on the darker locks of Italy. His features were regular and handsome, lips mostly curved in a merry smile. He was vivacious and witty, and they found him charming. They had a delightful party.

It was in a quite different mood, however, that the officers gathered in small knots after seeing their spouses home.

"What think you of this voyage, Don Felipe?" asked Lieutenant Ybarra.

The other looked about him carefully. "You probably know that I tried to be transferred. I'm not ashamed to admit that I have little stomach for this attempt. Oh, by choosing our weather carefully we can run up the coast to the Low Countries, putting into harbor to wait out any spells of unfavorable or overly strong winds. But operations in or near the Channel are nothing for us to look forward to."

"The ships of northern Europe operate there regularly," Ybarra took up, "but they are great ships, more strongly built and decked than these. Even in our relatively calm Mediterranean we voyage only during the more clement months of the year. The English and the Dutch ships can keep the sea for nine months, and twelve if necessary."

"The Norse galleys cruised in season with no decks at all; but they too were differently built. They were heavier, and had no fear of breaking their backs by hogging or sagging."

"Similarly, the few Dutch and English galleys are likewise, I have reason to believe, of different construction."

The like discussions were going on in other clusters of officers.

"I am as loyal a subject of the king as any other." Idiaquez was saying, "and if his majesty appoints Senor Don Federigo as my captain, I obey him. But the prospect of sailing against the English and the Dutch in their home waters, far from the places and conditions that we know and understand, gives me no pleasure."

"Nor me either. I think I should rather venture on an ocean crossing and operate in our American waters than in those wild northern seas whose bottoms are paved with the timbers of ships and the bones of men."

These men were not cowards. They would have faced an enemy - even one of superior numbers - unflinchingly. And they did not fear the sea more than a prudent mariner should. But in their judgment - and they could have found many to agree with them - their vessels were not fit for this sort of duty, and had never been intended for it. The combination of northern weather and the heavy northern men-of-war was something beyond all reason. Besides which, their overweening Spanish pride made them distrust their Italian commander.

It was the seventh of August. Spinola's squadron lay moored in the Tagus river. It was still night; only the anchor watch stirred aboard the galleys. In the clear atmosphere the stars shone brightly.

A faint greyness appeared over the hills to the east, and grew. Ashore, the birds began their twittering. A light northerly air breathed over the water.

On the Capitana, the ship's boy of the watch turned the sand glass, struck the bell, and sang in the treble of boyhood:

"Blessed be the dawnlight good,
Blessed be the Holy Rood,
Bless the Lord of all the Host,
Father, Son, and Holy Ghost!
Blessed be both flesh and soul,
And the God Who made the whole;
Bless the daylight in the skies
And the Lord Who bids it rise!"

Accompanied by the members of the watch, he sang the

Pater-noster and the Ave Maria.

After they scrubbed down the decks, the crew assembled and heard mass. Then the steward and his men dispensed a breakfast of bread, water, and a few sardines. The seven to eleven o'clock watch began. Men scattered to their tasks; there were the usual earthy jests about visiting the choicest view points and the showers from below as some supplied themselves with tarred rope ends and sought the relief of seats built outboard at the bow.

The last kegs of gunpowder, the last hogsheads of drinking water were taken aboard. The last rowers and troops filed up the gangways. Finally, a great treasure for the army in the Netherlands was loaded. Federigo Spinola, Captain General of the squadron, led his ships down the Tagus and out to sea. At his mastheads fluttered the banners of the cross, the castles of Castile, and the lions of Leon.

Naturally, both Spinola and the ministry had tried to keep the preparations, and still more their purpose, a secret. They need not have bothered. It was a period of a fantastic chain of action and reaction, panic and resolution, in England.

Once out of the harbor, Spinola set half of his rowers to the oars and led his squadron in line astern at three knots up the coast.

It was a blue and gold morning. The many-legged ships crawled over the long Atlantic rollers, rising alternately at bow and stern, and rolling as the large waves lifted the middle of each galley; in this unsteady position the center of gravity was high, so that the ship heeled until the sinking side immersed enough air space for its flotation to counter the moment of heel. This happened whenever ships were rowed directly into the wind or proceeded directly downwind under oars or sail.

The weather was balmy; except for the slaves at their toil and those others subject to motion sickness, it was a pleasurable sensation.

At noon the meal of hardtack, cheese, water instead of wine, and a mouthful of sardines was distributed. There was of course better food for the officers, fresh meat or fish while it lasted, to be replaced later by the salted variety. The seamen had much besides rowing and steering to do. They kept busy at marlinspike seamanship (plain or fancy ropework), last minute stowage of cargo and gear and housekeeping operations. The surgeon oversaw the placement of his materials and supplies. The soldiers engaged in the eternal cleaning of steel weapons so necessary in the salt-laden atmosphere.

Presently a fire was kindled, and salt pork and beans were set to boil. As the sun sank toward the western horizon they were distributed as the mainstay of the evening meal, with some onions and the usual hard bread and cheap wine. The galley slaves received none of the meat, but with the evening meal were given each a taste of wine.

By now, they had rounded Cape Roca, and stood north-northeastward following the trend of the Portuguese coast; except that the commodore ordered a slightly more seaward course to avoid the possibility of a disaster in the hours of darkness. The running lights were lit. The watch took its post; the rowers who had finished their four hour stint lay down for what sleep they could get on the benches, while others relieved them; and except for the hiss of the bow wave and a gurgle under the keel, silence descended upon the ship.

The commodore retired to his low, tiny cabin, the patron to the equally tiny one which he shared with the sailing master. The latter took the evening watch. A few officers and men found scanty room to wrap up in their cloaks on deck, and the rest of those off duty slept perforce in the almost impossibly crowded spaces below.

They put in for a night at Vigo, where Spinola gathered his captains and held a critique on the performance thus far.

A golden day of calm. The ships continued northward under the drive of half of her rowers. Experience had shown that over a period of days, in the absence of a useful wind, such shifts covered the greatest distance, and the oarsmen would still have reserves of strength to meet an emergency.

At mealtimes, a few of the rowers were unchained to pass the mess kits to their fellows. Forward the "good boys" served in this function. "Good boys," "buenos boyas," was a corruption of "bueno voglie," good or free will. These were men of such wretchedness, endurance or both that they enlisted as rowers without constraint. Naturally, their treatment was relatively good. They received the rations of seamen rather than of slaves, and a pittance of salary, were not chained, and when the ship was laid up they had the freedom of the shore. In combat, when an enemy was made fast, they were expected to join in the fighting. Their positions were at oars numbers one and two.

With them, and enjoying similar indulgence, except for freedom ashore, were men who had been sentenced for crime to a limited period of servitude, and whose sentences had expired, but by reason of the shortage of rowers, or perhaps merely because of the location of the ship, it was not considered practicable to free them promptly. They too would take part in hand-to-hand combat. And so, insofar as their fetters would allow, would some of those with time yet to serve, in hope of pardon or shortening of sentence. This sometimes happened.

All day the calm continued, and through most of the night. The ships had settled down into a routine. Such drill as the limited space permitted was carried on by the lieutenant of marines in the flagship, and by his sergeant-major on the others. The barber coiffed and shaved the officers at their leisure, and shaved the heads of the rowers in the monthly routine to hold vermin in check. On each ship the clergy conducted their matins and vespers, heard confession, and occasionally made perfunctory attempts at conversion of Protestants, Moors, and Jews.

At Ferol they refilled their water butts and took on food and fuel for cooking.

The northerly wind had resumed, slowing the galleys with its thrust and the pound of the surges. They continued to make good time nevertheless, and arrived at Cape Finisterre, where the coast of Spain turns northeastward, then eastward into the extremity of the Bay of Biscay. In case the fleet should be scattered by storm, Santander had been appointed as the rallying port.

Once having rounded the cape, the galleys could hoist sail and give the rowers some needed relief. This would have been more welcome if the good weather had continued; but rain squalls sprang up during the night. Motionless in harbor, the galleys would spread awnings for protection from sun and rain. This was of course impracticable at sea. The seamen and the troops could at times take refuge below decks. The even more inadequately garbed servants of the oar huddled in the soaking rain and slept as they could.

The Capitana led the squadron into the harbor of Santander on the north coast of Spain. A day of vigorous activity sufficed to replenish the food, water and fuel. But then, to the surprise of his officers, Spinola gave no order to sail. The wind was fair for Bayonne in France, up whose coast the galleys could then cruise in easy stages, finding shelter as they might. But the commodore had other plans.

A council attended by his patron and his captains sat in Spinola's cabin.

"Gentlemen," he said, "I am informed by Senor de Moreo and the sailing master that this wind should soon give way to a southerly. We shall lie here until that takes place. Thereupon, at whatever time of day or night, we set sail for Brittany. I need hardly mention that these orders are confidential.

"Request has been made to the French king for permission

for us to put in at Brest. This has been denied. We have been given unofficially to understand, however, that no notice will be taken if we make the much less conspicuous harbor of Le Conquet. This, therefore, will be our next place of reassembly should we need one, and there, in any case, we shall replenish our supplies and pick up a Norman pilot."

They stared at him in consternation. The route up the sandy southwest coast of France was treacherous enough. But the westerly trades had their seas deflected down from the northwest into the Bay of Biscay, and its expanse was swept by every gale from north to southwest. It had an ugly reputation. Many and many a skilled captain and stout ship had come to grief in its wild waters.

"Senoria," said Captain de Cerralbo, "you are, of course, aware of the great hazards of this voyage."

"Galleys accompanied the Armada of 1588," Spinola replied.

"Yes, Senoria - they accompanied it, and therefore had the protection of the great ships. And one out of four foundered with all aboard."

"Freight-carrying galleys have plied between Portugal and England."

"True, Senoria. But they were beamier, deeper, and, speed not being essential, of much heavier and stronger construction. I respectfully call your attention to the greater safety of running alongshore rather than cutting right across stormy Biscay of such evil reputation."

"I am aware of all this," Spinola replied. "But the great tactic is to take the English and the Dutch by surprise. We want no French Protestants rushing word of our progress ahead to our foes."

"Communications are faster, Senoria, by sea than by land."

"They are. And we want no fast pinnace racing at sea to report that we have been seen at Rochefort or St. Nazaire. Neither do we want relays of horsemen carrying the word overland while we, perhaps, lie stormbound in harbor.

"I refuse to insult you, senores, with the question as to whether your officers are afraid of this passage."

Before dawn on August 18 Spinola was awakened with the word that a southerly air had sprung up. He turned his ship to, and sent his captains his best wishes for the passage north.

The seamen took in the harbor awnings, and raised and set the sails. The officers' ladies - they were allowed on board, and incredibly, in the impossible stench, crowding, lack of privacy, and danger, love drove some of the younger, childless ones to share the adventure - lay and listened silently while the ships' boys sang the matins with the friars. Then the signal blazed from the galley's masthead:

"The Narrow Seas!"

VII. THE DAYS OF BISCAY

Thou Ocean-Star! thou port of joy!
From pain, and sadness, and annoy,
O, rescue me, O, comfort me,
Bright Lady of the Sky!

> *Hymn to the Virgin - From the Spanish of Juan Ruiz*

The weather shore gentled the sea for their departure. With an easy motion the ships left the harbor and stood to the north. Only wavelets ran along the sides, and for a while there was neither roll nor pitch as the squadron worked its way to sea.

Grey of dawn disclosed the graceful bunts of the wind-filled sails. The sailors set about washing down the decks, with an occasional adjustment of sheet or halyard. The rowers lounged and watched the straining canvas do their work. Gradually, as they worked up an offing, a sea rose; the ships became living, moving beings.

Now the golden glory of the sun appeared, commanding a deeper blue to enamel the face of the sea; little veins of white, delicate and transitory, began to overspread the cobalt water. An occasional larger wave would slap at a plunging bow, and the droplets under its sprit became jewels that arranged themselves into transient rainbows on either side. Scarlet fluttered at the mastheads with the lions of Leon and the turrets of Castile.

There was a breakfast of beans, bread and onions. The ships' companies were set to their tasks, and the day was well begun.

Don Estevan de Guzman was the son of a petty hidalgo of Valladolid. Although an inlander, he had been made very much aware of the bereavement in many local families caused by the terrible failure of the Great Armada. The sensitive lad had been led to shun violence, had turned to the Church, and found his vocation in the order of St. Francis. More even than his brethren, he lived thenceforth for the poor and the weak.

He really believed and lived what were commonly found as platitudes in mouths, but seldom as realities in hearts, and never, it seemed, in hands. Having noted the desperate positions of the particularly afflicted galley slaves, Moorish and Jewish, he made the usual attempt to bring them the salvation of the Faith. Rebuffed, he did not wash his hands of them but did his pitiful best, with unguents and bits of food, for their bodies.

His fellow was Sancho Padilla, a Dominican. The Padilla family were peasants near Valencia. The father had had the good fortune to take over the farm of a condemned Morisco. Not unnaturally, bigotry and self-interest united to reinforce a bias which he transmitted to his children. Sancho, gifted with a good intellect, impressed the local priest, had his chance, and took it. He became a regular clergyman, and joined the Dominicans in their hunt for heresy.

"I marvel, Don Estevan," he remarked that morning, "that you give yourself such care over the enemies of God and our gracious king."

"The blessed St. Francis would have called them his brothers."

"Brothers such as Cain or Esau."

"I have seen your Valencia, Brother Sancho," said the other. "And I know what it was before you expropriated the Moriscos. You have done Spain and yourselves no good service. I am not even sure that you have done Holy Mother Church good service."

The Dominican turned angry eyes. "We hounds of God" - for so by a word play *(Domini canes)* the members of the order often styled themselves - "are content to accept the knowledge and sanctity of those whom God has set over us, rather than to adjudicate all things ourselves. If we can rightly do our duty of inquiring into heresy, we shall have done well enough. I recommend to you, Don Estevan, some of that humility of which you make such good show."

The other sighed but did not answer. He rubbed his secret hair shirt over a raw place on his shoulder, and murmured, "Take it unto Thee, oh Lord! Pardon the blind!"

The wind freshened in the afternoon, and came from over the port quarter. The seas made up, and there was a corkscrewing pitch-and-roll combination that began to try the stomachs of some. The mountains of Biscay had been lost to sight, and only open sea could be seen. Spray began to whip over the row benches. The cooks made representations, and fires were not kindled for the evening meals; bread, some greens, dried cod, and olives were passed around.

Clouds attended the setting of the sun, and they donned their most glorious and colorful robes to do him honor. They gathered before his place, that none might behold the shame of his fall into the sea. The horizon too veiled herself in the west, and none could say at what moment the great lamp of daylight disappeared. Nevertheless, it was long ere twilight was done, and when the evening watch turned to at seven, there was still abundant light in the sky and on the sea.

Don Estevan gazed at the pageant of nightfall. The ship swam between two infinities. Or was it two? The demarcation was lost in the distance and the gathering darkness.

"The heavens are the heavens of the Lord," the psalmist had sung, "but the earth He hath given to the children of men." But did that earth include the sea? Had not the Lord divided the waters over the firmament from those beneath, and was it not the dry land that He had called earth, and had not the sea, therefore, come from heaven, been reserved to Himself? Man could harrow or mine the dry land; he could make the desert bloom; he could quarry a hill till it was level with the plain. But onto the sea he ventured only on sufferance, and at his peril. He could destroy nothing, change nothing. The sea rolled as it had since the Beginning. Was not this journey, therefore, a trespass into the realms of eternity?

The wind had not dropped at the approach of evening. It continued to mount, slowly. Now the galleys were forging northward with great leaping strides. The commodore and the sailing masters, the latter all former enlisted seamen whose years of meritorious service had been rewarded with such promotion, marked their traverse boards complacently, congratulating gazed appalled at the growing combers racing past the decks, the bending spars, and the iron-hard cords of the straining sheets.

And indeed, the motion grew wilder and less regular. Besides the waves that pursued them under the hounding wind, there were cross seas whose origins were elsewhere and it became hard indeed to keep one's footing. There were many anxious glances toward the unfriendly north into which they drove, and longing looks toward the unseen harbors in the east.

By morning, seas were beginning to board. They swept the decks and wet the legs of the idle rowers. The mariners shortened sail. All gear was lashed and double-lashed in place; not only topside but below as well, all things not well secured went adrift. The crowded hold began to assume a chaotic appearance. Men were stationed at the pumps; the ships were making water.

Friar Sancho, to do him justice, had no misgivings about the voyage. "We fare speedily, Brother Estevan," was his greeting. "By God's grace, we shall punish some of those stiff-necked Flemings who maintain the cities of Holland and Zeeland in rebellion against God and the king! Once let us suppress the main fount, and we shall see whether heresy will make further head against the peace of the realm!"

"God's work be done!" said the other. "Although I saw what

happened at Cordova last year. I do not greatly rejoice at the prospect of seeing the like befall any people - be they relapsed Jews, Moslems, or heretic Christians!"

"Do you pity those enemies of both heaven and earth? I think you hold dangerous doctrine!"

"Brother Francis bade supplicate the emperor even for less than men - 'Tell him to make a law,' he urged, 'that no man should take or kill our sisters the larks, or do them any harm!' And remember what Abelard wrote - 'God gives love to all peoples, Jews and heathen included. Heretics should be restrained by reason rather than by force.'"

"And he was roundly condemned for it by the great St. Bernard who said very well, 'The faith of the righteous believes, it does not dispute.'"

"Does it not? Thomas Aquinas was a lover even of the great non-Christian thinkers, such as Avicenna, Averroes, Isaac Israeli, and above all his beloved Rabbi Moyses Maimonides. 'The proper operation of man is to understand,' he taught, and 'Of all human pursuits the pursuit of wisdom is the most perfect, the most sublime, the most profitable, the most delightful.' And does he not prove that God loves all? 'Deus autem peccatores amat'; and if he loves even the sinners, can we not show mercy?"

"Thomism is a heady draught, my brother! He himself knew that well. Did he not write, 'Since error in matters of faith may lead many to hell, tolerance should not be shown to unbelief except to avoid a greater evil'?"

"Even belief may lead to evil. Erasmus, you remember, wrote, 'They are not as impious who deny the existence of God as are those who picture Him as inexorable.' And did he not consider even such pagans as Plato, Cicero and Seneca to have been divinely inspired? To say nothing of his 'St. Socrates'? He even wrote to His Holiness concerning the Adversary, Luther himself, 'Those counsel you best who advise gentle measures...The question is not what heresy deserves, but how to deal with it wisely.'"

"Have a care, Don Estevan! You know well that the Holy Office has looked with a jaundiced eye upon the teachings of your Erasmus - as more than one has found to his cost! The Inquisition of the Galleys might take your words very ill! I stand with Loyola - 'I want to be where there are no Moslems or Jews. Give me out-and-out pagans!' He knew that the last were far more amenable to enlightenment and conversion."

The blow told. Don Estevan trembled with visions of the

stake. And he had flirted with doctrines of the Illuminati; who knew what an investigation might dredge up! He was thoroughly orthodox in his submission to Rome. But that was no guarantee that an unsympathetic tribunal might not find otherwise! But he mastered himself, and showed no outward sign of his disturbance.

"Yet even the blessed Loyola," he muttered as he turned away, said, 'More prudence and less piety were better than more piety and less prudence.'"

The friar's humanity was not assumed, or a tenet of his order. In fact, originally the Franciscans along with the Dominicans had been charged with the investigation of heresy. But the greatness of heart was part of the man, as ineradicable as his very backbone.

Spinola had come up unobserved behind them.

"Shall I venture to tell you what I think is the great desideratum, reverend brothers?" he asked. "Every man should aspire to be able on his death bed to say after Nero - 'Qualis artifex pereo!' What an artist perishes in me!"

But to the merciful Franciscan this was no mere intellectual exercise. Privacy was hard to come by in the crowded galley; but he found it. And as often before, he swung a knotted cord in agony against his back, groaning, "Mercy, oh my God, for the sins of mankind! May this be unto Thee an acceptable sacrifice, oh my God and my Redeemer!"

"Red sky at night, sailor's delight!
Red sky at morning, sailor take warning!"
runs the old sailors' rhyme; but apparently this was not, or not always, applicable to the Bay of Biscay. The promise of the night before was not being kept. The sky was overcast and grey; grey too was the growling sea, its waves white-tipped where the wind tumbled their tops, and laced with snaky white streaks down their faces. The wind continued to grow, and there was first a whine, then a snarl, as it whipped past the standing rigging.

They had already unlaced a bonnet, a strip of sailcloth from along the foot of each sail, thus decreasing the area exposed to the wind; but now the sailing masters deemed it wise to remove a second one. This lessened the threat to the sorely taxed canvas (and possibly to the masts themselves), at the expense of some of the wind force that bore them on their way. But it was doubtful whether they lost by it. The ships were eased, the motion was much improved, and less of the primitive energy was expended in wrenching the punished hulls up and down, starboard and port, through the water.

Particularly for the slaves shivering at their stations, it was fortunate that the wind blew almost in their line of advance. The ships did not of course equal its speed; but the difference would have been greater with a beam wind, greater yet when lying hove to, and distressing indeed if they had been rowing against it, which in the present state of the sea would in any event have been impossible. But the feelings of cold and of violence would have been severe.

By now even the more fearless among them were eyeing the havoc of nature with a sober air. These were, after all, galleys, not galleons; they were light of frame, and those frames were being subjected to stresses that were incalculable. Many of the men, and most of the women, were too sick to demand or even care about an estimate of the situation. But it became necessary further to reduce the sail area by substituting smaller, stronger sails for the working canvas in the afternoon.

There were other reasons for disquiet. The sailing masters and pilots, and even some of the mates, were competent enough at dead reckoning. No heavenly bodies could be seen, and in any case the determination of the latitude was not yet the almost exact science that it not too long afterwards became. So Spinola had no means of knowing just how much northing he had made. The squadron should be closing the seaward reaches of Brittany in the area of Brest and the Iroise.

That area was nothing to mess around with in the dark - especially not with a rising sea and more than a capful of wind. For fifteen miles from shore to Ushant the sea was foul with islets and reefs; once upon them in this weather, the ships were lost (and, except for a stroke of very bad luck indeed, Spinola would perish too). Besides, what of the tides? To close this coast in a rising tide would mean risking the squadron in dangerous inshore currents.

They could alter course to the westward, making sure to clear Ushant. But even assuming that they saw and recognized the island as they passed it, there was no assurance that the rowers could work far and fast enough to weather again to make their port, Conquet, just to the north of the Iroise. And at Conquet they were to pick up a pilot for Normandy.

True, it would be possible, by accident or design, to omit the call at Brittany altogether. It would certainly give a greater advantage of surprise if he ran right on into the mouth of the Channel; he might make his easting before the Dutch and English fleets knew that he was among them. But the tides and rips of the English Channel and the Straits of Dover had a wicked, wicked reputation; and so did their shoals, and so did those of the whole coast from Brest to the Frisians. He needed that pilot.

As usual, fortune favored the brave. In the fading daylight the rugged coast of Brittany rose exactly where expected out of the sea. The pilots stated that the tide was high. They elected to pass close under St. Matthew's Point. The sails were run down the masts even as the oars gripped the suddenly smooth water of a lee. They rowed into harbor and dropped the anchors. It was evening, on the 19th of August. Sleep comforted the sea-worn crews.

VIII. The Days of Brittany

Lowering and dark, the stormy sky
Splits loudly in the east. A flash of light
Illuminates the sea. Unearthly bright
It spreads its wild and yellow glare on high.

Wild blows the wind; the seas in torment run;
Against the gleaming of the troubled day
Sparkle the dollops of the flying spray,
And in the sea still shines the dying sun.

Marina. From the Spanish of Juan Ramon Jimenez

Nature smiled on Brittany with clear, beautiful summer days.

Spinola made the necessary petty repairs. He established contact with his pilot for Normandy. He paid the necessary but sub-rosa call upon the French governor of the port. Above all, he gathered news of enemy ships.

With a full heart, Don Estevan celebrated the mass. The rite was omitted at sea on the lively galleys and even on the larger but still heaving galleons, lest the precious blood of the Savior should by ill chance be spilled on the decks. Now he could again supply the delight to his soul and to his flock.

There were priests in whom the fires of faith, even though not extinct, burned low, and who ran through their offices in rote fashion. But in Don Estevan, time and use had not diminished the glory of the Eucharist. Grateful for the high privilege that God and Holy Mother Church had granted him, however unworthy, he performed the miracle of transubstantiation; and as the wine and host became the blood and flesh of the Son, so it seemed to the priest that he too was for the moment at least changed from weak, sinful man to a member of the heavenly host!

Stout George Fenner commanded an English observation squadron - his own galleon, Dreadnought; Swiftsure, under Matthew Bredgate; and the pinnace Advice. On being informed that Spanish galleys had left Lisbon for the north, he had set out to find them. And here he came, cutting across the wind like a coursing hound; and like a coursing hound he scented his prey! The pinnace by his order fluttered away with the news for England. But off Conquet, Dreadnought and Swiftsure settled grimly down to a death watch.

There was a fine, strong sailing wind for the English, and theirs were two fine, strong, well gunned ships. It would be their kind of fight. Spinola settled as grimly down to out-wait them. His kind of weather would come. Meanwhile, all sorts of useful intelligence was coming in.

But his officers lost heart.

The secret little conferences began again.

"Tell me frankly, senor Teniente, what think you of this campaign?

"I can tell you very simply, Don Roberto. I think we are all dead men."

"I, too."

"Mark you, senor, I am not afraid to die. I was the last to leave the Boqueron fort at Puerto Rico, and it was there that I got this wound. But that was the kind of fighting that we knew and understood."

"This Spinola does not know whether he is soldier or seaman."

"Or banker," sneered the other.

"He might easily have drowned us but now, with our ladies. He is like to do it yet. And militarily he has no judgment at all. As you can see, the English know all about us. That means that the Dutch do, too - or they will. He has lost the game, and is too stupid to see it. Besides, as any man of understanding can tell you, these are not the ships even for cruising in the Channel, let alone fighting. Could you have imagined an action under yesterday's conditions? And in the Channel they will be worse."

And, "What do you think, Don Gil, of the new way of waging warfare by inviting your foe to set a trap and then walking into it?"

"About the same as you do, I daresay, Senor de Olivares. The Narrow Seas will be aswarm with Dutch and English ships waiting to pounce. I fear no enemy on equal terms - or even unequal, for that matter, so they be at least possible. I got these wounds at Corunna. But is a man to walk right up to an enemy, thrust out his head, and invite the other to cut it off?"

And, "Senor Ybarra, do you enjoy bowing and scraping to the foreigner?"

"My forefather was with King Jaime at the taking of Murcia. And yours, Don Rigoberto, was in the vanguard when Santarem fell. Is there no hidalgueria from which to choose the leadership of this expedition - if indeed this expedition must be?"

"Indeed, senores, the adelantado has not taken up for us as we had the right to expect. Today we serve a Genovese; tomorrow, perhaps, a German!"

"Are you minded, senores, to follow mildly after this young madman until we are all killed? Is that what our loyalty to the king should mean? Loyalty should work two ways, senores. It is for his gracious majesty the king - whom God protects - to give us leadership that we understand and trust."

"Aye, our lives are his. But his to use, not his to throw away. I can interpret this mad, rash campaign in no other way than as a repudiation of his duty by the king."

"I agree. When the king dishonors a gentleman's arms, the gentleman may withhold their gift. When the king treats too lightly a chevalier's gift of his life, the subject may refuse this too."

Another nodded. "Many a time it has happened that good and loyal soldiers of the king have refused in their wisdom to follow where he led in his folly."

On the second morning in Conquet, an officer on Federigo's ship and one on each of two others was missing. The commodore was puzzled. The absentees' valuables and some of their clothing were missing with them.

On the following morning over a half dozen were absent without leave. The commodore looked sharply at the junior officers of the watch who reported having seen no irregularities; three watch officers were among those unaccounted for. It was not always wise for a junior, or even a senior, of undistinguished background to oppose the designs of a gentleman of one of the great houses of Spain; and one of the missing was the son of a grandee.

So the commodore changed the manner of moorage; in a well protected area all galleys were moored together, and he himself took the night watch. There were no more desertions.

Some would have set the ladies ashore at this place; but the governor of Brest, close by, was of the English party, and it did not seem wise.

Fenner's pinnace brought England the news that six or seven galleys were at Conquet. The roll of the ships that the admirals led from the Thames to Margate Roads rings like a trumpet call through the mists of time. Triumph, Merhonour, Repulse, Bonaventure, Nonpareil, Defiance, Foresight, Mercury, Rainbow, Crane, Mary Rose and Hope followed them to join Leveson in the Channel. Proudly at their mastheads they bore the Tudor lions.

Thirty thousand men mustered to defend their queen at London.

Howard decided to sail for the "Trade," as the waters of the Gulf of Iroise off Brest were known, to investigate and challenge the enemy. But he remained wind bound in home waters.

Andrew Felton was a ship chandler and victualler of no great intelligence or honesty. He became aware of the fact that a supplier had foisted upon him some salt beef and other provisions of bad quality. He saw no reason why he should stand the loss; so when the rapid mobilization gave him his chance, he took it.

It therefore befell that in the ships of George Fenner, seeking valiantly to contain and ultimately bring to action the intrusive Genovese, men began to sicken. Soon there were not enough left on their feet to fight the ships - barely enough even to sail them. On the evening of the twenty-third of August, therefore, Spinola's lookout saw Fenner's ships bear off for Plymouth and reprovisioning.

In England, a ludicrous play and counterplay of military intelligence went on. The powerful Spanish fleet entering the Channel turned into Gerbrandtsen's returning Hollanders. But what of the galleys? A dash up the Thames to destroy property and shipping with a large troop contingent was not impossible. So all day on the twenty-fifth the burghers of London, armed and assembled, kept formation through a pouring rain, and so did the cavalry; but to no purpose.

After four days at Conquet, the galleys had put to sea. Spinola worked his way along that dangerous coast. One hundred miles to the north the Lizard marked the opening of the Channel; the interval was wide enough for every bit of dirty weather from the west to hurl its hatred at the hapless craft in its way.

Swiftly but safely their pilot took them through the night-bound menace of the northern Finisterre. They opened the Bay of Morlaix, then the Bay of Lannion. Past the Seven Isles they raced in a flaming dawn, to where the Gulf of St. Malo makes widely into the land.

The decks were dry of dew that morning - like the red dawn, a sign in Brittany of a coming westerly gale. It was sixty miles of open water to the Cherbourg peninsula, and the wind was rising at his back; but Spinola did not hesitate. Men paled and crossed themselves, and women collapsed into pitiful piles of terror. But the squadron commander led boldly northeastward, and there was nothing to do but follow. Far to the east a furious surf was beating on the shoals of Dover Rocks.

Guernsey took shape ahead. Like a stampeding herd the galleys flung themselves on their wildly rolling way. So close did they pass around the western side of Guernsey that its governor thought they intended a landing. But as night drew on they ran off toward the overfalls of the distant Casquets.

Plunging, rolling, pitching, their decks continually awash, they steered a course to clear those dangerous banks. Seamen gazed in horror toward the unseen mountains of vicious surf that they knew were reaching for them.

But now even the tough, stolid Breton pilot spoke to Spinola, shaking his head. Federigo was fearless and stubborn. But, despite the opinions of some of his associates, he was not a madman. So over went the helms in the darkness, and the pilot set a course for Cape La Hogue. Like a herd of frantic wild horses they dashed for its lee, and like quieted horses that have run their course they furled sail and took to the oars. They had run a little too far north, and it took some hard pulling, even in relatively calm waters, to make harbor.

Finally the anchors plunged overside. It was the twenty-fifth day of August.

The Dutch Admiral Justinus joined Howard, so that together they mustered some sixty sail. They beat for the Downs against the same southwest gale of which Spinola had made such excellent use. Although the report of the great Spanish power was soon proven erroneous, there were still those six galleys on the coast of France.

Lord Howard sent Leveson and the Dutch to Calais to intercept them on their further way, though Howard feared it might be difficult "by reason the baggages will ever keep near the shore." And indeed the galleys drew much less water than the huge and heavy galleons.

Fenner meanwhile had been revictualling at Plymouth.
There in the west he had a better chance at the enemy, now thought to
be at La Hogue. Howard, Hunsdon, and Cecil of the council wrote
Fenner to seek them out, alone or with the Dutch. "Tarry not, good
George," they wrote, "but do the best you can; for we would be very
glad these might be catched or canvassed. Assure yourself that your
ship and the Truelove will beat them if there were no more to assist
you."

On the twenty-eighth the orders were written, and Fenner
acted, when he received them on the second day thereafter, with
exemplary quickness and vigor. Surely the Genovese, with his light,
vulnerable vessels, had been lying up at La Hogue out of the storm
that was blowing from the southwest, and he in his more seaworthy
ships would trap them like rats.

He little knew his man.

IX. THE DAYS OF NORMANDY

Now all to heaven are hoisted by the fury
And rage of Neptune, terrible and fell:
Now to the bottom of his waves all hurry,
As if their keels would knock the gates of hell.
The east, west, south, and northern winds (to worry
The world by turns) from ev'ry corner swell.
The Lusiads. From the Portuguese of Luis Camoens.

The weather was bad - very bad. A southwesterly gale raged
up channel. Gutierrez' ship was making heavy weather of a wild sea.
It beat upon her planking, it wrenched at her timbers, it drove the
water in through her seams at a rate that kept the weary mariners
pumping for very lives. Again and again seas swept the deck, leaving
wreckage in their wake, and carrying men off to die where no human
eye could see.

All winds vary somewhat from minute to minute in strength
and direction. The waves they raise vary accordingly in size, therefore
in speed. They overtake and pass one another. As they do, the hollow

of one may neutralize the crest of another. Or they may summate and produce a wave of frightful height.

There was another storm - a norther - off Ireland. It sent a sullen swell to the south.

The tempest grew ever worse. In a lifetime at sea, Gutierrez had seen nothing to surpass it. Again and again he crossed himself and prayed. He was weary keeping the deck, weary of the battering of the gale.

Two waves synchronized for a moment, and a swell from the north summated with them. Higher and higher rose an enormous wave. This is a rare phenomenon - in a lifetime at sea one may never see the like. And well that it is so!

The galleon rose to a crest. Turning his head, Gutierrez saw a sight of horror. It was not the monstrous size of the mountain of water, apparently higher than his masts, that wrenched a scream from his throat. The face that bore down upon him was sheer up - and - down!

The captain gazed aghast upon his death. Stout and buoyant as his ship was, he knew that she could never rise to such a sea.

Nor did she. Around and above the ship swept that impossible wall of water. It clasped and held her in an embrace of death. With a weight of a hundred and a half tons it beat in a ten foot square hatch cover and poured irresistibly into her hull.

She never rose again.

At La Hogue Spinola had picked up his Dunkirk pilot, and the last intelligence on enemy ships. Here the women on board could be left in safety before the desperate business ahead. They could expect hostilities now; he had to rid himself of them, and gave the order. Those who still wished to enjoy their husbands' company could travel overland to the Spanish Netherlands. Gladly would Leonora Mondego have been of their number. But he had known that her presence aboard among the officers' ladies would have created an impossible situation.

The blundering little bride of a junior officer remarked to the commodore, in saying good-bye, that she was proceeding to Antwerp, where she was to be the guest of her kinswoman, Senora de Lanza, nee Alisette de Vlaine. Her husband looked blackly at her, but Federigo merely smiled and wished her well. He realized suddenly that Leonora had had much to do with his final recovery from that business. In fact, better than that. He was cured of the malady, but it had changed his life. Although the cause and effect relationship was

broken, he was still committed to the grand design that his love-
sickness had initiated. He was not turning back. The great guiding
star of his life was, and would continue to be, the Enterprise of
England!

Spinola respected the sea and its storms. He did not fear
them. While he lay supposedly immobilized at La Hogue Bay, and
the boys marked the passage of time by reversing the half-hour sand
glasses regularly (clocks were still very new), he studied the gale and
he studied his charts. And he conferred with his pilots and sailing
masters.

The contours of the coast, he decided, were favorable to his
plan. The gale swept off the land, but that same land would give him
an excellent protective lee for a long way. And the pilots assured him
that the wind was very unlikely to change direction.

So he ignored it. This rat would not be trapped! On the
twenty-eighth he put to sea again, standing along the generally
eastward trending shore, while the great gale blew harmlessly over his
head and the wavelets had not yet, where he went, sufficient fetch to
grow to any dangerous size or strength.

He might have had trouble on the approaches to Harfleur,
where the reefs forced him some four miles offshore; but the very
shoaling also prevented the seas from reaching their growth.

The galleys moored for the night in the Bay of Carentan. In
the morning the Capitana almost lost an anchor, so firmly was it
embedded by the racing tide. But a doubled detail lined up on the
cable. A chanteyman chanted, in an all but toneless recitative, and the
men responded and pulled:

       "O-o-oh God"......"We pray to Thee!"
       "O-o-oh our task" ...... "To serve Thee."
       "O-o-oh let us serve Thee." .... "First and last."
       "O-o-oh the Faith." .... "To hold it fast."
       "O-o-oh the Faith." .... "The Christian creed."
       "Curse the heathen." .... "And his seed."

The bottom yielded, the anchor came free, and the ship and fleet were
under way.

They proceeded across the wide, sandy Bay of the Seine. So
easy was the motion that at eleven o'clock the officers responded with
particular enthusiasm to the cabin servant's summons. "Table, table,
sir captain and patron and worthy company! Table set, meat ready;
usual water for sir captain and patron and worthy company. Long live
the King of Spain by land and by sea! Who says him war, cut off his

head! Who says not amen, give him no drink. Table set; who comes not, eats not."

Spinola raised his glass. "Wine, gentlemen! The next few days will show what manner of men we be. Victory to the King, and confusion to his enemies!"

They downed the wine, the stringy salt beef, the lentils, the rice, oil, and garlic. On deck, for the hundredth time they examined the rigging, the oars, the guns and ammunition, the small arms, the condition of the men.

The three to seven o'clock watch was dogged - that is to say, it was divided into two-hour watches, so that neither group of watch standers might consistently have the rugged middle of the night assignments. In the second dog watch, with the setting sun, the youngest of the ship's boys led evening prayers for all hands with, "Amen, and God give us a good night, a good voyage, may the ship make a good passage, sir captain and patron and worthy company!" All recited the Pater-noster, the Ave Maria, and the Credo. Then the boy's voice rang out in the Salve Regina, as they reached for Le Havre.

On the thirtieth Spinola was on his way again, keeping close to the beaches as the dying storm left a subsiding thunder on the strand. The shoals were treacherous. After every storm the shifting sands changed the bottom contours, and the pilots had to study them again. But they were a protection against deep-draft ships, and it was the violence of man, not that of angry nature, that presented the greater peril.

The squadron spent a motionless night at Dieppe. Progress had been slower than expected; with some disquiet Spinola realized that he would have no darkness for the final dash. And indeed it was not until three o'clock in the morning that he made Boulogne. But so close to the English he dared not delay for another night.

X. Dover Straits

From the great sea of Earth that veiled in mists,
Stretches out here at thy feet its vast desert,
Flew adventurous vultures
To the conquest of El Dorado.

On Gredos. From the Spanish of Miguel de Unamuno.

For Spinola, speed was now essential. The Tudor lions were on the hunt. At the straits he was presumably to face the greatest concentration of his enemies, in the smallest search area, where long, sandy beaches, mostly without coves or bays, offered no possibilities of concealment.

He had to determine his further course in view of the daylight. In among the sands his light draft would enable him to keep out of range of the galleons. He would have to run more slowly and cautiously than in open water, however; the galleons might easily be able to pace him, keeping outside the shoals; and if he should become embayed, or if a channel should run out into deep water, he might well be forced right into the iron embrace of the great ships. If on the other hand he ran in clear water, there was no telling at this point what forces might encounter and overwhelm him.

A haze, he saw, was going to lessen the full visibility of daylight. The wind was fair for the Netherland coast, and freshening. He gave his pilot the order.

"Midchannel!"

The lions of Leon at his mastheads whipped in the breeze as he steered widely around Cape Gris Nez, well out into the Pas de Calais; and off Calais they should have caught him.

But there for two days and more Leveson's squadron had tossed in the furious gale; he had perforce sailed to shepherd his stricken lighter ships on the voyage home; and only Justinus with his Dutch squadron lay in wait. Justinus saw the galleys pass; he cut his cable and hoisted sail in pursuit. But Spinola's craft were swift greyhounds of the sea, whereas Justinus had complained bitterly about his "very slugs" of ships, and his only hope was that another squadron, blockading Dunkirk, might head the galleys off, and bring them to action.

A watcher ashore at Calais had seen the Spanish squadron,

and brought word to the governor. When, therefore, on that very afternoon the relieving English ships came to resume the watch at Calais, their captains, dining with the governor, learned that their quarry had escaped them; and bitter brew they drank at his table.

Hunters and hunted ran on past Gravelines, and then indeed they saw the blockading ships off Dunkirk. But Spinola ran wide of them, six leagues and more to sea. He ran past Nieuwport, past the long beaches of Ostend, of Blankenbergh, of Zeebrugge, and as the sun grew low he turned into a narrow waterway, and the protective guns of Sluys thundered in friendly salute.

He had passed through the narrow seas in despite of all the power of the enemy's ships!

XI. A TALE OF TWO BROTHERS

> .....Brothers, proud and high
> Masters, who in prosperity
> Might rival kings,
> Who made the bravest and the best
> The bondsmen of their high behest,
> Their underlings.

From the Spanish of Don Jorge Manrique

Federigo Spinola, now Captain General of Galleys on the Coast of Flanders, set himself to harry the allied shipping with his augmented power.

But not for a moment did he forget the grand design. He would act as the moment demanded, until the time should come to point again toward what had become the lodestar of his life - the Enterprise of England!

On the very day after his arrival he sallied out from his lair and snatched a prize. Grief, loss and shame befell the Dutch and the English. Whensoever their ships passed along that coast, peril awaited.

A large Anglo-Dutch army marched on Dunkirk and Sluys, and a well-guarded flotilla carried its supplies. But the wind fell. Spinola swooped down upon them like a falcon on fat ducks. The convoying galleon under Captain Adrien Blancker made heroic resistance, and when they abandoned the attack on him he lay dying and his ship was all but a wreck. Spinola carried off over a score of his flotilla. And the allied expedition was a failure.

After the first battle of the Dunes, when the convoy of Maurice of Nassau was becalmed, Spinola's squadron fell upon its rearguard. Much damage was done the allied merchantmen, and the galleys attacked the flagship at bow and stern, where her guns could not bear. The men of the galleys swarmed aboard in overwhelming numbers, beat down all opposition, and cut her out of the fleet. Her sisters lacked wind to come to her aid.

Leonora had traveled northward through Germany. Spinola was surprised at his own delight in their reunion; he found himself thinking up ways to please and intrigue her. She on her part was by no means indifferent to the quality of the man who had become her lover, and pride, gratitude, and the mysterious working of nature combined to make her fall deeply in love. She shut her eyes to a clouded future, and lived intensely in the present.

Juan de Idiaquez, former lieutenant in the army of Spain, had been condemned by a court martial to disgrace and poverty.

The family of Don Felipe de Feria, for its own good name, had rallied to his support. Its power had secured his acquittal; but his naval career was at an end, and he became a monk.

Guillermo del Valle sold his sword to an obscure condottiere of Umbria.

They had been afraid at Brest. Worse, they had been disloyal. Worst of all, they had been mistaken.

Spinola kept his deadly station. Elizabeth's heavy oared crompsters, specially built for service against the galleys, were useless against his mastery of his art. The English even, in a moment of folly, resolved to build galleys of their own, to meet him on even terms. The Dutch built three galleasses, huge oared vessels, slow but heavily armed, to ban the harbor mouths to their foe. But the man seemed unbeatable.

Unbeatable or no - Spinola had not come to Flanders merely to be a thorn in the side of the English and the Dutch. It was now the year 1601 - time for more ambitious projects. He needed only a suitable partner in the enterprise who should exercise command in the army and exhibit a devotion that matched his own. He sought and obtained permission to approach the throne once more.

And now it seemed as though he were indeed the child of fortune.

First he went home and visited his brother.

"Federico," said the elder, "I have some news that will surprise you - pleasantly, I believe."

"I am all ears, Ambrogio."

"The affairs of the House of Spinola go well. The bank is making money. I am making money. But that is not enough.

"I do not know whether I should have thought of this if you had not chosen the career you have. But I grow less interested in piling up pieces of gold. While I am still a young man, I want to do something very different.

"Your successes have suggested to me that perhaps the time has come for the family Spinola to take the rank in Genoa that the Dorias have attained. Why should not the name Spinola be not merely among the four greatest in Genoa, but the first?

"The family can run the bank very well without me. I need not worry about that. I have fathered my sons - the line will, by God's grace, go on after me.

"I have decided to take up the sword!"

A flash of lightning in the dark!

An intelligent and competent man would have asked certain questions. Had Ambrogio any talent for warfare? Was there any reason, other than the man's vanity, to believe that this prisoner of the counting house would be master - could even live - in camp and field? If so, would he fall in with his younger brother's plans? Could Federigo depend on Ambrogio's ability to dovetail one complicated and unfamiliar operation with another? Even brotherly love could be stretched too far. Could he depend on Ambrogio for the very extraordinary loyalty that would be needed when - as they would - parts of the plan went awry?

But Federigo was not merely an intelligent and competent man. He was a genius. And he knew, even before raising them, the answers to his questions.

Two weeks later the Spinolas were in the audience chamber of Philip III. Federigo presented his brother.

"Your majesty," he said, "two years ago I requested your majesty's most gracious permission to turn the naval war in the north against the rebels. I think I may say that I have done so."

"You have indeed, Don Federigo. We are very well pleased with your devotion to the crown. We remember your exploits after the battle of the Dunes."

"I now come on a different errand. Your majesty, I request permission to make you a gift of the throne of England!"

The king, his minister of state, and his minister of marine stared.

"Your royal father, of glorious memory, launched a great armada against the English. In their northern seas, the English were masters of the weather. They used the winds of God against the ships of Spain. Our power, once committed to the Channel, had no choice but to drive forward.

"Ill advised, he then considered an invasion by small craft. This could not even be attempted.

"My brother Ambrogio wishes to enter upon your majesty's service."

Ambrogio spoke in turn. "Your majesty, I am prepared to raise, at my own expense, five thousand foot and one thousand horse, with artillery, ammunition, and supplies, in your majesty's Duchy of Milan. I will march them through German lands to the Low Countries!"

"We did not know that you were in military service," remarked the king.

"I have not been, your majesty! Therefore, I crave permission to do all this at my own cost, lest your majesty's ministers think it unwise to entrust to me the royal troops."

"It is a princely offer," answered Philip.

"In connection with it," Federigo went on, "I ask your majesty for another eight galleys and two thousand troops. I will rendezvous with my brother at Sluys - or it may be Dunkirk. We will pick our weather. In a calm, when the galleons of England are powerless, we will row across the Channel and land your majesty's expeditionary force in England!

"If their ships try to interfere, we will destroy them. If they do not, we will later capture them at our leisure.

"Once Ambrogio's army is established on English soil, with ports in our possession, we will return for the troops of your majesty's Netherlands army - or any others!"

"An astounding plan!"

"Your majesty, I have shown what I can do with galleys. By picking my time and place, I can crush any opposition afloat - as I have crushed it. With God's help, the English Catholics will come in their thousands to serve under your majesty's banner. You will give to God a wholly Catholic England!"

The Duke of Lerma was convinced; which meant that the Council would approve. "Your majesty, our means are stretched all too thin. Without the gracious offers of the Spinolas, we cannot find the funds to carry on."

The king was persuaded. "Go, Senoria, and do as you have spoken. We appoint you Grand Admiral of Spain!"

Only the minister of marine looked at Federigo with skepticism. "And I suppose that you will say, senor, that you cannot fail?"

"Better than that, senor. I <u>will</u> not fail!"

Not all of Spinola's energy could at once overcome the discouragement, the inertia, and the disorganization of the Spanish shipyards. But slowly his squadron took shape. In the first days of June of 1602 he was ready to sail from Santa Maria. His crews were complete, and he took on board a regiment of infantry.

Ambrogio too had encountered more trouble than he had looked for. The jealous governor of Milan had put all sorts of difficulties in his way. Nevertheless, he finally made up his force, and marched for Flanders.

The Enterprise of England was on its way!

XII. THE MEN OF OARS 7 AND 9

The salt made oar-handles like sharkskin; our knees
were cut to the bone with salt-cracks; our hair
stuck to our foreheads; and our lips were cut to
the gums, and you whipped us because we could not row.
           Will you never let us go?
But, in a little time, we shall run out of the portholes
 as the water runs along the oar-blades,
and though you tell the others to row after us
you will never catch us till you catch the oar-thresh
and tie up the winds in the belly of the sail. Aho!
           Will you never let us go?

Song of the galley slaves. Rudyard Kipling

By the end of the sixteenth century, four-man oars were standard in the galleys of Spain. Spinola's flag galley, San Luis, however, although in other respects similar to the rest of the squadron, seated five men to each oar. Spinola numbered his oars odd on the starboard side, even on the port. Beside the usual scouring of Spanish jails, there were in the ship certain rowers of different antecedents.

Outboard on number seven sat Yussuf Ibraheimi. He was a

Morisco; that is to say, he was a descendant of a Moorish family which, after the Christian reconquest of Spain a century earlier, had accepted conversion to Christianity as the bitter alternative to exile or death. The Moriscos were the most industrious segment of the population. Even to the most ragged hidalgo any form of manual toil was demeaning; and while the peasantry of Spain had no pretensions to gentility, the attitude filtered down and made them averse to any work except for the barest necessities of life. The best farms, the best managed flocks were those of the Moriscos, which roused both the jealousy and the contempt of their neighbors. Partly on this account, and partly for good reason (forced conversions often take poorly), their orthodoxy was suspect to the surrounding laity and clergy alike; when a case could be made against one of them, he would find the course of justice a rough one.

The plough horse of a neighbor had been found on Yussuf's property. His plea that it had strayed of its own accord did him no good. He was torn from his wife and children and sentenced to six years at the oar.

Rashid Ibn Daoud pulled next to Yussuf. Rashid had been the son of a peasant in Tunis. His share of the paternal plot, divided among many sons, would have been so inconsiderable that he had given no thought to claiming it. At loose ends in the country's main seaport, he had taken a berth on a trading felluca. The boy was active, intelligent and energetic. He demonstrated these qualities to such good effect that several years later he was second mate when the captain of a raider took passage to Cairo. Impressed by the young man, he made a proposition which, while it entailed loss of rank, offered better prospects in the long run.

Forty years old and captain of his own galley, Rashid was cornered between two converging Christian fleets. There was nothing to do but transfer from a captain's cabin to a rower's bench, and from the society ashore of his fellow captains and his girls to the almost bestial company of his fellow slaves.

Inboard of him sat Suleiman Ibn Khalid. Suleiman had been a deckhand on a Turkish merchantman which had been snatched up by a Genovese galley. From a sailor, enjoying a reasonable stint of work and the freedom of the port when he was ashore, he became a slave of the oar and the lash, fettered like the rest to his seat, changing it only for a place in a chain gang on very heavy labor ashore in winter.

Arturo Mendoza was the scion of a long line of Toledo rabbis and poets. His great-grandfather had fled from Spain to Portugal under the terror of the Inquisition. There had been subsequent removals for the same reason. The line had gone to seed in Arturo, who as an ambitious young man had made his bargain with the Church.

Unfortunately, he had been materially successful, and had aroused the jealousy of a neighbor. When on a Friday evening (the beginning of the Jewish Sabbath) a bribed serving maid set a white cloth on the table and illuminated it with a pair of candles, this was evidence enough to bring the charge of Judaizing. Of course, more evidence than this was required to obtain a conviction of heresy; of course, it was supplied. There was enough doubt so that when he was "relayed to the secular arm" the usual recommendation that no blood be shed was omitted. He escaped the stake accordingly, but endured what in the long run was possibly even greater suffering in the galleys. The informer pocketed the usual half of the heretic's wealth. Mendoza pulled beside Suleiman.

Yehudah ben Maimon sat beside the catwalk. A Jew of Algiers, he had been a passenger in a Turkish vessel that fell to a ship of Malta. They didn't return to Algiers to bother with proceedings for ransom; and in any case Yehudah was not a rich man. The Jewish community of Algiers might have helped, but a purchasing officer of the Spanish crown bid him in for the navy.

Christian Younkerman had been born to the hangman of Oberdortfeld.

There were few more tragically isolated children than the offspring of such fathers. The trade was a legal and necessary one, but was not unnaturally regarded with loathing. (The hangman was the torturer as well.) People approved of his work, and might even enjoy the spectacles he provided; but no one would associate with him. Boys and girls of his family were not permitted to play with other children when they were young, still less to court them when they were grown. For temporary female companionship the young men had only the abandoned women of the town. For wives they would have to seek daughters of their fathers' colleagues, or other pariahs. The girls had only the choice between similar marriages or lives of vice. The fate could not be avoided. The youths were forced by the authorities to follow their fathers' abhorred calling.

Young Christian at some eighteen years of age had courted an outcast of another kind - a wandering Gypsy girl. They had not wedded. A baby died at birth, and the hapless mother was charged, tried, and convicted of infanticide. She was sentenced to the gallows.

Her mother contrived to get word to Christian. There was an old law that a criminal could be saved from the rope if at the gallows' foot a citizen offered marriage. Christian did, and the girl was saved. They married.

But the idyll was not to last. A man of some influence had had his own eye on the girl for a light-o'-love, and put a hired assassin on Christian's trail. In the event, the would-be murderer fell victim to his intended prey. But it was not too difficult for the villainous employer to maneuver an accusation against Christian. A·week later the royal representative pleaded a shortage of rowers, and Christian was led in chains to the inboard seat on bench number nine.

Amyas Merrill was a Devonshire fisherman who had left his nets for the promise of glory and gain in the galleons. In a hot engagement a Spanish ship had been carried, and he was one of the prize crew. Other Spanish vessels coming up, however, his captain was beaten off; Amyas and his fellows had to yield to overwhelming force. Ultimately, he arrived at the bench beside Christian.

Jan de Hertog came from a burgher's family in the city of Gertruydenberg. Patriotism had impelled him to take up a musket in defense of his city. Upon the fall of the town, organized resistance ceased. Jan arrived at his home in time to see a few Spanish troops making free with his wife and his sister-in-law. As he attempted to interfere, a fortunate blow with a gunstock laid him unconscious - fortunate, because it forestalled the sword thrust that would have ended his life. When, finished with the young women, the ravishers discovered that Jan was still alive, they tied him up for sale to a slaver. He in turn sold him to a noble who wished to make a present to the king. So Jan found himself pulling alongside Amyas.

Outboard of him sat Francis Morton. Morton had been a businessman who, although English, had been licensed for some necessary importation in the city of Ferol. It became apparent to the Spanish authorities that he could develop access to information concerning English coastal defenses. Morton had an eye to the main chance. He had no objection to betraying his queen and country if the price were right. For some years important data passed through his hands to those of the Spanish intelligence staff.

Unfortunately for him, he had a high quotient of greed and a low one of judgment. He proceeded to play both ends against the middle. It was only a question of time before either the English or the Spanish would find out what he was up to. It turned out to be the latter.

The presiding judge at his trial rather fancied himself as a humorist. "The prisoner has been interested in garnering information concerning our naval establishment for his friends abroad. Let us send him where he will have ready access to the facts. The prisoner is hereby sentenced to the galleys for life."

A squadron of three galleys of Sali in Morocco adventured far to the north and made a landing near Penzance. Marching inland, they made a rich haul by surrounding a church in which William Blount had just taken as his bride the lovely Alice Faversham. The wedding was well attended, and the corsairs seized a large number of young men and women for the slave markets. On the way back to the ships the prisoners had a last glimpse of their homes as the captors rifled them of plate and other valuables.

The bashaw himself commanded, and was rich enough to allow himself luxuries. He took fair Alice for his own. Blount, embarked in another of the ships, was never to see his bride again.

So at first he hardly minded the hardships and brutalities of a Moorish galley for the unendurable visions of Alice and her fate that tortured his imagination. But he learned in time that even the most desperate misery does not, unfortunately, kill. And when one day a Spanish victory changed his seat from inboard at a Moorish oar to outboard at a Spanish one, it hardly mattered.

Yussuf and Rashid preserved an uncompromising silence to the friars' efforts. It was they who suffered most. Spanish policy was to single out two classes of galley slaves for especially brutal treatment. These were the former captains of Moorish ships, whose fighting and leadership qualities made them particularly dangerous if any chance of revolt should come their way, and the Moriscos, feared and hated because their knowledge of Spanish ways and terrain might make them useful guides in a possible raid or invasion.

The rowmaster's mates, therefore, walking up and down the midships catwalk, would flick their whips with particular venom and frequency upon these unfortunates; and the latter were denied the occasional supplements to the rations, and any extra rest periods. Such slaves were not expected to survive for long, and seldom did.

Suleiman had no more inclination to change his religion than the other two. Seated as he was, however, he thought it wise to emphasize the difference of his position from theirs; so he strove to give the impression that he might ultimately become vulnerable to persuasion.

Mendoza received the attentions of the clergy with unctuous gratitude. He hoped for amelioration of the conditions, if not shortening of the time, of his servitude. In the hearing of Friar Estevan (Spinola had requested that the Franciscan sail with him again) he urged receptiveness upon Ben Maimon. Yehuda looked at him contemptuously.

"You are dying of thirst," Mendoza said, "and you reject the living water that is being offered to your lips."

"It would have been more to the purpose," the other replied, "if water had been applied to the flames that were devouring our brethren at the stakes."

"Can you not believe that the Saviour died for you?"

"Of course he did," was the unexpected reply. "So did Rabbi Akiba, and King Saul on Mount Gilboa, and every man who has given his life in defence of human betterment or freedom."

"The Man of Nazareth opened the gates of heaven itself. He taught the doctrine of mercy and of love."

"Assuredly he did. Why should he not have? Was he not of our people? Had not Moses our teacher bade him love his neighbor as himself?"

"But what of forgiveness and remission of sin?"

"What of them? 'Though your sins be as scarlet,' said Isaiah, 'they shall be washed whiter than snow.'"

"Granted. But these things need to be taught again and again. Why can you not honor Him who promised them on the long road to Calvary?"

"I can. I do. In fact, I might even accept him among the prophets. But the stern New Testament God who delights in the odor of roasting flesh, and who has dealt so horribly with my people and with so many others, I cannot accept. And," with an expression of utter contempt, "I do not spit upon my fathers' graves."

"Has it ever occurred to you that the miseries of Israel may be a punishment for having rejected the divinity and the service of the Son of God?"

"It will surprise you to hear that, yes, I am enough of a mystic that it has. And shall I tell you the result of my reflections?"

"Do."

"We are taught that the judgments of the Lord are true and righteous altogether. But nowhere are we taught the same concerning the judgments of man. It is not the Lord whose hand has been heavy upon us in Christian and even in Moslem lands. He has bestowed upon us health and long life - when we are permitted to enjoy them. Less than our neighbors do we suffer from disease. Our affairs prosper. We have the delights, more perhaps than other peoples, of poetry and of study. It is only the hand of man that is raised against us."

Blount was still immersed in a private world of misery over the fate of his beloved, even more than over the loss of his freedom.

The stubborn Hertog preserved his morale. He had English enough to converse with the two Englishmen. Neither of the others knew of the duplicity of the forsworn merchant Morton. As for Merrill, his period of captivity had been long enough so that he had recovered from his crushing despair and had not yet given up all hope for a better life. All knew by looking at the sun that they were bound for northern waters. There, anything might happen.

Among the relatively favored rowers, the buenos boyas, was one who had found his way to the bench in even stranger fashion There was in the Spanish army a grim gamble, wherein soldiers who had come by a little money would put it up for a toss of the dice. The winner gained the purse; the loser went to the galleys!

XIII. CEZIMBRA ROADS

What new disaster dire intendest thou
To lead these kingdoms, and these folk into?
What deaths, what horrors must they swallow now,
Under pretense to spread religion true?
What holdings, earth of golden mines, and how
Great kingdoms shall be conquered by a few?

The Lusiads. From the Portuguese of Luis Camoens

William Monson's life story reads like a tale of romance.

He had left Oxford to go to sea in a privateer. His first cruise culminated in a bloody action with the taking of the first Spanish prize of war. Thereafter, it had been one voyage after another, until eleven years ago he had suffered what for most men would have been final disaster; he had been captured and sentenced to the galleys.

But Monson never despaired. He used his service at the oar to acquire all manner of new information; and when, incredibly, fortune freed him, he was so useful that he served as flag captain to the Earl of Cumberland in the exploits of 1593, and to Essex in the famous action at Cadiz three years later. It was there that he was knighted. He did good service as commander of Rainbow in the war that followed, and he commanded a galleon in a later crisis. Now, three years later, at the age of forty-three, he flew his vice-admiral's flag for the first time as second to Admiral Sir Richard Leveson.

After cruising about the eastern Atlantic to little purpose, Leveson and Monson found themselves in early June with a rich prize at hand - if they could take it. A great carrack from the East Indies lay in Cezimbra Roads, a short day's sail south of Lisbon. She carried a cargo worth two million. Her homeward course had been a two-year odyssey of disaster; only thirty of her crew of six hundred odd men were still alive.

The governor of Portugal had done his duty. He had put four hundred volunteer fighting men into her, and he had ordered Spinola with his eight galleys, and the young Marquis of Santa Cruz with his three, to rally round the trapped vessel.

Leveson had insufficient power for such an attack. The carrack faced them with a picked, reinforced crew; she was three times the size of the greatest of the five English ships. On the one flank frowned a strong fort with a dozen large caliber guns. On the other, in line abeam, lay the eleven galleys, each one with a sixty-pounder, heavier than anything the English carried, in her bow, as well as four lesser pieces; beyond them were rocks. High overhead rose one of the fortified monasteries so characteristic of Portugal. And on the beach the governor had mustered his troops.

The taking of the carrack therefore, was a desperate project indeed. But there were two factors that favored the English.

After years of mediocre achievement, Leveson had performed brilliantly at Castlehaven in Ireland the year before. He was not going to lose his hard won reputation now.

Monson saw the hated galleys of Spain within range of his guns. More, one of them was the very ship on which he had suffered such bitter servitude; the very officers were still aboard. The old lash scars on his back burned for revenge.

In Leveson's cabin there was a council of war. The admiral was for trial of their fortune. But one after another, through most of that long June day, his captains pointed out the folly of trying to cut out a ship from under the guns of so strong a fort - and of eleven galleys as well. The prize was a tempting one, but they would lose men and ships for nothing. They might, at most, burn her; capture was impossible.

But Monson's raging hate drove him to support his chief. The carrack? There were men aboard her, admittedly, but they were not yet a crew. The galleys? Had not Drake shown at Cadiz that nothing could stand up to the English broadside? Forts? Was not one function of a galleon to stand in and silence shore batteries? Stout oak would absorb a tremendous amount of punishment. Were they to return home and report to their royal mistress that she had been defrauded of her prize by pusillanimous hearts bred in the English earth?

"Gentlemen," Monson said at last, "if Sir Richard and I, in our two ships and prizes, will undertake to carry the enemy without other aid, will you engage the forts and galleys, that we may not have an insupportable fire playing upon ourselves?"

For very shame they could hardly refuse.

Rashid sat impassively at his oar and watched the English power come on. It was ten in the morning; there would be much hot fighting. To him the outcome was immaterial. If the Spanish won, his lot would not change. If the English won, he would no longer be in a galley - the English had no slaves - but things were not likely to be any better. He had seen nothing to give him faith in any Christian mercy. In any case, all things were in the hands of Allah.

Was it error, or was it by reason of faintheartedness, that he saw her sailing master let the English flagship drift down to leeward and out of the battle? No matter. The raging English admiral transferred his flag to another ship, and the battle was joined. Rashid felt the galley leap as she loosed her powerful armament against the northerners.

That other great galleon, with the banners that proclaimed a rear admiral aboard, had taken station where she could use both her broadsides against carrack, galleys and fort. Especially the galleys, as though her commander nursed a special hatred for the oared ships. His shot raked one after another of them. Men were screaming, now, in the crowded rowing benches as the English fire told. Rashid saw a mast fall, and another. A hit on the superstructure drove huge splinters of wood like missiles through the air, and there were screams again from the hapless flesh that stopped them.

Galleys, fort and carrack were pounding the rear admiral's ship; but she proudly held the position of honor. Her guns poured death into the carrack. The gallant young men who had marshalled for her defense were lying redly about the decks. The East Indiaman's fire had noticeably slackened.

So had that of the galleys. Guns had been dismounted. Gunners drooped dead or dying over their useless artillery. One galley was awash; another drifted out of line with her. The English boarded them, and there was little fight left in the crews.

An English cannon ball came over Spinola's bow. It tore the shoulder from Rashid, sent a splinter flying into Yehudah's throat, and the chest of young Blount simply disappeared. Blount would grieve no more over lost Alice; he went where there was neither marrying nor giving in marriage; the glory of the Lord delighted his soul. Rashid rose joyfully to his feet and clasped to his bosom two of the houris, the dark-eyed virgin daughters of Paradise, whose bodies were created of purest musk. Yehudah had been taught to do God's will, as far as he could; what followed was unknowable, and God's business, not man's. He advanced to whatever might be.

The wounded Marquis of Santa Cruz had withdrawn with his shattered hulls. There was nothing more that Spinola could accomplish. To remain would simply be to sacrifice his six remaining ships to no purpose. As a fighting force, for the time being, they were finished. His surviving oarsmen began to pull for Lisbon.

But the carrack was still not English prey. The fort still

poured down a fire that interdicted approach. It was five in the afternoon; the admiral decided to burn her. For this he called upon two German prizes.

Naturally, they were reluctant to brave the fortress' guns. But he made them very sure that what risk they might run thereby was less than what they would incur by refusing. Strange though it seems, that was a lawful practice at the time.

Not unnaturally, they did poorly, and their mission miscarried. But a flag of truce summoned an English party to the great ship, and in the event she was surrendered with her cargo. What was left of her people were to withdraw with their arms. "So the matter ended," says Corbett, "and Monson carried the captain and all his gentlemen back to supper on the Garland, where with a variety of music they spent the night in great jollity together."

Well might the English rejoice. It had been a tremendous feat of arms, not equalled in the whole course of the war. They sailed their prize triumphantly to England.

Scarcely less gratifying was their victory over the galleys. Not only did Monson taste the sweetness of revenge, but the redoubtable Spinola, who for two long years had thrust like a lance into their shipping in their very home waters, had been beaten. His reign of terror was over. His galleys smashed, himself defeated and humbled, he would trouble her majesty's subjects on the high seas no more. In London, Plymouth, Bristol, and Hull, in Amsterdam and Utrecht, merchants and shipmasters lifted their bumpers and rejoiced. Spinola was finished.

Only Spinola did not know it. He spared not a thought to the past. Galleys were never meant to stand up to galleons when any kind of wind was blowing, and fight it out toe to toe. He had done as he had been ordered, but the decision to fight had not been his. Given a calm, he would face the great ships; but to do it otherwise was madness.

With his formidable energy he set himself to the restoration of his squadron. The shipwrights of Lisbon worked long hours upon his battered craft. By September, dead and wounded personnel were replaced, and his complement of 250 rowers per ship sat again at the oars. Nearly a thousand soldiers of Spain filed aboard. After two months, he was ready for sea.

He made provision for Leonora against the chances of his death - or marriage. He was now thirty-one years old.

By spies, by merchant seamen, by neutral diplomatic channels, the word went forth to the Dutch and the English: Spinola is coming! The Genovese is on the prowl! The long, lean galleys point their prows to the north once more!

XIV. THE NARROW SEAS

No one said those last words due the dead;
No one closed their widely staring eyes;
But, in their final agonies, they returned
Each to his mother's house to pace unseen,
Or like a shadow, and a chill wind blew
Quenching the flame that leaped upon the hearth.

From the Spanish of Oscar Lamas

In his flag galley, San Luis, Spinola led his squadron northward. With him were San Felipe, Lucero, San Juan, Hyacinth, and Padilla. Trinity and Opportunity had been lost at Cezimbra Roads.

Yehudah's place at the oar had been filled by a recruit known only as "El Cordovano." He too, as it happened, had been an executioner, in the service of the government of Spain.

Those who habitually apply torture are likely to experience one of two reactions. A minority come to find it unendurable; they begin with severe conflicts of conscience, go on to minor illnesses of one sort or another, and progress to a complete moral and physical breakdown. Most, however, at first regard torture as a means to an end; thereafter, they look upon it as routine; and finally they get to enjoy it. El Cordovano was of the latter.

He insisted on regaling Christian with accounts of his more "successful" procedures.

"You can do very well for yourself," he told the others, "if you are careful; but it is dangerous. You can arrange things so that the condemned will suffer less or more; and the family will often be glad to make a financial accommodation. Considerable money can be made in this fashion."

He paused and grinned. "More than money. As you know, women are often strangled before being burned. If a pretty girl is accommodating, well and good; if not, there can be an accident. I remember one convicted of Judaizing. She was a real beauty. She wouldn't come across. It just happened that the rope that should have strangled her burnt through too fast. She screamed for almost three hours!" He paused again. "But I got careless. They caught up with me. That's why I'm here."

Brother Estevan had overheard in the dark. He groaned. On the next day at mealtimes instead of eating he went below and swung the knotted cord. "Forgive us, Father! Forgive us and have mercy!"

Christian was also outraged. He was an honest workman. He voiced his indignation.

The other grinned again. "Look here, pal. You are so particular. But we've come to the same place; and I at least have had something to show for it!" This was enough to silence Mendoza, who had been about to make some self-righteous remark.

Mansell, with only his flagship Hope and two of the oared, three masted, heavily gunned smaller crompsters, would be unable to trap Spinola. But in early September Admiral Opdam came by Plymouth, on his way back to Holland; and he left his Vice-Admiral, Jan Cant, with two fine ships and two large flyboats, under Mansell's orders. He knew about the enemy's progress.

In mid-month came the warning: Spinola is on the Breton coast! Cant put to sea and joined Mansell off Dungeness for a council of war. Dunkirk and Sluys had each its blockading squadron; but they looked for the Genovese to favor the coast of England. So Cant with half the force was to lie in the Downs, while Mansell was to keep station on Dungeness. They still trusted in the power of the great ships.

From Dungeness Mansell reached out his arm far into the waters of the Channel; the flyboats were his fingertips. And by first light of a misty dawn on the 3rd of October the flyboats saw the six galleys running up the Channel on a stiff southwesterly, closing the English coast. They gave chase, a little further to seaward, but converging. Spinola stood defiantly on course until the brightening dawn revealed powerful Hope athwart his way.

Down went his sails, and down his helms; the mighty oarsmen began pulling dead to windward, where the sailing vessels could not follow. But as well as they could, they too put themselves on a windward leg, and away went the crompster Advantage to warn the Dutch squadrons.

Mansell stood for mid-Channel. All day Spinola's brilliant maneuvering kept the foe at a distance. The hours wore on; suddenly

Spinola turned downwind again, and close to the coast hoisted sail, slipped inside his enemies and raced for the Downs.

Dover appeared at five in the afternoon; as they left it astern their master-at-arms unchained Hertog, Morton, and Weston, Blount's English replacement, to hand the mess kits. But then they passed the South Foreland close aboard; and of a sudden the three flung themselves into the sea and swam for it. They all made the shore.

Mansell's squadron was still pursuing in the dropping wind and failing light. They were further out from the coast, herding the galleys toward the Downs, to the narrow waters between the coast of Kent and the deadly Goodwin Sands. There the guns of Bredgate and of Cant were waiting for them. Mansell steered further to sea to cut off Spinola's escape. But his wind dropped.

On rowed Spinola in the gathering darkness. The moon rose, and a breeze sprang up. Suddenly, there was the flash of guns off the port bow as Cant tried the range! On the west side of Cant was the shore; somewhere on his east side was Mansell; dead ahead were the dreaded Goodwin Sands!

But this was Spinola; now came the fortune that favored the brave - and the clever. The wind dropped - not long, but possibly long enough. While the Downs squadron drifted impotently, the oarsmen carried the galleys around the south end of the sand toward the Flemish coast.

But the wind rose again, and there was Mansell, coursing, coursing in the darkness. Suddenly, his lookout sang out for a galley almost under his bowsprit! The darkness gave way to a line of fire as he poured in a devastating broadside; there were screams and the crash of falling spars. Mansell would have offered quarter; but suddenly the other five galleys were all about him, and he had to look to himself lest he fall prey to boarding in overwhelming force. So he drew off, and the galleys disappeared in the night.

Spinola had escaped a cunning trap. His way was open to the Netherlands coast. There, he was home free if, as once before, he could evade the Dutch blockade. But his rowers were tiring, and he had a crippled ship to nurse; he must run the gauntlet of the aroused fleets of two nations. He no longer knew where all his ships were, and he dared not light a rallying signal.

Never did fortune more deserve the name of fickle jade. One after another, the Dutch ships encountered the much lighter galleys. The great object of their gunners was to cripple the enemy, so that they could despatch him at leisure. So they emptied their cannon into the massed galley slaves at pistol shot range. Pieces of row benches and of human bodies flew through the air. The beautiful galleys became floating heaps of wreckage manned by the wounded and the dead. Two of them fell athwart the bows of the heavy Dutch ships; the latter crashed into them, smashed them under foot and sank them. Two drifted as wrecks onto the Flemish sands; one ran ashore as a heap of useless wood just outside of Calais.

Only the flagship San Luis was still afloat. At dawn they caught her, and forced her deep into the Flemish shoals; then they drew off to watch her death agonies.

In the wind and surf, she heeled so far over that now on one, now on the other side, the rowers sat in the bitterly cold water to their waists. It did not matter. Utter exhaustion had taken its toll. There was no more work left in them. In vain the sailing master shouted that if they did not row they would drown beside their Spanish masters. In vain the master-at-arms' mates walked the catwalk, whips swinging viciously. The slaves had accepted death. Christian, Suleiman, and Yussuf and the rest would serve the oar no more.

Still Spinola was not beaten. Overboard went the guns; over went the shot; over went the stores; over went everything not needed for flotation or propulsion. Then the admiral addressed the slaves. He spoke one sentence only.

"Men of the oar! When this galley reaches Dunkirk or Sluys, every one of you will walk ashore a free man!"

A great cheer rose. Muscles cramped in agony unknotted to take one more stroke, and another, and another, and another; gasping lungs filled again. They pulled as though fresh and unwearied; and they pulled her into Dunkirk with her treasure.

San Luis alone of the flotilla reached safety.

As Spinola had promised, her slaves were given their freedom.

Only not Yussuf. He had been found dead, still chained to his oar.

XV. APOTHEOSIS

All habited in mourning weeds
Come marching from afar
By four and four, the valiant men
Who fought with Aliatar.

All mournfully and slowly
The afflicted warriors come
To the deep wail of the trumpet
And beat of muffled drum.

From the Spanish of an unknown Poet.

Not his recent failure, nor the covert sneers of Duke Albert's army, nor the arms of Leonora could distract Spinola from his duties. A new squadron of eight galleys and two smaller oared frigates began to take shape. Proud England would yet bow to the Spanish crown and the holy apostolic Church!

Ambrogio, arrived in the Low Countries, had already demonstrated his brilliance at the siege of Ostend. They two would yet bring it off!

But on the staff of the governor there was scant sympathy with Federigo's ideas. Even in Sluys, the base for so many of his triumphs, men looked askance at the galley admiral. Disesteem led to delay, and delay became sabotage. Weeks wore on; it was May, and he had accomplished nothing.

There was a function one evening, to which Spinola - unwisely, perhaps - escorted Leonora Mondego. She was snubbed by some ladies of the archducal court. Furious, Federigo complained to the governor.

"I regret the offence, senor, if offense there was," the cardinal replied. "Perhaps it would be as well if the lady absented herself."

Spinola's temper, grown more and more taut under the hostility that surrounded him, could brook no more. "Perhaps, your grace, it would be even better if I did the same."

Albert shrugged. "Perhaps," he agreed.

Furious, Spinola left with his companion. He brooded on the insult. He would have to effect some great exploit to shame his enemies.

A Dutch fleet of two big, powerful galleons and the two

galleys that they had built specifically to operate against Spinola was blockading the port. Spinola sallied out and took up a favorable position. It was a windless day. He had ideal conditions. He attacked at daybreak.

But the indomitable Dutch did not know that their situation was hopeless. Michelzoon's famous Black Galley moved bravely forward. Two of Spinola's vessels rammed her at speed, and stuck fast.

There ensued an incredible fight with guns and steel between the sailors of Spain and those of Holland, and between four hundred soldiers of Spain against thirty-six musketeers of Flushing. Manfully the Hollanders presented their breasts to the missiles, pikes and cutlasses of Spain. Their gunners poured artillery fire at close range into the packed rowing benches of Spinola's galleys, with ghastly results. Michelzoon fell dead; but Hart, his lieutenant, was just as determined. Himself severely wounded, he carried on the fight on the bloody decks. Finally the Black Galley broke away, the two Spanish bowsprits stuck in her sides, and her opponents were glad enough to let her go.

Meanwhile, four galleys hurled themselves on Logier's galleon, and another terrible boarding action began. But her people were of the same heroic temper as Michelzoon's, and threw off the Spanish storm. So hot was her fire that they willingly left her to join Spinola in a fresh assault on the bleeding Black Galley. This would have been her end; but Logier drifted near, and added his fire to hers.

Spinola, conspicuous in handsome armor, had been, as always, heedless of danger. He stood prominently in sight encouraging his men.

The guns of the Black Galley spoke again. A ball crashed in; it tore off Spinola's arm just below the shoulder. He fell with twenty-four wounds in his body.

A breeze sprang up, and the galleons closed to assist their lighter sisters. The Spanish galleys fled with their dead toward the safety of Sluys. Their admiral died in less than an hour.

So fell Federigo Spinola. In his thirty-two years he had dared much, and achieved much. But his great goal, the Enterprise of England, was never attained, either by him or by any other. He deserved better of fortune. His exploits by sea stand as a memorial to the greatness of both Spain and his native Genoa. Let me put him among the stars, for alas! He is all but forgotten.

With him died the doctrine of the galley. Thereafter, the great sailing ship was supreme.

The Fourth Wager

The religious wars were over. In the north, the soldiers of Great Britain, Prussia, Scandinavia, and Holland had maintained the Reformation. The souls of John Knox and Martin Luther had looked on disapprovingly as Federigo Spinola made his great run from Lisbon to the Low Countries.

"The judgments of the Lord are true and righteous altogether," Knox quoted. "They are not for me to question. But I wish I could understand why He makes no distinction between true believer and Papist."

Luther nodded agreement. "Like it or not, we must accept what He ordains."

"No other man will ever defy British sea power in that fashion. Despite what Spinola and Godwin, and perhaps forgotten captains, achieved, the emerging Britain of today is another sort of antagonist."

Luther raised his eyebrows. "Still the Scottish chauvinist! I see no reason why another should not do as well or better. A man of German speech, perhaps! What has happened, will happen again."

"I tell you that it is impossible."

Let us see. Shall we try to arrange for another confrontation in the Channel? If the Throne grants permission, then we shall view a new defiance of the British men-of-war by an inferior naval force. If it wins, then I shall forego the bliss of delighting in the divine presence for 100 days. If it loses, it will be you who deprive yourself."

"Agreed."

In the dark souls of the men who seized power in what came to be known as the Axis, there was no place for saints, for angels, or even for God.

THE BLACKNESS OF THE EAGLE

A wind arose. Westward it blew over the fair fields and firesides of freedom; and where it passed, it left the fetid smell of blood. Faintly to the ear it bore the moans of the tormented, and the daunting tramp of hosts of marshalled men. It spread fear over the face of Europe.

Inspired by the fascism of Italy, a mad tyrant evoked a foul brown slime from the hidden places of the German soul. Not the least of the horror was the responsive loosing of the same feral pollution in other lands. The brown shirts of Adolf Hitler ranged themselves beside the black shirts of Mussolini. Now the cagoulards of France arose to join in the wolfish chorus, and the green shirts of Romania and Hungary, and even, to our shame be it written, the silver shirts of the United States.

In all human hearts lurks the love of evil. Woe to mankind when it is unchained - woe first to the victims, then to the perpetrators!

1

The Laying of the Keel

I sense the winds that are coming, I must live them...
For already I know the storms and am stirred like the
seas.

Presentiment. From the German of Rainer Maria Rilke.

The armored cruiser Scharnhorst, of the German Asiatic
Squadron, had done her emperor good service in action against a
British force off Chile at the outbreak of World War I. Now the
victorious ships stood to the east to destroy the enemy's radio station
in the Falkland Islands. This would disrupt communications in the
South Atlantic; thereafter the Kaiser's squadron could raid Allied
shipping for a long time before reports of their activities, still less of
their whereabouts, could reach the Admiralty in London.

But in that cold, lonely, far-off sea they were trapped and
brought to action by the much more powerful British "Invincible" and
"Inflexible." On August 12, 1914, after three hours of desperate but
hopeless struggle, Scharnhorst sank with all on board.

Eventually, the rest of the German navy was lost or scuttled.
And that was to have been the end of German naval power.

But within a decade the nations of the west, paralyzed by
their fear of Russia and Communism, were turning a blind eye to
Germany's steps toward rearmament. A small military establishment
was permitted her by treaty. But her soldiers went secretly to Russia
for further training (the masters of the Kremlin were even more
paranoid about the west), and her naval architects worked elaborately
to design ships that in the parlance of yacht racing could be known as
"rule cheaters."

The German naval leaders dreamed of a newer, more
powerful, and more fortunate Scharnhorst. They were permitted
cruisers of 10,000 tons, eleven inches of armor plate, and a main
battery of eleven inch guns. This was slightly liberalized in
subsequent agreements. But what they designed, in great secrecy, was
a battleship of 38,000 tons. And the German admiralty worked in

every possible improvement in offensive and defensive power.

So on the shipways of Wilhelmshafen, in the year 1934, a mighty ship began to take form. First the shipwrights set up a line of huge wooden blocks. On this they laid a long, narrow steel keelplate, over which they fastened a girder.

In the heart of the beautiful city of Hamburg was the lovely Lake Alster. On one bank rose the ornate old city hall; from a quay before it small passenger boats ran through a network of canals. On another bank was the apartment of Herr Professor Dr. Herman Hartmann of the Department of European History at the University. In this home, in the war year of 1917, his wife Elsa bore him a healthy, well-favored son. They christened him Emil.

11

THE BUILDING OF THE SHIP

We need hate, and more hate, and yet more hate!
(Speech). From the German of Adolf Hitler.

For two years the ship gradually took shape in the yard. Along its length, transversely across the keel, the floors were laid. Slowly and with much effort ribs arose from their lateral extremities; stem and sternposts were added, and when the beams joined the tops of the ribs from side to side, the skeleton of a great denizen of the sea lay along the way. Seven hundred and seventy-four feet she measured overall and ninety-eight in beam, and if her designer were correct, she should draw thirty-four and a half feet of water.

Now a skin of steel plates began to grow fast to the bottom and sides of the framework, and against the perils of stranding, collision, torpedo, or mine, another on the inside of her bottom. Men swarmed within her, dividing the cavernous space into some twenty watertight compartments against the same dangers. Eleven and a half inches of armor grew fast to her sides. Deck plates closed in the hull, and wooden planks dressed their surface.

Scharnhorst received her engines. Meticulously the

machinists installed and fastened them, lining them up with the propeller shafts. Two turrets, each with eleven inch guns, were built into the hull forward and one aft. Four twin turrets with two six inch guns each and four more such guns separately were welded and bolted in position. Fourteen four inch and sixteen one-and-half-inch flak guns were added, and ten (later there would be thirty-eight) guns of four-fifths inch caliber. Six torpedo tubes completed her formidable armament. There was hangar space and launching apparatus for two scouting planes.

When the last turret was added, and higher pressure steam engines were given her, Scharnhorst could outface anything but the heaviest units afloat.

Men in uniform began to gather in Scharnhorst - seamen, a prospective commanding officer, a medical officer, machinist's mates, cooks, gunners.

A great seaport has something international about it; the ocean currents carried all sorts of freight and ideas from all over the world into Hamburg, and into the apartment on Scheidegger Street. The growing boy heard in the conversations between his father and guests repeated presentations of points of view that ranged widely over the political and economic worlds. Not a few who shared the Hartmann hospitality were visiting foreigners. So the boy grew as in some sense a citizen of the world.

In some sense. In school, of course, the emphasis was on uncritical support and admiration of all things German. And when at the age of eleven he left primary school for Gymnasium, this attitude was intensified both within and without the academic halls. As he progressed in what in America would be a combination of high school and junior college, among the boys, as among their elders, the threefold lines became drawn between those who, like the Hartmanns, supported the republic and the status quo, the dedicated Communists, and the fire-eating National Socialists or Nazis.

Germany, alone among the nations of the west, had never freed her spirit from the shackles of the feudal system, in which in theory the serfs obeyed the freemen, the freemen the barons, and the last the king. When the democracy that succeeded to the Kaiser's rule after World War I was unable to solve all problems within a few years, many in the land yearned after the pristine simplicity of being told what to do, and having all difficult decisions made for them by their superiors and handed down through the chain of command. So when Adolf Hitler offered himself as the power and conscience of

Germany, there were enough who were more than willing to hand over their independence and freedom, and force the reluctant ones to accept the National Socialist regime.

The National Socialists' Hitler Youth reached out for the growing lads. But in educated circles they had initially little success.

There was no explanation when an ill prepared, loutish young man appeared suddenly as dozent - instructor - in economics at the university. He propagandized vigorously for the new order. He visited Professor Hartmann one day in the latter's office.

"It is high time, professor, that your son gave some evidence of his patriotism," he said, "and that of his family. The Hitler Youth is the ideal training school, and he should join."

"Emil is young for political activity."

"They start much younger, professor, as you know. Our day is coming. Our friends will enjoy the fruits of the struggle; those who have been against us will rue it."

Hartmann became angry. "Are you threatening me, sir?"

"Not yet. But I think that the threats will come soon. A wise man will make them unnecessary."

The better part of Emil viewed the extremists of both right and left camps with aversion. But part of him yearned after the relief of wildly enthusiastic fellowship with his comrades, and the drowning of all painful questionings in blind worship of the Fuehrer - the Leader - and the nation. Especially after Hitler became Chancellor.

Then the glove came off the iron hand. There was a summons to the office of the Rector of the university for Professor Hartmann and others.

"We must adjust to new times," the older man told them. "A new soul is growing in Germany. Our country is going to take her place in the sun, and we must all support her."

"Hamburg is the only state of Germany that did not vote in Adolf Hitler," Hartmann objected. "Are we nevertheless to submit to this blackmail?"

"We did not vote the Nazis in." the other agreed. "So what happened? The storm troopers simply marched into the state legislature and threw the elected members out. Do you want that in the university? Your son, Herr Professor, had better join the Hitler Youth."

"I am still my son's father, and I decide on his activities."

The rector smiled wanly. "Do you? Let me tell you of the things that will happen if Emil remains outside the Hitler Youth. You will probably lose your post. No, the threat does not come from me - I have become a mere messenger. And you will lose Emil. Oh, yes, they can - and I assure you they will. The boy will be taken from you. And what of his future? If he remains on the outside, I assure you that he will not have one."

It would have availed little if Hartmann had continued to resist. Enrollment in the organization soon thereafter became compulsory.

So, in addition to his studies, his sport - Emil was a solid and dependable soccer player - and his piano, Emil foregathered regularly with a chapter of the Hitler Youth. He knew better than to repeat his father's remarks on criminal idiocy among his new companions, even though, to a large extent, he shared the older man's ideas of the evil of the death-obsessed movement. The mass hypnosis of his fellows could not however be wholly withstood; he thrilled with the rest over the national triumphs won by the Leader through the supineness of the democracies, sang the songs, and longed despite himself, at times, to be one with his generation.

As for instance when the unit attended the rally at the medieval city of Nuremberg.

The brown clad ranks of the Hitler Youth stood motionless as Adolf Hitler addressed them. He was finishing his peroration.

"And so we march forward against the satanic enemy who would destroy our sacred Germany. We march - in our hands, steel! In our minds, steel! Deutschland uber alles!"

He stood at the podium while a forest of red banners waved overhead, and thousands of young lusty voices cried, as arms shot rhythmically forward in the Nazi salute, "Victory, hail! Victory, hail! Victory, hail!"

Despite all doubts, the orator's hypnotic voice had its effect on young Hartmann; and as he cheered with the rest, he felt for the moment the excitement of being one among many - the comforting solidarity with the mass of his fellows.

But in the following week he watched helplessly as a squad of brown uniformed storm troopers beat a hapless gypsy into a mass of bloody, tormented flesh.

ᘔᘔᘔ

Launching.

Who that height of bliss has proved
Once a friend of friends to be,
Who has won a maid beloved
Join us in our jubilee!

Ode to Joy. From the German of Johann Schiller.

 Two years had gone by when before a festive assemblage a lady broke a bottle of champagne against the gleaming bow. Simultaneously, a workman swung a mighty sledge hammer, and as the fair sponsor intoned, "I christen you Scharnhorst, and may your career be as glorious as that of your namesake," the ship slid majestically down the ways and entered the water that would thenceforth be her natural element.

 Quickening came to the ship. When a stronger gale than usual set the waves dancing even in the protected waters of the harbor, the ship stirred faintly, beginning at long last to be a creature of the sea.

 In the year 1936, Emil, aged 18, graduated from the Gymnasium.

 The city of Hamburg sits on the Elbe River, very near the sea. It had been a leading member of the medieval Hanseatic League, and its ships had fared widely with the freights of northern Europe. In the days of the Weimar republic, after World War I, it was one of the three German towns which retained their rights as members of the league - with its tiny hinterland it formed a state of the federal republic - and it proudly carried on with its maritime tradition. The estuary of the Elbe was also a base for the small but rapidly growing German navy.

 Despite its freedom of thought, the Hartmann family had always been a patriotic one; and under and with the influence of an uncle in the service, Emil applied for admission to the naval academy. His grades had been excellent, his personality unexceptionable, his heritage solid. He was accepted. He made his farewells to the city of his birth, entrained for Flensburg, and embarked upon his career.

 The academy town was situated on an arm of the Baltic, just at the Danish border. Behind the gate with its eagle insigne rose the castle-like brick Gothic towers with tiled roofs - buildings such as the Teutonic knights had raised along the length of the Baltic. About them grew fir and beech. Wide meadows sloped down to the waterfront. Emil gazed enthralled at the academy flotilla. Where once Viking galleys had put to sea, rode ships whose rowers were steel and flame, and whose screw-shaped oars were of bronze. The training barks Horst Wessel and Gorch Gock dominated the numerous small craft.

At Flensburg, the two hundred sixty odd Officer Aspirants spent their first ten weeks as though they were in the army. There were close order drill, practice with various weapons, physical training, and, with heavy packs or without them, marching, marching, marching. Some of the youths, unable or unwilling to endure the rugged regime, dropped from the academy.

There followed weeks on the two square-rigged ships.

It was at the end of this year that Professor Hartmann died of a heart attack. Emil's mother had been ill with influenza; she insisted nevertheless on following her husband's remains to the cemetery on a cold, wet, blustery day. Within the week she joined him in death.

Emil had loved his parents, and was deeply affected by their passing. No one ever really recovers from the loss of those he loves. One adjusts, however, after a fashion, and learns to laugh again.

And he met Leni that year.

He had some time coming to him, late in the year; and in a sporting goods store in nearby Kiel he saw a notice of a week's course in skiing, to be offered in the Ore Mountains, on the Czech border. Emil had a relative in Dresden, a few hours further west, and he decided to combine the outing with a visit to his kin.

Dresden was beautiful, especially the banks of the Elbe. He watched fascinated as the barges made their way upstream by winding a chain lying on the river bottom around drums on their decks. There was the opera, which he had learned at home to appreciate, and the theater, both of high quality; and the collection in the ornate Zwinger, especially the Sistine Madonna. Dresden had not long ago been the cultural center of Germany.

He found the skiers to be a small group of young or youngish, mostly middle-class people. The little hotel offered simple but adequate accommodations and meals. The whitened landscape of coniferous forest with slopes at all angles served excellently both for practice and pleasure of the eye.

Hartmann was agile and enterprising, and quickly became the star pupil of the instructress. Leni Ketterman was two years his senior. Petite, trim, well favored in face and voice and with curly, shoulder-length dark brown hair she was easy to admire. He found great pleasure in following her through the fairy-tale forest. When they came to a slope, she was off and away with a ringing "Lo-o-os!"

It was a delight to sweep after her down a mist-shrouded hillside studded with trees grotesquely deformed by snow and frost, where one expected at any moment to witness the emergence of a gnome from under the weighted-down branches, or to watch as, locks flying in the wind of her motion, she eased gracefully around tight turns in a forest trail, or arced sinuously down a hill through the, hitherto, unmarred whiteness of a snowy meadow.

The others, with their imperfect mastery of stem turn and even snow plough, would hesitate, but Emil swept right into her wake.

"You can make a good skier," she told him. "You are stronger and more enduring on the trail than most. And, not surprising in a military man, you've more courage."

"I suppose that I have as much courage as the next one," he replied. "But I haven't demonstrated it here. What you think was courage, was simply common sense. When you tell us to do something that looks dangerous, the others hesitate. But I realize that if it were really dangerous, you would not order beginners to do it."

"Be that as it may, you get the credit for performing. We owe it not only to ourselves, but to our Germany, to make ourselves as fit as we can."

And again, when some one had proposed an evening sleigh ride and some one else had objected on the grounds that one could see nothing at night, his "It's not a matter of seeing, but of feeling" brought her vigorous agreement. "It is probably the same sensitivity to feeling that determines your attachment to a sea-faring life. We have a saying, 'The boat and the ski are sisters.'"

"I think you'd look as charming in a boat as you do on the boards," he mused.

She laughed. "I love the skis and the mountains. If I could pick the manner of my death, I should like to be on my skis, in the hills."

He grimaced. "I love the sea and ships. But I have no objection to serving out my time afloat, and dying thereafter - not too soon thereafter - in bed. But Let's talk about something less morbid."

"I saw 'Wilhem Tell' recently. I am far from being a

dramatic critic, but it seemed to me to be poorly done."

"My father and his friends used to say that actors no longer take plays of that genre seriously; they just don't give themselves the trouble to play them well."

"Another illustration of the demoralization of which our Leader complains."

"Let us hope," he murmured, "that he will change such things."

"He will! He will! And he will free us from the chains of our Versailles Treaty!"

"It was a bad treaty," he agreed. "But let's not go overboard in our thinking. Too many of our countrymen wallow in self-pity, and never consider the distress that occurs everywhere."

"Not like ours," she replied. "You know how we have been victimized by the devilish Versailles Treaty slavery. Only recently the director of the municipal laboratory was complaining to my father about the quality of the microscopes. He said that on account of the reparations, all the good microscopes are in France or Britain!"

Emil nodded. "We have been well indoctrinated regarding the evils of the Versailles Treaty. But the loans from America, I am told, more than make up for the reparations - loans which probably will never be repaid."

"There have been unemployment and want in Germany. They swept away jobs and income, and the people suffered."

"But that the phenomenon is world wide does not occur to most Germans; and, when it is called to their attention, they can't believe it. Don't American motion pictures show luxurious mansions and motor cars? That those who service these things are obviously not wealthy, never crosses most minds."

"Don't talk to me about the sufferings of the poor American millionaires," Leni exclaimed, "or the impoverished British, with their whole empire to support them! Even if the want is real, and I don't believe it is, I'm just not interested."

Emil had a feeling of irritation. But Leni was really very pretty, and he changed the subject.

Such was supposedly their conversation. Did a youth in Hitler's Germany actually woo a maid with talk of economics and world politics? One cannot aver that that was so, any more than one can assert that in Stalin's Russia a swain would tell his sweetheart that he loved her because her labor team had broken the factory's record for the production of 6 centimeter bolts. As Herodotus observed, one is duty bound to record what is reported, but one cannot guarantee its correctness.

Leni's home was in Kiel, near Flensburg; so it was possible for Emil to see her after their return.

Upon his visit, Leni was proud of her dashing cavalier, with his narrow silver shoulder straps, officer's belt and buckle, and sword. And a happy reunion they made of it.

Leni was very sweet in the park that afternoon. Now she sat opposite him in the restaurant. A man at the next table told a Jewish joke which dissolved his companions in laughter.

Leni turned appreciatively to her companion. "Thank God that the glorious Adolf Hitler has opened our eyes to the nature of the Jews. They are parasites upon society. They are destroyers of culture."

"Are they? They seem to live and work like every one else. I have heard Dr. Heinrichs say that if you take away their contribution to medicine, even our German medicine, great as it is, would collapse like a building from which one has removed every tenth brick or girder. All of our ethics comes from their bible. Every young German woos his sweetheart with the poetry of Heine. And can you imagine a cruise down the Rhine without a rendition of Lorelei?"

"What you say cannot be true. Why would the Fuehrer be against them?"

"The master propagandists of the party know that if they can drag their fellow nationals to a common delight in human degradation, suffering and death, they will have a mass following that will become addicted to the drug of sadism, and so can be controlled." He was quoting his father. "Man has always been reluctant to take the blame for his own faults and stupidity. One scapegoat has always been available - the Jew. He is everywhere and always outnumbered. He has no homeland. A Christian or a Muslim, ill treated at home or abroad, can always hope that coreligionists in a powerful government will give him assistance, or at least a refuge. Likewise a Buddhist, a Confucianist, or what have you. But there is no Jewish state to espouse that cause.

"The Jew has survived over a thousand years of our torture, pillage, rape, and massacre. Why should we not continue so glorious an achievement?"

"But the Fuehrer has justified his hatred and his measures against the Jew," she objected.

"Of course he has. The Jews as a class, they tell us, are Communists, dedicated to the destruction of the capitalist system.

"The Jews as a class, they tell us, live and can live only as capitalists - which is to say, as exploiters of the labor of others.

"That these two postulates are mutually incompatible troubles no one.

"The Jews as a class, they say, are crass materialists, interested in none of the higher purposes of life.

"The Jews as a class, they say, have forced themselves into the cultural life of Germany to an extent utterly disproportionate to their numbers.

"That this pair of postulates too is mutually incompatible likewise goes unnoticed.

"All of these charges are published in the journals of the Party, again and again. If any perceive their fallacies, they keep their pens unused - or live to regret it."

"Granting what you say, I don't like them anyway!" Her eyes flashed. "Innocent or guilty, what matters it? All this milk-and-water righteousness and love one another stuff turns my stomach, and we have it ultimately from Judaism! I agree with Ludendorf - we should do away with Judaism and its offspring Christianity too! Strength alone is what we should respect, and let the weak suffer! Back to the worship of Odin and Thor! Furthermore, despite what you say, there must be good reasons for enmity to the Jews!"

"Yes. Those of them from eastern Europe speak a vile and inharmonious tongue known as Yiddish, condemned and ridiculed by Aryans. The fact that this is essentially Rhineland German of the eleventh century, carried eastward by the Jews as they fled massacre and spoliation, and therefore our own ancestral language, makes no difference.

"A German, in pain or distress, cries 'Ei, ei!' A Yiddish-speaking Jew under those circumstances cries, 'Oi, oi!' This of course is something that a manly, self-respecting German cannot possibly endure, and must be punished!"

Shocked, she exclaimed, "Are you saying that we are ruining them for no reason?"

"Certainly not. There is an excellent reason. Hatred of them has helped to unify the German people, and to give it needed emotional stimulation. That the Jews are sacrificed is their misfortune. Innocence is no protection in this world. Not that all of them are innocent; they too have their scoundrels."

"Don't they have all the money?"

"Who is the richest man in Germany?"

"Hugo Stinnes, I suppose."

"Who is a good Aryan, with no Hebrew blood. And, believe

it or not, there are many poor Jews. Naturally, you do not know of them - the names of the poor are not famous.

"But there are certainly rich ones. We closed every occupation to them but commerce, until recently, and business is the way to riches. And now we blame them for it, and, as so frequently in the past, we fleece them of their wealth."

As was remarked before, this is neither the theme nor the language of courtship. But young people who are aware, concerned, intelligent and articulate do not limit their interchange to sweet nothings. These of course constitute part of their speech, but by no means all.

Every reader knows the immemorial parlance of lovers, and has no need to learn it here. We can, therefore, safely rely on imagination to supply what is common to all men and women, and pass on only that which specifically illuminates the individualities of our youthful pair.

In the final year of academic work for the young men of the academy, navigation was still emphasized. Athletic standards were still maintained. Emil's performance continued more than adequate.

The year ended. Now they were rotated through the special schools of the service - torpedo, coast artillery, mine, signal, naval infantry (corresponding to the British or American marine corps), spending about two months in each.

IV

SEA TRIALS

The sea is fate and law.
The Sea Eagle. From the German of Felix von Luckner

With prospective commanding officer and crew aboard, Scharnhorst put to sea - first in the landlocked Baltic, then in the stormy North Sea. She tested herself in all weathers, on all points of sailing, throughout her range of speeds, and even through firing trials. Stability, seaworthiness, weatherliness (ability to work to windward), rate and moment of heel, structural rigidity were carefully evaluated.

Hartmann's training too included time at sea. In the Horst Wessel (she had been named for a thug and pimp who, having early identified with the Nazi party, lost his life in a street brawl but was seized on by Hitler as a convenient martyr to his unsavory cause), Hartmann made a training cruise to Capetown. Seafaring under square sail leads to keener appreciation of the forces of wind and wave. Suffice it to say that Emil stood up well under the taxing toil, and returned with even greater commitment to the sea and the navy.

A longer cruise followed, this time in the light cruiser Emden. In her he was assigned to gunnery. The young men had classes, with much drill in foreign languages, notably in English. And since a naval officer was expected to represent his country creditably, there was much exposure in port to social functions.

Hartmann enjoyed being afloat. At least, under most circumstances he did. But there was an atrociously hot day in the Gulf of Oman, when the burning wind blew in the same direction as their course, and at almost the same rate, so that it seemed as though they were becalmed, with no relief from the heat; and Emil had hard physical work to do. And there was the time when they lay in an exposed road with a steep sea beating at her bow, so that the ship stretched her rode to rigidity on each wave with a sickening shock, and then rolled far over; so that everybody aboard was nauseated by the relentless motion, even the Kapitan-Leutnants. But there was the excitement of far and exotic places, and of entering ports that one might some day force for Germany!

Moored in Southampton, England, when the voyage was almost over, they sat for the comprehensive examination. Of the four possible grades - excellent, good, satisfactory, and unsatisfactory, Emil achieved the second. He now became a midshipman of the German navy!

As passed midshipmen Emil and his fellows were ordered to sea for their final testing. He was assigned to the destroyer Ernst Witthoeft. As a junior officer of the watch he took part in the working of the ship. He was under the scrutiny of the officers, and upon their report his commission would finally depend. The ship operated in the North Sea, so from time to time he could be with Leni.

v

THE COMMISSIONING

It is necessary to sail. It is not necessary to live.
Motto of the Hanseatic League. From the Latin.

On a clear, cold day in January, navy notables and their ladies assembled on Scharnhorst's deck. The crew was mustered. There was a speech. Orders were read, and an admiral turned the ship over to her captain. The band played the national anthem, the commissioning colors ran up the mast, and the ship came fully alive.

After six months the officers of the Witthoeft unanimously elected Hartmann to commissioned officer status. He became a Leutnant-zur-See, and swaggered ashore with the stripes upon his shoulder.

And then, suddenly, Germany was at war! She had invaded Poland, and the British and French at long last (perhaps too late) stood by their treaties, and the armies marched.

It may readily be imagined how excitement and - yes - elation ran through Emil and his fellows. The years of preparation had not been for naught. Now the testing was to come, with the dear spice of danger! And with the sudden surge of increased loyalty to their country came a lessened inclination to look critically upon the Leader.

Emil received orders transferring him to the battleship Scharnhorst at Kiel.

Leni, charming in a lavender evening gown, swept across the floor and extended her hands. They kissed.

"I had heard of the ugly duckling that turned into a swan," Emil told her, "but I never knew before that a swan could become a bird of paradise!"

She laughed. "For a moment I thought that you had considered me an ugly duckling!"

"Duckling or whatever, every man here envies me! And I would not change places with any other man alive!"

The orchestra began a lively tango, and she accepted his arms. She danced well; so did he. Many eyes were upon them as they circled the floor.

"I have been so proud since hearing about your commission! Things must be very different now!"

"Well, I have the same duties. The difference is mostly in status and authority, and of course pay. It is mostly a matter of intangibles - of which, however, I am very conscious, and others too."

"Now you are fully launched on your career."

He nodded. "The rest is up to me - and luck."

Her eyes danced. "I see you as captain of your old destroyer, then of a battleship."

He laughed. "Why not as admiral?"

"Of course as admiral! But I am looking forward only a few years."

"Meanwhile, let me just enjoy being a lieutenant."

Presently the music stopped, and they went to a table. "Look about you," said Leni. "Every woman here is jealous of me."

"Yes. Of your looks."

They studied a menu, ordered, and danced again - a slow, dreamy waltz.

"How long do you think that the war will last?" She asked.

"Long, I think. Until our enemies are starving, or out of oil and other supplies. Our navy will sink ships faster than they can build. But I would be happier nevertheless if the western peoples had less reason than I fear they have to condemn us for our treatment of both Aryan and non-Aryan prisoners."

Leni's mouth twisted into an expression of scorn. It was still a beautiful face, but less so now. "Hypocrisy," she replied. "Sheer hypocrisy! You don't see them begging us to ship our Gypsies and Jews to them! And you know, or should know, in what terms they themselves speak of outsiders. 'Wops' and 'Honkies' are the mildest of them. And you know about the blacks and the Indians in America, the extermination of the Tasmanians by the British, and the Canary Islanders and all the other peoples who have been wiped off the face of the earth!"

"Yes, I know. But must such things be forever?" He suddenly remembered something his father had said. "It is bad that we commit or even tolerate evil. But the great thing, if we cannot press forward, is not to take a backward step. That is the unforgivable sin."

"But not all party members approve of illegality or cruelty, Emil! And some excess always occurs, especially in times of stress."

"It can. The important point is how often, and how sincerely the authorities try to stop it (instead of even sponsoring it, if all tales be true). Then guilt lies not only with the perpetrators, but with all of us."

It did not occur to either of them that it did not matter whether the charges against Jews, Gypsies and others were true or not; that to give absolute power to a man and a party who avowedly hated human beings, was to deliver them helpless into the hands of the executioner, the torturer, the rapist, without any recourse. (Hitler's law actually forbade charges of atrocity!) All followed inevitably.

"I admit, mein lieber," she conceded, "that some of the stories I have heard are disquieting. I'd rather not know about them."

"And I admit that with the successes of our Fuehrer I become more accepting of him and the movement."

Indeed, even among the military, who cherished their independence and prestige, the status of Adolf Hitler had risen with each of his triumphs. His defiance of the West in Germany's rearmament; the occupation of the Rhineland; the union with Austria, longed for by the pan-Germans for almost a century; the disgusting self-abasement of Britain and France, coming cap-in-hand to Munich to implore his indulgence; the seizure of the Sudetenland, followed by the overrunning and annexation of the whole of Czecho-Slovakia; the swift conquest of western Poland; all of this transformed the support that Hitler had enjoyed into worship.

Even in the proud armed forces the regained prestige and power had their effect. The younger officers looked to Hitler as the saviour of the nation. And Hartmann was not wholly immune.

Leutnant-zur-See Emil Hartmann of the German battleship Scharnhorst sat at the tiny desk in his third of the stateroom. He had to make out the watch, quarter and station bill for the gunnery division. By this every man would know his rightful position and duty when standing watch, at general quarters for combat, or in such other conditions as fire, collision, fueling, taking on ammunition, etc. It was not an inspiring job; it was not made more so by the suspicion that, as a newly joined officer, he had been assigned the task merely for training, and that the finished listings would find their way directly into a waste paper basket.

With the roster of all gunnery personnel before him, he set about assigning post and duty to each enlisted man. He did his best to see to it that each duty station would be manned by various ratings, in such fashion that no unskilled seaman should act on his own initiative, and that no higher petty officer should be burdened by the scut work for which those of lesser training were available. Personality too played a role; he had to make sure that fools and incompetents, so far as he knew them - despite best efforts there were always a few of these - were not left to their own devices; and conversely he did not want to waste talent by duplicating the assignment and efforts of technically efficient personnel.

Hartmann finished the task, made a neat copy, and carried it to the office of the gunnery officer, Commander Erwin von und zu Raupenheid. (The prepositions indicated that the commander not only bore the title of an ancestral estate, but actually possessed and occupied it as well.) He knocked, and upon invitation took off his hat and entered.

"Heil Hitler!"

"Heil Hitler!" The tall, muscular but slender, hawk-faced man responded. Did Hartmann imagine it, or was there something ironic in the tone?

"The watch, quarter, and station bill, sir!"

"Very good!" and the senior nodded dismissal.

"Chow time!" in the passageway. Hartmann turned to see a roommate, Heinrich Berg. "How are you getting along with Old Stately?"

Raupenheid's old-school formality and generally aristocratic air had given him his nickname. He came of an ancient East Prussian landed family, and his education and training had been of the expected type. A lesser connection of such a family might have entered upon a university career; but for an oldest or even a second son of the main stock there were but two pathways open; the officer corps, or politics. Erwin had no inclination toward the forum. He had diverged from tradition only to enter the naval rather than the army academy.

Hartmann returned to the stateroom and donned his tunic, then went to the junior officers' mess room. He sat down next to Berg, rose again as the mess president, its senior member, entered, and the meal was served.

Berg shot a hostile glance at the cabbage soup. "What is this, a Russian army mess?" he asked. Hartmann laughed, and began eating with zest. "Yes, you Hamburg men can enjoy anything," Berg continued.

"Naturally - we are a cosmopolitan seaport, and all sorts of foods are commonly known and eaten at home."

"All sorts of ideas have currency there, too."

Hartmann judged it unwise to enter into a discussion. He finished, changed, and went ashore.

A waiter had been particularly stupid, and Leni sighed in vexation. "And such people, in the republic, were entitled to decide our destiny!"

Emil laughed. "That is democracy, Leni! All have the vote alike!"

"How can anyone expect to run a country, or even a village, with such idiots? How can anybody help seeing that it is far better to give power to those who are most competent to make decisions?"

"My father used to say that democracy is the most inefficient form of government known to man, and a benevolent despot is the best. But, he would add, every benevolent despot is either corrupted or succeeded, sooner or later, by one that is not benevolent, and that is terrible indeed."

"It may be so; but, as our Fuehrer has remarked, "Who would die for a republic?"

"The history of World War I will give you the answer to that."

"I can't see it. But," changing the subject, "I confess that I find some of the things you have been saying disquieting - very disquieting. Nevertheless, even if our movement is indeed founded on injustice, we must have the resolution and courage to disregard it, and press on! No matter at what cost, Germany must win! And this time, Emil, our armies will be allowed to fight to victory, and not be stabbed in the back by the socialists, as happened in the last war!"

Emil opened his mouth to say, "That is more of Hitler's ravings! Our armies simply could no longer get men - or even materiel - to replace losses!" But he remained silent. Particularly in his uniform, it began to seem improper to voice some of these sentiments.

What was he to do about Leni? She was warm and sweet. She had character. Without much formal education, she was a girl of serious interests. He could not marry yet; and in any event, he knew that she would not find acceptance in his circle. A German officer's life, even his personal life, was not his own. Emil had been aware of reactions by the military, and even more, by their spouses, to any woman of a lower social class who dared to marry above herself - "Wo kommt die her? Sie spricht nicht einmal Franzosich!"

VI

MAIDEN VOYAGE

The white, widening line of waves
Pulled by the urging tide
Rolled in and rumbled nearer and nearer,
A resonance weird of wailing and whistling,
Of laughing and murmuring, sighing and shouting,
And, under it all, the strange croon of the ocean.

Twilight. From the German of Heinrich Heine.

Weeks became months, and it was still drill, drill, drill.
Neither ship nor men were given the chance to show what they could
achieve. They swung at moorings, or cruised in the peaceful Baltic.
A few men came and went; a new captain, Hoffmann, took over
command and had to familiarize himself with ship and crew.

Then at last, in the fall of 1939, accompanied by the sister
ship Gneisenau and destroyers, they were standing out through the
Skagerrak for open sea. A foray into Icelandic waters was under way!

Emil had of course been to sea before. But this was his first
wartime cruise, and the wine of danger delighted his nostrils!

Men turned to in the mornings, lashed and stowed their
hammocks, breakfasted and dispersed to their tasks. At various times
in the day or night the signal sounded "General quarters!" or "Fire in
the after starboard berthing space!" or "Explosion in the number two
port ammunition space!" and men raced madly in apparent chaos
through the passages and up and down the ladders; but in a few
minutes all was in order, and reports were telephoned to the bridge
that all stations were manned and ready. After evening meal,
darkened ship meant a movie for some, a sing for others, and personal
tasks of washing, mending, or letter writing.

Northwestward they stood, through the gray windy sea of late
November. The North Sea is seldom calm or warm, the Arctic Ocean
practically never. Even the great ships began to dance to the lively
combers. Men were cold on the weather decks or aloft, and some
stomachs paid unwilling tribute to the sea-god's power.

It was on the fifth evening, between Iceland and the Faroes,
that they sighted the expected British man-o-war. She was the
auxiliary cruiser Rawalpindi, formerly a passenger liner, with six inch

guns against Scharnhorst's eleven inch rifles, and three hundred officers and men to oppose the nineteen hundred Germans. And no armor.

And she was alone. Captain Hoffmann's challenge was ignored. The Royal Navy ship sent out a radio report of contact, refused to heave to, and made a hopeless attempt to evade. The unequal battle was joined.

The lighter ship could not long survive. Afire and sinking, she nevertheless got a few damaging hits on her mighty opponent before Gneisenau closed and administered the coup de grace. Scharnhorst picked up a boatload of prisoners before the approach of other enemy units drove her off. Their countrymen completed the rescue of the few survivors in the icy sea.

One-sided as the fight had been, a victory is a victory; a nation sends its champions to war not to perform deeds of derring-do, but to savage the foe until it is unable further to resist. An enemy warship had been destroyed, with much of its crew. So Hartmann and his fellows slept well (those of them not on watch), happy in the consciousness of duty performed.

In a rising storm they returned to home waters.

But in April of 1940 they had harder fighting.

The ships of both countries were out in the north, and the prize was Norway - Norway with her island-sheltered route for the steel mined in Sweden's western mountains, and carried to a Norwegian port. Scharnhorst and Gneisenau, with the heavy cruiser "Admiral Hipper" and a dozen destroyers, set their course for Narvik and the Lofoten Islands to land mountain troops in support of the conquest of Norway.

There are two kinds of weather in those seas - bad and impossible. In a spell of the latter there was heavy fighting with ships of which the battleship "Renown" was the most formidable, and she inflicted much damage and many casualties on the Gneisenau. The rising gale became a hurricane, and they broke off the action.

June found Scharnhorst in the Arctic in support of the Narvik operation. They sank the British carrier "Glorious" and a destroyer. But Scharnhorst suffered severe torpedo damage, and was fortunate to make port. Repairs took long.

Leni was less exuberant than usual.

"No. I am not happy, Emil. I have but now heard from an old friend. Her father was a middle-of-the-road man. Nevertheless, the police came pounding on the door at three in the morning, and took him away. When her mother persisted in her questions, she was badly beaten, and so was my friend who attempted to shield her. Two days later they received his ashes."

"I am distressed to hear it, Leni."

"I am deeply troubled. Are our people more careless of the truth, and more brutal, than they should be? I have always been skeptical of such complaints, but now - I wonder!"

"I hope that this was an exceptional miscarriage of justice. When these things hit us personally, or through those we know and like, they produce an inordinate effect, and color our thinking if we are not careful."

He comforted her as well as he could. But the atmosphere for the romantic interlude for which he had hoped was irretrievably ruined.

The French had constructed a magnificent fortification along their German frontier - the Maginot line. Despite the scorn often shown it, this line was never breached. But the French had economized by leaving open their friendly Belgian border.

In that same summer of 1940 the Germans launched an assault through Holland, Belgium and Luxembourg. Their column of irresistible armor swept like a torrent through northern France (and incidentally, through Denmark and the rest of Norway). Treason played a great role in the north.

In January of 1941 Scharnhorst and Gueisenau left home waters on a fateful raid into the Atlantic. They entered the ocean through the Straits of Denmark, between Greenland and Iceland. Rendezvous had been arranged with tankers, so that they could be long at sea. In a cruise of eight weeks they had no fighting, but sank 116,000 tons of Allied shipping. Thereafter, they took shelter at Brest, in occupied France.

And there for over ten months they remained.

VII

INTERLUDE IN FRANCE

And ships that lay at anchor by strange rocks
Tossed in their sleep and dreamed of distant docks,
The ports of home, now small and far.

Sea-Monster. From the German of Gertrude Kolmer.

In June the German armies in another treacherous surprise attack crossed the border into Russia on a two thousand mile long front. They penetrated deeply. Murmansk in the north was the only western port still available to Russian shipping.

The British were not long in discovering the whereabouts of the "Ugly Sisters." Against the pair, and against the heavy cruiser "Prinz Eugen" that came in soon after, they sent raiding planes, day after day and night after night; and not wholly without success.

In the councils in Berlin, Hitler several times fumed over the apparent uselessness of the ships at Brest, and wanted to move them; but the naval command talked him out of it. For all his success in military operations, it was a great boon to the West that Hitler had no understanding of sea power. His admirals told him that not only would the removal of the ships to German waters involve an unacceptable risk, but its accomplishment would be a strategic error. While at Brest they constituted a "Fleet in Being," a standing threat to the British, who were forced to keep available in the Atlantic naval forces strong enough to deal with a possible renewed raid on shipping. Were the three to join the German force in home waters, the same British fleet that covered the German naval vessels in the Elbe and the Baltic could deal with these additional units without extra strain.

Early in the stay of the ships at Brest, an aerial torpedo found its way to Gneisenau, sending her to dry dock for months of refitting. In a later attack five bombs hit Scharnhorst, and one landed on Prinz Eugen. Scharnhorst had to seek the dock in her turn.

All this meant work for Hartmann, not only at his guns repelling the raiders, but before, seeing to everything in preparation, and afterwards, overseeing the cleaning and the constant recalibration of his weapons.

There was work for the quartermasters, as well. The firing always amounted to less than a broadside, but even so the magnetic field of the ship might have been altered by it, which meant correcting the magnetic compass again. Of course, their main reliance was on the gyrocompass; but one had to keep the more primitive means of navigating available. Despite the greater usefulness of the more sophisticated equipment, one never knew when it might fail.

The commanding officer of the Brest squadron made it a policy to keep ashore those of its crews not needed for the work at hand, in order to reduce casualties from the continual British air raids. Even so, one hundred forty lives were lost to the aerial weapons. So when off duty, Hartmann and his shipmates strolled through the streets and lanes of Brest, admiring, those of them who were sensitive to such things, the Breton architecture and the ancient church. They marched to and fro on the heaths outside of town, and played organized and impromptu games of soccer. Some cultivated those of the town folk who would accept them.

On December 7 of the same year of 1941 was the debacle of Pearl Harbor. Tragic though it was, it brought back hope to the British Empire. America had become an ally!

The German commandant had engaged the facilities of a seaside hotel for the recreation of his officers. It had a splendid cuisine, an exceptionally well stocked cellar, and a very good location.

Hartmann entered one day, only to find the dining room with tables almost full. Raupenheid, however, sitting alone, caught his eye, and beckoned him over.

"This is not too unlike my home in East Prussia," the older man remarked. "I have not seen it in two years."

"I hope you'll be able to go there long before another two, sir."

"Perhaps. It depends largely on the British. We'll make it, but not simply on the basis of our fighting quality."

"What do you mean?"

"The Fuehrer was right about one important point. A rot has spread in the democracies. They have been unwilling to use their strength in time. Do you remember the Naval Armaments Treaty of 1922?"

"Yes, sir!"

"Then you remember the formula adopted - naval strengths of the powers was to be in a 5:5:3:1 2/3:1 2/3 ratio, for Britain, the U.S.A., Japan, France, and Italy, respectively. The Americans in particular were fools. They not only had more money than the others, but endless coal and iron. They could have and should have outbuilt the world. Not only that, but they agreed with the Japanese on a limit on fortifications in the Pacific. Having so agreed, they were even greater fools to be the only ones in the Pacific to keep their word. They broke up large, new ships on the way, and dismantled partly built forts in their island possessions."

"I remember."

"They committed the further incredible folly of ignoring reports that the Japanese were building ships beyond the treaty limitations, and illegally fortifying the trust territories assigned them by the Treaty of Versailles."

"I know, sir. But I have never understood why the American military did not see the folly of it."

"The American admirals and generals knew better. But when they protested, they were called 'Warmongers,' 'Militarists,' and 'Empire Builders.' As a result, not only don't they have the ships that went unbuilt, but the Japanese with their large naval establishment destroyed most of the American navy at Pearl Harbor. So there will be no American assistance for the British here. And the Americans will have to expend oceans of blood to reduce those island fortifications. Now the British are stretched woefully thin."

"But they are still strong."

"Yes, but not strong enough. They threw away too many chances. They should have crushed our ally, Italy, at the time of the Ethiopian war. But the slogans so successfully used by our friends in England, 'We have no business in Ethiopia! We won't have our boys fighting and dying for a distant autocrat!' did the job. A show of strength by them at that time would have wrecked the whole fascist movement.

"Again, they should have marched when we reoccupied the Ruhr, or on any of the other occasions when we flexed our growing muscles. They feared a war, in which they might have lost some thousands dead. Their casualties in this war already amount to a hundred times that figure."

"They certainly erred."

"They did worse. The failure was not one of judgment, but of heart. Did you ever hear of the Oxford pledge?"

"No, sir."

"In the famous Oxford debating society one year - about 1932, I guess, the proposition was, 'Resolved, that this house will not fight for king and country.' It won!"

"Why, do you suppose?"

"Very simple. The world has two kinds of people - those who mentally and emotionally take it easy, and those who do not allow themselves the luxury of believing what they want to believe when facts are unpleasant or dangerous. The anti-war agitators had persuaded themselves that if they felt good will, others would reciprocate. 'We must trust them,' they loved to say. 'If nobody leads the way, how will peace come?' Well, they have this for their trouble. The greatest maker of war, Hartmann, is the pacifist. Give me foes who value life too highly to take it, and I will show you a blood bath."

"They are fighting now, though."

"Yes, and bravely. But as Hitler foretold, it is late. Even if they win, which of course they won't, it will be a disaster for them - a disaster which could have been easily prevented by more resolution and courage at the right time!"

VIII

BATTLE PLAN

>*The Robbers. From the German of Friedrich Schiller.*

A courier was needed, and Emil managed to procure the
assignment. He had time for a stop at Kiel.

Leni was tense and unsettled.

"I have been hearing stories that, if true, would horrify me. If
they are false, steps should certainly be taken to punish those responsible
for such cruel propaganda. About children, some still alive when they
were cast into the fire. About slow drownings. I do not believe them. But
I am troubled."

Emil looked around. No one was within earshot.

"When great events take place," he said to her, "we must be
willing to pay a great price. Look at what we have had to make us proud!"

Leni should keep things in proportion. Ursula Bormann, the
attractive daughter of Gneisenau's captain, would have had more sense.
He certainly did not approve of burning children - or anyone else, for that
matter - alive. But he was not to be diverted from following the grand
design by a few outrages, assuming that they had really occurred!

There was a sense of strain throughout the evening.

Hitler did not forget about the three capital ships. One day he
called a staff meeting to settle the matter. In the cold wind of late fall
in this third year of war, several men accordingly made their way to
the "Wolf's Redoubt." From this East Prussian base the Fuehrer
conducted the Russian campaign.

"Meine Herren," Hitler began, "the time has come to
conclude our discussions on the battleships Scharnhorst and
Gneisenau and the heavy cruiser Prinz Eugen."

Admiral Raeder replied.

"Mein Fuehrer, the Atlantic war will decide the fate of the
nations. If we can destroy enough of Britain's commerce, then more
surely than by troop action we will bring her to her knees."

The Fuehrer looked at him with dislike. "For months the ships have lain idle."

"Mein Fuehrer, they have been idle but not useless. They tie down enemy ships which must be ready to counter a breakout. A breakout to raid their commerce is nevertheless not impossible."

"And I tell you that it is on land that the issue will be decided. The chief duty of the navy is to support our armies. Our soldiers are not fighting on Atlantic shores. It is the sea off Norway that is critical. The British are preparing to invade Norway by force."

"May I ask how you know that, mein Fuehrer?"

Hitler became angry. "I know it because I understand such things. My intuition tells me that they are about to mount an invasion of Norway to cut off our access to Swedish steel and perhaps to threaten Finland, as well, and take our forces in Russia on the flank. The three ships, therefore, must be taken to Norway to participate in its defense."

There was a moment of silence. Then, "Mein Fuehrer, the passage would be so dangerous that it is probably not possible. The British fleet is out guarding the Straits of Denmark to the west of Iceland, and in even greater strength to the east of it. Our crews would have to be retrained for such a passage, and the Luftwaffe could give us no air support there. As to the English Channel, that is not to be thought of. Not for centuries has the British navy been successfully challenged by an enemy fleet passing through its home waters."

Hitler went into a rage. "Either you bring the ships back to Germany, for use off Norway, or I shall dismount their guns, send them to Norway, and junk your ships."

Vice Admiral Ciliax, commander of the Brest battle squadron, spoke. "Mein Fuehrer, the Naval Command in France has considered the possibility of a Channel passage. As against a more northerly route, it has several advantages. The traverse is shorter than the northern voyage; we could offer both surface and air support; we could jam the enemy radar by new methods of which they are still unaware; there would be no enemy ships stronger than ours nearer than Scapa Flow in Scotland - they have all been withdrawn there to avoid our bombers; and there are numerous harbors in our hands along the route that could offer shelter at need. That is not to say that I contradict my colleagues who advise against the operation. It is certainly one of utmost risk."

"The risk is diminished by one important factor," the Fuehrer rejoined. "The British are not capable of rapid and effective improvisation in an emergency." He paused. "Three conditions, however, are essential to success. First, there must be as little preliminary movement as possible to suggest that we might sail. Second, you must transit the Channel by daylight for the most effective defense, which means you sail from Brest in the evening. Third, throughout daylight hours we must provide maximum fighter cover. Can you do that, General?"

Colonel General Jeschonnek, Goering's chief of staff, rose to the occasion. "We shall commit all available aircraft, Mein Fuehrer!"

Adolf Galland, General of fighters, seconded his chief. "Some two hundred fifty planes are on the Channel coast. They cannot guarantee complete protection, but we will use them all!"

Raeder perforce swallowed his pride. "The navy will provide destroyers, E boats, and mine sweepers."

Vice Admiral Ciliax departed to plan the operation that, win or lose, would be the turning point of his career.

Otto Ciliax was a born martinet. From his student days on - he had learned his trade at the Naval Academy - he had been a stickler for the minutiae of form and discipline. He spared no one's feelings, and had won the sobriquet of the "Black Czar." A former commanding officer in Scharnhorst, only with great difficulty did he restrain himself from interfering with the working of the ship.

Ciliax' plan "Cerberus" was a brilliant one. All eventualities were foreseen; it covered one hundred and twenty closely typed pages and left nothing to chance or improvisation. The duties of each man were prescribed in detail, for all possibilities and situations.

Above all, his reliance would be on speed. The fewer hours of exposure to British attacks, the greater chance of a successful passage. The battleships, the slowest units, could do thirty-one and a half knots or thirty six land miles per hour.

The breakout would be at night. The fleet would transit the Channel in daylight; this would give the gunners maximal effectiveness. The British would probably look for a passage of that most dangerous sector in darkness, and he would catch them unawares.

For several days previously, mine sweepers would clear a fairway, which would be marked by anchored boats. There would be a continuous umbrella of fighter planes to take out enemy assailants. The fleet would include destroyers as escorts; these were new, large, powerful vessels which outclassed any the British had to offer at the time and place. There would also be E boats, the larger, faster, improved German answer to the motor torpedo boats of the enemy navy. The combined fire power of the three capital ships plus that of all the escorts would, he expected, be overwhelming.

Only the admiral, his chief of staff, the commanding officer of each of the three capital ships, and the senior destroyer commander were informed of the plan. No others would know.

Six large destroyers were to join the fleet at Brest. At Cherbourg two E boat flotillas of five units each would reinforce the screen; off Cape Gris Nez the escort would increase by twenty-four more E boats of the Channel command, plus gunboats and mine sweepers. Here the fighters and bombers could form a protective umbrella.

It would go hard with any British, air or sea-borne, who might try to breach that array!

Hartmann sat down in his stateroom to read Leni's letter.

"Sweetheart! I used to love the winters, even when I could not ski. But now I find the season cheerless. When you are away, not only is there nothing to relieve the drabness of grey skies and rain, but I think that even if it were spring, there would be no spring in my heart with you far off. I think of you day and night. Oh, why did the Japanese have to make their strike and bring America into the war when we thought that it was as good as won!

"I am saddened by something else as well. My cousin Rudolph, with whom in childhood I was so close, is, as you know, a lieutenant in the S.S. He was home on leave, and we met.

"He was in his cups, and said more than otherwise he would have. He told of some of our procedures in the east. Dear God, I would not wish such things on anybody, even an enemy! I never thought that Germans could do such things to human beings! And he said that those practises were not exceptional - that they were occurring by the thousands, perhaps by the tens of thousands!

"Even if it meant the difference between victory and defeat, I could not countenance that kind of horror. I am greatly disillusioned about our Leader; I tried to believe that he knew nothing of it, but I cannot convince myself that that is so.

"I feel spiritually isolated. If only you were here, and I could talk to you!"

There was more, but he paused in alarm and irritation- no, anger. In war, one should steel oneself against such morbid ideas. But aside from that, was she mad, to put such things on paper? Suppose the letter had come unsealed before reaching his hands! Or suppose that he had received and opened it, and then been called away to General Quarters or some other urgent duty, and left it lying around to be read by any chance comer! Not only would it have been the end of Leni, but he himself might well have been ruined! A more prudent girl, Ursula, for instance, would never have written so!

Vice Admiral Sir Bertram Ramsay had been born in the beautiful palace of Hampton Court, which Cardinal Wolsey had presented to Henry VIII. His father, and therefore, his mother, had gone to India on Her Majesty's service. The boy, sent by British custom to a "public school" at a tender age, saw little of his parents, and from his thirteenth year on was practically his own master.

At sixteen he was commissioned a midshipman in the navy. He was not a tall lad, but well built and fond of sports. He took easily to naval life. In his first command, a monitor in the Dover patrol, he spent two years off the Belgian coast. Promoted to commander, he was given the famous fighting destroyer Broke. He made captain, then Rear Admiral, and became Chief of Staff of the Home Fleet. The outbreak of the war found him again in Dover, as vice admiral in command of naval forces on the coast.

This, then, was the man upon whom lay the chief responsibility for thwarting the German plans.

At No. 10 Downing Street he sat facing the Prime Minister.

"You have, of course, made plans against the possibility of an attempt by the Ugly Sisters to run for home," Churchill stated, rather than insult the other by asking.

Sir Bertram nodded. "Indeed, yes. Our estimate of the situation leads to the conclusion, however, that they will not attempt it. If there is an attempt, it will be by a northerly route, and you know our dispositions both to the east and to the west of Iceland. It is hardly possible that they will attempt anything so foolhardy as to try to run the Channel. If they do, it will certainly be by darkness, which means departure from Brest at dawn. Our preparations for the night battle are made. We will have ample notice."

Churchill raised his eyebrows.

"We have a former lieutenant in the French navy, now a British agent, as a worker in the dockyard of Brest - naturally under an assumed name. He is, supposedly, carrying on a romance with the daughter of a farmer who lives a moderate bicycle ride from town. In the cellar of the farmhouse is a small radio transmitter, used only for the most urgent messages, and then briefly, lest the German radio direction finders pinpoint its location.

"In the Gulf of the Iroise, outside of Brest, the submarine

Sealion keeps station, both for observation and in the hope of a torpedo shot when one of the Ugly Sisters ventures out.

"The coast from Brest to Ushant is patrolled by one plane. From Ushant as far as northeast Brittany, surveillance is the responsibility of a second plane. At Havre a third takes over, to cover the sea as far as Boulogne."

"And your forces in the Channel?"

"No capital ships, of course; our counter will be by light, swift units that can operate effectively at night. The German heavy guns will be useless at a distance, in the dark, against small targets; whereas our people will have huge, relatively slow targets. Heavy ships, as you know, need the protection of a screen of lighter vessels to protect them against swift, light, torpedo-carrying assailants."

"Pray God your precautions are adequate."

There were thirty-six British torpedo bombers. These were slow - their top speed, loaded, was only ninety miles per hour, so that they were completely dependent on darkness, cloud, or heavy air cover to get them close enough to their intended prey with any hope of firing, let alone survival. They were dispersed from Cornwall to Scotland. There were also a fighter group and a hundred bombers.

Six ancient World War I destroyers were based at Harwich. There was a flotilla of six motor torpedo boats at Dover, and another at Ramsgate.

The British had planted innumerable mines, and were always increasing their number with mine-laying surface ships, submarines, and planes.

Finally, two great guns at Dover could range the whole width of the straits to deliver devastating blows at any surface craft.

These were but scanty forces. Hard pressed, Britain had to distribute her strength over miles of sea lanes and many distant countries as well as on her own coasts. There was therefore, a great lack of adequate numbers of units of all kinds in the first place, and lack of back-up ships and planes in the second. Furthermore, ship for ship they were inferior to their newer opposite numbers on the German side; and they were outnumbered in destroyers and motor torpedo boats, and enormously in planes. There were no ships in Channel waters that could stand up to the battleships, or even the Prinz Eugen, in a slugging fight. The heavy British capital ships, those of them that were not defending the empire in remote waters, had been withdrawn as far as Scottish havens to remove them from the hazard of German bombers. Given an early warning, they could intercept the

Germans off Holland. A proposal by a relatively junior staff officer to bring them near enough for action in the Channel during the present peril had met with rejection.

It is difficult to understand how the admiralty expected, with the slim forces available, to crush the powerful German men-of-war. Perhaps they did not consider the possibility of reinforcement of the German heavy ships by so many smaller units; even so, they were playing with a poor hand.

They assumed furthermore, that the enemy would certainly time his outbreak to transit the straits during the hours of darkness, and made only minimal arrangements for the opposite contingency. Details not only of tactics but even of concentration of forces at a given area were left to chance or improvisation.

The planning of the engagement was incredibly inept. Success, if possible, would require most complete knowledge by at least the commanders of all units. But for the sake of secrecy, only the high command was given any information.

Ramsay's plan was for fighter bombers to drop flares that would illuminate the targets for torpedo attacks by planes and motor torpedo boats. The destroyers would thereafter attack under cover of fighters and bombers. How this "simple battle" developed, we shall see.

IX

BREAKOUT

The night is starless and cold,
The ocean yawns.
And, flat on his belly, the monstrous north-wind
Sprawls upon the sea.

Night on the Strand. From the German of Heinrich Heine

Ciliax fixed on 7:30 p.m. of February eleventh for sailing. It would be four days before the new moon; the night would be dark, which would not only screen them from detection, but would hinder any British attack by air or by heavy surface units. And the spring tides would increase their speed, and the greater depth of water would decrease the danger from mines.

The British admiralty was quite aware that the Brest squadron was making preparations to break out. Flights of bombers that regularly visited Brest had photographic reconnaissance planes among them, and espionage provided further information. Destroyers and E boats had been observed proceeding eastwards through the Channel, and some were photographed at Brest itself.

The Germans took every precaution to conceal their prospective time of departure. Besides the usual secrecy, they laid a dense smoke screen in the form of an invitation from the admiral commanding the western group to the commanding officers of all ships to dine in Paris on the evening of the eleventh.

Hartmann watched the evening flag ceremony for the last time in Brest. The band played; they stood at attention as the flag descended the mast, whipping in the chill wind.

The British agent in Brest was not deceived. After years of experience afloat he had only to use his eyes to know that the ships were making ready for sea. As soon as he was off duty, he took his bicycle and started for his hidden radio.

At the edge of town there was a German road block. No one was permitted to leave. He tried to talk his way through, but in vain. He pedalled back and tried another route - with the same result. A third and a fourth try were similarly frustrated.

Britain's first warning system had been countered.

The British submarine Sealion lay in wait off the harbor. She could not be evaded. With luck, she might send one or more torpedoes into the enemy at the very outset of their intended exploit. At worst, she would radio the news to the admiralty. She waited grimly while the hour drew near.

Just before the planned departure time came a British air raid. Normal practice would have sent sea-ready ships out at once, rather than let them be motionless targets. But this would disclose to the observant planes the fact of their departure and the British might well follow up such information with further reconnaissance. So the ships remained at their mooring, luckily without damage, for two extra hours.

Over the loudspeakers of all ships came the word of Admiral Ciliax:

"Fighters of the Brest group! The Fuehrer has summoned us for a new assignment in other waters.

"After our great successes in the Atlantic, despite all attempts of the enemy to put and keep us out of action, the tireless work of every one of you has made the ships again ready for sea.

"A task lies before us. Orders are: 'Proceed through the English Channel eastward to German waters!'

"The Fuehrer expects his whole duty from each of us.

"What awaits us after we have passed through the Channel, does not now concern us. The present task must occupy our minds and hearts completely.

"I lead the fleet in the knowledge that each of you will do his duty to the utmost!"

In darkness the fleet put to sea. (It had, in the last days, been augmented by six destroyers and five torpedo boats.) The die was cast.

Hartmann was beside himself with excitement and pride. The most daring operation of the war, and he was in it! He felt, personally and as part of the task force, invincible! And if he should fall in the action, how better could he die? *Es lebe Deutschland!*

They put out, of course, in darkened ship condition; not so much as a cigarette glow could be seen. There was also a ban on any unnecessary noise. Ghost-like the ships glided through the water, without benefit of moonlight. The navigator behind the bridge pored over his charts with ruler and dividers in hand; the assistant navigator strained to see through the blackness; his quartermasters were staring as though their eyes would start from the sockets. They had to find a safe channel through the nasty reefs for which this bay was infamous. It would have been no child's play in any case; but the estimate of the forward motion imparted by the screws had to be corrected for the tidal currents, different at each hour and on each day, that tried to sweep a ship off her plotted course. In the narrowing angle between the coasts of France and Britain, the tidal wave that circled the world climbed up on itself to greater heights and rates of flow. And this was close to new moon, when it would be at its greatest! Many a goodly ship had come to grief in the Iroise, and many under more favorable circumstances.

The great need of the ships was for speed. And the greater their speed, the less the error imparted by wind and drift. But the greater their speed, the more disastrous would be any encounter with rock or shoal. In the more open stretches of the fairway, therefore, the officers who had the con ordered more turns of the screws per minute; in the areas more beset with dangers, they diminished them. This complicated the already difficult problem of estimating their "course made good." And always the sounding machines told the changing depths for what hints they might give of position.

Destroyers nosed ahead and out at the flank, where bottom contours permitted, their sonars ranging in search of lurking submarines.

Signalmen kept communication with their lights, which cast a beam not visible except within a narrow angle, and with the steam whistles. Radio silence had to be observed, and signal flags were of course invisible at night.

Hartmann stood in the turret that housed his two fifteen centimeter guns, and tried to send his thoughts as messengers to the similar turret for which he was responsible. Shells were at hand, and replacements would be there within seconds from the magazine below. He strained his ears, but could hear only the rush of wind of their passage and the deep, dull rumble of the engines. Or did he feel them, rather? It was hard to say. He could see few stars, and barely, when he stepped out upon the deck; they were remote and small against the black sky. There was the Dipper, and there frost-loving Orion. Already he felt chilly, despite layers of wool, and he knew that it would be worse toward morning.

Any second might bring the terrific blow of a torpedo hit.

The submarine Sealion had repeatedly braved the rushing tides and numerous dangers of the Iroise, to say nothing of depth charges, where there was little deep water to hide in. She had just found it necessary to retire in order to recharge her batteries. Unseen, therefore, the Germans cleared the mouth of the bay. By the time Sealion was back on station the fleet had passed by. The delay in departure had played into the German hands. The second sentry had failed in her task.

The destroyers and E boats took station as an inner and an outer screen, respectively, about the capital ships. At last the hobbled engines were released. Roaring, they sprang into their desperate race. Full speed ahead for Ushant and the narrow seas!

Kapitan zur See Hoffmann stood high on Scharnhorst's bridge. His was the pride of power. In his arm was the strength of twice a thousand men; in his legs, motionless though they were, the speed of horses by the hundred thousand. His word would hurl monstrous engines of destruction upon an enemy ship; or he could darken the skies with bursting metal against a hostile plane. If he should fail, the audacity of what they had undertaken would be his shield against accusers. And if he should get through, the greater would be his glory!

Thus far, the British had been unfortunate. What followed

was a tragedy of errors.

Stopper, a British Coastal Command radar reconnaissance plane, had the duty of patrolling by night from Brest to Ushant. The poor visibility could not thwart the magic eye of radar. But after almost colliding with a German, the pilot switched off his radar for a moment. In attempting to start it again, he unknowingly blew a fuse. Blinded, he returned to base; and after forty minutes of useless tinkering, the crew manned another plane. It would not start for another fifty minutes; there was, they finally discovered, a "damp, cloggy plug." By the time they were back on station, the hostile fleet had come and gone.

The third line of warning had been found wanting.

Unknown to the British, the Germans had perfected a device for jamming radar in such fashion as to make it appear that atmospheric conditions were responsible for the failure in performance.

"Line S.E.," the second patrol, flew out according to plan. The radar apparatus was inoperative due to "weather interference." There was no eye visibility in the mist, so the completely blind plane returned. No other took over the duty.

The fourth sentry had been evaded.

"Habo" covered the Havre-Boulogne sector nightly until dawn. Because of the menace of increasing fog, the unwise orders were to fly only two circuits and return. So return they did - an hour early. An hour later, the German fleet raced through the area unseen.

So much for the fifth monitor.

It was eight a.m. Dawn of a cloudy, rainy day was at hand. The racing German fleet, aided by a strong favoring tide, had made up almost all of the delay caused by the air raid over Brest. Admiral Ciliax had seen nothing of his foes, but he dared not assume that he had gone undetected. In any case, the enemy would certainly find him now, if they had not hitherto. But the success thus far was heartening, and he felt confident in his growing strength.

With the dawn came more destroyers and E boats, raising his force to ten of each. He was past Cherbourg now. A slight rain helped in his concealment; a calm sea and lightness of wind aided in the piloting.

Daylight brought a measure of relaxation to all topside personnel. They could hear the friendly protective fighters overhead. Hartmann rubbed his eyes and congratulated himself on being still alive (but not wholly without a youth's romantic regret at the lack of action).

He permitted his thoughts to wander. His father's remarks returned to his mind's ear. Surely, the older man had been wrong! And yet, an almost forgotten breadth of sympathy warned him that not all was false. Had so many Germans laid down their lives for unscrupulous lies? Had Poland been destroyed, France humbled, Britain put to sore travail, so many other countries invaded, and so much of Russia devastated and covered by her dead, on a piratical looting expedition?

It was troubling. He wanted to think well of his country. Was he a dupe?

There was Norway. The Fuehrer had called the occupation an "action to defend the neutrality of Norway." But the Norwegians were singularly unappreciative. They stood to gain by the subjection of the lesser races to the superior Aryans. But they had fought bitterly, outnumbered as they were, and were still fighting. How could they not see that the Fuehrer's policies would raise their status? Or could they see things to which he was blind?

He dismissed the subject from his mind and thought about breakfast.

With all their 160,000 horsepower the huge engines forced the hulls through the resisting water. There was a five mile visibility.

In England, radar had detected a large number of aircraft circling off Le Havre. The inference drawn was that these were an escort for coastal shipping. There was much interference, which Radar Filter Room ascribed to weather influence. Admiral Ramsay signaled the end of the pre-dawn alert. The chance of a daylight transit of the straits by the foe was, he still thought, remote.

At 8:45 the daily reconnaissance patrol flew to investigate the area from Ostend to the Somme. The two Spitfires noted E boats standing out - the mustering of Ciliax' reinforcements. British doctrine insisted on radio silence; the planes flew home to report. The Group Controller decided that a German air-sea rescue was under way.

More radar sightings of aircraft were reported, and more "weather" interference. But a station operating new, improved radar perceived that the enemy planes were moving up-channel at over twenty knots. No enemy freighters would be moving so fast; this must be technical error. As more such reports came in, practice or rescue flights seemed the explanation. No one passed these reports to the admiralty!

Only Wing Commander Jarvis was not satisfied. He

assumed that something was up but he could not convince his superiors.

The Beachy Head Radar Station picked up two surface vessels off Boulogne! Attempts to report by telephone and by scrambler to Ramsay's headquarters at Dover were unsuccessful. Further attempts, when the ships' course was plotted, were likewise fruitless. Investigation revealed that both phones were routed through a public trunk, and had been available to any listener!

The weather was still moderate, with five miles' visibility and an overcast sky.

Irrepressible Group Captain Victor Beamish was too senior for operations. He could not, however, be kept on the ground; and today, as often, he took to the air in his Spitfire to stir up trouble. Wing Commander Boyd followed loyally in his own plane. It was cold, cloudy, and now rainy.

They found trouble. Pursuing a pair of Germans, they broke out of the clouds to see Ciliax' driving armada below them!

Thorough indoctrination had its disadvantages. If they had radioed their observation, the British command would have known a precious twenty minutes earlier about the breakout. But the doctrine was radio silence, and the officers could not bring themselves to disobey. Under attack, they streaked for home.

Meanwhile, a second reconnaissance flight had taken off. Squadron Leader Oxspring and Sergeant Beaumont, about fifteen miles west of Le Touquet, suddenly saw large numbers of fighting craft, including big ships, in the sea below! Attacked by a swarm of German fighters, they made off for their base at top speed. They too, unfortunately, remembered and obeyed the injunction to radio silence.

After half an hour's delay, the Beachy Head radar reports finally got through to Dover; so did a report from Fairlight station of a plot of two ships off Boulogne. Wing Commander Constable-Roberts was the first, apparently, to suspect the truth, and he tried his best to convince his superiors. With the electronic data and the visual sightings, even the most reluctant belatedly saw the light.

At long last, at 11:25 a.m., the code word crackled along the wires.

"Fuller!"

X

MOTOR TORPEDO BOATS

What marvels of fire in the billows are flashing
That, sparkling, against one another are crashing?
It beams and hitherward wavers, and bright
All forms are aglow.

Faust II. From the German of Johann Wolgang von Goethe.

Throughout the morning, Admiral Ciliax' mood had varied from confidence to a suspicion that a trap had been laid for his fleet. Given timely warning, the great ships moored at Scapa Flow could intercept and crush him before he reached the Elbe. Surely, he could not have escaped observation all this long while!

Speed, speed! But now, at the end of the morning, he had to slow down to transit a very narrow swept channel between the still threatening mines and the shoals off the Belgian shore. He had charts showing the coast. But only rocks were fixed; sands shifted with every gale, almost with every tide. Silently, unseen, they would build dangerous shoals where the mariner had been wont to find safe depths. Sand could be more deadly than rock; a hole could be mended, but sand could pile up around an errant hull almost - sometimes quite - beyond the possibility of salvage. Not that in such case he would be given any time for salvage! An immobile ship would be quickly pounded into ruin by the enemy. He dared not skirt the threatening sandy shore except at a cautious speed.

On its other side the passage menaced with an even swifter destruction. The sweeping had necessarily been done in haste; who knew which isolated mine had been missed, and was waiting for his hulls?

Worst of all, on attack in this narrow fairway, there would be no room for maneuver! If a torpedo were seen approaching, he would have to hold his course helplessly until it either hit or missed! If planes threatened, he could take no evasive action, but would have to steer right into the path of their bombs!

But a welcome misty rain had begun, to shield him.

The entire fleet company was tense and apprehensive. But nothing happened. Ciliax passed through the dangerous stretch, and the great screws whirled madly again.

It was noon. Where were the English? He was practically through the Strait of Dover - there was Cape Gris Nez to starboard. He had come three hundred miles; there were two hundred forty to go. Would he get home without a fight? As to his already formidable force fifteen torpedo boats and three flotillas of E boats added themselves, he ordered the port-side destroyers to make a smoke screen to confuse possible assailants.

Now - too late - the great guns of Dover opened fire. It was 12:20 p.m. Visibility was bad, and the radar had been expertly jammed. And he was almost out of range. Not one of the thirty shells hit within a mile of his ships.

The men of the island kingdom - the Englishmen, the Scots, the Welsh, the Irish - loved their misty green land with a passion. They came charging out to defend the inviolability of her seas, whose watery borders compressed them into a proud, loyal fellowship, fearing conquest more than they feared death. Suddenly Ciliax was made aware of a flotilla of five motor torpedo boats dashing at their full thirty-six knots from the hidden English shore through the whitecaps. He marvelled at their temerity. They had only machine guns to answer the twnety millimeter cannon of the E boats alone. Outnumbered thirty to five and outgunned by the more modern German small craft, prey to the formidable destroyers and the great guns of the capital ships, harried by the greatest aerial cover any ship had ever known, without air or even gunboat protection of their own, they would never get past his outer screen.

But they did! Guns blazing at the stinging fighter planes and E boats, the first British MTB (that of the flotilla commander, Lieutenant Commander Pumphrey) bored right into the deadly German fire, until she had Scharnhorst within range; and she got off her two torpedoes. The mighty battleship herself had to acknowledge the daring pigmy with her secondary batteries. Hartmann was beside himself with eagerness and excitement as he worked his guns.

Two more of the assailants, under punishing fire, fought their way to within four hundred yards, and withdrew.

The fourth, despite severe hits, fired her missiles at Prinz Eugen, then retired, pursued by the destroyer Friedrich Ihn.

Number five had been delayed by engine trouble. Now she came up fast, penetrated the screen, and let go at Prinz Eugen at three thousand yards. Destroyer Herman Schoemann attacked her. But two British motor gun boats, armed with twnety millimeter Oerlikons and half inch machine guns, appeared on the scene and rescued MTBs four and five by feigning a depth charge attack.

All torpedoes missed or were evaded. Conditions were unfavorable for torpedo work.

Lieutenant Long came with three motor torpedo boats from Ramsgate. Misdirected, he was too far astern; and all three boats developed engine trouble. In the rising sea and thickening overcast he returned to base.

Below decks in the German ships, the black gang nursed their engines to coax yet another turn of the huge propeller shafts. Their position in the bowels of the ship was one of greater peril than most; not only could enemy explosives make their own engines into dealers of death, but the steam at seven hundred pounds of pressure, if it escaped even through a narrow opening, could shear off a limb like a meat axe.

XI

SWORDFISH

Ours is this ground by thousand-year possession.
Dare hirelings of an alien tyrant come,
Forge chains, and shame us here upon our earth?
William Tell. From the German of Johann Schiller.

Eugene Esmonde was the scion of an Irish Catholic family that had fought for England abroad and against her at home for over a hundred and fifty years. Born at the great house of Drominagh in Tipperary, he had spent his boyhood on the forested shores of Lough Derg. His father had been a fervent Irish nationalist; but, as indicated, there was a double tradition in the ancient family. Short, athletic, intelligent, fun-loving, Esmonde joined the Royal Air Force, and was always ready for a risky assignment.

When in 1939 Hitler emerged, even to those reluctant to believe it, as a clear and present danger, he accepted a commission as lieutenant commander in the Fleet Air Arm. He was assigned to the command of a Swordfish training squadron. It had been his squadron, with himself in command, that crippled the Bismarck with a torpedo and doomed her to destruction. He was now one of the finest pilots in

Britain. More important, he had a sense of duty which he expressed in a letter home: "I can think of no greater honor, nor a better way of passing into eternity, than in the cause for which the allies are fighting this war."

This was the man who commanded six Swordfish torpedo planes at Manston. This was the man whom the wing commander ordered to attack.

Esmonde had been training his crews for a night attack, which would have been dangerous enough. In broad daylight the lumbering Swordfish, slowed to eighty-five knots by the weight of their armament, would be overtaking the thirty-knot enemy ships at a relative rate of only fifty-five knots. At this low speed they would have to fly into flak and the concentrated fire of three capital ships and the Lord only knew how many planes, destroyers, and E boats. He would be ordering his unit to their deaths. Constable-Roberts, his commanding officer, told Esmonde that in view of the unexpected daylight operation, the decision to sortie or not was his to make. Of course he accepted the orders, despite his foreknowledge of doom. There were six planes, each with a crew of three, but there were seven pilots. The two most junior tossed a coin for the privilege of making the flight.

There was anguish even in the high command. The air marshals and the admirals knew that they were ordering men to almost certain death, and perhaps in vain. But there was now no alternative.

Thus far the British misadventures had been grim comedy. What was to follow was stark tragedy.

The group commander assured Esmonde that five fighter squadrons would escort his Swordfish, and that three more would strafe the vessels of the German screen immediately before contact.

The main fighter station of southern England was Biggin Hill. Here there was an action plan for the situation. But it was locked in a safe, and the intelligence officer had the key. He had gone on twenty-four hours leave.

They finally worked something out. A fighter escort was to rendezvous with the Swordfish over Manston. Some fighters, the word went out belatedly, might be late by a few minutes.

The few other men on the field watched darkly as the Swordfish crews emplaned. A pretty WAAF from the office came running for a quick kiss with her sweetheart.

As Esmonde approached his plane, the field commander wished him good luck. Afterwards he said of Esmonde's appearance, "It was the face of a man already dead."

At 12:25 the Swordfish took off in the thickening mists, in what the wing commander called "Calculated suicide." As the planes circled the field, only ten of the promised fighters appeared. They had no information concerning their mission, except that they were to protect the Swordfish!

Off the doomed torpedo planes flew to attack two battleships, a heavy cruiser, six destroyers, thirty-four E boats, a number of other craft, and scores of enemy planes.

Ten miles from Ramsgate, Messerschmidt 109's attacked. The escort fighters drove them off, but another German flight took their places. The Spitfires returned to deal with these. Now twenty 109's dove and fired on Esmonde and his second plane, piloted by Brian Rose. The two took evasive action, but thereby slowed to fifty knots. There were many hits on both planes, but the shells went harmlessly through the fabric of wings and fuselages.

Then they sighted the dismayingly large German fleet - and over it circled the most immense umbrella that any of them had ever seen! The Swordfish crews knew then for a certainty that they must die. Not one flinched.

The rest of the belated Spitfires were now attacking the umbrella, but too far in the rear to take any pressure off the Swordfish. By now their ten escorts were lost to sight in dogfights. Another flight of Spitfires despatched still later to protect the torpedo planes missed the direction, flew to Calais, and returned.

Assailed by fighters, then by flak, then by fighters again, the torpedo planes bored in. Esmonde's fuselage was set afire by tracer bullets. Clinton, the gunner, climbed out of the cockpit and, sitting astride the fuselage, beat out the flames with his hands, then returned to his gun.

A new hazard presented itself. The battleships' eleven inch guns dropped shell after shell into the water ahead of the planes, creating water spouts that could well overwhelm the vulnerable aircraft. For torpedo work, they had to fly low - not more than fifty feet over the water.

Esmonde's lower port wing was shot away. He was wounded in the back and head; his observer and gunner were killed. Inside both outer and inner screens, the dying pilot released his torpedo and crashed into the sea.

Waves of FW 190's, faster and more maneuverable than the 109's, assailed Brian Rose. Their cannon killed his gunner and wounded him. Lee, his observer, standing in the cockpit, directed him in weaving and dodging to avoid the German fire and to approach his target. A shell exploded against the steel plating at the pilot's back; Rose was wounded again, severely. He still flew. A shell exploded in the main gas tank; he switched to the reserve with its fifteen gallons. At a thousand yards he fired his torpedo at Prinz Eugen, and made a belly landing in the water.

Kingsmill's Swordfish was next. He passed the destroyer screen, but was badly hit by flak. The fighters attacked; they shot away the top two cylinders of his single engine and set his port wing afire. All three aboard were severely wounded. Kingsmill managed nevertheless to release his torpedo, again at Prinz Eugen, at two thousand yards, then turned toward the rear of the fleet. His engine went dead, and he pancaked into the water. The three succeeded in leaving the plane. Their dinghy had been destroyed, so they had only their life jackets.

Thompson with his three Swordfish of the second flight pressed through the flak, and three FW 190's poured their cannon fire into the doomed planes. Fabric torn from the skeletons, the Swordfish fought valiantly to stay in the air. They flew over the outer and inner screens, and approached the dreadful waterspouts of the heavy guns. They were seen to fly dauntlessly from the clear air into that frightful windrow, and from time into eternity.

Lee, working frantically, got the half conscious Brian Rose out of the sinking plane and into the rubber dinghy. He could not disengage the body of gunner Johnson. The Swordfish sank, carrying Johnson to the depths. As the two bobbed in the rising sea, one after another the E boats fired on them. And after, there was the bitter cold of the wintry sea.

A motor gunboat reached them in time. Another boat rescued the wounded Kingsmill and his two companions. There were five survivors of the eighteen who had set out, all but one badly wounded. At Manston, a WAAF sobbed brokenly.

Not one torpedo hit its target.

Admiral Ramsay was furious at the loss of those young men, and bitter at the failure to provide them with proper cover. "Had I known," he said, "that the fighter escorts might not keep their rendezvous... I would have forbidden that flight."

The poor consolation of a decoration was afforded the families of the living and the dead. Eugene Esmonde's sacrifice has been taken as type and symbol of the deeds of all the brave men who fell fighting at desperate odds for Britain in the war.

XII

MINE

There is a gash
of two hundred yards
underneath the waterline
in the steel-plated hull, slit
by a giant's knife.
The water is rushing into the bulkheads.
The Sinking of the Titanic. From the German of Hans Enzensberge.

Emil Hartmann greeted the cessation of torpedo plane attacks with relief. Despite the wintry weather, he found that he was sweating. It would do his gun barrels no harm to cool, either. Sandwiches were passed, and he ate appreciatively.

He was hurled violently off his feet as a roar smote his eardrums. So a torpedo had finally hit!

But he was mistaken. Scharnhorst had struck a mine. The propeller shafts were damaged, the engines stopped. Her compartmentation should enable her to suffer much additional damage before sinking. But she was dead in the water; she could not, as hitherto, evade any torpedo or bomb that the British might send her way. It was 2:30 p.m.

The young man felt a sudden great rage at the enemy. Why had not the English understood that Germany was fighting their war? That Britain too stood to gain by the relegation of the lesser breeds - Poles, Russians, etc. - to the position of subordination and servitude that would permit the more highly gifted Germans to use to the full their superior talents for the good of the world? And if thereby the Reich recovered her colonies and exploited their wealth, was it not right and proper that the higher people should enjoy the luxuries of the world, in return for permitting their inferiors to reap some of the fruits of the German genius?

And if Poland, Czechoslovakia, Lithuania, and other countries should cease to exist as sovereign nations, what then? Had they the right to stand in the way of German achievement and consequent aggrandizement? And if the Jews and Gypsies had to disappear, would that not solve a problem for the world? Not that the decent, useful Jews he knew or knew of need go down in the wreck.

Like most men, Hartmann was capable of believing two diametrically opposite doctrines at the same time.

The German government did not publicize the true nature of the death camps, or of the forcing of large numbers of Jewish, Polish, Russian, and other women into army brothels; and torture was of course denied. Rumors passed around nevertheless, which one believed or not according to personal orientation. Hartmann was among the skeptics; but it was an uneasy skepticism.

These thoughts ran half realized through his head while he waited like the rest of the ship's company for the attacks that might signal the end.

The damage control details and the engineers were working frantically. There was of course a great hole in the ship's side, and the worst damaged areas were flooded and inaccessible. A mat was gotten overside with difficulty (what was without difficulty in that desperate time?), and auxiliary engines were put to the task of pumping out the sea water from within the flooded compartments. There was a fire - burning paint and stores - above the water level, and fire fighters worked to extinguish it. Bulkheads were reinforced against the possibility of an advance by the sea. The engineers toiled frantically on the bent propeller shafts. It would require the facilities of a navy yard to repair them, if indeed it were possible. But the object was to enable them to turn even in their present almost impossible state. Speed, speed!

Admiral Ciliax quickly decided that Scharnhorst's chances of survival were desperate. He transferred, with difficulty in the rising sea, to a destroyer. But it was three o'clock before the enemy struck again.

XIII

THE BEAUFORTS

.. *The wild and all-subduing forces of a nature working in a state of chaos.*

Critique of Judgment. From the German of Immanuel Kant

The goddess Chance had only been playing with the British hitherto. The web of ill that she now spun was truly fantastic.

Seven Beaufort torpedo bombers had been ordered south from a distant station. Bad weather had delayed them; then they had landed at a field without torpedoes. Now they were at Thorney Island, near Portsmouth, almost ready to fly. They were to rendezvous with their fighter escort over Manston at 1:30. (Had their attack been coordinated with that of the Swordfish, the Germans might not have evaded all of the torpedoes.) At this time their commander learned that two of the planes were armed with bombs instead of torpedoes. There was something else wrong with a third.

The remaining four were ordered to Manston, thence to be led to their targets by the fighters. What this target was, nobody told them. During the delay in their take-off, the fighters arrived over Manston and were ordered to fly toward the German fleet and there to watch for the Beauforts' arrival. The Beauforts were to be informed of this change of plan.

Nobody remembered that the Beauforts had recently installed a voice communication system in place of the Morse. When, therefore, they arrived over Manston twenty minutes late, they could not be contacted, and began circling, waiting for the already departed fighters to come and show them their target. After a quarter of an hour of this, Pilot Carson, in command, headed out to sea in the direction being taken by many fighters. Only his wing man followed: other fighters had intruded between them and the remaining Beauforts, whose pilots therefore had momentarily lost sight of their leader. They continued to orbit. There were repeated fruitless attempts to communicate with them from the ground.

Carson and his two planes never found the German fleet. In fact, they never even knew what they were looking for.

After circling for three quarters of an hour, the second pair was running low on fuel. They landed an hour and a quarter after the original rendezvous time.

The conversation on the ground can be imagined. The pilots of the two Beauforts were briefed, given fuel and despatched.

They tracked their invisible prey through fog and rain by radar. They encountered the same fighter opposition as the Swordfish, but they were faster, better armed and more maneuverable. They penetrated both screens and sought their foe in smoke and cloud. He revealed himself by a burst of tracer bullets; they followed these down and burst through the thickening fog upon Prinz Eugen. The fierce flak barrage interfered with a good shot at the prize. They fought through three times, sustaining many hits before they got the torpedoes off.

The three that had been left behind at Thorney Island became airborne, flew to Manston, and landed for briefing. In the air again, they found the German fleet with their radar, and drove in against the defense and the bad weather. The first, badly shot up, was unable to release his torpedo. On the impossible flight home he was mistakenly attacked by English coastal batteries, but landed safely. The second had a similar experience over target, except that not only was his torpedo release mechanism rendered inoperative, but the undercarriage was jammed above it. The pilot flew home, and landed at a remote corner of the air field; the torpedo was knocked off and lay harmless on the ground. The third pilot, Sergeant Rowe, was in aerial combat for the first time. He fired off his torpedo in the midst of flying lead and shells; but as he withdrew the German fighters seriously wounded his two mates, and drove a piece of shattered windshield into his eye. The plane caught fire; in their agony the crew fought and extinguished the blaze. They returned safely.

Carson and his companion, back from their fruitless flight, learned for the first time of their intended mission. Dauntlessly Carson took off while the other was still refueling. The German fighter planes and flak ships would be able to give him their undivided attention. He made it to the target area nevertheless, and sent his fish speeding toward Gneisenau.

Again there were no hits by any of the torpedoes.

Fourteen Beauforts of Number 42 Squadron at Leuchars, Scotland, had been ordered south for the operation several days before. Severe snow conditions had delayed their departure. Three of them had no torpedoes, when in flight, they received word that North Coates, the field with torpedoes, was snowed in. They finally landed at Coltishall, in East Anglia. A mobile torpedo servicing unit was ordered to rush the three missing torpedoes to the planes. It was unable to accomplish the mission until far too late. Two more of the planes were unable to take off.

The remaining nine, likewise with no idea of their mission, flew to Manston to join their protecting fighters and bombers. They found there eleven Hudson bombers flying about, similarly uninformed. Many fighters circled above them, waiting to land and refuel. The Beauforts entered the circle with the Hudsons, but these turned after the Beauforts. So the planes played like a dog chasing his tail for a half hour, to the amazement and consternation of the field authorities. Attempts to contact them were fruitless. Each pilot was following, as he thought, the confused instructions he had received.

Finally, at 3:35 p.m., the Beaufort leader knew that something was very wrong. He used his own initiative. He led his planes out toward the position he had been given an hour earlier. Six of the Hudsons followed; the other five went on orbiting until, a half hour later, they returned bewildered to their base.

In the thick weather over the sea, the flights of Hudsons and Beauforts became separated. The former sighted the enemy fleet and attacked the screen according to plan. Two of them were destroyed. Six of the Beauforts found and attacked Gneisenau. The other three had lost the squadron, but found and loosed their torpedoes at three "big" ships. There was, strangely, no defensive fire. The ships were British destroyers.

XIV

DESTROYERS

Yet he, like a man, stands by his tiller.
With the bark are sporting wind and water.
Wind and water sport not with his bosom:
On the fierce deep looks he as a master.
> *The Sea Voyage.*
> *From the German of Johann Wolfgang von Goethe*

At 11:45 a.m. Admiral Ramsay had signalled Captain C.T.M. Pizey, D.S.O., commander of destroyers at Harwich, "Enemy battle cruisers passing Boulogne, speed about twenty knots. Proceed in execution of previous orders."

Pizey had in his command six old destroyers. These too, it had been expected, would have had a chance to torpedo the enemy ships and perhaps withdraw. The Germans would have had the extra hazard of possibly firing on one another in the confusion of the darkness.

By good fortune the destroyers were exercising at sea when the order came, which saved two hours of preparation. Even so, to set forth by the safe circuitous route would have put them hopelessly behind their prey. So Pizey, greatly daring, cut right through the mine field in the hope that the mines might be missed, or that they would have been set too deep to contact the relatively shallow draft. destroyers. Tension was very great. One destroyer captain eased it on two ships by sending a challenge to the captain of the vessel ahead to play "Battleships", a favorite navy game.

They passed the minefield without damage. But ahead loomed a fight so desperate that survival seemed unlikely. An attack by one of their own Hampden bombers gave a foretaste of the peril to come.

Soon friend and foe fired on them and on each other in a confused melee with poor visibility. The weather was getting worse; waves washed over the shivering gun crews on the decks.

Visibility was about four miles in the mist and rain. Their radar found the German fleet. They closed the enemy at twenty-eight knots. All German ships of course took part in the defense. Hartmann pointed his guns lower to put the surface vessels in his sights; he poured in as rapid and accurate a fire as possible. A battleship's main batteries were for offense. Their blow was devastating, but huge and heavy as they were, their rate of fire was relatively slow. Secondary batteries and smaller units were therefore necessary to protect the capital ships, lest a lucky torpedo or shell strike a magazine or other vital area. A Goliath could fight off many Davids, or another giant, but a single well placed missile from a sling felled the monster.

Pizey's Campbell, with Vivacious, Worcester, and Whitshed, made for Gneisenau. She had been absorbed in fighting off plane attacks, and the destroyers had the advantage of a measure of surprise. At 3,300 yards nevertheless, the concentrated German fire was so heavy that Campbell and Vivacious fired their torpedoes and retired. It was not a question of saving their skins; the captains had to consider that if they pressed home the attack more closely, they would be destroyed, and the torpedoes would not be released.

Worcester, Whitshed and Mackay got slightly closer. At 3,000 yards they let go their fish. The two latter miraculously withdrew with little damage. But in the concentrated barrage Gneisenau's great primary batteries shot away Worcester's starboard bridge and blew up numbers one and two boiler rooms. The ship reeled and stopped. Four salvos from Prinz Eugen hit her again. Captain Fein of Gneisenau broke off the action, considering that no destroyer so punished could possibly live.

Worcester's bows were burnt out, what was left of the bridge was honeycombed with hits, the radio shack, mast, and funnels were gone, her hull was holed above the waterline, and what remained was a mass of wreckage.

Captain Coates' order, "Prepare to abandon ship!" was misheard as "Abandon ship!", and many did so. Y turret, however, was still operative and continued to fire until its crew fell. So did the two pompoms amidships. The crews of the Oerlikon guns were all casualties. Campbell and Vivacious approached and, although dive-bombed, rescued the men overside.

Worcester's struggle for life that night is material for a great epic of the ocean. Left as a sinking ship after her engagement with a battleship, a heavy cruiser, and various destroyers and planes, she wallowed in a rising and hungry sea. She made slow headway; she could make, at different times, three to five knots, when she could make any. From time to time her maltreated engines stopped, and at such times her people feared that she would roll a little further to starboard and not come back. Once for an hour and a half, off the Dutch coast, she lay dead in the water.

But slowly, like a gravely wounded sea beast, she struggled toward England and safety.

In the bitter cold her people on the weather decks wore long, heavy underwear, and flannel shirts over that, and sweaters, and uniforms sewed of good woolen cloth, and overcoats. But it didn't seem to do any good.

There were thirteen dead aboard, and some dying. Men had been blown overboard by the devastating shells from the great German guns, to be seen no more. The doctor worked desperately with hands bleeding from shell splinters. The wounded were everywhere; the sick bay had been destroyed, and would have been far too small in any case. The dead were sewn into their hammocks, weighted, and after a brief service were buried at sea.

The captain kept on a course reciprocal to the one he had followed earlier in the day. Only the need to bring his ship back kept him from breaking under the strain. Below, the engineers battled magnificently. Back they drove her over the same mined area that she had traversed on the way out. But she drifted, and channel tides are swift. The navigator could not know his exact position. They finally saw and recognized a light - thank God, the Admiralty had ordered the Orfordness light rekindled from its wartime blackout against this very possibility.

Dawn of February 13 came, and they could see the fields of England!

The little fleet, steaming at eight knots, made port in the morning. Off Harwich, a destroyer issuing from the port inquired of the floating wreck whether assistance were needed; the captain proudly rejected it. To the cheers of the crews of moored ships and of shore parties, she waved off the tugs, crept up to her berth, and made fast unassisted. Then the engine definitely quit. Worcester was given the name, "The Ship That Wouldn't Die."

But her crew would. Of one hundred thirty, over half were casualties.

Later, they learned that the minefields had been cleared the day before, but the word had not yet been passed.

XV

BOMBERS AND FIGHTERS

The face and bosom of the endless sea
Too wide were for my beaten mind, too frightful and too
high;
The monstrous burden of its waters wrenched my soul
awry,
Yet thrilled me even so with intimation of its ancientry,
That spring eternal of all floods, that source whence came
the sea.

    The Stormy Sea. From the German of Barthold Heinrich Brockes.

Bomber Command had been requested to keep all available planes in readiness for this operation. But that ruled out current operations and training; so it withdrew two hundred and kept one hundred bombers up and on four hours' readiness. The admiralty was not informed of the changed procedure.

At 9.00 a.m. on this February 12, Sir Richard Peirse of Bomber Command had looked at the weather and ruled out a German passage on that day. He made one of the great misstatements of the time - "It looks like one of the quiet days of the war." At 11:40, when he changed his mind, two hundred forty bombers were available.

The weapon for attacking armored ships from the air, of course, was the armor-piercing bomb. This, however, had to be dropped from seven thousand feet to be effective, and the ceiling at that time was seven hundred to two thousand feet. The visibility was only a mile. So the hundred standby planes had to rearm with general purpose bombs, which would merely raise some havoc above decks. They might distract the German gunners from the torpedo planes.

At 2:20 p.m. a wave of seventy-three bombers took off. Their attack should have been coordinated with that of the coastal command Beauforts at Manston. Under the prevailing conditions, it was hard for the pilots to find the Germans; most never did. Some bombed the E boats.

In the late afternoon the R.A.F., finally ready, attacked the enemy fleet continuously. Even then, the attacks were not coordinated, and did relatively little damage. Two motor torpedo boats were put out of action, two German seamen were killed and a few seriously wounded.

Within three hours, more than two hundred bombers had taken off. Only thirty-nine returned having sighted and engaged the racing Germans; one hundred forty-eight returned after a fruitless search; fifteen were lost and another crashed on landing.

Almost certainly, more than the thirty-nine British bombers encountered the enemy; the Germans reported shooting some of their assailants out of the air. It seems likely too that a few pilots succumbed to a strange but well authenticated phenomenon; unable to distinguish between grey, misty air and grey, mist-shrouded water, they flew into the sea.

At 11.00 p.m. twenty bombers took off to drop mines in the mouth of the Elbe. Twelve succeeded.

The British had at their disposal some five hundred fifty to six hundred fighters. Air Vice-Marshal Leigh-Mallory expected no calls for them until 2.00 p.m. at the earliest. But at 1:40, ten Hurricanes made the first sortie and attacked some small ships. After them, wave after wave took off, some to escort other types of air or surface craft, some independently. Altogether, of the almost six hundred that should have been available, three hundred ninety-eight went on their missions. The Germans shot down seventeen. For them, the British flyers shot down sixteen enemy fighters and probably three more, damaged seventeen others, sank a six hundred ton German vessel and an E boat and damaged eight surface craft of various types.

XVI

THE PARTHIAN SHOT

Who helped me against the Titans' insolence?
Who rescued me from death, from slavery?
Prometheus. From the German of Johann Wolfgang von Goethe

Scharnhorst had accomplished temporary repairs, and was rushing at full speed after her sisters. The British had missed their great chance. She stood repeated air attacks between three and six o'clock in the afternoon, but the only results were that a few men were wounded by shell splinters and machine gun fire. Two of Hartmann's gunners fell to ricocheting projectiles from strafing planes.

Night fell at last. The airplanes, British and German, broke off the action, except for the dropping of British mines in the estuary. Like his shipmates, Hartmann was utterly weary. He had stood to his guns for twenty-four hours.

When Ciliax had transferred to destroyer Z-29, he had felt that his fleet's chances of completing its mission without serious damage were poor. Nevertheless, he had taken station at the head of his column and continued the homeward dash. But at 4:20 p.m. an AA shell exploded, cut an oil line, and reduced the ship's speed to twenty-five knots. Despite a bad sea, Ciliax transferred by cutter to the destroyer Hermann Schoemann.

They were now in a shallow area of the sea. The passage of a ship displaces water, which flows around and under the hull to come to rest astern of it. In very shallow water, the bottom resists this flow; in effect, the water moves through a narrower channel. The ship's speed is accordingly affected. The fleet lost about two knots, but in relative safety steamed determinedly on.

Then another mine gave forth a triumphant roar, and Gneisenau leaped in agony.

The starboard engine was damaged and stopped, the other two jammed. Thousands of tons of water flooded in, giving her a seven degree list. Her lighting system went out, and emergency lights were used. There was much damage to guns and instruments. Snow flurries fell on topside personnel as her engineers toiled mightily. At 10:39 she was able to resume course at twelve knots, shepherded by Ciliax' destroyer toward Wilhelmshafen.

Gneisenau and Prinz Eugen were ordered to Brunsbuttel. Arriving off the harbor, they were informed that neither tugs nor pilot vessels were available! They had been supplied with detailed charts of the approaches to French harbors on their route, but none to this!

Gneisenau anchored for the night in a sea that was turning to thickening ice. Captain Fein preferred the danger of a British plane attack to that of running aground, or, worse, hitting a mine. Captain Brinkmann of Prinz Eugen made the opposite decision, and stood to and fro all night.

At dawn Gneisenau determined to enter without assistance. The wind and tide swept the crippled ship against a wreck, inflicting further damage; but she finally made a successful entry, followed by Prinz Eugen. Scharnhorst too could get no assistance on arrival, except for a tug which tried to pilot her in, and another which brought back Admiral Ciliax. In the intense cold and thickening ice Captain Hoffmann demonstrated his seamanship by entering a dock unassisted.

Admiral Ciliax first informed naval headquarters at Berlin that the operation had been successfully concluded. He then addressed Scharnhorst's crew. His words were coldly received. They felt that he had deserted the ship. A ditty, contemptuous of the admiral, began to be sung.

But nothing could affect the great feeling of pride among the German crews. They had passed successfully through British waters! They had forced the Channel! They had achieved the impossible - they had beaten the mightiest sea power in the world!

Emil was blissfully happy. They had won. He had proven himself again in the crucible of battle, and more dramatically than hitherto! Surely so successful a cause must be right. Those who could not see it must pay the penalty. As for him, he would doubt no more. Heil Hitler! Deutschland uber alles!

XVII

DEATH AND THE MAIDEN

Mephistopheles. She is judged.
Voice (from above). She is saved!
> Faust I. From the German of Johann Wolfgang von Goethe.

It was not until three days later that the mail was forwarded from Brest. A letter was handed to Hartmann. It bore Leni's return address. He opened it.

But it was not from Leni, but from her sister.

"...And so Leni, in her wrong but understandable indignation, attended a meeting of whose true purpose I am sure she was unaware. It was raided; she was arrested. I fear that she will be sentenced to a disciplinary camp, which she may not survive, but which will in any case be a horrible experience. I need not go into details, I know.

"Perhaps if you, as an officer of the navy, vouch for her, it will prevent or mitigate her sentence. Please write to ..... and for God's sake, hurry! ...."

He thought for a long moment. Then he slowly tore the letter to pieces and dropped it over the side.

XVIII

END OF A QUEEN

The god of Greenland is lonely
In the mountains of ice.
The Figure of Fulfillment.
From the German of Emil Lerperger.

The ships were hurt worse than their people knew. And the British bombers gave them no rest. So the German admiralty sent them further east, to Gotenhaven, for repairs. They never did completely restore Scharnhorst to her pristine condition. And as to Gneisenau, they simply gave up. The damage was too great. They dismounted her guns for use elsewhere, and sank her as a channel barrier.

Hitler now decided to attack Murmansk, to cut off the flow of supplies to Russia through this northern port. "Any ship of the navy not in Norway," he proclaimed, "is out of place."

Twice Scharnhorst and an accompanying fleet started for the north on voyages that for one reason or another had to be canceled. Hitler disliked Raeder, a surface ship admiral, and replaced him as supreme commander at sea with Donitz, partisan of the U boats. Donitz gave Scharnhorst six months to show what she could do.

On August 3 in the year 1943, Scharnhorst put out with ten destroyers and eight torpedo boats. Almost immediately, the weather changed for the worse. The wind increased to force ten. It was too much for the smaller vessels. First the wallowing older torpedo boats, then the newer ones, then destroyers had to be detached to seek shelter.

Arrived in Langfiord, near Narvik, Scharnhorst settled herself with her one remaining destroyer to wait for news of an allied Russia-bound convoy. The British planes did not neglect her, though they scored no signal success. But for a while she lay idle; the western allies dared not send supply ships to Russia during the long, light days of the summer half of the year.

The high command ordered the battleships Scharnhorst and Tirpitz and nine destroyers to Spitzbergen to ruin that island's weather and fueling stations and her mines. The mission was accomplished; but Tirpitz succumbed to enemy submarine attack. Scharnhorst was now the only battleship left in the German navy.

𝔏t was the beginning of the long, bitter Arctic winter. Scharnhorst, in far northern waters, received information of a Russia-bound allied convoy. This should be game for the hunter! Escorted by cruisers and destroyers, the battleship put to sea. It was a clear night, with the northern lights dancing overhead, but the wind was rising. In the bitter cold the ships, especially the wave-swept destroyers, began to ice up.

The fleet did not know about a returning convoy, shepherded by a powerful force, and a few enemy units slightly further north - the great battleship Duke of York, cruisers Belfast, Norfolk, Sheffield, Jamaica, twenty destroyers, three corvettes, and a mine sweeper.

Ignorant of the odds against her, Scharnhorst drove in to attack and sink the slow, laden merchantmen. But it was she who first came under fire, from unseen foes. Two hits knocked out her forward ranging installation. Scharnhorst managed two hits on a cruiser, but her forward heavy turret was wrecked by York's terrible counter; then she suffered a hit below the water line. Her speed dropped to eight knots. It was a half hour before her sweating black gang was able to get twenty-two knots out of the stricken engines.

But by that time the British destroyers, unseen in the dark, had taken positions. Scorpion loosed her torpedoes and blew in the stricken champion's side, and Savage and Saumarez stung her, and each again and yet again.

Scharnhorst slowed. She was afire. Her B turret had three shells more, her C turret none. "We fight till we have no more ammunition," shouted Captain Hintze. Enemy guns were hurling their shot into her, despite the impossible seas.

On Dec. 26, at 7:40 p.m., Scharnhorst ended her brave but evil career. She sank at latitude seventy-two degrees north, longitude twenty-eight degrees and forty-one minutes east.

Thirty-six men were rescued.

Emil Hartmann was not among them.

AUTHOR'S NOTE

Wulfnoth, Thane of Sussex, probably the father of Earl Godwin, committed the treason of 1009. His motivation, and everything else concerning him in this story, are the invention of the author.

Queen Emma's coldness to her sons is factual. Its reference to disenchantment with their father is the author's suggestion.

Godwin's passage of the Channel in despite of the royal fleet is history. The manner of it is greatly embellished herein.

The Saxon tale is based mainly on the Anglo-Saxon Chronicle.

Spinola's log books have disappeared. His voyages to Holland are reconstructed from British and Dutch reports. His childhood is described, very roughly, from the biography of his more famous brother.

The characters of Alisette de Vlaine, Leonora Mondego and of Gutierrez are my invention. Spinola apparently never married; I have seen at Simanca, Spain, a letter from the Genovese ambassador, written after the tragic end, suggesting that the king might want to write a letter of condolence to Spinola's mother. There is no mention of a widow.

Spinola did have as goal the Enterprise of England. He died as I have reported.

There are two views of him; the one that I have presented, and another that he was rash and incompetent.

There is the statement that he saw service against pirates. I have assumed that both Mediterranean and Low Country pirates were the objects of his zeal.

I have searched, mostly unsuccessfully, for details concerning Spinola in the Library of Congress, the British Museum, the Vatican Library, the library of the Maritime Museum of Madrid, and the libraries of his native Genoa. There are some letters and reports, although none that I have found on personal matters, at the University of London. The best account of his exploits that I know of is that by Julian S. Corbett (*The Successors of Drake*. Longmans, Green and Co., London, 1900).

Ambrogio, despite his lack of early training in war, became one of the great generals of the age.

In the writing of the last part of my history I have been dependent for my information on the works of Terence Robertson (*Channel Dash*, E.P. Dutton Co., New York, 1958), John Deane Potter (*Durchbruch*, Paul Zsolnay Verlag, Vienna and Hamburg, 1970), and Heinrich Bredemeier (*Schlachtschiff Scharnhorst*, Koehlers Verlags GmbH, Herford, 1962). They differ on some minor points.

In his debate with the German admirals, Hitler, as shown, was tactically correct. The passage was made. But in the larger framework, the admirals had been right. It was a victory for the Germans, but a strategic error. Gneisenau was finished; the other two capital ships played no further important role in the war. The British navy was relieved of responsibility for them in the eastern Atlantic. It is very fortunate that Hitler, despite his undeniable other gifts, had no understanding of sea power.

It is difficult to understand the utter ineptness of the British planning and execution, relieved only by the selfless courage with which the pitifully inadequate forces hurled themselves on the foe. Probably there was a concatenation of all errors that each tactical administrator would commit in a lifetime, compressed into this little time. If this were typical of British thinking, they could never have won the wars that they did. No light will be thrown by supercilious sneers at "muddling through" or the "military mind."

The German operation by contrast was brilliant in conception and execution.

I have followed the German designation in calling the two largest ships battleships (*Schlachtschiffe*) rather than battle cruisers, as the British did.

Emil and Leni, of course, are my inventions.